The Gailean Quartet, Book II

SERENADE OF KINGS

Christine E. Schulze

Words Matter Publishing
P.O. Box 531
Salem, Il 62881
www.wordsmatterpublishing.com

Map Illustration Copyright © 2021 Stacey Hummel
Edited by Kira Lerner

ISBN: 978-1-949809-54-1

Library of Congress Catalog Card Number: 2020930087

The Gailean Quartet

Prelude of Fire
Serenade of Kings
Symphony of Crowns
Requiem of Dragons

Table of Contents

✳

Map of the Four Realms

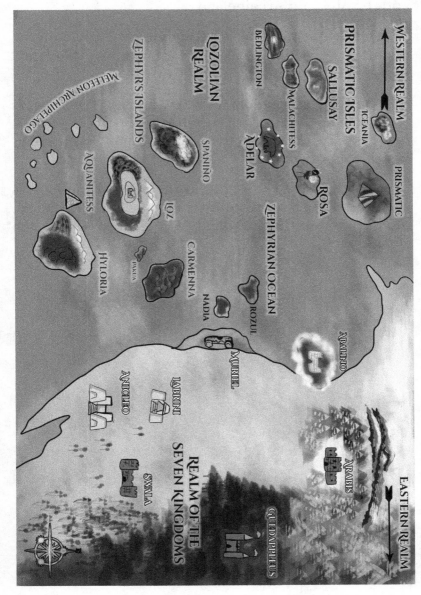

The Lozolian Realm encompasses all the islands in the Zephyrian Ocean, including Loz, the Prismatic Isles, and the Meleeon Archipelago.

The Realm of the Seven Kingdoms is located on the mainland, sometimes called "The Surpriser Mainland" from the time of the 100 Years' Curse.

The Western Realm lies far beyond Zephyrian waters and includes Asian, African, and European countries. Several explorers from the Lozolian and Seven Kingdoms Realms have ventured to this mysterious realm.

The Eastern Realm beyond the Seven Kingdoms is considered even more mysterious and little explored, though rumors tell of Giants living deep within the woods.

To my brilliant family,
both blood-born and chosen;
To Kira, who helped me birth this book
From the ashes of its original form
So that it could soar like a phoenix renewed;
And to all my wonderful readers:
Remember always that it is
the choices of your heart,
not your circumstances,
that create the "you"
who you become.

CHAPTER 1

THE GIRL IN THE WOODS

The hunt had just begun.

As Crispin raced through the woods, trees half-stripped of color from winter's approach whipped past him in a steady, gray-brown blur. He pushed his mess of fiery red curls out of his face and grinned at Tytonn, who ran beside him, before bursting ahead.

A grin broke out across the taller, broad-built, blond boy's face.

"Oh, no, you won't!" Tytonn picked up speed.

When Crispin's lungs burned so hard he was certain the warm sun must have set them ablaze, he staggered to a halt and doubled over. Clutching his knees, he gasped for breath and then laughed as Tytonn toppled with a dramatic somersault before sprawling flat on his back.

Crispin followed suit and fell to the earth beside Tytonn. Propping himself lazily on one elbow, Tytonn laughed, "All right, you win again. But you won't win the *true* challenge."

"You think we've outrun the others, at least?" Crispin looked behind and ran a hand through his sweat-dampened hair. "We're pretty far ahead."

Tytonn nodded. "Without a doubt. Most of them wouldn't even know to reach this side of the thorn brambles. We're close now to several places where deer like to feed. Should be a simple enough task to find one. For *me*, anyway..." He sat up all the way, and his freckled face brightened with an impish grin. "Care to make a wager on who can finish the challenge first?"

"Mm, I suppose it *is* a big deal—becoming a man. Perhaps we *should* make a bet. Although..." Crispin frowned. "I'm not certain. You *do* have an unfair advantage..."

In fact, Tytonn was already at it, murmuring a soft melody to a mongoose that had just scurried nearby. The small, brown creature sniffled cautiously in Tytonn's direction, seemingly mesmerized by Tytonn's sun-bleached gold hair before approaching. Tytonn continued to serenade the animal and gently stroked its back.

"See there?" Crispin said. "This is exactly what I'm talking about."

Tytonn ceased his song, and the mongoose scurried toward the trees. "Well, if you'd hurry up and get your fire powers already, *you* could blast any beast from afar."

"*If* I get my powers," Crispin muttered. "Maybe I'm doomed to be like Queen Marlis, growing plants for the rest of my life. Then again, at least that would be *something*..."

"She's only your aunt by marriage; you couldn't take after her. Just wait, it'll come to you," Tytonn assured, looking remorseful for his jab. "I know it. You just turned sixteen, after all. My grandfather didn't get his powers till nearly eighteen. You'll be setting things on fire with the best in no time, just like Lord Alistor."

A grin broke through Crispin's momentary gloom. "And in the meantime, I can at least rival you when it comes to archery. So, back to this wager then?"

"Indeed. Though, despite all this talk of becoming a man, I don't exactly make the *wages* of a man yet—or at least, I don't possess the coinage of a higher-ranking member of court like yourself." He smirked at Crispin.

Crispin rolled his eyes and jumped to his feet. "Being the King's nephew may have advantages, but being rich isn't one of them. Perhaps a bet isn't such a keen idea after all." If he lost this bet with Tytonn and had to beg his uncle Alistor for the coinage necessary to settle the score, Alistor would never let him hear the end of it.

Tytonn stood up with a lazy stretch. "We don't have to. But lots of the other boys are making bets. Perhaps just a small one to liven things up and turn this chore into more of a challenge?"

Crispin crossed his arms and glared skeptically at his best friend. "There's still the matter of your animal charming."

"I'd never use my gift for such a purpose. It would seem a foul thing—almost like betraying a friend, pretending to be kind to someone only to lead them straight to the slaughter. At any rate, if it's a fair hunt you're after, you'll get one from me, rest assured."

Crispin squinted into the sun, judging the time. He suspected—though would not admit aloud—that neither of them was likely to excel above the others. Tytonn possessed all the necessary skills for a hunt and then some, but he lacked the heart. As for Crispin himself, while he enjoyed nature and studying all the sciences behind it, the art of hunting bored him. He preferred to limit his archery skills to games and tournaments.

"Very well, then," Crispin said, extending his hand. "Five coppers?"

Tytonn grasped his hand and squeezed firmly. "It's on. Let the race commence."

He darted off through the woods again, moving lithely. Crispin followed, shaking his head. If one couldn't see Tytonn only a few yards away, it'd be impossible to detect that the older boy was there: not a single twig snapped beneath his boots, not a single leaf rustled. Tytonn really could win this challenge, if he had more of an inclination toward killing for sport.

Crispin branched in a different direction. Silence soon engulfed him, broken only by the distant singing of birds. Reaching behind him, he drew his bow and crept deeper into the woods, weaving between sunlight and shadows.

A huge shadow suddenly shrouded Crispin, making him shiver; how he hated coming to the king's wood. He stared up at the daunting immensity of Astyrian—the island floating some thousand feet above, atop of which the king's castle rested. The magic supporting it was extraordinarily powerful, but Crispin knew that with the right spell, the entire castle could likely crumble from the sky and slam down on top of them, killing their entire hunting party and every living thing below.

A birdcall snared his attention, and his head snapped toward a water-hopper gliding overhead. They often dwelled near the shores of lakes and rivers—also the perfect location for a deer to find refreshment. Crispin quickened his pace, following the bird's melancholy whistling—

The bird's singing abruptly ceased, and Crispin paused. For a moment, he stood stunned, as though the descending quiet was a spell that had knocked his breath away. Then he stretched forth his hand, feeling the air until his fingers grazed something invisible, something solid and fluid at once. Strumming his fingers delicately across its transparent surface, he watched as the faintest silver ripples danced up and down midair, just hinting at the existence of the protective barrier circling King Moragon's woods.

He glanced up, tilting his head back and straining his neck. Miles above, streamers of the silvery substance stretched from Astyrian down to the silvery barrier, holding the castle in place. Briefly, Crispin wondered what would happen if those silver ropes were severed. Would the castle come crashing after all, or might it simply float away like a balloon?

The light shifted; Astyrian had moved to the side. The floating island adjusted positions every hour, to allow enough sunlight and rain to reach every part of the forest.

The light shifted again—this time, straight ahead. Crispin crept forward, locking his gaze between two thick trees wrapped in vines and moss. One of the tree's gnarled roots arched up like a small bridge, and he climbed under, catching his footing on the slippery moss. Hunching down, he peered through the narrow gap in the bushes ahead and held his breath.

A stream babbled some feet away, glinting in the sunlight. Just beyond, a doe grazed with her fawn. Crispin smiled. Perfect. He'd already beaten Tytonn at their wager. He decided magnanimously that he wouldn't ask his friend for payment. Weeks of mocking Tytonn would be well worth the conquest on its own.

Except that there *was* no conquest. He had not won yet. The terms of the ceremony did not dictate that each young man merely find a deer in the woods. He must slay the creature, defeat and claim it as his own.

Crispin reached behind and drew one of his arrows, slowly as to make no sound. Nocking the arrow, he stretched the drawstring back, aimed...

And then lowered the notch a little. He'd always avoided hunting with his uncles when he could help it. Hunting for food and clothing was a necessity. But King Moragon hunted only for sport—a needless, messy business, Alistor always said. Crispin had never seen any animal slain for any purpose, and while the chase had been fun, the game now turned into a harsh reality. If he killed the doe, the fawn would die too. No one would care for such a helpless creature. And if he killed the fawn, a disgusting notion in and of itself, might not the doe suffer from a broken heart? Did animals feel such things as people did—?

Footsteps crashed through the underbrush, distant but rapidly growing louder. The doe's head rose, and its ears perked. Crispin lifted the bow and aimed again. It was now or never. Maybe if he only wounded the animal, it would be enough to satisfy the demands of the ceremony—

A high whistling shrieked in Crispin's ears. At once his hands pulsed with fiery pain, flames erupted from his fingertips, and he stumbled, crying out. Throwing the bow to the ground, he collapsed to his knees and clapped his hands over his ears, trying to drown the shrill noise, but it seemed to emanate from inside him.

With a groan, he made himself look up. At first, the only movement he saw was the fawn bounding away into the trees. Then a green blur darted past, and without thinking, Crispin growled and stretched his arm out toward the shape. Fire erupted from his palm, and the figure screamed before falling to the ground.

Crispin stared at his hands, bewildered. Had he really just produced fire, or had he only imagined it because of his talk with Tytonn? His thoughts jumbled as the shrill sound continued to ring in his ears. Trying to ignore it, he crawled over to the person—female, by her shape—who'd already scrambled to her feet and started to run. She slipped, and Crispin snatched her wrist, drawing her to him.

"What was the meaning of that? Making me lose my catch? Who are you, and what devilry did you use? Answer me, or you will answer to my uncle, the king—"

The young woman's lips parted and sang a quiet tune, distracting him, and she wrenched away from his grasp. Covered head to toe with dirt and leaves, and with skin gleaming a faint green, she looked more like a kelpie or siren than a human. She did not run from him but instead stood straight, fists clenched, body poised to spring at any given moment. Her blue-green eyes watched him steadily and, he thought, a bit wildly.

"You've some effrontery," Crispin said, "meeting the gaze of your superior, considering that creeping around the forest during the coming-of-age hunt is more than enough grounds for punishment."

She narrowed her gaze at him, and he took a few steps back. Her skin was still caked with leaves and dirt. Her skin had morphed from its greenish hue into a more human skin tone, fair like his own. Was she a nymph of some sort? Some guardian spirit of the wood?

"Instead of wasting your focus on threats," she said quietly, "why don't you figure out what to do with your catch?"

Crispin scoffed. "I think we've both established by now that *you're* the cause of my losing my catch."

"Oh, am I?"

As her gaze strayed across the brook, she frowned and flinched as if something had struck her. Crispin followed her gaze and gasped. The deer lay on its side, its limbs crumpled beneath it. Its tongue lolled, and its chest rose and fell unevenly. Blood trickled from its wound, and the arrow smoked from the strange fire that had burst from Crispin's hands, filling the air with the stench of burning flesh.

Crispin splashed through the brook and fell at the deer's side. He rested a hand on the creature's flank, which trembled with failing breath. The girl hurried over and knelt beside him.

Crispin studied the girl's mournful expression and asked quietly, "Can you do anything for her?"

"Maybe...if I had the right supplies..."

"My uncle," Crispin said, rising to his feet. "Lord Alistor—he always keeps a stock of healing tonics. Perhaps he has something—"

"Crispin?"

Tytonn rushed into the clearing and stopped, breathless and with a stare alternating between Crispin and the mud-and-leaf-covered girl. Rustling trees and thudding footsteps announced the arrival of several more boys, some with bows, others with daggers stained with blood, and most with what appeared to be blood streaked across their foreheads.

Behind them, a man with the same fiery red curls as Crispin hurried into the clearing—Alistor. His confident, leonine manner set him apart from the group of young hunters even more than his gold and purple robes. His sharp eyes fixated on the girl, and curiosity filled his still youthful face, softening its sharply chiseled features.

Then, crossing his arms and looking sternly at Crispin, he said, "Nephew, what's going on here? And you there, girl—why are you not in the castle, fulfilling your duties to your king? Surely you know it is forbidden for females to step foot in the king's wood during a hunt."

The girl narrowed her gaze at Alistor, showing neither remorse nor deference. While he only smiled at her politely, his servant beside him reached forward and slapped her. She stumbled back, touching the reddening spot on her cheek.

The servant drew back his hand to slap her again, but Alistor grabbed his arm. "Hold, Hadrian. No true harm has been done here. I will give my nephew a chance to explain." He turned to Crispin and arched an anticipatory brow.

Crispin winced. "I—I found this deer during the hunt. This girl startled me, and my shot went amiss."

"Not entirely, I'd say." Alistor gestured toward the panting beast.

"I didn't intend to harm her. She had a fawn, and I meant to choose another target instead."

"A noble aspiration, but its chance has already passed. You cannot simply leave the beast here to suffer. The fawn will now be motherless either way. If you wound an animal, the merciful thing is to finish the job, not to leave it in needless torment."

Crispin stared up at his uncle, mortified. He looked at the girl who met his gaze and gave the subtlest nod. Beyond the daubs of green and brown paint masking her face—at least, he thought it was paint—he noted the bright red handprint on her cheek and glanced away. She might be an insolent servant, but he didn't wish to see her punished again any more than he wanted to see the innocent beast before him slain.

Numbly, he drew another arrow, but Alistor snatched it. "What are you doing? If death is the sole mercy you can afford this creature, best to make it swift and complete. Use your knife."

Crispin drew a long breath. Was this another of his uncle's tests? Why must Alistor always be so hard on him in front of the others? Crispin glanced at Tytonn, who looked remorseful on his behalf, then back at his increasingly impatient uncle.

Crispin took his dagger and swallowed hard. Pressing the knife close to the deer's neck, he closed his eyes and slashed. As warm blood flowed over his hand, he recoiled, breathing slowly in and out and suppressing a shudder. This was still a man's rite, and disgusting though it may be, this was the last place he should display any weakness. Without making himself look at the slain creature, he opened his eyes and rose to his feet, wiping its blood on his tunic.

"Well done, Crispin," Alistor said.

His uncle knelt slightly, then rose and reached to smear something warm and wet across Crispin's forehead. Crispin lifted his hand to touch it, and when he pulled back to see the red staining his fingertips, he knew it was the deer's blood. He knew also that this should excite him—many of the boys who wore blood looked proud and eager at this symbol of their success—but as its coppery smell bit his nostrils, his stomach churned. He dropped his hand, vowing not to show his revulsion.

"Let this be a lesson to all of you," Alistor said. "Sometimes, there is no mercy, save in the shedding of blood. Every choice has consequences, and those consequences serve to mold a man's heart. Thus, your choices reflect what kind of man you will become."

Alistor met Crispin's gaze. Then, setting his sights on the girl, he said, "You. Hadrian here will escort you back to the castle. Wash up and report to your mistress. She will decide a rightful punishment for you."

She glanced briefly at him then back at the ground. "Yes, Lord Ragnar."

"Ah, good. So, you *can* submit. The Head Housekeeper has said you're still a wild thing, but perhaps there is hope yet for your taming. The rest of you follow me. We've one last rite of passage to take in the woods, and then we'll return above to complete our ceremony in the Shrine."

Hadrian grabbed the girl's arm and yanked her after him. Alistor cleared his throat to catch Hadrian's attention and shook his head with a warning glare. Hadrian released the girl, who trailed behind him, without looking back. Within moments, her forest-clad figure had blended with the trees and out of sight.

The other boys had already begun following Alistor from the clearing. Crispin hurried to catch up, taking the rear with Tytonn. His friend had lagged behind, watching him.

"I'm sorry," Tytonn whispered as they walked. "I'd found the doe too, but I couldn't bring myself to kill her. You showed up right afterward, and I thought it was fair to at least let you have your chance."

"Perhaps not," Crispin muttered. "At least you wouldn't have made such a mess of things." He felt his forehead again. The blood had now dried and cooled. It served as a small trophy of his false victory, as though the disaster had never occurred.

Alistor's rich, melodious voice rang out ahead. "Here we are, lads." He spread his arms wide.

They had stopped before a massive tree whose trunk stretched many times thicker than the others', with hundreds of tiny notches carved in its side.

"This is the Druce Tree." Alistor nodded at it with respect. "A sacred place where many lads before you have crossed that final threshold into manhood. These notches..." He traced his fingers across them. "...represent each boy who has made that transformation. Today, each of you was given a test. Some were successful, others less so..."

His gaze shifted to each of the boys, ending upon Crispin and Tytonn.

"However, as I said earlier, your choices this day

11

merely dictate what *kind* of man you will choose to become. There are no true failures here. You are all of age, and you will all now pass into the next stage of life. As men, you will now be given the rights to obtain your own properties, govern your own lands, and marry. Those of you who succeeded in today's hunt have each been marked with the blood of your success and will wear this symbol for the rest of the night as a sign to all of what has taken place this day. To those who did not succeed, no fears—you will find these useful as your tokens instead."

Alistor nodded toward a bouquet of white moon blossoms set beside the tree. Tytonn and the other boys who had not won the hunt each began weaving one of the flowers onto their tunics or cloaks. Some, like Tytonn, were solemn. Others were brooding, and still others complacent.

Crispin found it strange that those who'd failed should win an eternal token of their manhood; moon blossoms never wilted. He scowled at those who, like him, bore the mark of blood on their foreheads. He felt just as shamed as those who wore no blood and was suddenly glad his mark would not endure. Perhaps he'd slain the deer, but only by another's order; in that, he'd still failed his task, and he wanted no reminders of this.

"Now," Alistor said, "the final rite is for each of you to step forward and mark your completion of today's ritual on the Druce Tree. Observe."

Alistor revealed a dagger. Choosing one of the larger notches in the tree, he dug his dagger in and carved it a little wider. Crispin wondered if this was his original mark from when he'd completed his own ceremony.

One by one, the boys stepped forward to create new notches.

"Well done," Alistor said, once they'd finished the task and lined themselves once more. "Now come. We head back to the Shrine to receive the clerics' blessings. Then, as the sun sets on your boyhood, you will rise—as new beings, men of Adelar."

As they followed Alistor through the woods once more, Crispin darted ahead.

"Uncle..."

"Yes, nephew? What is it? How are you feeling?"

"Disgusted," Crispin admitted. "How did *your* first hunt go?"

"Flawlessly," Alistor said. "I remember it now, fifteen years later, and will likely fifty years hence—if I am graced to see eighty. I found the perfect catch only an hour or so in—a massive stag. I knew what had to be done. I took him out with one shot."

Alistor's smile faded, and he lowered his voice before continuing, "In that, your uncle the king and I differ. He has never appreciated what he has. He has never had to struggle or suffer for anything and cannot empathize with those who do. He would have likely chosen the fawn and made it suffer."

"That isn't all," Crispin said. "In the woods, during the hunt. Something...something *happened* to me..."

"*What* happened?" Alistor asked, his voice still quiet but suddenly intense.

"I'd aimed my arrow and was prepared to release the string, but I heard this shrill noise, almost like screaming but sort of musical. Then these—these flames erupted from my hand! That was what made the shot go amiss. The fire hurt, but not enough to burn or leave any scars. It all happened so abruptly, and it was over just as quickly. If I didn't remember it with such clarity, I'd swear it had been nothing but a dream or mirage."

Crispin waited till his uncle's silence made him ache with anticipation. Finally, he looked up; Alistor looked thoughtful but otherwise unreadable.

13

"I am proud of you," Alistor said at last. "You've become a man this day in more ways than one. However, this must be our secret for now. No sharing with friends, and especially not his majesty."

Crispin stared, his face beginning to burn. "But—but manifestations of powers are to be reported to the king. If I—"

"I am familiar with the law." Alistor's voice was thick with irony. "But my brother need not be notified of what might simply have been a fluke. Trust my instinct in such matters. In the meantime, we'll discuss everything in greater depth at tomorrow morning's lesson."

Crispin nodded and fell back in line, joining Tytonn. He couldn't help feeling impatient. His other uncle, King Moragon, was fond of mocking Crispin's late-developing powers, and it would be beyond satisfaction to stop such jokes with a flash of flame—if Crispin could reproduce the effort. But Alistor knew the tapestry of palace intrigue and politics far better than Crispin and had never steered Crispin wrong. So, for now, Crispin could delay sharing the news until after tomorrow. Even if it meant having to first survive yet another dinner at the high table.

For the past couple of years, he'd only ever been able to produce a pathetic red glow in his hands, and despite Alistor's encouragement, Crispin's hopes of ever gaining his magic had continued to spiral.

Then, today had happened. Fire had burst from his fingertips. What random miracle in all the five Greater Worlds might have triggered such an abruptly strong response inside him today?

They reached the part of the woods that was dotted with vertical spheres of soft white light and surrounded by guards. One by one, Alistor and the young men stepped inside the portals of light. Crispin entered one and, in the blink of an eye, now stood atop the floating Astyrian, pulling his cloak tightly around him as a sharp wind blew. Trumpets sang a triumphant melody from the watchtowers to announce their return. The sun shone upon the castle's high towers and turrets, and dozens of purple flags waved with the king's sigil—a phoenix spreading its flaming wings over a golden harp. Crispin followed his uncle and the other boys toward the Shrine housed inside the castle's inner courtyard.

Now closer to the sun, Crispin reached for its power, muttering some of the Fyre spells he'd heard Alistor say before. Nothing happened. The sun's rays didn't spiral down and strike him with some dramatic, glorious gift. No fire danced along his skin. He didn't feel even the slightest bit of warmth, not so much as a tingling. Maybe the fire had only been released by whatever spell the girl had used—a fluke, as Alistor had warned. Maybe, instead of passing into true manhood, the ritual was indeed just a ritual.

Maybe he would never become a true man after all.

CHAPTER 2

CASTLE SECRETS

Her slim frame no longer in her woodsy garments, young Gailea watched as her sister finished mixing herbs in a small bowl on the stool beside her. Darice then added them to the wet mass of flour and tied the concoction shut with a bit of cloth and twine.

"All right then, hold still..." She swept Gailea's disheveled blonde braid aside and then pressed the poultice to her cheek.

"Ouch!" Gailea cried, automatically responding with a playfully vengeful tug on the older girl's brunette braid. "Being slapped once today was enough, thank you."

"Well, it's got to be pressed on there!" Darice plonked the poultice in Gailea's palm. "Do it yourself if you've developed such a delicate constitution!" She swept her braid back up to its usual neat bun. "Let the herbs do their work..."

As the kitchen door opened and closed, a sharp chill drafted inside. Gailea shivered, hugged herself, and glanced at her sister's clothes with a prickle of envy. While still humble in style, Darice's wool dress and apron were far less shabby than Gailea's essential rags.

"I know," Darice said, rubbing Gailea's arm to warm it. "Mama sent a letter—I'll let you look at it later when you're done with your work—and she's working on making you a new dress."

"She can't afford that," Gailea protested, though a part of her felt just a tad warmer by daring to hope. Their mother, Brynn, was the finest seamstress she had ever known, and Gailea had seen her fair share within the castle walls.

"If you stopped skulking about the caves and woods like a dryad, the dresses Mama sends you might last longer," Darice teased. But her eyes were soft with sympathy. "Don't worry. It would seem business has picked up a bit lately. She says she'll be able to send it before winter sets in too hard."

Gailea grimaced. She loathed this time of year. While winter was just creeping in to steal autumn away, for her, winter had already begun. For the next four months, she would always feel cold; there was no way around it.

While never eager to perform her scullery tasks, today Gailea was ready to move around and get some semblance of heat flowing through her. Darice tended her in the kitchen, but away from the steady heat of the stoves, here in the corner near the pantry where herbs, spices, and other dry goods were kept. Cook assistants hurried in and out for supplies, but all were too absorbed in their work to pay the two sisters any mind.

As the scents of a rich roasted boar wafted to Gailea, she swallowed hard, her dry mouth watering. An ache punched at her stomach, and she grabbed at it, groaning a little. As servants and cooks bustled about the kitchen, kneading dough, adding spices to various sauces, and chopping slews of colorful vegetables, Gailea's glance strayed to a loaf of bread set on the edge of one of the tables. Perhaps she could swipe a bit on her way to begin her cleaning duties...

"Don't even think it," Darice scolded in a sharp whisper. "I've already taken care of it..." With her free hand, she passed Gailea a thick slice of bread. It was cool and lacked any fresh aroma. It was likely close to stale, but neither Gailea nor her stomach could afford to complain. Her stomach lurched as she took the precious gift and wrapped it in her apron for later.

"Thank you," Gailea said.

"Of course. Besides, I think you've had enough recklessness for one day. I know you always think you can handle things, but..." Darice lowered her voice to a quieter whisper and leaned close. "This is different. The way your magic is changing lately, you shouldn't be using it so openly—especially without having it under control. Mama is caused enough grief by us being kept here in the first place, never getting to see us except on—"

" 'On a merciful holiday' now and then," Gailea finished along with her, mocking the Head Housekeeper.

The sisters shared a grin before Darice turned stern again. "Really though. I heard talk the other day that the king has been on the search again for music mages—not that he ever stopped, but he seems to have intensified his interest again. You *must* be wary. He's up to something."

"In all of ten years," Gailea huffed, "he's never taken a special interest in *me*."

Darice raised her brows. "You sound almost insulted."

"No! Of course, I don't really want the king's attention. But it's also frustrating at times, having to portray ignorance and watch others gain a warmer bed and better food. The king chose Niall from last year's music test, if you recall. *Niall*, of all people!"

19

"Yes, and he was also placed under the king's close watch because of his more advanced musical skills—or whatever exactly his majesty is looking for. I don't think you want that being your fate. Which is why carelessness like today—"

"I didn't even do that much," Gailea whispered back. "Just a simple charm to change my skin color. And a shrill note to distract Lord Crispin from killing the deer, and one could easily argue that that was just an annoying sound instead of one of my—"

Darice pinched her sharply, and Gailea suppressed a cry.

"That's enough!" Darice snapped, her words quieter still but lacking none of the sisterly reprimand filling her face. "Just imagine if your powers continue to grow and the king discovered your full potential. Thank the blessed Lord Amiel above, thus far he hasn't spotted you yet. Draw attention to that, and it's only a matter of time before he would discover the *whole* truth about you. And then you'd be dead—or worse, like that pale wraith who follows the king about like a faithful dog."

"*Now* who's being reckless with her words?"

Darice made a face but ignored the question. "What were you even doing out in the woods anyway?" Taking the poultice back from Gailea, she eyed the result and nodded, clearly pleased with her work.

Gailea shrugged. "Lady Aline needed some herbs for her aches. I told her I'd fetch them. She said to wait till after the hunt, but I didn't see the point of making her suffer a whole day. And besides, I wanted to test out what I'd learned from our lessons."

"Kind as that may be," Darice said as she gathered the spare herbs and bits of cloth, "it was still foolish. I doubt Lady Aline teaches you with the intention of you getting a big head and running wild for all the court to see—never you mind if it was for noble intentions." She paused. "I hope it was at least worth it. Is she feeling better?"

"Yes. It's just this winter weather. But can we be done with this talk? I'm likely to hear at least as long a scolding from her."

"But not as harsh of one. I'm your big sister. And without Mama close by, someone's got to shake reason into you. Please promise you'll be careful. Do well in your studies, as always—but, as always, do not stand out by doing anything too extraordinary. Promise me."

Gailea promised dutifully, and Darice did a quick scan of the room. Gailea looked too. Nessa and the others seemed yet fully occupied in their cooking and boisterous gossip. Who would care to eavesdrop on a poor scullery maid and her sister anyway?

"I've got to get back to work," Darice said, "and so should you before the Head Housekeeper finds something else to punish you for and makes you skip another meal. I can't guarantee that I'd be able to spare more bread without getting reprimanded myself—and that would help neither of us."

Gailea touched the lump of bread in her large pocket. "Thank you, really. I'd better hurry now with the water so I can make myself somewhat presentable before having to serve in the great hall."

Darice frowned. "Why would they ask you to serve?"

"They've asked several women. Some of the men are taken ill with some stomach sickness. It seems the king doesn't want to take any risks getting ill himself."

"Nor his queen, I trust."

"You mean the heir she's carrying." Gailea scowled. "I doubt he cares for his wife's actual health any more than he does that of his brood mares; in fact, he probably cares for the horses even more—"

"Off with you!" Darice released an exasperated sigh. "You've said enough to get us in trouble for life. Get to work and mind yourself." She kissed Gailea's forehead and jumped to her feet with a final warning glance before bustling off to join the cooking fray.

Gailea gingerly touched her temple. Despite the relief her sister's poultice had brought, a dull pain persisted in her cheek and began to form a headache. She would likely boast an impressive bruise tomorrow. Perhaps such a sight wasn't very elegant or pretty, but she would accept it as a fitting prize for standing up to that stupid boy and his uncle.

With a sigh, she jumped up and headed out the small side door into the courtyard beyond. Winter's approaching chill blasted through the thin layers of her frayed dress and undergarments, and the icy air bit at her toes through a gap that flapped in one of her boots. The boots themselves had been a mercy, passed down by Nessa, a former scullery maid who had since risen to the appointment of cook's assistant.

As Gailea hefted two of the large wooden buckets and lugged them toward the well, she wished she were inside as a cook's assistant or any other position. Nessa always fussed about the kitchen draft, but its chill was like one of the warm, southwest islands Gailea had read about, at least compared to drudging outside in the bitterness of Adelaran winters. Especially since their winters were spent suspended a thousand feet in the air.

With her knack for cooking and the knowledge of herbs that Darice had taught her, Gailea could have requested the position herself, but Darice had persuaded her to keep their mother's warning: *Remain a scullery maid. Don't seek attention from unwanted eyes*. The higher Gailea rose in station, the closer she might get to the king. And such proximity meant danger—especially now that her musical magic began to manifest itself more noticeably.

Gailea lowered the buckets one by one into the well and then hoisted them back up, wincing as the cold cracked her reddened hands, reopening wounds that wouldn't have a chance to heal now till spring. Splaying her fingers, she noted the tiny slices and dried blood, along with smudges of dirt and lye. She scoffed. Who in all the Spectrum Isles would ever dare to suspect that royal blood flowed through her veins?

She could picture now the sweet, spring evenings back home, when after supper her adoptive mother, Brynn, would share stories about Gailea's heritage. Her grandfather, King Cenric, had passed the Adelaran throne to his cousin, Lord Gareth—before Moragon had usurped it. Should Moragon die, the throne should belong to Gareth, if he still lived. Rumors suggested that Moragon had already found and killed both him and his son, Donyon, in secret.

Still, while Gareth might own a legal claim to the throne, Gailea had a blood claim. That made her the greater threat, should Moragon find out. And so, Brynn had always warned both Gailea and Darice—her own birth child—from revealing anything about Gailea's potential claim to the throne.

Gailea hefted the buckets of water back toward the castle, all the while wondering how a poor maid with powers she hardly knew how to comprehend could ever prove a threat to a master mental magician like King Moragon. Even were she bold—or stupid—enough to start openly making claims on the throne, such a notion would likely prove the biggest jest that anyone in the castle had ever heard.

***

The irony of the great hall always amused Crispin. Blacks and whites decorated the entire room, from its checkered marble floor to its long, silk curtains flanking the large windows that stretched nearly to the top of the massive ceiling, displaying the millions of twinkling stars beyond.

More amusing was the fact that even though Moragon seemed to think himself superior to everyone he'd ever come in contact with, he still insisted on surrounding himself with ludicrously large amounts of people. The lords and ladies of the court dined at many tables that formed an arc around the high table—an arc formed many yards away, making the high table feel like a distant island in their midst.

Despite the large number of courtiers and the dozens of servants bustling about, Crispin also felt that the high table was dwarfed by the ridiculously cavernous size of the room. This juxtaposition made him feel very small and cornered—much as he often felt under the king's scrutinizing stare. Crispin wished he could go join the other tables, with their merry talk and laughter. There weren't even dogs to pet or throw scraps to; the king considered animals dirty, disgusting things, except for his horses, which he groomed and treated like gods.

Apart from the tables, the other half of the gigantic room was occupied by a vast collection of musical instruments, all sealed inside glass cases suspended mid-air—all the work of King Moragon. He was a great collector, but while he excelled at playing many of them, he had begrudgingly never shown any signs of the musical magic that so fascinated him. Crispin assumed this obsession was his main reason for keeping a number of music mages about the castle, granting even the poorest of them private lessons with the best tutors he could find.

Candlelight from the elegant chandeliers above and the gleaming candelabras on the tables cast a soft, orange glow upon the small party gathered with Crispin at the high table tonight: his uncles—Moragon the king, and his younger half-brother, Alistor, to his left. To Moragon's right was his wife, Marlis, and Master Chevalier, who despite being no relation, was—as the king's head magician—a favorite guest. He seemed to play the part of the king's eternal shadow, seen more constantly at the king's side than the queen herself.

Not far from the high table, a small orchestra played music that Crispin thought might have soothed him under any other circumstances. Instead, the music set him on edge. As was not uncommon, ever since the meal had begun, something had seemed amiss.

"If I may say, your majesty," Crispin said to his aunt Marlis, attempting to slice the tension, "You look in excellent health tonight. You and your child are well, I trust?"

Marlis beamed at him, the red flush in her cheeks even deeper than her burnished-copper curls. Touching her swelling stomach, she said, "The babe is quite well, nephew. It's so gracious of you to ask."

"Yes, quite well indeed," Moragon said, "and better still, if my seers speak the truth and she bears a son as strong as his father."

"And," Marlis added, "Amiel-willing, the strength of his grandfather."

Moragon snorted. "I would dare to hope, except I think hoping, in this case, would prove worse than foolish. Seeing as *you*, my dear, did *not* inherit your grandfather's strength..."

The king drew himself up proudly. He was a tall man, lean but muscular like Alistor; he wore a smile of necessary politeness, though it did not expel the annoyance in his eyes. Their dark color—brown, nearly black like a raven's feathers—matched his hair, trimmed short and perfectly contrasted with his fair skin. With his icy complexion and hardened face, he looked almost like a marble statue.

"Then again," he added, with a challenging glare at Alistor, "perhaps we've enough Fyres running amuck as it is."

"I did inherit my *mother's* strength," Marlis persisted. "*Botanica* can be just as great a strength as fire—"

"What strength is there in growing herbs and flowers? The fields and forests accomplish the same, all on their own."

"But healing—"

Moragon set his wine goblet down with a harsh thud. "There are more than enough healers in the world. We need more men of power, of true talent. Talents of the *mind*. I cannot understand why you would not have more ambition for our child—why must I have it for the both of us? Amiel forbid our child should inherit the less admirable characteristics of your family—let alone their looks. Really, if I were to chop off her hair, it would be like waking up beside *Alistor* every day."

Crispin looked at his plate and stabbed a potato with his fork, trying to hide his surprise at the king's blatant rudeness toward his wife. Even after all this time, he still found himself caught off guard by the variety of insults his majesty managed to conjure.

Moragon smiled wryly at his brother before skewering a piece of meat and shoving it in his mouth. Alistor looked equally annoyed; the grip on his knife had tightened. The queen only stared at her place setting. Everyone knew why the king hated Marlis so vehemently: she reminded him so much of his half-brothers, Alistor and Merritt—Crispin's late father, who had died in battle just before Crispin was born. Moragon made no attempt to conceal his loathing toward his younger brothers' Fyre heritage and everything associated with that side of the royal family. But there were some contracts—arranged marriages included—that even kings could not break.

"And your parents and sister?" Chevalier asked, looking at the queen, his voice as even and pleasant as though there had been no interruption in the flow of conversation. Tilting his head, he watched the queen with a polite smile. His green hair was plaited in its usual fashion—a thick, elegant braid that stretched long down his back. His willowy frame and cream-colored robes made him look almost like some guardian spirit of the earth. Crispin thought briefly of the servant girl from yesterday, but Chevalier was far more refined; the girl had fit more naturally into the woods.

"Have you any word from Hyloria as of late?" he added.

"Yes—yes." The queen sipped from her goblet and tilted it toward Chevalier with a gentle smile before setting it back down. "They're doing splendidly. The Aquanites have helped to establish trade routes. We've discovered that the land is rich in many types of minerals and gems and have set to mining them. Our Fyre magic excels in crafting the gems into all sorts of treasures, and so our trade continues to grow—"

"A fool's business!" Moragon snapped loudly; several heads turned in their direction from the surrounding tables. "I tire of hearing about your flashy race and their obsession with vulgar colors and shiny things. True riches are those of the mind—the arts!" He flung his arms wide toward his collection of floating instruments before returning a disapproving glare to his wife. "Truly, you are base in your pursuits."

The queen sat with her mouth agape. Then, she closed it and looked down at her plate, her smile extinguished, and returned to delicately eating her meal.

Moragon carved off another sliver of boar and waved his fork at her. "You should keep your sights set on Adelar, my dear; its prosperity and power far outweigh those of your petty kingdom with its fire-breathing heathens, spreading their heresy of equal religions—a country from which I rescued you, though you're ever incapable of showing any gratitude..."

Alistor breathed deeply beside Crispin, who felt a sudden warmth radiating through his hands. He didn't think twice about the familiar sensation until he caught Alistor's stern glance and followed it. Tiny flames rippled along Crispin's fingertips, singeing the tablecloth. Drawing his hand beneath the table, he focused until the unexpected flames drew back inside his skin—

"How goes your evening, Crispin?"

Crispin jumped at the loud greeting but quickly redrew his composure and turned to his least favorite uncle. "Your majesty?"

"Forgive me for not yet greeting you after what I'm sure has been a long day."

Crispin stared evenly at the king. Ordinarily, his commanding demeanor was intimidating. Tonight, Crispin's flare of anger lingered, especially after Moragon had berated the Fyre race yet again before him and his aunt and uncle.

"Good evening, your grace," he returned politely.

Marlis smiled. "I have been meaning to ask after your sister. When will dear Elda return to us? She is much missed by me and my ladies—her company *and* her skill with a needle. And she herself has not a few young swains amongst the courtiers pining, I dare say—"

"You must please excuse the queen," Moragon broke in. "She is yet as incapable of knowing what kind of talk is appropriate as your other uncle here is of knowing how to properly instruct his own nephew in a simple hunt."

Alistor sat more straightly beside Crispin. "The hunt was a success, sire. If someone misinformed you—"

"On the contrary, my more loyal servants corrected *your* misinformation." The king's smile tightened. "They tell me that the boy blundered through and you had to convince him to complete the job. But perhaps he should tell his own tale and clear up the matter for us."

All eyes turned to Crispin whose face burned under the scrutiny.

"The arrow simply went amiss," he said, as evenly as he could. "I completed the job with a knife, to finish the rite and show the creature mercy."

"You finished the job while quaking like a girl. And with the vulgarity of the common folk; no one of royal blood should stoop to getting his hands dirty. A pity your fire powers haven't manifested yet. You could've destroyed the creature instantly."

"That would have wasted both the venison and the hide," Alistor retorted.

"The task was not to cook venison or sew deerskin trousers like some servant wench. It was to make the kill—*without* aid from others. If I were in charge, I would've made half those boys redo the trial. It's disappointing, if not surprising. The Ragnars have always been known to get what they want by bending and twisting the rules. Anyone who possessed the blood of my Vorlaire kin would have taken what belonged to him, without question. But don't feel too badly, Crispin. It's not entirely your fault. Perhaps I would have done better placing you in the care of someone more capable, such as Chevalier. Alas, that he's only joined us more recently."

Moragon's trained smile softened a little, but not so much with sincerity. Rather, he seemed to pity Crispin, as though he was some kind of infidel incapable of making his own choices.

"You there, girl," Moragon called, throwing a bone down on his plate and motioning with one hand. "Why are you just standing there? I require more wine."

The girl hurried to obey but, the next moment, she was jerked forward through the air. Moragon smirked, and Crispin shifted uncomfortably; he never had gotten used to how the king enjoyed using his mental magic to toy with the servants. Moragon released the girl so abruptly that she had to catch herself on the edge of the table to prevent herself from falling into the king's lap; wine sloshed from the tumbler she held, splashing across the king's tunic.

Moragon slapped her across the face.

"Clumsy wench."

Crispin felt a strong urge to turn the king's meal to cinders, but Alistor held him in check with a strongly meaningful glance.

As the girl filled the king's goblet, she kept her face turned to the floor, looking more angry than embarrassed. Her blue-green eyes sparked something inside Crispin's memory, and he gasped. The girl from today, the nymph-like creature from the woods. She had a lovely figure, and her face, while not exceptional, held a natural prettiness when not covered with dirt and leaves. She glanced briefly at him, narrowed her gaze, and then finished cleaning the spilled wine before hurrying away.

"That's the trouble with sending a woman to do a man's job. But then again, we couldn't risk any disease coming to our perfect heir?" He arched a brow in Marlis' direction, and she granted a small nod and smile.

"If my eyes did not deceive me, I think the girl may have pleased Crispin," Moragon added, looking amused. "You *are* a man now, and while Vorlaire blood may not flow through your veins as thickly as it does mine, it does flow. You are entitled to her, if you so desire."

"No, your grace. I only thought I recognized her."

Moragon scoffed. "Likely not. She's merely a kitchen drudge, nothing more. Honestly, Alistor, what have you been teaching the boy? He's as incapable of entertaining speech as is the queen. Just because he's a Ragnar doesn't mean he need become an impotent fool dependent on others for his every success."

"No, indeed," Alistor said, "though up until a few months ago, it was not the Ragnar line that was in danger of coming up short..." He smiled politely and let his glance drift to the queen, then back to Moragon.

Moragon scowled and called for the servant girl again. As she brought out a fresh pot of betony tea and began pouring it, he watched her with a vicious glare.

"Honestly," Alistor said, "it's a shame the pretty girl is reduced to such a state. Isn't she also one of your music students?"

"Yes..." the king released a long, frustrated sigh. "But her abilities are as disappointing as your nephew's. Simple at best. At this rate, I fear we may never find a suitable match."

"A match for what?" Crispin asked.

"Nothing of your concern. Just a special magic Chevalier has been kind enough to educate me in. He, at least, has this family's best interests at heart."

The remainder of the meal passed with gratifyingly little other conversation. Moragon spoke mostly to Chevalier. Alistor hardly ate; more than anything, he stared out the window as if bored. Everyone ignored the queen, except for Chevalier, who would send her an occasional nod or smile.

At last, supper ended, and Moragon announced he must attend royal duties.

Everyone rose, and Moragon's gaze locked on Chevalier. "Master Magician, do not forget tomorrow morning. We've much to discuss about our newest developments."

Chevalier nodded. "Your grace."

The king strode from the room. The queen forced a polite smile before curtsying and following after her husband.

Alistor paused before nodding toward the black and white floor. "A pretty chess board we have here," he murmured to Crispin. "With a king and queen and knights and castles and pawns..." With a glance at the white-robed figure of Chevalier, he chuckled. "And even sort of a bishop."

As if bidden, Chevalier took a few steps toward Crispin, but Alistor quickly swept up beside him and wrapped an arm around his shoulder. "Well, nephew, shall we?"

"Indeed, uncle."

Alistor drew Crispin into the hallway. Once they'd come to a secluded corridor, Alistor stopped Crispin, faced him, and said, "Tomorrow morning. Don't forget. We've much to discuss. And keep our secret well. You are no longer a child; it's imperative that you stop thinking like one. Moragon may begin to see you as a threat—especially if he knows you've discovered your magic. Be on your guard, and share our secret with no one."

Nodding, Crispin arrived at the corridor that would take him to his chamber, but he paused to turn back toward Alistor. "Uncle. In the game of chess, you said there were pawns. Whom would you cast in that role?"

Lord Ragnar stood tall, elegant and marked by ever-changing shadows in the flickering candlelight. "We are all of us pawns. The problem is that no one ever seems to advance. Yet."

CHAPTER 3

A SCULLERY MAID'S INTERESTS

Gailea gave the cold stone floor a few more vigorous strokes with the scrub brush before pausing, wiping her brow, and glancing about the kitchen. Servants scurried between the tall wooden cabinets and the giant counter set in the long room's midst. Women young and old measured herbs and spices and kneaded dough, preparing the next day's bread. Fragrant scents wafted around the kitchen, overwhelming Gailea's senses almost to the point of reeling—likely because she'd eaten nothing all day except the bit of bread her sister had snatched for her. Not that she wasn't grateful, but what little of her stomach it had filled was long since empty again, and the tempting aromas churned her stomach even more than usual.

As Gailea scrubbed, she inhaled the fresh, warm scents with a quiver. Some yards away, at the far end of the room, Nessa's tall, spindly frame stood turned away from her. She hummed and stirred a stew in the giant iron pot nestled over roaring flames. As the courtiers had already eaten, the stew was likely for castle staff, but due to her punishment, Gailea would never taste a drop.

The fire's warmth reached Gailea too faintly to prove helpful. As she plunged her brush into the bucket full of icy water and lye, her hands ached, and she shivered all over. It was a wonder she hadn't ever caught her death.

The smaller kitchen door banged open, and Gailea looked up as Darice entered. Another giant bucket of icy water floated into the room behind her; Gailea could just detect the tune her sister hummed to make it levitate. As her song ceased, the bucket set itself beside Gailea with a groan.

"Here you go, love."

"Thank you," Gailea said, trembling once more as the water sloshed on her hands, slicing into the raw cracks etched along her knuckles.

Darice knelt before her with a grin. "And this."

She quickly passed a small half loaf to Gailea who wrapped it gratefully in her apron pocket. Then, with a disdainful glance at the bucket of water, she said quietly, "I wish I could make the water float myself. We just learned how to with Lady Aline."

"But you will not display even the slightest skills in front of so many eyes," Darice reminded sternly.

Gailea sighed but nodded her agreement, and Darice bustled off to rejoin the kitchen staff in cooking.

Gailea returned to her scrubbing duties, singing softly to herself. One thing that wouldn't bring any notice or harm to her was the lullaby Brynn had taught them as young children. Apparently, it was also a special charm that Gillian, Gailea's birth mother, had taught Brynn before her passing. Gailea sang it ever so quietly now to grant some relief to her raw hands, which had started to crack and bleed.

Gailea scrubbed harder. Maybe her music helped her hands, but what she really needed was a song that could steal some of the roaring fire's warmth into her body. She shivered rather violently now. Her head reeled, her vision faded in and out, and she had to catch herself on the wall.

"Are you all right?" Nessa glanced over her shoulder; the herbs she was using continued to shred themselves into the pot mid-air. Nessa possessed no musical magic but knew a few basic charms with powders and herbs. Perhaps Gailea could find a way to learn levitation that way instead and therefore draw less attention to herself.

Gailea turned her face toward the flames' warmth. The rich smell of the stew made her mouth water; her dry lips parted, and she imagined stealing a spoonful—

The idea passed as Nessa narrowed her gaze and turned back to the stew, shifting in front of the pot as if guarding it with her life. Nessa was just as poor as the rest of them but terribly anxious about following every rule to a tee. She'd never risk giving Gailea the tiniest morsel.

"*Are* you all right?" Darice repeated the question as she stood kneading dough.

Gailea nodded. "Just weak. But the day's almost done."

Darice's gaze brooded with its usual concern. "You know how I worry about you. You're of age now—perhaps it's time you start looking to attract a husband. You're pretty enough, and intelligent."

Nessa scoffed and pointed to her head. "No man cares what's up *here*, if you understand my meaning. And that goes for his wench as well as himself."

Darice shot an irritated glare at Nessa's back, then looked at Gailea. "I think *some* men like a clever girl. Lord Ragnar, for instance. According to Geoffrey, he seemed quite interested in you at supper."

"You know how Geoffrey exaggerates."

"Lord Alistor Ragnar might be a nice one to cultivate," Nessa said. "Better than his majesty, anyway. My sister, Anya, was once a servant to the queen, and the king took quite the fancy to her. Promised her jewels and estates and all sorts of nice things. Then he took interest in another, and not a single one of those promises ever came true. But Milord Alistor—he's wealthy, he has *some* power, and he's certainly handsome. And they say he is a man of his word."

"He *may* be attractive, but he could be more so if he didn't parade so arrogantly."

"You're one to talk," Darice sniffed. "Always thinking you can handle situations like the one tonight and getting in over your head."

Gailea lifted her chin. "One might call that confidence, not arrogance."

"And I'm sure Lord Alistor would argue the same."

Gailea's cheeks burned while Darice returned to her cooking.

"You're both a bore," Nessa said, "especially you, a scullery maid. You don't even *deserve* someone like him."

"I never said I care to."

"You know," Darice said with a sudden playful smirk, "Geoffrey mentioned one other sitting at the high table this evening—Lord Crispin. Apparently, *he* didn't look at you like you were a tasty joint of meat on a platter."

"No, he did not look at me at all, and that pleases me more. *He* is the reason I was punished."

Darice frowned, looking skeptical, and Gailea turned away. She wasn't trying to be stubborn. But despite the boy's reluctance to kill an innocent creature, he was still part of Moragon's family and thus not to be trusted.

Hunger gnawed more painfully at Gailea's stomach, which growled loudly. She glanced up and made a quick survey of her remaining work. Still half a floor to scrub and the Head Housekeeper had also asked her to tend to a pair of chambers upstairs before finishing for the night.

"Enough of this madness," she muttered beneath her breath.

She faced away from the nearest servants and toward Nessa, who was yet occupied with her stew. Keeping a steady eye on Nessa, she crouched over, scrubbing with one hand while diving her other into her pocket and stripping off bits of bread.

She carried on this way, washing and sneaking and nibbling in corners, till the bread was spent. It was much fresher than the one Darice had secured for her earlier in the day, and it gave her just the spark of energy she needed to finish her task. She all the while wondered if perhaps, at tomorrow's lesson, she might ask Lady Aline if there was some combination of notes that could grow a loaf of bread into a whole feast. If such a song did not yet exist, it seemed to her that someone really ought to compose one.

Gailea brushed any traces of crumbs from her dress and hurried to empty the water buckets outside. Then, she grabbed some fresh herbs and rushes and scurried upstairs to the rooms the Head Housekeeper had indicated earlier.

The first was one of the sewing rooms. A bout of illness had recently swept through the castle, and many of the servants who had fallen prey to it had been confined here until they recovered. The usual *Botanica* mage, Leo, was himself ill and unable to perform the tasks.

As Gailea entered, human stench bombarded her senses. She reeled but quickly recovered. Nothing would make her lose the precious meal she'd just consumed. Breathing carefully through her mouth to take in less of the scent, she swept up the old rushes before spreading new, along with a fresh mix of basil, sage, and fennel.

Once finished, Gailea stood in the room's entrance and inhaled deeply. Traces of the foul odors lingered, but the herbs masked most of them.

"Honestly," she murmured to herself while carefully closing the door. "I've probably done a better job of things than old Leo usually does anyway."

"I'd concur with that—it's a very thorough job indeed."

Gailea whirled and nearly dropped the basket of herbs.

"Good evening. Gailea, isn't it?"

Gailea hummed her lullaby ever so softly to quell her trembling nerves. Lord Alistor Ragnar stood in the nearby archway. She quickly turned her gaze to the floor and curtsied.

"Good evening, Lord Ragnar."

"You look needlessly weary, Gailea. Is there not a less onerous way for such a delicate lady like yourself to perform your tasks?"

Gailea frowned at the floor, confused. She had no desire to risk further consequences by stepping out of line again. What was he getting at?

"It's all right," he continued. "Don't be afraid to look at me, to talk to me. Not here. We're the only ones in this hall. Some rules only apply when there are those around to see whether or not they are being kept. I won't tell."

Gailea was taken aback. That afternoon, her fury had forbidden her from paying him much heed. But now, as he leaned against the opposite doorway with a tilted chin and knowing smirk, his eyes glistened like amethysts from the moonlight shining in the windows in the hall behind him, and a crown of light seemed to ring his fiery curls. Nessa was right—he *was* handsome and more than most. But Gailea was more right in knowing that he was still dangerous.

"What?" Lord Ragnar shrugged. "Have you no words of gratitude for the one who came to your rescue after today's misadventure?"

Gailea remained silent. Was he trying to play some sort of trick, or simply mocking her?

"I spared you, you know," Lord Ragnar continued. "The Head Housekeeper wanted you whipped for leaving your post without permission, let alone entering the king's wood during the hunt. But I thought that defacing such elegance like yours even further was a far greater crime than what you committed."

Gailea lifted her chin, her lingering hunger and frustration fueling her boldness. "So, you suggested starving me? Knowing what kind of work I perform every day?"

"You'd be little good working if your body was broken."

"A broken body can still do some work. A body without strength is useless."

Lord Ragnar's brows rose in a subtle sign of possible amusement. "I can concede to that. And yet, a body need worry about neither sustenance nor physical strength if he or she possesses the right sorts of tricks to work around such challenges."

His smile remained pleasant, though his searching gaze made Gailea tense. Did he know about the food Darice had stolen for her?

"Your hands," Lord Ragnar said, stepping into the room. "They're so worn for such a lovely creature. May I?"

Gailea's heart thundered in her throat as he inched closer, partly with terror and partly with a small thrill, the latter of which she admitted with annoyance. He watched her so intently—not in a grossly lustful way as did many of the young men about the castle, but with true curiosity, as if he wished to puzzle her out. If the look came from anyone else, she might've found it attractive. Thank Amiel he didn't possess the king's mental magic, or she'd have sworn such an intent look could see her every thought.

As Alistor reached toward her, Gailea's mind raced for some song she could use to defend herself if need be.

Instead, he took the basket of herbs and set them on a small table. Gailea could only stare—a lord, performing a servant's gesture? He took her hands, and she started in further surprise, especially at the gentleness of his touch. Warmth began to flow from his hands into hers, and she flinched. Just as she prepared to jerk away, she realized the cracks were melting away from her sore flesh. Within moments, her hands felt as smooth as a newborn babe's skin. He released them, and she turned them over, spellbound.

"My lord," she breathed, staring up at him, "thank you. But what thanks do I owe such a generous mercy?"

"None at all," Alistor said. "Having enjoyed your company for a moment is thanks enough. You were so brave yesterday with my nephew. Might you be as brave with other members of his family, if given the chance?"

Gailea swallowed. Her lips parted, but her words froze in her throat. Swallowing again, she pushed the words out. "Lord Crispin doesn't seem to be quite in tune with the rest of your family."

Lord Ragnar tilted his head, traced her cheek, and smirked. "'In tune...'" He laughed quietly. "Crispin is a good lad. Strong-willed, determined—much like you. I commend you for standing up to him, even if it was impolitic. You may be just the sort of influence Crispin needs. And you could do worse than having him for an ally—and me of course, as his uncle and mentor."

Gailea still wasn't sure what he was getting at. Perhaps he sought some particular response, but what and why? Was he making some advance on her, or trying to arrange an improper liaison for his nephew?

"I won't keep you any longer," Lord Ragnar said. "I'm sure you want to be well-rested for tomorrow's studies. Good night then, Gailea."

He nodded at her, and she curtsied in turn before watching him breeze down the long corridor.

She stood stunned a moment before rousing herself to make sure the chamber door was properly closed. She then turned back toward Lord Ragnar's departing figure—

But he was already gone, vanished from the hall as though he'd been a mere vision or trick of one of the will-o-the-wisps that the servants always spun grand tales about.

Much grander was the idea that Lord Ragnar, the king's brother, had just spoken with her, a simple scullery maid, as an equal...and, more so, that he implied the king's nephew had taken some interest in her as well.

CHAPTER 4
VOICES AND VESSELS

Gailea hurried that next morning from the kitchen as fast as her feet would take her. Though she had overslept, she had refused to dash off to Lady Aline's chambers without snaring a sufficient breakfast of bread, a bit of cheese, and one of the apples picked fresh from the orchards. She could perform manual labor all day with no food, but she refused to attend lessons without being at her best. Both she and Lady Aline deserved that much.

Gailea had studied with Lady Aline for several years now. The king required every music mage in the castle, regardless of wealth or status, to take classes. Beyond his obsession with musical magic, no one was certain why his majesty made such a demand, but despite some unsettling rumors—and her sister's worries—Gailea was glad. She loved learning and looked forward to the reprieve from her duties two mornings a week.

As she picked up the pace into a sprint, last night's encounter with Lord Ragnar seemed merely a dream conjured by her tired imagination. She twisted her braided hair up into a tight bun and pinned it in place, all the while remembering his surprisingly gentle demeanor and his implications about Lord Crispin's interest in her. She still didn't trust any of it, but she couldn't help but feel intrigued. A noble taking interest in her could help her rise from her awful scullery position, never mind her mother and sister's warnings. If the king had taken no special notice of her music abilities after all these years, certainly that danger was past. Besides, she didn't see how rising from scullery to housemaid would make anyone suddenly unravel her true lineage.

Gailea finished her last bite of apple, tossed the core in her pocket, and rounded a corner where two familiar faces, Macha and Sorcha, twins just one year her junior, stood waiting beside the closed wooden door.

Skidding to a stop, Gailea fell against the wall and said breathlessly, "The boys' lessons running over again?"

"Luckily for you," Macha sniffed with a disapproving glance.

"That was an impressive run," Sorcha said brightly. "I'm excited today, aren't you? I hope we learn a new charm. Something that'll make our jobs easier. My fingers aren't used to sewing yet, and they've been aching so."

"Try scrubbing floors with ice and lye for hours on end," Gailea said with a wry grin.

Sorcha's smile faltered.

"Of course," Gailea added quickly, "our jobs are all difficult in one way or another. I couldn't imagine doing your job all day either; I don't even like sewing."

Sorcha perked up again. "Honestly, I don't care much for it either. But Mama says the accommodations are better than for some of the other servants—"

The door burst open, and two boys scurried out. They waved and smiled at the girls before darting down the hall, shoving at each other and laughing at some se-cret joke.

"Well then," Macha said. "If you two are done play-ing around, we best get inside and get to work before someone sees us and gives us some chore to do."

Immediately upon entering Lady Aline's chambers, a certain tranquility descended, wrapping around Gailea's shoulders like a warm cloak—of course, it also helped that a large fireplace always roared in the lady's hearth, melting away even the harshest winter chill. Her study chambers provided a safe haven, besides being a place of discovery.

Gailea's calm turned to excitement as her attention was drawn to the elderly woman standing at the large table on the far side of the room. She examined vials of colorful powders while mumbling at one of her thick books sprawled open.

The girls glanced at each other in curiosity, and Gailea opened her mouth to announce their presence, when Lady Aline motioned toward them and said, "Come in, come in, ladies. Come closer."

Sorcha shut the door behind them, and the three of them breezed over to stand around Lady Aline, watching wide-eyed as her hands, weathered with age, still moved nimbly, mixing bits of purple and blue powders into a small clay bowl before using a pestle to crush them finer still. Several vials filled with similar powders lay scat-tered across the table, along with shimmering rocks of the same colors and small baskets of fresh herbs. Gailea deeply inhaled their sweet scents. Besides the warmth and calm of Lady Aline's chambers, the amazing fra-grance had to be her favorite thing. She doubted any other place in the castle smelled so divine, not even the king's chambers.

Lady Aline took some of the herbs, crushed them in

her hand, and added them to the mixture. With a satisfied nod, she poured the mix into a fresh bit of cloth and tied it up with twine.

"There now," she said, smiling up at them at last. A sprig of her graying raven hair fell from her cap, and she pushed it back. "A gift for the queen. She's been having nightmares since being with child, headaches. Hopefully, this will ease her mind."

"Are we learning healing charms today?" Sorcha asked, bouncing on her heels.

"No, my dear. One day, if we've time, I'll show you a thing or two. But today we must focus on music, as his majesty demands. However, I believe that this morning's lessons won't be without interest. We've been working on how various note combinations can affect our environment, yes?"

The girls nodded. "Yes, Lady Aline."

"Take this flame, for example." She lifted a small candle and set it closer to them. "By focusing on the flame and singing notes that ascend and descend, we can make it burn brighter or softer. Observe…"

Lady Aline plucked a note on a beautifully polished lute beside her, which Gailea and the others instantly recognized as a C. Then the mage started singing "Ah," beginning with the note C and climbing her way up the scale—D, E, F, a higher A, and so on—and gradually, the flame expanded until it was the size of her fist. She held the note she'd ended with—the C an octave higher than the first—letting the bright flame crackle and shine, holding the girls spellbound. Then, she sang the same notes backward, and the flame shrunk to its regular size once more.

"Remember that concentration is key," Lady Aline said. "Whatever you want to manipulate must hold your full attention. When I was in the court orchestra, I recall this one musical mage, Silas. Oh, he was brilliant; he could lift a whole room to happiness with his songs…"

The three girls smiled knowingly at each other. Lady Aline often got distracted with tales of her youth, but none of them minded. Rather, it was nice to have someone who not only spoke to them as equals but made them feel so welcome.

"…But Silas had a wandering mind. When enough accidents happened—people getting knocked off their seats, one of the nobles nearly catching fire from a blaze in the hearth—he was promptly removed. Shame. I still miss his music to this day. But my point here is this: don't be a Silas! Focus and control are the most important tools you can learn for any type of magic, but especially magic of the mind, lest you misuse your gift. Now, let's see what you can do, eh?"

Lady Aline lit two more candles. Together, the girls stepped forward and began singing ascending scales. The flames expanded and shrunk. They repeated the exercise several times.

Gailea wondered what would happen if she sang a much lower note. She sang the lowest note she could—and gasped as her flame extinguished altogether. She quickly tried the opposite—singing a very high note—but the flame did not reappear.

"Well done," Lady Aline said, "using logic to snuff the flame. But here also you learn an important lesson—it is easier to destroy than to create. A different song would be needed to recreate a *new* flame, a different level of concentration altogether. But that's for another time. Instead, let's practice our scales on a different task…"

Lady Aline set three leaves on the table and reminded them of a previous lesson in which they made the leaves float mid-air. Sorcha giggled in delight, and even Macha grinned through her usual serious expression.

This had been a favorite lesson.

The girls again sang ascending scales, making the leaves rise higher and higher. As Macha's leaf brushed the ceiling, Sorcha exhaled in frustration. "That's not fair, you can sing higher than any of us."

"With practice," Lady Aline reminded her, "you can learn to increase your range."

Determined, Gailea focused harder on her leaf, which hovered just inches from the ceiling. She couldn't sing any higher a note than she already did, so instead, she sang louder and more forcefully. The leaf whooshed up, colliding with Macha's. Both girls ceased singing in surprise, and the leaves spiraled down and landed on the table together.

Lady Aline laughed. "Or you can always figure out another way."

"Isn't that cheating?" Macha pouted. "It's not how the magic is supposed to work."

"That's the beauty of musical magic," Lady Aline said. "There are rules, but we're not always as boxed in by them as elemental beings and other magic types. Well done to you all. Now, I would like each of you to choose one of our previous lessons to demonstrate, and we'll see if you've still got it properly mastered."

One by one, the girls demonstrated a favorite skill.

Macha sang an ascending scale that made the heat from the fireplace intensify, then shrink enough to make them shiver a bit, before returning it to its natural state. Sorcha sang a combination of notes—C, E, and G, up and down and up again—that induced a happy feeling in each of them, so much so that even Macha started to giggle.

When Gailea's turn came, she held out her arms, sang a chipper melody, and grinned as her arms changed to a bright, leafy green color. Macha stared, alarmed, while

Sorcha clapped her hands together in delight.

"How did you do that?" Sorcha breathed.

"I don't remember this one." Macha seemed quite displeased with herself.

"That *is* something." Lady Aline's smile seemed forced, and Gailea's faded as she sang her song to return her arms to their normal color. "Our lesson time is drawing to a close, and I've just remembered that I was meant to bring that calming tonic to the queen. I've kept the poor thing waiting. Macha, could you and your sister deliver it? Gailea, you stay for a moment. I know your duties await, but I need just a word."

Gailea nodded, her stomach twisting inside her. Short of her getting into a competitive quarrel with Macha, she had never seen her mentor display such a concerning look.

As Lady Aline handed the small earthy bundle to Macha, Sorcha asked, "May I please borrow another book?"

"As long as you don't let it interfere with your duties."

"Of course." Sorcha scanned the shelves and snatched a smaller volume before curtsying and hurrying after her sister.

Lady Aline shut the door quietly behind them and motioned Gailea toward the sitting area beside the fireplace. While Lady Aline eased onto the sofa, Gailea perched in one of the cushy chairs. For once, she wasn't comforted by their softness but rather sat on edge.

Studying her seriously, Lady Aline said, "I didn't teach you that. The song-spell you just showed us, the changing colors—that was never one of my lessons."

"No, I taught myself from one of your books. You said to pick a favorite, and it's one of my favorite song-spells I've ever used."

"When you say you taught yourself, how did you accomplish this?"

"The book talked about different note combinations and the colors they can create. And then I composed a short song for applying that color to my skin. I could sing it again if you like—?"

"You *composed*?" Lady Aline demanded, her voice suddenly so sharp that Gailea sat rigidly, caught off-guard.

"Yes, ma'am. If I've inadvertently shown disrespect toward you by going too far in my lessons—"

"Disrespect? No, child." Lady Aline's stern voice softened a bit. "Not at all. But I must ask, for your own safety, not to repeat that word—'composed'—ever again. Especially not outside this chamber."

"Why?" Gailea asked. "Does his majesty have some rule against…against performing that act?"

Lady Aline breathed deeply as if preparing herself for some great spell or speech. Then, she patted the cushion beside her. Gailea didn't need to be asked twice to accept an invitation so near the blazing hearth. Jumping up from her spot on the chair, she joined her teacher on the sofa.

"It has, this morning, become pertinent," Lady Aline said, "for me to tell you some things. Things most of the others do not know. But you have just proven your need to know. We have worked together for a few years now, Gailea. And you've always been bright, studious…

"But in these past couple of months, there has been a change. Perhaps due to your coming-of-age—some natural-born music mages like yourself find their powers enhanced around this time. Of course, I would owe it mostly to your curious and hard-working nature, your joy of learning. But whatever the cause, it matters not. What does matter is the fact that creating your own song-spells is a gift. A rare gift that many a music mage well advanced in years still struggles with. I don't wish to deter that gift. But it must be protected—*you* must be protected."

"Protected?" Gailea thought perhaps she should fear the intense concern on her teacher's face, but she couldn't comprehend it. "From what? Or whom? What harm can a simple charm for changing skin color do?"

"It isn't the charm itself, but rather the knowledge of its creation—the fact that you took music already established and from it, created something new."

Lady Aline sidled closer, so close that Gailea could practically taste the berry cordial on her breath. Her mentor seemed to hesitate, and for a few long moments, the only thing breaking the anticipatory silence was the crackling of the fire. A log shifted and popped, making Gailea fidget.

"I don't wish to worry you," Lady Aline said, "but I must warn you. For some time now, even before you and your sister and the other musically inclined children came to the castle, the king has been seeking to harness a forbidden magic. He is trying to craft some sort of vessel. I don't know the details, but I do know from a very reliable source that he would seek to use someone—a music mage of exceptional talent—to create this 'vessel.' Essentially, he would seek to bend their musical magic to his will, turn them into his puppet. Were he to know you possess the level of talent you've been displaying as of late, he may turn his sights to you. He cannot know."

"My sister has expressed concerns of late as well, in regard to the king's plans, but I didn't realize how...how devious they were. What do I do? Do I stop learning?"

"No. Quite the opposite. We will continue your lessons here, to maintain a sense of normalcy. The last thing we want is any attention drawn to you. But I propose also private lessons. Secret lessons, that will teach you ways to defend yourself, should the need arise. I will find a way to get these lessons to you. I have my own spies and secret servants. But you must reveal these lessons to no one—including here, in class. You must pretend to be on the same level as the others."

"Of course," Gailea said, her head spinning. Suddenly, she wished she hadn't been so reckless in the woods. Then again, the only one who'd heard her use any kind of music was Lord Crispin, and he had seemed far too absorbed in his hunting ritual to notice much else. "Has the king tried to use anyone else before? To craft this musical vessel?"

Aline nodded. "There was one. Many years ago, when you were still young. Another girl. He pushed one of the other mentors to teach her. He pushed her to her limits, and beyond…and then he tried to control her."

Gailea swallowed and dared to ask, "What happened to her?"

"She went mad. And then she was never seen again. He may have had her killed, or he may have had her locked away. Before she disappeared, she was never herself again. He couldn't control her mind fully, nor was she able to fully fight against his mental magic. Her mind was broken. It was a tragic disaster. One I could never bear to witness *you* go through."

"Won't…won't it be dangerous for you too? If you're using special books or scrolls or borrowing things to help me learn?"

Lady Aline smiled gently. "Perhaps if I was a young thing that the king could cultivate for his whims and obsessions. But an old fool like me, who has never neared the level of skill I've seen you possess? No."

"You're a brilliant teacher. Certainly no fool!"

"And neither must you be. Which is why we must endeavor to get your magic under control and well-hidden—and getting that impulsive stubbornness under control wouldn't hurt either." She and Gailea shared a grin. "This is a most vulnerable time for you, but also the most important. If you can master the art of control now, while your powers are at their most unpredictable, you'll have learned a great lesson that can help you all your life. From there, it's just continuing to learn new songs, combinations of notes—and crafting your own, secret song-spells, which you can then use to protect yourself as well."

Gailea smiled at Lady Aline. "Thank you. For everything. But I think I should be going now. The kitchen will miss me soon."

Lady Aline nodded, and the two ladies rose to their feet. "Of course. Go, be safe. Amiel keep you, my child, 'til next we meet."

***

Crispin wound after Alistor through the many corridors lined with lofty windows, dazzling tapestries, and rugs crafted from animal furs and brightly colored dyes.

Their path soon took a downward spiral, and after several sets of stairs, they curved down a long corridor flanked with torches whose flames provided the only light. A chilly breeze waved down the hall, and the cool, damp air made Crispin's nose twitch. He glanced warily at the sconces crafted from onyx stone, shaped into fairies playing flutes and sprites strumming harps. Fire blazed from their scalps as if their hair was formed of flame. Strangely, as their hollow eyes pierced Crispin, he thought of the girl from the woods.

Finally, they stood before the plain wooden door, and Alistor slipped a key from around his neck. Holding it in one hand, he muttered a spell; its metal glowed bright gold and then shifted, reshaping into the key that would fit the lock. Alistor slipped it inside and turned. Together, he and Crispin entered the older man's quarters.

As Crispin shut the door behind them, Alistor breathed a few words, and a fire blazed to life in the hearth, bouncing soft shadows along the bookshelves lining one wall and the many scientific contraptions scattered across his mammoth desk, along with stacks of papers and quills and bottles of ink.

"What a night last night, eh?" Alistor riffled through a book sprawled on his desk. "And quite an important one at that for *you*, nephew."

Alistor scrawled a note in his book, closed it, and then smiled up at Crispin.

Crispin could only frown. He touched one of the silver contraptions on the desk; it spun around in a silver blur, singing a high, whistling note, like an arrow whizzing through the air.

After Crispin's mother had died in childbirth and his father was slain in battle, Alistor had shielded him under his wing and practically raised him as his own. Moragon had never taken much notice of Crispin and without Alistor's guidance and education, Crispin wouldn't be half the man he had become.

But after yesterday, Crispin didn't feel man *enough*. It was like he'd taken all of Alistor's painstaking lessons and nurturing and, in one moment of uncertainty, cast them aside like a careless master throwing the best of his feast to his hounds.

What was more, despite his best efforts last night and this morning, it seemed his surge of power from yesterday had been little more than a fluke, pure luck—or perhaps not so lucky at all if he must now bear the shame of having lost his powers already.

Crispin's frown deepened. "Uncle Alistor, about the ceremony yesterday. Why a hunt? Why must becoming a man involve needless cruelties like killing for sport?"

Alistor paced slowly around his desk, hands clasped behind his back, and wandered to the table set between two cushy armchairs by the fire. A chess board displayed a game in mid-play, and Crispin wondered who Alistor's opponent was; he didn't think his uncle had many visitors. Alistor picked up a white knight and considered a few moments before claiming a black rook.

"We spoke of chess last night, and you asked of pawns. Well. Joining the adult world means sometimes viewing people as pawns who must be guided, or strategically placed...or even eliminated." Alistor shifted his attention to the black side of the board. "Growing up means letting go of the innocence of childhood and learning how to play the game of life. Unfortunately, only winners survive." He used the white knight again, this time stealing the black queen.

"Check," Crispin observed.

Alistor flicked the black king onto his side. "Mate."

Crispin looked again. "You're right. But how? The black king was still surrounded."

"A man may be surrounded by many so-called 'allies,' but many are out only for their own intentions. A good king—or any leader, any man—knows how to both detect and protect his closest allies, while keeping his wits about him and his shields raised on all fronts at all times. Complacency can be just as dangerous as recklessness."

Crispin folded his arms, his attention still drawn to the chess board as he tried to puzzle out how his uncle took the board so swiftly. "Yesterday, when I told you about my magic, you said Moragon might feel threatened. But I still don't understand. Moragon's mental magic is far more powerful than mine."

"Recall that you are in line as an heir to the throne—especially depending on whether or not Marlis produces a male heir. Even lions murder their princes to remain king. If you found a way to surround yourself with powerful allies like a king in a game of chess, you could pose a valid enough threat to the king."

"But I've no desire for the throne," Crispin said, looking up at his uncle, "and I have you besides. You're the best ally I could need."

"A flattering yet naive statement," Alistor said. "Remember that you left your boyhood behind you yesterday. You must start thinking like a man. And a man knows that once the knife is already at your throat, your chances for saving yourself from being slit open have already grown dismally slim. You do have my allegiance, but it may be time you start rallying the support of others in high power and position."

"And to start honing my Fyre powers?" Crispin suggested hopefully. "That is, if they come back. I can't seem to produce much beyond small embers this morning."

"Your powers will show again when they're ready. Don't force them; that won't help the process along."

"But they *will* return?" Crispin frowned at his hands; he made tiny flames dance along his fingertips, but they wouldn't intensify as they had yesterday.

"They'll come back," Alistor reassured him. "Note how they first displayed themselves in the heat of emotion. Eventually, you'll need to learn how lure them out at will—while also learning to keep them in check during those impassioned times. But in the meanwhile, don't think on it too hard. As your mind and body mature, your powers will start manifesting more readily. Then, we can start proper training."

"I hope they return soon…" Crispin waved his hands through the air, watching as the tiny flames flickered and danced before drawing them back inside his skin. "It was the best feeling in the world."

"I do commend you," Alistor said, "for keeping yourself in check at the high table last night, despite the king's provocation. I could tell that was difficult for you. But, as with a snake, there's a time for silence, a time to rattle in warning, and a time to strike. Silence is the proper course now."

"I suppose..." Crispin smiled crookedly. "His majesty isn't a snake. He's more like the boar we ate at last night's feast—all brute force and aggression."

"Do not underestimate him. He was wise *and* brutal enough to gain the services of the most powerful weapon in Adelar."

"What weapon?"

"The one that he keeps ever by his side, that would seem harmless with his graceful airs and serene grin."

"Chevalier? But isn't he just an advisor?"

"He is far more than that. So dangerous a weapon that Moragon must control him entirely. Without the collar Moragon uses to keep him in check, he could rise up, annihilate us all, and recreate a brand new Adelar none of us would ever live to see."

Crispin drank all this in, hardly believing the portrait Alistor painted of the slim, passive, ever-polite Chevalier. Alistor went on, his tone dark. "Remember that it was a sorcerer who murdered your grandfather. Moragon won't take any chances of the same happening to him. But he would certainly use Chevalier to bring all under his own dominion."

"My grandfather," Crispin repeated. "What has Chevalier to do with—" The words choked in his throat. Eyes widening, he leaned back as if bracing for an attack. "Chevalier's a *sorcerer*?"

His uncle nodded. Stunned, Crispin shook his head. Sorcerers were alien, heretical. Evil. And they were outlawed, banished, *purged* from the realm long ago.

As if he'd spoken the words aloud, Alistor murmured, "Kings make their own laws. And follow them, or not, as they please."

"Am I the only one who doesn't know? The queen, the court—do they know?"

"Some, perhaps. It's not general knowledge. Those who have figured it out have kept wisely silent."

A sorcerer in the castle. Crispin looked at the walls, imagined the stones behind them, and shuddered inwardly. No wall was thick enough protection from the power a sorcerer wielded. But...

"You said Moragon has him under control," he said slowly. "You said a collar... You're speaking of the king's mental magic?"

"Yes and no. Moragon created a literal, physical collar—some mental magic requires a conduit, especially more intense types—that he uses to keep Chevalier's powers muted, through his mental magic, yes."

"So, all this is why you so greatly despise Chevalier?"

Alistor chuckled lightly. "Is it that plainly obvious?"

Crispin laughed himself but felt uneasy; Alistor no longer looked quite as amused as he had moments ago. "As obvious as is the fact that you and his grace are also not the closest of comrades. That, I can understand; the king is no easy person for anyone to contend with. But Chevalier on the other hand...He's always seemed pleasant enough, even for a sorcerer," he added shakily.

"A serpent seems pleasant enough...until its fangs inject venom into your arm."

"What about the collar? If he can only bite when Moragon commands him—"

"Observant as you are," Alistor said, leaning casually against the bookshelf, "it's your naivety that will either spare or kill you—only Amiel knows which. Chevalier may appear harmless enough for now...and that's just what he wants everyone to believe." He paused then added quietly, "It *is* difficult at times, serving alongside such an abomination of a man."

"If he's such an abomination," Crispin began, "why does Moragon allow him to live, useful or no? The rest of the sorcerers were destroyed years ago. Moragon himself led one of the scourings, didn't he?"

"Moragon *is* a hypocrite," Alistor admitted, "for using the man's powers while scourging the land of the few others like him. But my brother keeps his pet alive because Chevalier knows things that Moragon does not, things that he lusts after. Once he obtains those things, he'll likely see Chevalier as a threat needfully purged as well."

"But what's so bad about them?" Crispin asked. "Sorcerers? I know what I've been taught, I know what everyone says. I know history. But speak plainly, uncle. After all, they didn't choose what magic they were born with. How then are they different from you or me?"

"Because they are almost impossibly powerful and thus easily corrupted."

Alistor lifted his hand, palm facing up; a small bit of flame erupted from his skin, making Crispin jump. Alistor let the fire dance along his fingertips and curl around his hand, shifting from orange to red to blue to purple, and back again.

"They are a bit like chameleons," he went on hypnotically, "in that they can naturally take on *all* types of magic. Most people are born with only one type of magic—like yourself. You could study other types and learn them through hard work. But a sorcerer is naturally born already possessing many kinds of magic."

The flame in his palm shaped into a tiny person and began to dance, still changing colors. Crispin leaned forward, fascinated. Tiny flames burst along his own fingertips as if responding with excitement to his uncle's magic. He waved the little flames in the air, trying to imitate Alistor's movements. His flames remained orange and shapeless, but he kept them burning, enjoying the sensation.

"Chevalier is young, quite young, for a sorcerer. His strength is not fully formed. I suspect that is the only way our mighty king managed to 'domesticate' him." Alistor smiled thinly. "Eventually he could gain enough power and knowledge to outmatch even the king's strongest mental powers. Then, only two choices would remain; either the king would be overrun and a new tyrant would take the throne or, before things came to that, Chevalier's threat must be extinguished." Alistor curled his hand into a fist, snuffing the flame.

Crispin swallowed, his throat suddenly dry, and the flames flickering along his fingertips reduced to a pale glow.

"I prefer the latter option," Alistor said. "Personally, given the choice, I'd rather contend with my brother than a fully matured sorcerer. I might call Chevalier out for heresy myself if I didn't think Moragon would use it as an excuse to take my own head."

Crispin's stomach dropped. After all, the king could easily turn such wrath not only upon his uncle but upon Crispin himself. Hadn't the king done away with plenty of others he'd perceived as threats? In times past, rumors had flown about the castle that not everyone Moragon had claimed to annihilate in the name of sorcery was truly guilty of the crime. Any new law might be made, any virtue turned on its head to be declared blasphemy and treason.

"Do not trouble yourself, dear nephew," Alistor said. "All we need do is make ourselves useful, not interfere in the king's business, and our lives will be secure. But

I think that's more than enough on today's cheery little life lessons." He guided Crispin to the door. "Why don't you stretch your legs, go and collect some herbs for today's botany study?"

"I will." Crispin fought against his nerves and finally voiced his question, pausing in the doorway. "Just one more thing. That girl who served us in the great hall, the one from the woods. You talked like she had some significance. Does she?"

"You may be old enough for some questions, but others require more than a certain age for revelation. You'll find out in due time, Crispin, I assure you—especially if my suspicions prove correct." Alistor lifted his eyebrows and nodded to the corridor, letting Crispin exit his chamber. Then, he laid a hand on Crispin's shoulder, squeezing gently. "Allow me to simply offer a final word of caution: You've been given many secrets to keep this morning. But sometimes, ignorance is truly bliss."

CHAPTER 5

HIDDEN GIFTS

✳

G ailea lugged the bucket of water into one of the castle's many bedchambers with a sigh. Then, hurrying over to the fireplace—larger than that in any of the servants' shared rooms—she started brushing the ashes from the hearth.

She hated how the black soot stained her clothes. Her dingy frocks weren't much to speak of, but she took pride in her appearance as best she could. At this rate, she may as well ask Mama to make her a black mourning dress.

Once she'd swept every bit of the ashes she could reach into her cloth-lined basket, she scrubbed the stones with water and lye, all the while humming her lullaby to soothe her dry, red hands. At least they hadn't cracked or bled since Lord Ragnar had healed them with his fire a few days ago. Gailea had since sung the lullaby as often as she could to keep the damage from growing too severe again.

Setting the bucket of ashes and now-filthy water aside, she grabbed some wood and oil from the nearby basket and set them ablaze in the hearth. She stirred the embers, and within moments, a steady blaze warmed her skin.

Gailea smiled, pleased with her work. Despite the unfavorable task, she felt grateful to be away from the kitchen's drafts and the constant bite of cold from making so many trips to the well; there was another servant in her place to fetch water today.

Gailea grabbed her basket of soaps and brushes, prepared to fetch a fresh bucket of water for the next room, when a noise made her pause—an unexpected, pleasant noise; rather, a song.

She listened intently. Someone played a sweet, almost melancholy tune on some sort of flute. Setting down her basket, she moved toward the opposite door, from which the music seemed to flow.

At first, she only listened, soothed by the flute's fluid melody. Then, she cracked the door open just enough to peer inside—

She covered her mouth, drowning a gasp, and nearly staggered back in surprise. Then, she leaned forward intently, watching as King Moragon himself continued to play. He sat in a small room on a chair beside a small table, where a book sprawled open. Sheet music set on a stand before him. His attention seemed to shift between the two, and he played with such grace and precision that Gailea wondered that she had never heard him play before.

The song shifted from graceful to frantic, till at last he jumped up with a roar, flipped the table, and flung away the flute, which pinged against the wall.

Gailea threw herself back from the door and pressed against the wall, quietly singing her color-changing song-spell to make her skin blend in with the gray stones. Between this disguise and the ash covering her dress, she hoped she would go undetected by the king and his rage.

She waited, trembling against the wall, until a loud slamming noise echoed in the room beyond. She waited a little longer, breathing quickly like a frightened doe ready to bolt. But she didn't bolt quite yet. Curiosity dared her to glance inside the door once more.

The room was a mess but empty of any human presence. Slowly, she opened the door a little more and crept inside. The king must have stormed out the door on the opposite side of the room.

The room itself seemed to be a library of sorts, two of its walls lined with what seemed like thousands of books. Her glance fell to the book that had fallen when the king turned the table. *The Art of Transformation, Volume 4: Music into Magic.*

So that was what had infuriated the king so. Despite his affinity for mental magic and his obvious musical talent, he still could not combine the two into musical magic.

A glint from the sunlight streaming through the window caught Gailea's attention, and she found the flute lying in the corner, lonesome, discarded as if it were nothing more than the ashes she'd just swept from the fireplace. She knelt, glanced around cautiously as if even the walls might have eyes, and then picked it up. Placing it to her lips, she played a few notes, savoring its smooth and calming sound.

Gailea hesitated. She knew what she wanted to do, but she must decide quickly before someone found her doing exactly that. Her mind flew to her lesson with Lady Aline a few days back—her urge for caution, the possible dangers she proposed, Lord Ragnar's sudden interest in her—were they all linked? Perhaps Lord Ragnar had suspected her musical talents and acted as some sort of spy for his majesty...

It could be dangerous to take the instrument for more reasons than one. And yet she couldn't protect herself without taking some risks. Learning how to harness her magic through another instrument could prove a powerful tool.

She carefully slipped the flute inside her apron pocket and prepared to leave—

There, standing in the doorway, was Lord Crispin, looking just as bewildered as she felt.

"I—pardon me," Lord Crispin said. "I was just passing by and heard music, and I was intrigued. I didn't mean to interrupt."

Gailea arched a brow. "You didn't mean to interrupt me stealing?" It wasn't the politest way to address a member of the royal family, but he stood looking so much like such an anxious altar boy that the words fell from her lips before her mind could stop them.

"I won't tell," he assured her with a shake of his head. "I've seen a dozen such tantrums; his majesty would likely just throw it out or forget about it. At any rate, such instruments are a dime a dozen to him. Best it's in capable hands, someone who will take care of it, treasure it. I heard you playing—you have some talent."

"Thank you. Though I've honestly little knowledge of what to do with it." She ran her hands lovingly along the flute.

"If I promise not to tell," Lord Crispin said with a lift of his chin, "as I already have, will you promise to learn how to play it? Perhaps you could play for me sometime."

Gailea couldn't help but smile at his playfulness. When he wasn't whining arrogantly as during the hunt, there was a certain charm about him—similar to his uncle's, but more boyish and genuine.

"I promise, my lord."

Lord Crispin nodded. "Good. Then, till we meet again—and perhaps next time, I might see your actual face. Good day, miss."

"Milord," she said with a curtsy.

With a smile, he bowed and turned to leave, but then he quickly turned back.

"Wait."

"Yes, milord?"

"I want to apologize—for my behavior in the woods and for the king's harsh treatment of you in the great hall the other night. Both were unwarranted."

"Thank you, though I'm quite used to it."

"Well...you shouldn't be. And for my part, I would not harm such a lovely creature." His cheeks flushed the moment the words left him. Looking flummoxed, he quickly bid her good day again before stealing from the room.

Gailea stood bemused. She'd been caught by either the best or worst person to catch her, as only time would tell. She may as well take the flute, at least. Lord Crispin could still break his word and tell on her—though a part of her felt that he wouldn't—so she may as well make it worth her while.

In that case, best she hide the flute now instead of carrying it with her all day for her to accidentally drop or damage.

She scurried from the room and down corridors and stairs until she reached the drafty, empty hall near the kitchen. She opened a small wooden door, slipped inside, and shut it firmly behind her. Only then did she sing her song again to return her skin to its normal shade.

Gailea's room was a tiny, cramped, humble space she had made from an old pantry. Many of the lower servants, like herself, chose to band together in one of the sewing rooms or corridors or even the kitchen itself.

They liked huddling against each other for warmth or having someone to share the latest gossip with. As for Gailea, she preferred her solitude, and now even more so if she was to start practicing her music with a stolen flute.

Carefully, she shoved the flute under her straw pallet and laid the blanket across it. She turned to leave—but then noticed something out of place. On the chair that doubled as her writing desk, a small scroll tied with a bit of twine nestled neatly between her candles, parchment, and quill.

Gailea picked up the scroll and unrolled it with a gasp. Across the top, a lovely, elegant script declared: *Your first lesson. Use it well.* Beneath that was a brief lesson on how to combine various note patterns to make noises louder or softer, as well as a small charm for creating warmth on a cold winter's day; the latter was not a musical spell, but rather a simple herbal remedy. She smiled at Lady Aline's thoughtfulness.

She memorized the ingredient list before shoving the scroll under the pallet. With any luck, by tonight, she'd be both a little warmer and a little wiser in her studies as a music mage.

***

Crispin hurried toward the garden enclosed by the inner courtyard's sturdy walls. Today had been one of those rare opportunities where his history lesson with Alistor had been cut short, thanks to the king's summoning him for some duty or other. Alistor had left Crispin with clear reluctance, promising to finish their studies later. Moments after, Crispin had received word that his sister, Elda, had returned to court at last and wished to see him in the garden.

The timing could not have proven more providential. Besides being excited to see Elda, Crispin was grateful for a distraction from the past few days' mundane routine. He tired of fetching herbs like an old woman, learning practical magics when he would much rather be practicing his Fyre magic. And yet, since the day of the hunt, he still could summon no more than mere sparks.

Even thinking about the girl and the flute—which had also well been on his mind—couldn't stir the proper passion in him. Letting her have the flute was the least he could do to repay her for the king's insults. Besides, if he admitted it to himself, she really was rather pretty, even if he had seen her mostly with green or gray skin. What he had noticed most the other day were her eyes—bright, observant, a little wild. He wagered that she would have fought him over the flute if need be.

Emerging into the garden, he stopped short and gulped the fresh, cold air. Though still surrounded by walls, the free air and trees granted him the release he needed when he felt suffocated inside the castle walls and couldn't journey down below into the woods or town.

Elda already sat on the bench beneath their favorite tree, facing away from him. Sunlight glinted on her long golden hair; whereas his was curly, hers was perfectly straight, trailing long down her back.

Crispin approached and sat beside her. She glanced up with alarm, then smiled and hugged him close. He returned the embrace, and warmth flooded his heart. Elda's presence always soothed him, even on the gloomiest day.

When they pulled back, Crispin smiled directly at her and said, "Dearest sister. It's so wonderful to have you back at court. I trust your commission was successful?"

Elda nodded and grabbed the slate beside her. She touched it with the tip of her pointer finger, which glowed gold and then illuminated with white and blue sparks. As she ran her finger across the slate, her lightning crackled, etching words that appeared in an elegant calligraphy.

Crispin watched her with a grin. Even after all these years, he still admired his sister's clever way of communicating. She had lost her hearing at a young age due to illness, but that had never stopped her from speaking her mind.

Once finished, Elda turned the message toward Crispin, and he read:

Very successful. Lady Nora was especially pleased with her new gown.

Crispin grinned at the words on the slate and then looked at his sister again, making certain to catch her gaze. "You're making quite the name for yourself. I'm proud."

Elda's smile faded into a cynical frown, and she wrote: *I wouldn't be too proud. I'm becoming renowned for reasons far less noble.*

"Vicious gossip," Crispin said, hating to see his sister possess the tiniest inkling of a doubt in herself. "Rumors—*not* reasons. Don't let their talk bother you. Anyone who knows you knows that you are truly a woman of virtue."

Elda shrugged and wrote: *I'm an easy target. They think I don't know. I know well enough. I just try not to care.*

"As well you shouldn't." Crispin squeezed her hand.

His thoughts began to stray then, as did his gaze. Staring up into the sun shining beyond the tangled, bare branches, he muttered, "I wish *I* could care less sometimes..."

Elda nudged him, and he glanced at her slate.

You look troubled.

Crispin shook his head and, certain to look at her this time, said, "It's nothing. I'm just tired."

Perhaps this will waken you.

Elda set the slate aside and cupped her hands. Soon, her hands glowed bright, making them look as if they were clad in golden armor. Tiny lightning bolts rippled from her fingers and palms. The sparks rose up and took shape until a tiny horse stood in her palm, its every detail crafted so delicately. It reared up, its mane crackling. Just as Crispin leaned close, Elda clapped her hands together, and the horse vanished.

Crispin leaned back, instantly disappointed. His sister was always teasing him with tricks like that, giving him just a taste. As a child, he had begged her to show him more, but she'd always said it wasn't wise to waste power on frivolous tricks, that it was better to conserve energy and learn how to use it for true purpose.

Crispin stared at her empty hands with a frown. He felt no jealousy toward Elda, but her talent brought his incompetence over the last few days to the forefront of his memory, twisting the embarrassment just a little deeper inside his heart.

Elda lifted the slate before him: *Now I know you are troubled. My new tricks always please you. What is wrong?*

Crispin took a deep breath and then studied her face—full of a motherly sort of concern, and certainly demanding. She would not have peace until he explained all.

"The other day, I engaged in my coming-of-age hunt." Elda's eyes widened, and she quickly wrote: *Forgive me! I'd forgotten. How did it go?*

Crispin explained briefly what happened in the woods, with the mysterious girl and the strange burst of fire that he'd produced. Elda watched him with rapt attention.

71

"Our uncle—Alistor—thinks I'm finally coming into my powers. He warned me not to talk of it though. He seems to think that the king might be jealous about having another relative around the castle as powerful as himself." Crispin said the words with a lightheartedness he didn't feel; he didn't want to involve his sister too deeply in palace intrigue. The less she knew, the safer she'd be if any serious contentions developed between himself and Moragon.

Elda studied him a while longer. Her intuition was right on target as she wrote: *Alistor thinks that, if your powers become like his, Moragon may start to see you as a threat to the throne.*

"Yes, Alistor fears that. But it doesn't even matter..." Crispin sighed deeply. "I've tried producing fire again since then, with no success. For all I know, it might have been a dream."

Elda shook her head and wrote: *I think something powerful is about to happen within you. Sometimes, the greatest powers are not born but cultivated. I think we've yet to see yours emerge fully, and when they do, they will surpass mine—and possibly even our uncle's.*

"I think that's what Alistor is worried about."

Elda's calm smile filled her face. *You know my philosophy: to be prepared, but not to worry until there is need to. Keep your eyes and ears open—and your mind, when it comes to your magic. But until then, don't fret. All good things happen in their own time.* She grinned warmly and added, *I've missed being away. It's good to be back here again with you.*

Crispin smiled back, despite himself. "You always know how to grant comfort. It's your gift. I think the queen has sensed it as well—she speaks highly of you. And honestly, it's been torture, eating at the high table without you. I'll be more than glad of your cheerful presence."

CHAPTER 6

PAWNS AND PROSPECTS

Gailea lay on her pallet, snuggled beneath her thin blanket, admiring the flute that had become one of her best friends and a true source of solace over the past few days.

She had told Lady Aline of her discovery, and the mentor had since passed to her one of their secret scroll lessons on how to channel musical energy into an instrument.

The concept was similar to using one's voice for song-spells but required a different level of concentration. Much like training a horse, one had to practice and form a bond with a musical instrument in order to fully bend it to one's will; otherwise, any song-spells attempted might turn chaotic and have unpredictable—possibly unfavorable—results. The first time Gailea had attempted to play the flute, she'd played an ascending scale to brighten her candle flame. She had played too fast and sparks had erupted, much like tiny fireworks. The embers had set fire to her skirt; thankfully she was able to drop to the floor and roll in time to snuff them.

Now, as she lay in bed, she slowly and gently played scales up and down: A, B, C#, D, E, F#, G#, and back again. The candle flame waxed and waned, waxed and waned.

Gailea glanced out her small window—another reason she had chosen the pantry for her home. Beside the moon, she could glimpse her favorite constellation—the Arion, a horse with powerful magic found in many of Adelar's legends. The Arion was said to harness the power to fly inside its silver hooves. Gailea often wished she could stretch forth her hand, grab hold of the stars, and let the majestic beast carry her far away.

Gailea practiced a little longer before storing the flute under her pallet alongside the scrolls. She wished she had a more secure hiding spot, but then again, who would bother to spy on a scullery maid in her tiny hole in the wall?

At last, her small reprieve ended, she blew out her flame and left the coziness of her room behind for the great hall. While she had finished her regular duties early for the day, she had been requested yet again to replace one of the servants at dinner for the royal family. As she picked up the pace, so did her heart as she wondered: Would Lord Crispin be there? And had he kept their secret safely between them?

***

The moon shone high outside, illuminating the black-and-white checkered floor of the great hall with a pale, ethereal glow. Torches surrounding the room provided the familiar golden-orange pallor, crowning the heads of all gathered around the high table. Crispin absently stirred the food on his plate and glanced briefly at his family—Elda shared a smile with him—but his gaze lingered upon the king, who studied him intensely.

"So, Crispin," Moragon said. "How have your studies been going?"

"Very well, your grace," Crispin said.

"Our nephew has a remarkable mind," Alistor said. "His curiosity is vast, and he can retain new knowledge and skills with seemingly no effort at all."

"As to be expected of one sharing Vorlaire blood. But I think perhaps, Crispin, a higher challenge may be in order. A young man like you *must* be starving for a higher challenge than that which mere books and essays can provide. I need a new tithe collector. I've been considering you for the task. What say you?"

Crispin stared, trying to decipher what wheels spun inside the king's head beyond his complacent expression, without revealing too much of his own surprise and curiosity. Since his talk with Alistor, Crispin had paid closer attention to his interactions with the king. Moragon continued to speak to him little more than he spoke to his wife, though he did so with a more obviously growing politeness. Was Moragon trying to play now as an enemy or a friend?

As the king continued to study Crispin, Crispin thought he detected hints of a smile pulling at the corners of his mouth and shivered. It was a fast-growing, dire wish of his that he could learn to guard against Moragon's mental magic. As king, Moragon had the right to read anyone's vulnerable thoughts at any time. Did Moragon hear him now? Did he listen to Crispin's doubts with hidden glee?

It was impossible to know. Crispin straightened, trying to look confident, before glancing with question at

Alistor who only shrugged and said, "You're a man now. Such decisions are up to you."

Looking back at the king, Crispin said, "I thank you for this honor. I accept and will try my best to fulfill the duties of the position you've so graciously extended."

Moragon nodded. "I think you can handle it. You'll mostly attend to collecting taxes. It might not be the most favorable position, but it's a start."

"Might I be able to have an assistant?" Crispin said. Moragon arched a brow, and Crispin quickly added, "Not that I couldn't handle the job alone, but a good friend of mine, Tytonn Grayfell, could make good use of an opportunity like this. He's clever, very skilled in mathematics. If he was permitted to help me, we could share our wages—"

Moragon held up his hand and then waved it in a dismissive gesture. "Let it be done. And you shall each have your own wage. It's a noble suggestion. It shows a certain maturity to pay your debts by helping those most faithful to you."

The king shared a grin that Crispin politely returned.

Moragon then motioned for someone to refill his wine. Crispin did a double-take—the girl from the woods again. As she poured the wine, she looked up and met his glance briefly. He nodded ever so subtly, hoping she understood that their secret was still safe between them.

"If you would be so kind," Chevalier said, extending his goblet toward the girl.

"Put that down, Chevalier," Moragon said, "and let the wench do her job. You're *my* servant, not hers. Girl—" He grabbed her wrist, but she didn't look at him. "Go to the kitchen and tell someone to bring me another pie. This one's burnt nearly to cinders."

He released her, and she curtsied before hurrying from the room.

"We've been seeing an awful lot of her around here lately," Chevalier mused in his soft, silvery voice. He spoke so rarely at the table that Crispin was always surprised to hear him—and as their chairs were so far apart, he had to strain to do so. "Strange, for a woman—let alone a scullery maid—to be sent on such errands."

"Tonight, I was the one to set up her service. I want to keep a closer watch on her. Observe her. My spies found something earlier today in her room—a flute, stolen from my personal collection."

Crispin choked on the gulp of wine he had just taken. He gasped for breath and quickly took another sip, hoping to wash it down and not draw attention to himself. Elda glanced at him in concern, while Moragon said, "Slow down, nephew. You just became a man—not one of the animals you hunted."

For once, Crispin didn't mind the jab. Better an insult from the king than a suspicion. He returned to his meal, eating slowly as he listened.

"If she is a thief, as you say," Alistor said, "then why is she afforded the honor of serving in your hall? Why not have her locked up or punished?"

"Because this same spy discovered the flute by hearing her play it," the king said. "She's one of the youths whom I've been allowing private lessons—with Lady Aline, in particular. You're acquainted with her, yes?"

"Of course. But why? Has she mentioned the girl displaying any particular gifts?"

The king shook his head. "None yet. But I believe she may be one to watch..." His gaze strayed to Chevalier, who nodded, looking intrigued.

Alistor scoffed. "Why the keen interest? If she hasn't shown signs of being an impressive music mage after all these years, our only reason for watching her is because of her tendency to steal."

"There are rumors too," the king added. "One of the boys from the hunt claims to have seen and heard a peculiar interaction between her and *you*, Crispin."

Crispin stopped himself from choking on his food this time but felt his face—and fingertips—turn red. Drawing his hands beneath the table just in case his flames chose now, of all times, to present themselves, he said, "I only recall her whistling loudly, to throw off my kill. If something else was amiss, I was too consumed in my hunt."

"Yes—too consumed with making a shoddy job of it."

"A stale conversation," Alistor said with a wave of his hand. "As stale as your proposal that some lowly wench shirking her duties to gallivant through the woods could hold some special significance when she's shown herself to be no more than a careless thief—a child messing around with a toy she's stolen."

"Do not question my intuition," Moragon said. "The other night, and now, when I touched her, I felt something. Our minds linked just long enough—I have an inkling about this girl. And my mind has never yet failed me."

"If it pleases your grace," Marlis spoke up, "if you wish to keep a closer watch on the girl, one or two of my ladies-in-waiting are in need of attendants. Perhaps she might do?"

Moragon scoffed but didn't look up at her. Shoving a piece of venison into his mouth, he said, "Whatever for? Haven't I given you enough wenches to perform your every task and whim? Do my gifts displease you? What of Lady Elda here?" He motioned in Elda's direction. "Do you not find her company sufficient?"

"Of course, your grace," the queen said quickly, and with a sweet smile at Elda. "But with the baby becoming more of a burden, I thought it might be helpful—"

"Our child is no burden." Moragon glared up at her; she stared at him, looking stunned, as though slapped. "However, if you are so incapable of fulfilling your duties on your own, I will grant you a new lady—dozens, if you need them—but not her. She may be of interest, but she's wild, untamed. Likely bad blood. She'll place more stress on you than I'm willing to tolerate for my heir's sake. I won't allow it."

"My ladies have watched her. She's a hard worker. She doesn't flirt with the young men or attempt anything that might be considered unclean or—"

"*Enough*," Moragon said.

Marlis drew a deep breath and began to retort, but Moragon snapped his fingers and her lips shut, pinched tightly together; she squirmed, and her face twisted in pain.

When Moragon finally lowered his hand, Marlis slumped against the back of her chair, gasping several deep breaths before regaining her composure and returning her gaze to her plate. She reached for her fork, but Moragon said, "I grow weary of your presence, my dear. You know how I hate being forced to waste my magic talents on tethering your little tantrums. Go and rest in your chambers, or whatever will please my child."

He forced a smile, his lips drawn into such a thin line he might as well have grimaced.

Rising to her feet, Marlis curtsied. "Your grace," she said quietly and left the room.

Moragon sighed and fell back in his chair, rapping his knuckles on the table.

"You there, my nerves—I need you to soothe them." He motioned to one of the servants who held a lute strapped around his shoulder. The musician stood near the king and began to play a quiet, happy tune, and Moragon turned to Chevalier.

"There are some things we must discuss. Alistor, Crispin, Elda, you are all dismissed."

Crispin rose quickly—Elda's glance had strayed across the room, and she seemed not to have seen the king give his command—but when Alistor did not stand either, Crispin glanced with question at his uncle.

"Why are you still sitting there, Alistor?" Moragon asked. "Are you becoming deaf as well as dumb? I said only Chevalier is welcome at this table."

"You may have whipped your good wife the Queen like a cur, to obey your every whim," Alistor said, "but I still have dignity and will enough left in me to resist your mind tricks. As for Crispin—he's become a man, as you said. I believe he is old enough to be included in important court matters."

Moragon's sigh was almost a growl. "Very well then. You heard your uncle, boy—sit. I expect Elda may stay as well since everyone is intent on obeying the commands of others before their king's."

While Crispin cautiously sank back into his chair, Chevalier murmured, "I actually think the queen's idea is worth considering, sire. The girl would make an excellent attendant, even perhaps a lady-in-waiting if she proves herself suitably dignified and gracious. What better way to keep her close?"

"Have we really reduced ourselves to rewarding thievery?" Alistor asked.

"Enough," Moragon said. "If you're to join us, you'll do so in silence. Your ignorance of good manners shames you and sets an awful example for our nephew."

Alistor's smile was cool. "Is it truly my ignorance that irritates you, or is it my knowledge that intimidates you—your grace?"

Moragon narrowed his gaze at his brother and slammed his fist on the table, which shook violently. Goblets fell; food spilled. Crispin's gaze darted to Elda, who looked as alarmed as he felt. The tremors traveled up the wood toward Alistor whose hand shot up, bright red flames dancing along his fingertips. The flames waved from the impact of Moragon's little spell which abruptly ceased. Then, all lay still.

Alistor extinguished his flames. With a smirk, he leaned back in his chair and shook his head. "Temper, temper. You always *were* the most spoiled—the curse of the eldest, I suppose."

At a loss, Crispin just stared at his closer uncle. Had Alistor lost all sense? Why provoke Moragon so boldly, so pointlessly? Over the queen's potential *attendant*?

"If I may," Chevalier said, raising his voice a little— and shocking Crispin in so doing, "turning back to the girl, if you truly are suspicious about her magic, then keeping her closer, surrounded by many ladies who already serve as your spies—is it not worth it? Perhaps she hasn't displayed any significant powers yet, but if she does, think what it will mean. Think of everything we've been working toward."

Moragon's gaze narrowed a little more, whether with disgust or intrigue, Crispin couldn't tell. He took a deep breath, and his fists, resting on the table, clenched tightly.

"By increasing her position," Chevalier continued in his most sinuous voice, "she becomes more important. And important people are more closely watched. If she is so skilled in music, she will have to slip up at some point."

"Or," Alistor said, "by increasing her position, we simply give her more leave to steal further from us or perform some other unsavory feat."

"I will consider your words," Moragon said to Chevalier, ignoring Alistor. "Chevalier, please remove yourself. I would have a word with my brother."

Chevalier rose from the table and departed with a bow.

Moragon turned then to Alistor. Crispin could sense the tension emanating between them, as though they might leap across the table at any moment, throwing spells and grappling at each other's throats.

Moragon tapped his fingers on the table, seeming almost to claw at the tablecloth. "Why do you insist on insulting and embarrassing me?"

"Perhaps because it continues to insult and embarrass *me*," Alistor said, "that you would trust me with some matters but leave others, vastly more important, in the hands of a veritable stranger in comparison."

"Strangers can prove far more loyal friends than family. Chevalier has more to lose and more to fear— and thus more reason to be on his best behavior."

"But this is no matter of a simple spell," Alistor pressed, leaning forward in his chair. "I *know* what magic you're dabbling in. It is dark, and it is powerful beyond imagining. Do you honestly think your precious little protégé can handle it? While your favorite fool may be admittedly skilled and ambitious, it takes more than simple ambition and skill to unlock such an ancient art. Do you really think he won't balk when things go awry—?"

"Silence, snake!" Moragon hissed. "I should not have to remind you that you are not as close to this family as others and that it would be shamefully easy for you to be accused of treason for speaking against one of my closest advisors."

Alistor studied his brother for a few moments more, seeming to consider. Then, rising to his feet, he said, "I seem to have overstayed my welcome, as usual. Your grace."

Crispin and Elda rose too. Alistor bowed and hurried from the room. Crispin followed suit, as did Elda with a curtsy. Crispin could hear the king calling for more wine and a merrier tune.

Elda grabbed Crispin's arm then and hastily wrote on her slate: *Do you know the girl? I saw your face when you saw her tonight.*

Crispin took the chalk his sister offered and wrote back. *I've met her before.*

Do you have an interest in her?

Crispin tried to feign ignorance, but Elda smiled and wrote, *If she becomes one of the queen's ladies, I'll do my best to keep an eye on her.*

Crispin grinned and said quietly, "Thank you. But now let us retire to our chambers before someone finds a reason to accuse *us* of some mischief."

CHAPTER 7

PRETTY BOWS AND WARM BEDS

Summoned. The king has summoned you to his chambers.
As two guards led Gailea through the corridors toward the king's chambers, the word rang in her ears, hollow and piercing. Did his grace *know*? Had he finally gained an inkling of her musical affinity? Or perhaps someone had found the flute? She couldn't be certain, as she hadn't returned to her room since that morning.

Perhaps Lady Aline had told the king about her gift of composing; Gailea wouldn't hold it against her, as she may have been threatened or otherwise forced. Or perhaps the royal nephew had betrayed his word to her after all.

Or perhaps it didn't really matter who, but only what would come next and how Gailea must prepare herself.

The castle's décor grew gradually more elaborate. Tapestries woven from shimmering gold, silver, red, and purple threads adorned the walls. Furs padded her way as she crossed, a relief to her old shoes and the new blisters on the feet within them. She smoothed the nonexistent wrinkles from her carefully kept plain dress and forced a smile. Making herself look truly presentable to any king, let alone one who despised her as much as Moragon seemed to, was likely a hopeless case. At least she'd been granted the privilege of washing up and re-braiding her hair. Mama always said that being poor in coins didn't mean one had to be poor in manners and self-worth.

Upon rounding a bend, she found double doors towering at the hall's end, painted a regal purple with ornate golden swirls that formed a musical staff with notes and a great golden harp, above which a phoenix spread its wide, flaming wings. When they'd nearly reached the doors, the two guards flanking them opened them wide. Gailea crossed over the threshold into a new world and slowly took in her breath.

The throne room was not as vast as the great hall, but its ceilings were just as lofty, and everything dripped with the king's dramatic flair. Golden pillars supported arched ceilings. Gold, black, purple, and blood-red covered everything, from the walls and floor to the carpets, the fireplace, and the throne set atop a dais, upon which his grace sat.

The guards led Gailea over, and Moragon met her gaze with a smug smile. She glanced away; she didn't fear him, but she didn't yet know for what purpose she'd been summoned and didn't want to press her luck one way or another.

"The maid Gailea to see you, your grace, upon your request."

The guards stopped, and Gailea behind them. Moragon waved the guards aside, and as they dispersed to the far walls, Gailea looked up again and suppressed a gasp. Two smaller thrones flanked Moragon's. The one on his right was empty, but the one on his left was occupied. Lord Alistor sat tall and poised, elbow propped on the throne's armrest, chin resting on his palm. He smiled at Gailea, a slight but steady expression, and his gaze locked intently on her. Why did he study her with such rapt interest? Was it his doing that she stood here now? Did he delight in whatever punishment would soon be granted her?

Gailea drew her focus once more to the floor and waited, hands folded before her.

At last, the king said, "Lift your eyes, girl. What a turn of events. Did the Head Housekeeper explain to you why I've chosen to see you this morning?"

Somehow, she raised her chin and met the king's stare, which was even cooler than his brother's. "No, your grace."

"Good." Moragon gave a curt nod. "My instructions were that I should tell you the good news myself. You are aware of your queen's condition. She is eager for the aid of some new attendants and ladies-in-waiting. My wife tells me you are a good worker, or so she has heard; at any rate, she encouraged me to enlist you."

Gailea stood stunned for a moment. She glanced at Alistor but could read nothing beyond his steady amusement.

"*Me*, your grace? That is a great honor."

"Indeed. I must say I cannot fathom what she sees in you. Her judgment is not very sound, made even less so by her condition. Honestly, I've never seen a woman so incapable of just carrying on with it; bearing children is a woman's purpose in life, after all.

"But I digress. My advisor, Sir Chevalier, also sees some merit in you, and his counsel is almost always wise. And, after some debate, Lord Alistor here concurs as well. Our Head Housekeeper says that you are strong and diligent. She also reports that your spirit can be a bit wild, but I'm certain with proper grooming, we can help tame such tendencies, possibly even make a lady out of you. What say you?"

Gailea felt a twinge of irritation. The king as much as called her a wild beast to her face. She also knew what Mama and Darice would say: it's not worth it. It's a trap. Being closer to the king will make it far too easy to trip up in front of him.

But she also knew enough of court protocol to recognize that turning down such an offer, made by the king himself, would look ignorant and ungrateful at best and treasonous at worst. This was a command disguised as a choice, wrapped up in the pretty bows of better food and living quarters.

She didn't trust it. But all she could do now was accept and make the most of it.

With a curtsy, she said, "I am most honored to accept, your grace."

Moragon nodded again. "Good. My guards will escort you to your chambers, where you may have a day to settle in and get accustomed to your new quarters. Tomorrow, you will meet the queen and may thank her in person for her generosity. Then, you will begin your new duties. None of the old will apply to you—except, of course, for your musical studies." He looked at her intently.

Gailea only curtsied and said, "Thank you, sire."

Moragon waved his hand dismissively. Two guards stepped forward, ready to lead Gailea to her new home. Gailea threw a glance at Lord Alistor, wondering why he had felt the need to debate with the king concerning her promotion. Perhaps he really had been making advances a couple of weeks back and was insulted at her lack of interest.

Gailea couldn't stop the anxiousness churning in her stomach as, instead of being led back down to the servants' quarters, she was led a few corridors over, down a stair, and made to stop before two double doors, much smaller in size than the king's but painted with similar golden designs.

"Your new quarters, my lady," one guard announced. "You'll find Lady Bronia inside. She will give you further instruction."

"Thank you." The words were out before she realized how he had addressed her. *My lady.* Her skin tingled with a flush at an honor that had never before been bestowed upon her.

Gailea spun to watch as the guards marched back down the hall and out of sight. Then, she turned toward the door, touched the handle, and took a huge breath. Her head spun. This was her first time entering any chamber outside her own or the kitchen or Lady Aline's without having to stoke the fire or scrub the walls. She could hardly believe this was happening, that she wasn't standing outside herself, watching another girl. Gathering her bearings, she opened the door and walked inside.

Blues, purples, and golds surrounded her. A small four-poster bed with rich velvet curtains, along with a wardrobe, desk, and dresser, all shone like gold in the sunlight pouring through one of three tall glass windows. A plump young woman with dark purple curls and wearing a simple, red gown smiled at her, hurried over, and took her hands.

"Hello, my dear. I'm Lady Bronia, the First Lady of the Bedchamber. It's so good to have you among us. You'll be attending me, and of course, the Queen as well, if she wishes." The older woman scrutinized Gailea for a second or two. "You're from the kitchens, I understand. I am not sure how much you know about the court…"

This seemed to be a question, and so Gailea shook her head.

"Ah. Never you mind, you'll learn soon enough. I and all the women of the bedchamber are closest to her grace, of course. Dressing, bathing, making sure her garments are carefully tended...all her personal needs. Of course, you attendants do some of the more, well, physical tasks, but there's no shame in doing anything that makes our sweet queen comfortable, especially now."

After drawing breath at last, Lady Bronia clasped her hands together. "Well then. I'll introduce you to the queen tomorrow as right now she's sleeping. For now, let's get you out of these drab things and into something more suitable!"

Gailea nodded and let herself be led along, all the while drinking in every detail of the elaborate room. She was led into an adjoining room where a small, blonde wisp of a pale-skinned girl stood pouring buckets of steaming water into a large porcelain tub. Gailea almost rushed over to help her but quickly staved her instincts and, the next moment, stood furthermore speechless as she realized the bath was for *her*.

"This is Tory," Bronia explained. The petite girl curtsied; her eyes, wide as saucers, didn't meet Gailea's. Gailea thought the poor thing must be hardly thirteen. "She will be your personal maidservant. Anything you need is hers to provide. I will leave the two of you to get acquainted. Some refreshments will be sent up later. If you need anything else, just let Tory know."

With that, Bronia breezed back into the bedchamber.

"Thank you," Gailea called after her, finally finding her voice.

Bronia threw a smile over her shoulder and then slipped out of sight.

Gailea glanced back at the tub. She'd been so anxious

that she only just now realized she wasn't cold. She was so used to being cold, but here, a toasty warmth surrounded her. The fire roaring in the hearth back in the main room explained her comfort.

Then she looked at Tory, who had begun to tremble. Gailea walked over and placed a hand on her shoulder. Tory flinched, but Gailea said, "Don't worry. I'm scared as well. This is all new to me. Take a look—we're almost twins in our dresses."

Tory looked up, still wide-eyed. She studied Gailea's dress, and her fear seemed to subside a little. It was true enough; the girl's gown was every bit as plain as Gailea's. They shared mutually shaky smiles.

"There, that's better," Gailea said. "If you want, go ahead and rest in the bed chamber. I'll finish the bath. And I can certainly wash myself."

Tory's eyes widened, and again she looked terrified. "Sit...sit in *your* chambers? And do nothing?"

Gailea hesitated. She wanted the girl to be comfortable, but if she was anxious the entire time with nothing to do, that wouldn't do her any good.

"What do you usually do?" Gailea asked. "I'm afraid I don't know much about personal servants—not yet. Maybe there is some other task that could make you less nervous? Perhaps..." Gailea's gaze strayed about the room till it found the wardrobe. "My clothes. I haven't had more than a simple shift and overskirts and aprons. Not since I was very, very small," she added wistfully. Her days with Mama and Darice were shrouded by time. "Perhaps you could select something and lay them out for me?"

Tory's face brightened with relief. "Gladly, milady!"

She hurried off to obey, and Gailea smiled.

She then turned back to the tub. This pool of steaming hot water was *hers*. She'd only ever known icy baths in winter, cool at best in summer. A thrill coursed through her. Closing the door, she slipped hurriedly from her thin gown and practically jumped inside the tub, splashing water across the floor. She almost wanted to mop it up but remembered that she didn't need to anymore. She laughed and splashed again, and then lay still; no need to flood the room and create extra work for Tory.

She slid beneath the hot water until only her head rested above. It burned her skin a little, but she didn't care. She couldn't recall being wrapped in this kind of warmth from anything—not even a blanket—and couldn't get enough of the simple sensation now. There was no reason why *all* the servants shouldn't be allowed such a luxury; they would have the task of boiling their own water anyway, which made them the most entitled, in Gailea's opinion. But she wasn't here to create leaps and bounds in the way the castle was run—not yet, anyway.

Gailea soaked in the tub until she was as red as the walls of Moragon's chambers. Her skin felt raw like she'd peeled out of her old self and into a newer, softer skin. The water began to grow lukewarm, and she realized she was still dirty. Sitting up, she found some herbs on a small table, with a jar of soft, creamy soap beside. She sprinkled the herbs into the tub and inhaled their rich aroma. The scents would have been better released when the water was hot, but she would remember that for next time.

Taking the soap, she stood up and scrubbed from head to toe. Once satisfied and certain that she'd shed her skin a second time from all the scrubbing, she got out of the tub to dress, but only the servant's dress lay crumpled on the floor. Its dingy color and thin, rumpled form made it look like a mere rag. Strange, how one thing could seem so valuable in one setting, yet so unnecessary in another. Gailea grabbed the only other thing she saw, a robe, and stepped into the bedchamber.

Tory rushed over to draw the thick blue and purple velvet curtains closed, securing them with thick golden braided cords. The room grew darker but in a subdued, calming sort of way.

Tory quickly helped Gailea slip into a white petticoat; her hands moved hurriedly and clumsily. Gailea did her best to help Tory along, but it took her some thinking to puzzle out the various elements of the petticoats, as well as the corset, stockings, and boots. The gown, a soft blue-green velvet with a high waist and long, trailing sleeves, proved the easiest part of the ensemble, disregarding the long row of buttons down its back; Tory and Gailea battled them together, with a few good laughs.

Once dressed, Gailea stood before the oval mirror and admired herself, again as though she watched a completely different person. The face was hers but far cleaner, and with the hint of a rosy hue to her cheeks. Her braided hair smelled like sweet herbs. And while the corset was a bit tight, the gown's velvet hugged her body as if she lay in a field of soft flowers.

Gailea eased onto the edge of the bed with a sigh.

"Thank you, Tory," she said. "If you like, you may be dismissed for now—I *am* allowed a bit of privacy?"

"Of course, my lady," Tory said.

Gailea nodded. "You've been a great help."

Tory curtsied. "Thank you, ma'am. If you need anything, there's a cord beside the bed. Tug on it, and I'll come running at once."

This much of the castle's magic, Gailea knew. She had been on the other end of the cord many times. "Thank you. I'll remember that."

With a final curtsy, Tory turned and left the room.

Gailea sat thunderstruck by the sudden, intense quiet. Then, she flopped back on the bed and spread her arms wide, absorbing the serenity. No clanging dishes. No cranky maids shouting commands or whispering inappropriate rumors. She rubbed her hands together; they had been made a little smoother from the herbs' soothing. She could lie this way forever, with furs stretching warmly beneath her—

A knock on the door startled her, and she leapt off the bed. Then, quickly realizing how improper such an action was, she smoothed out her dress, attempted to straighten herself into a poised position, and said, "Yes, come in—please."

The door opened, and Gailea lit up as her sister walked in with a tray of food.

"Darice!"

Gailea rushed over and, the moment her sister set the food down, swept her up in a warm embrace. Darice hugged her back, laughing, and Gailea spun them about till they both crashed on the bed.

Darice chuckled. "I think you've a lot to learn about becoming a lady."

"His majesty *did* call me a wild beast! May as well live up to my reputation."

Darice's smile faded a little. "Careful what you say aloud. You're no longer in the secluded confines of your closet, my love."

The two sisters sat up, facing each other, and Darice squeezed Gailea's hand. "Look at you. You look so beautiful—and smell just as pretty."

"It hardly feels real, it's happened so fast. And I didn't expect to see *you*, of all people."

"I shouldn't really be here," Darice admitted. "And I can't stay long. But when I heard about your new position, I convinced your servant to let me bring your tray, just this once, to congratulate you, especially since I'll likely see less of you now. And I also came to give you this…"

She leaned over and grabbed a small wooden box from the tray of freshly steaming food. She opened the box, and at first, Gailea frowned.

"There's nothing in it."

Darice sang a little tune, and immediately, three items appeared—a flute and two tiny scrolls.

"My lessons," Gailea gasped. "And the flute—so they didn't find it after all."

"Don't be so certain." Darice's expression seemed to tighten. "I rescued these from your room the moment I heard they'd moved you here. But I feel something is amiss. They didn't raise your position out of the kindness of his majesty's heart. Perhaps his nephew's newfound affection swayed him…but I doubt even that."

"His nephew? Lord Crispin?"

"Tongues wag. It seems he's developed some fondness for you. But that won't outweigh the king's lust."

Gailea grimaced. "I've no interest in becoming one of his mistresses."

"As if you would have a choice!" Darice whispered harshly. She leaned close and grasped Gailea's hand so tightly that it pinched a little, but Gailea gave her full attention as Darice continued, "He has lured countless ladies to his bed through the bewitchment of his mental magic. Still, that's not what I speak of. Remember what his true ambition is. His lust is not of the body, but for music and all the power that it promises. We don't know why he really brought you here. He may have an inkling of your musical talents. Or, Amiel forbid, your true lineage—or both! Either way, he isn't safe. None of the royal family are. You must keep your wits about you and guard your talent. And that means keeping things like *this* more secure."

She held out the wooden box, and Gailea gladly took it and hugged it protectively to her chest.

"It's magic," Darice continued. "A gift from my music mentor long ago. I'll teach you the song that will allow its contents to remain unseen except to those who know the tune. Listen carefully."

Gailea copied Darice as she sang, making the items vanish and reappear several times before Darice was satisfied.

"I recommend keeping other trinkets inside that people *can* see, to make the box seem less suspicious, should anyone go prying."

"Of course," Gailea said, smiling at her sister's wiles. "Such deceptive art! You contain depths that still surprise me. And thank you."

"I hope I have many chances to surprise you in the years to come. And you're welcome. If I hear any valuable gossip, I'll come to you. And should you find yourself in need of any aid, come to me. Meanwhile..." Darice motioned about the room. "Enjoy all of this, as best you can. You deserve it. But don't get used to this personal service. All your other meals will be taken in the great hall."

Gailea sighed. "More opportunity for the king to glare at me in contempt."

"Or for his nephew—and others—to take a liking to you. I said you shouldn't trust anyone, but that doesn't mean you shouldn't make allies. People are harder to manipulate or harm when they're well-liked. You're here now; time to start making the best of it."

***

Hours later as the moon rose and peeked through the leaded glass windows, Gailea fell back onto her bed, sinking into the soft furs. Their warmth soaked deep inside her, as did that of the roaring hearth.

Dinner in the great hall hadn't proven nearly as nerve-wracking as she had feared. Many of the court ladies and their attendants had been friendly and welcoming, and she hadn't had to interact with anyone from the high table. The king didn't seem to pay her presence any mind, though Lord Ragnar stole an amused glance now and then. Lord Crispin tried to catch her gaze as well, but each time, she didn't allow herself the luxury; in such fine settings, it would be easy to get carried away by his handsome appearance and forget the potential dangers of growing too close.

She was drifting to sleep when a knock on her door jerked her awake. She hurried to the door, but before she could reach it, Lady Bronia stepped inside. Her round face was flushed red, her eyes wide with alarm.

"Forgive me, but it's the queen. She is troubled. His grace commanded that you tend her at once."

"Me?" Gailea said. "But I haven't even *met* the queen—"

"It is an order from the king!" Bronia snapped, grabbing Gailea's hand and pulling her into the corridor.

Gailea's mind spun. The security she'd felt moments ago faded away into the shadows of the dark hallway. She touched her churning stomach; its feeling of fullness now seemed a bane as she feared losing her supper. This was it. The king was already setting her up to fail, to display some weakness or ignorance. She must be alert and polite in all things; aiding the queen must be her singular focus.

They entered a bedchamber three times the size of Gailea's and far more elaborate. Gailea followed Bronia around the side of the bed and froze in place. Queen Marlis sat propped up on pillows. The sharp angles of

97

her face softened in the fire glow, and she smiled at the person she watched—a girl with long, golden hair sitting and sewing in a rocking chair in the corner.

"Your grace," Bronia said.

The queen turned her head. Her smile deepened when she recognized Gailea.

"Ah, you've brought her. Thank you, Bronia. That will be all for now."

Bronia curtsied and slipped from the room.

Gailea curtsied. "Your grace," she said, hoping her tone wasn't too stiff. Standing in the presence of the queen was somehow more unnerving than standing in the presence of the king, perhaps because her majesty seemed like such a delicate, fragile porcelain doll. Except for her bulging stomach, she looked thin for a woman at her stage of pregnancy, and very pale. Her red hair fanned wildly about her face like a lion's mane. Heavy shadows beneath her eyes showed that her body begged sleep.

"Elda..."

Gailea assumed the queen meant the girl in the corner, but the girl made no reply.

The queen turned her head toward her, waved to catch her attention, and said, "Elda. Could you please give us some privacy? We'll finish the dress tomorrow."

Elda smiled sweetly, nodded, and gathered her thread and needles into a small drawstring bag. Slinging the silver-blue dress over her arm, she curtsied toward the queen, bobbed her head at Gailea, and stole from the room.

The queen turned her weary but sincere smile back to Gailea. "My niece, Elda. A lovely girl."

"Niece," Gailea said. "Is she also related then to Lord Crispin?"

"His sister, yes. Ah—is *he* the lucky one who was able

to persuade his grace into letting you be one of my new attendants of the bedchamber?"

"I don't know, your grace," Gailea said, grateful that the shadows and fire-glow were both certain to conceal her reddening cheeks. "But I thank you for the opportunity, as I'm told the idea was yours."

"You needn't thank me, dear. Please, sit." She motioned to the chair by the hearth. Gailea drew the chair up to the queen's bed as she continued, "Elda is a thoughtful girl, and very bright. Her talent with a needle and thread is unmatched. Had she been born a man and wielded a sword instead, she'd likely be a deadly warrior." The queen smiled weakly. "Her presence soothes me, watching her passion, her talent...but I hear you too have some talent." She leaned toward Gailea and whispered. "Do you know why I chose you, my dear?"

Gailea hesitated. "I don't know, madam."

"I chose you..." Queen Marlis reached across the bed and took Gailea's hand "...because I know what you are."

Gailea wanted to jerk her hand away. Instead, she gripped the side of the chair with her other hand, forcing herself not to jump up and rush from the room.

"You're one of the king's music students," the queen continued. "I was hoping that, like Elda, your presence might also grant some relief. And I believe I was quite right."

Gailea inwardly sighed relief; the queen knew no more than anyone else.

"I do hope," the queen added, "that we can be friends. Two ladies, repressed in our own homes, trapped within the roles set for us..." She glanced at her bedside table. "That brush there, if you don't mind—Elda usually does it for me, before bed."

Gailea helped the queen sit up, propping pillows behind her back. Then, she gently ran the brush through the queen's hair, careful to make each stroke slow and delicate. The queen's trained smile remained constant but couldn't wash away the weary sadness in her eyes—though, as she touched her stomach, her smile grew a little more genuine.

After a time, the queen turned and smiled up at Gailea. Taking the brush, she laid it aside, then took Gailea's hands in hers and said, "Thank you. I think we will be wonderful friends."

"Thank you, madam," Gailea said, "though I hardly think a few minutes are enough to pass such a gracious judgment."

"With some, yes. But I can tell you're special." After a pause, the queen asked, "Will you sing to me?"

"Why, yes, ma'am," Gailea whispered back.

The queen nodded, sank against the pillows, and closed her eyes.

Then, Gailea sang:

"Close your eyes
My precious little treasure;
When you wake
The dawn will shine anew.
May you nestle
Safe beneath the covers
And may Amiel have mercy on you."

The song was a prayer and lullaby in one—and a spell of gentle healing, the same Gailea so often used to soothe her weary hands.

The queen's lips parted, and she sighed, "I will sing that to him when he is born..."

Her breathing slowed as she drifted to sleep, hands folded prayerfully across her stomach.

Gailea stole quietly from the room and lingered outside the door. She waited a few minutes, to ensure that the queen slept soundly. All the while, she admired the queen's strength and hoped she would find joy in being a mother where she could not find joy in being a wife.

Snickering sparked Gailea's attention. From the corner of her eye, she glimpsed three of the other girls also meant to wait in the outer room beyond the queen's bedchamber door. They'd huddled in the far corner, muffling their giggles with cupped hands while eyeing the queen's bedchamber. Gailea inched a bit closer, till she could just catch their words:

"Really," a slim golden-haired beauty said. "All she does is cry and go on about the baby..."

The green-haired girl scoffed. "No *wonder* the king can't stand her. Men hate a woman who mopes about."

"Mind you hold your tongues," Lady Bronia ordered. "In her condition, you—and *he*—" This word was a whisper. "Might well have compassionate hearts for once. Stop your cackling, Lyla."

"Some say it's illegitimate, you know," Lyla, the green-haired girl, hissed. "And I half believe them. We see her bedclothes, don't we? I haven't seen him near her in *months*."

The blonde giggled. "Amiel knows his majesty has been in plenty of other beds."

"Anya! You'd blaspheme while mocking our dear lady's marriage?"

"Their marriage has been a mockery for some time. I vow it's not all his fault. He's actually quite passionate." Anya lifted her chin. "At least, when able to bed someone, he's actually drawn to..."

Anya—I know that name...Nessa's sister! Gailea prepared to come out of hiding and attempt to engage in some friendly conversation, but at Lyla's next words, she froze:

"What about that new girl? The blonde from the

kitchens? Everyone knows the only reason his majesty elevated her station so abruptly is because he desires her. He's fascinated with her, for one reason or another."

"I'll hear no more of this prattle," Lady Bronia's voice snapped. "If you cannot speak with respect, stick to your needlepoint and sew your mouths shut."

Aghast, Gailea slipped noiselessly in the opposite direction and let the women's voices vanish into silence. Once out of their view, she hurried back to her chambers and shut the door firmly behind her. For some moments, she stood leaning up against it, breathing quickly like a frightened doe.

Her heart lurched again as her glance fell on the object lying on her bed, illuminated by the hearth's golden firelight. Trembling, she walked over, sank onto the edge of the bed, and opened the tiny scroll:

In light of your new position, his majesty has altered the time for our lessons. Come to my chambers Friday morning at eleven.

~ Lady Aline

Gailea hardly knew whether this should make her feel more secure or more suspicious. Of course, Lady Aline would have been informed of her new position. But what if the scrolls were being intercepted by some spy? What if this was how his majesty learned of her enhanced musical talent?

The ladies' conversation taunted her brain, along with Darice's warnings. The king had brought her here for a purpose. No matter what that purpose was, it couldn't be favorable. Even something as simple as her soothing the queen with a lullaby could be reported to his majesty and spark his interest.

She must be extra on her guard.

CHAPTER 8

EXPECTATIONS

✳

The courtyard bustled with activity as Crispin boarded the giant, gilded sky ship that would take him and Tytonn to the city of Delosaia below. Tytonn had rushed over to help load the last of the horses, which pawed nervously, pulling against their reins as their masters led them up the ramp onto the huge vessel that hovered just a few feet above the ground. As Tytonn sang a merry tune and the horses began to calm, Crispin couldn't blame them. It had been some time since he'd last traveled this way, and the ship's constant swaying motion was strange to him as well. Sailing the skies felt different than sailing on water.

The final boxes of cargo were loaded, and someone shouted orders. The sails turned to catch a giant puff of wind, and the ship rose steadily into the sky. Crispin clung to the railing, watching with wonder as they ascended above the castle walls. As his stomach turned exhilarated flips, one of the horses began to shake its head, whinnying and stamping the ground, but Tytonn continued his song while gently petting its muzzle.

"I wish your song set *my* nerves at ease," Crispin called over his shoulder.

"We didn't *need* to take the sky ship," Tytonn reminded with a playful grin. "Could've just taken the caves like always."

"The caves are boring," Crispin said. "We're on the king's official business. Might as well make a proper entrance, eh? Besides, the ship only travels once every couple of weeks to Delosaia; the timing was simply too perfect to pass up."

"Aha, then admit it!" Tytonn pointed a challenging finger at him. "You don't care about making a 'proper' entrance. You're just doing it for the fun."

Crispin laughed. "Maybe. This *has* always been my favorite way to travel. I feel like the great explorer Jorah from Muriel."

"Only he never sailed a *flying* ship, far as we know."

"Exactly. Which makes us a leg up on him already."

More orders were shouted between the captain and several crewmen manning one of the lookouts atop a tall mast. Still gripping the rail as the ship swayed and turned, Crispin turned his sights upward—this was his favorite part, after all.

Atop the mast, a massive white gemstone carved into many shimmering facets perched inside a golden cage. A brilliant light shone from the magic-infused gem. Crispin peered ahead, where the sunlight glinting along a transparent silvery surface told him that they approached the protective barrier surrounding the castle and king's woods.

The crew members up on the mast turned a crank, and the gemstone glowed, illuminating its cage and transforming the gold into pure white. The crew kept turning until the glow spread down the mast, across the deck, and lit the entire ship with its moon-like glow. The glow radiated outward, parting the silver barrier just enough for the ship to glide through with ease. As soon as they passed through, the barrier snapped shut, sealing them outside. The crew stopped turning the crank, and the glow vanished from the ship, contained once more inside the gemstone.

Once Delosaia loomed into view below them, Crispin took the opportunity to run to the port side of the ship and stare out toward the east. It was a flawless sunny day, and he could just make out a glint of gold. If he didn't know better, he might think it was an uncommonly bright star or comet, but it was actually the Kingdom of Abalino. The entirety of Abalino floated in the sky, just like the Adelaran castle.

In fact, it was the Abalinos' magic that Moragon had used to create his floating fortress in the first place. The Abalinos could naturally fly, but their ability to make other objects float required two things: liquid gold, which constituted both their city and the ship Crispin now flew on, as well as a special concentration of mental magic that the king was fascinated by. Crispin also thought that Moragon chose to suspend his castle midair because he likely reveled in the idea of hanging so loftily above all the common folk.

Delosaia neared ever closer, and so did the ocean horizon. Soon enough, they descended and landed gracefully on the waters, pulling up to the port alongside dozens of regular seaborne trading ships.

While Tytonn helped get the horses to shore, Crispin stared at the busy town, suddenly reminded of their purpose. He wished his friend would hurry up. Crispin disliked engaging in conversation with strangers, let alone on such an unpleasant topic as tax collecting. He was glad to have Tytonn along, with his amiable, diplomatic ways, but he also felt a twinge of doubt and envy. Tytonn might be able to tame beasts, but Crispin hoped Ty wouldn't get the best of him by handling his new commission just as well.

At last, Crispin and Tytonn emerged from the port into the busy town, where the marketplace buzzed with life. Crowds hurried between various shops. A woman rolled a cart overflowing with fresh fruits, shouting that they were on sale for cheap. The scent of burnt leather from the tanning shop mingled with the smell of smelted iron from the blacksmith's and the aroma of freshly cured pork from the butcher's.

The two young men turned down a street flanked by houses, where Crispin gulped a giant breath of air, spread his arms wide, and declared, "Isn't it refreshing to be free of the castle for once? To step beyond the boundaries of that silver shield that smothers everything?"

"It is—even if on a rather dry and not entirely favored sort of business." Tytonn grinned, his eyes dancing with impish pleasure, and Crispin laughed, elbowing him. Tytonn side-stepped, just missing the jab, and laughed too. Then, his smile ebbed into a more serious expression. "Thanks again for thinking of me. My mother will be grateful as well, with four mouths yet to feed at home."

Crispin shook his head. "I don't know how she manages."

"She's an amazing and steadfast woman. Speaking of the fairer sex, how is your sister doing?"

"Elda? Excelling as usual. And she was telling me just this morning about one of the queen's new ladies-in-waiting—that strange, nymph-like creature I told you about."

Tytonn's brows rose; turning and walking backward, he produced an apple from his pocket and took a huge bite out of it. "The girl from the woods?"

Crispin nodded. "His majesty was against it at first,

but he gave in—perhaps because Alistor hated the idea so much. Which I don't quite understand, because Alistor seems to think she's talented or has something special about her. You know how they are. There's always this strange competition between him and the king, subtle but very present. And then again, not *always* so subtle," he added darkly. "Now it's heating up over this girl."

Tytonn frowned. "Why do you think that would be?"

"Don't know. I've seen Alistor try to manipulate the king before when he's very ambitious about something. Maybe he wants to protect her from the king."

"Hmm...I've never known Alistor to be chivalrous just for the sake of chivalry."

"Neither have I. Which makes me wonder if perhaps he fancies her..." Crispin frowned, caught off guard by how much the notion bothered him.

"That's an odd conclusion to jump to," Tytonn said with a grin, still devouring the apple but turning to walk beside Crispin once more. "I don't think it's Alistor who fancies her at all. I think that's just your mind playing jealous tricks on you."

"Jealous? I don't know about all that. I hardly met her."

"You spared her from punishment when you caught her with that flute—yes, milord, you fancy her. But as you said, Alistor *is* ambitious. A lady from the scullery won't help him with ambitious plans, so I wouldn't worry."

"You're probably right, though it's hard to tell with him—with either of them, really."

As they turned onto a new street, the knot in Crispin's stomach twisted a little more tightly. "Almost there..."

"This'll be easy as pie," Tytonn said. "I don't know why you've been fussing over this assignment. You talk my ears off constantly. Just pretend you're still gushing about that girl."

"You're a trusted friend," Crispin reminded him. "And talking about girls and taxes are two such diametrically opposed subjects of interest that I don't think I could pretend if I wanted to—"

Crispin's mouth dried up when he stared up at the broad girth of house constructed from black-speckled brown stone and topped with a midnight blue shingle roof. He swallowed. "Well, here we are then."

"Are you ready for this?" Tytonn crossed his arms and gave Crispin an encouraging look.

Crispin studied the house, took a deep breath, and rapped on the door. "I suppose."

"No worries. If you find yourself at a loss for words, I'll fill in. And if they don't like what I have to say, I'll gladly take a beating in your place."

Crispin smiled at his friend and then looked at the door as it swung open. A round, fair face with black, thinning hair met their gaze. Blue and green robes draped over his figure, which though heavy was offset by his height. Despite his imposing frame, he gave a polite tilt of his head. "Can I help you?"

"Master Weston?"

"Aye, sir, that's me."

"I am Lord Crispin, the king's new tithe collector, and this is Tytonn Grayfell, my assistant. We've been sent to collect the month's taxes."

"A pleasure to meet you, my lord—and Tytonn, good to see such a friendly and familiar face." He nodded at Crispin and smiled at Tytonn in turn, though both gestures were done stiffly. For a moment, Weston stood awkwardly in the doorway. Crispin stared at him, uncertain what to do, but finally cleared his throat and said, "The tax money, sir?"

"Ah, yes, of course..." The older man chuckled nervously. "Well, you see, I'd intended to pay all in full *last* month, but we've fallen a bit on hard times. My wife is pregnant, and the matter isn't faring well. The healing expenses are mounting to quite a hefty sum. I could give you a small amount, with my promise to pay in full—with interest—next month. My son has taken on some extra labor, and we should be able to manage then. If only we could have a little more time..."

Crispin took a deep breath and released it slowly. Instinct made him want to grant mercy to this man—not only from kindness but from a desire to be done with the whole affair—but this was his uncle's first assignment. If he returned empty-handed, Moragon would have more reason to denigrate him than he already did, and Crispin's chance of rising in the king's eyes would be ended before it began.

"It's all right, Master Weston," Tytonn said brightly. "We're old friends, and I understand hard times. I'm sure my family owes you some debt or other that we never managed to repay. Keep your money and use it to help your wife get well. We'll return next month for the amount in full, as promised."

"Thank you, young Grayfell. My lord," Weston released the words in a large exhale, as though he'd been holding his breath. "May Amiel bless you, and as He is my witness, I will keep my word. Good day to you." With a sheepish grin, he closed the door, and before Crispin could even try to bid him farewell, the lock clicked.

Crispin stared at the door for a moment, dumbfounded. Then, irritated at the flush rising to his cheeks, he whirled and hurried down the street, joining the milling crowds.

"Crispin, wait!" Tytonn called, racing to catch up with him. Once they walked astride, he asked, "Are you angry with me? Did I handle myself poorly?"

"No," Crispin muttered. "You handled yourself quite

well—*too* well."

"I don't understand."

"What am I to tell my uncle? He'll think I'm a fool, a failure, a coward, that I—"

Tytonn grabbed Crispin's arm, dragged him to the side of the street, and stared at him. "What on earth has gotten into you? Since when do you care what your uncle thinks?"

"Since the coming-of-age ceremony, I can't seem to prove myself useful at all! I'm supposed to be a man, and I'd hoped this job would help me feel like one, but you handled that matter as gracefully as you tame beasts—and all I could do was stand there, ignorant as to how to handle myself. I'm not even worthy of the simplest job."

"That's not true. You did well, and you'll do better next time." Tytonn leaned close and lowered his voice. "Besides, it's not that complicated. We simply make a note that the vassal was confined for some ailment or other and that we couldn't enter his home. This sort of thing happens all the time."

"And if the king finds out the truth?" Crispin asked.

"The king doesn't take real note of those inferior to him—which, in his book, is basically everyone. In truth, he likely just wants *both* of us out of his way."

Crispin narrowed his gaze at Tytonn and tore away, but Tytonn blocked his path, his gaze imploring. "I didn't mean it as an insult. But you *know* it's likely true."

Crispin took a deep breath and released it slowly. "I know. But it's not just that. When Weston said he didn't have the money, I just froze. *You* carry yourself with such confidence and poise. Perhaps I should have just let Moragon hand *you* the job and then *I* could follow *you* around like a faithful dog. Perhaps Moragon places more faith in me than he should."

Tytonn's brows raised. "I follow you around because

you're my friend and I want to help. And I *have* to have such confidence. I've *always* had to. To take care of my mother and siblings, to defend them. There's no room for weakness and indecisiveness when you're used to taking care of others."

"So, you're calling me weak then?" Crispin muttered.

Tytonn opened his mouth and then quickly closed it, his cheeks flushing crimson.

"You'd probably be right," Crispin said. "I just...I don't know what role I'm meant to play in any of this. One moment, I was just living at court, studying history with my uncle. Now, things are *expected* of me...and I don't really know *what* yet. I can't even live up to my own expectations because my magic hasn't shown itself since."

"It will," Tytonn said, resting a hand on his shoulder. "As for the rest, you're not really any different from me. You're inexperienced. But you're every bit as smart. Don't be so worried about every possible terrible thing that could happen. We're in better positions than most. People in good positions are supposed to make other people's lives better; *that's* what you should be thinking about." He let his hand fall to his side and shrugged. "Worse comes to worst, you've got enough pocket money to pay Weston's taxes for three months."

Crispin frowned. "That's not what I bargained for. I took this job to have extra freedom, to have my own coinage, not to just hand it away, or..."

Tytonn crossed his arms and raised a skeptical brow, looking almost like a scolding parent waiting for their child to come to some revelation. Crispin's frustration rose, and he opened his mouth to retort, but Tytonn beat him to it, "What about that pretty new lady we were talking about earlier? When she defended the deer, did you look at that as a weakness or as a strength?"

Crispin fell silent, struck by his friend's words. The girl had risked her safety to defend something more helpless than herself. If people like her or Tytonn could find the courage to make others' lives better, perhaps he could too.

"You'll find your voice eventually," Tytonn said as if reading his mind. "You'll find your path, as long as you keep your eyes open." With a grin, he clapped Crispin on the back and started leading him down the street. "Maybe you'll even find the courage to talk to your pretty little sprite from the forest tomorrow night and ask her for a dance."

***

Gailea entered the hall leading to Lady Aline's chambers. She had spent the morning amusing the queen, along with some of the other ladies, by helping her with a quilt she was determined to finish before her child's birth. Lady Bronia and Anya had both been there, and the latter had watched Gailea with what had seemed mixed curiosity and jealousy. Gailea wished she could tell Anya that she'd overheard her conversation several nights ago and had no interest in stealing the king's interests—or especially his bed—from her but thought it wisest to keep silent.

Lady Elda had also been amongst the queen's ladies and had helped Gailea learn a few new stitches. Gailea's sewing knowledge was limited to simple repairs, but she learned fast, and the queen praised her for her precision with detail. While Elda herself could not speak, she had made Gailea feel welcome with her warm smiles or occasional encouragement written on her slate.

As Gailea reached the door, Sorcha and Macha stepped from Lady Aline's chambers. Macha gave Gailea her usual solemn frown, though Gailea detected a hint of curiosity in her gaze, while Sorcha's face instantly brightened.

"Oh, Gailea, it's so good to see you!" Sorcha cried. "I didn't think we ever would again. How is it, being one of the queen's favored ladies?"

"Favorable," Gailea said with a self-deprecating smile. "The food is certainly an improvement. And the queen and her niece have been very kind to me."

"Oh, Lady Elda. I've seen her about. Isn't she the crippled one—?"

"Sorcha!" Macha scolded harshly. "Show some respect! She is the queen's own niece, after all."

Gailea thought that his majesty likely wouldn't care enough to call treason for insulting one of the queen's relatives, but she gently corrected Sorcha, "Lady Elda isn't crippled. She just lost her ability to hear or speak because of illness when she was young. She's very intelligent—her written conversations show more wit than a lot of people's speech."

"And I suppose you know quite a few people by now?" Macha asked, looking intrigued despite herself.

"Not yet, really. But I should get to my lessons now. Good day to both of you."

"Good day!" Sorcha returned cheerily as her sister pulled her down the hall.

Gailea entered the chambers and shut the door behind her to find Lady Aline sitting in one of the cushy armchairs beside the fireplace. Flames roared in the hearth, their bright colors alternating between red, gold, and blue, and many hues in between.

Gailea walked over with a laugh, staring in wonder, and reached her hands toward the flames.

Then, turning to Lady Aline, she breathed, "How…?"

Lady Aline smiled and shrugged. "Simple charm made from various powders. The effect is temporary, of course. I had promised Sorcha and Macha a treat at today's lesson."

"I'm sorry I missed our last session. But I was told to learn my new duties and wait for further instruction. And then, when you sent word…I must admit I was rather relieved. It's good to be here, somewhere familiar."

Lady Aline motioned to the second armchair, where Gailea took a seat. Her tutor's intelligent gaze took measure of her. "And how are you getting on? I owe you congratulations on your new position, by the way."

Gailea smiled. "Thank you. I think…I think it's going well so far. But while my circumstances have certainly improved, I also feel…trapped. As if I'm being watched, or…I don't know. Maybe it's because I'm not used to the company of such fine people. I'm not always certain I'm doing the right thing."

"You are wise to show caution," Lady Aline said. "Before we start our regular lessons, I had actually wanted to give you this…" She reached into her pocket and presented a small scroll tied with a bit of twine.

Gailea took it with a curious frown. "This looks like one of our secret lessons." She opened the scroll and read its contents. "It *is* one of our lessons. Instructions on how to create a 'song-shield'?" She glanced up at her mentor in confusion.

"I knew you might not understand," Lady Aline said. "One reason for my wishing to give you this in person. But also, because now that you're closer to the queen—and thus the king—I'm not certain it is safe to deliver your lessons to your new chambers. Since we meet privately now, I thought this seemed the safest route. There are too many spies around court; any message could be easily intercepted and relayed to his majesty."

"I had worried about that too," Gailea said. "Not that I feel you would ever do anything to put me in danger; you know the inner workings of court life far better than I do. But it's just...while I want to be glad of this new position, I'm also afraid. Afraid that the king might have some deeper purpose for appointing me, afraid he might have suspicions about my musical talents..."

"All the more reason to start working on *that* immediately." Lady Aline motioned toward the scroll. "Whether he aims to see if you're fit for his vessel experiment or some other unsavory purpose, best to learn how to protect yourself as much as you can, whether or not the need to use that protection ever arises. You're very bright, Gailea. Perhaps not as learned as the king, but every bit as intelligent. And that song, when sung or played by a music mage—even if just inside your head—will act as a shield, a barrier to the influences of his mental magic."

Gailea studied the song and then looked at her teacher skeptically. "Can this really help keep his majesty out of my mind? How could such a simple melody be so strong?"

"Not just the melody, but the determination and focus of the one using it. The king has had many years to perfect his mental magic, so this song-shield will not work should he attempt directly to infiltrate your mind—you're not strong enough yet for that. But you've shown enough mental control to start practicing. For now, the song will allow you to raise a mental shield so that he cannot immediately hear your thoughts in passing. As long as he isn't purposely probing, the song will work. And if your thoughts are already guarded—via the song—nothing should spark his interest to probe further."

"But if he can sense no thoughts in my head at all, won't that give him more cause for suspicion?"

"That's why *you* do the choosing. As you master the song, it can serve as a kind of sieve. Only the thoughts you *want* to get out, will."

"I won't be able to do that at first?"

"Probably not. It'll take practice to be able to choose which thoughts to share or hide. But I've one other thing that may help you in the meanwhile. I must go away for a little while, but you having this will give me some peace of mind that you're safe; you're a smart girl, and so I trust you to use it to your full benefit."

"Why are you going away?" Gailea asked, an instant flare of panic fluttering inside her. "Is something wrong?"

Lady Aline smiled gently. "No, just a family matter I must attend to. Here we are then…"

She picked up a small box that Gailea hadn't noticed beside her and held it out. Gailea carefully took it and opened it with a gasp. Within, a gemstone shimmered with purple and red facets inside an elegant gold setting upon a golden chain.

"It's so beautiful," Gailea breathed. "I don't know if I can accept it."

"You must," Lady Aline said. "It won't do to argue with your elders. You're a lady now and must show the proper effects of one, after all." She shared a playful smile before continuing, "It's a saving stone. It's been infused with magic that allows one to save things inside— in this case, spells, and for you that means songs. You can sing the song-shield once and lock its power inside the gem. Of course, the gem's power lasts only for an hour or so at a time, and then it needs time to rest and restore its power; sunlight will help this along, if possible. Still, it's a useful tool if you think you might need to use a song-spell but don't want to exert yourself by having to constantly concentrate—tomorrow night being a good example."

"Tomorrow night?" Gailea said. "The king's birthday celebration? I hadn't even thought to attend."

"You must, my dear," Lady Aline said. "You're a lady of the court now. It will be expected. If the king is interested in you, he'll be much more likely to raise suspicions about your absence than your presence. Take the gem; wear it. Remember its powers are limited and time your use of it well."

"And what if his majesty—if anyone—asks where I received such a fine jewel?"

"Tell them the truth—inasmuch as is safe, of course. That your mentor granted you a gift as congratulations on your new position, and to please his majesty; the gem is purple and blood red, the king's colors."

"I suppose it is," Gailea said. As she turned it in the firelight, its colors shifted, and the stone shone almost like fire. "Although when I first looked at it, I was thinking more of the colors of the Fyres."

"Red hair and amethyst eyes? The stories hold some truth then?"

Gailea looked up, confused. "What stories?"

"That you've caught the fancy of the king's nephew?"

Gailea flushed hotly. "Even were that true, I've no intention of acting upon it. Catching his fancy can't be a good thing, can it?"

"It just might. When the time comes, he could prove a useful ally against the king. It all depends on how close he is to the king himself—though rumors would suggest he isn't very. I would consider cultivating this relationship, though always with caution until you're absolutely certain of his loyalties.

"But," she added with a grin, "do not dwell on such worries just yet. Focus on enjoying tomorrow night's celebration and everything it holds in store for you."

CHAPTER 9
A LORD'S FANCIES

Noise and color assailed Crispin and Tytonn on all sides as they entered the great hall.

The cavernous room had been entirely transformed. Streamers and fresh garlands wound with flowers strung all along the walls and ceiling and between the arching fronds of the golden chandeliers. The blossoms' sweet scent mingled with the aroma of perfumes, roasts, sweets, and sweat, making Crispin's head reel. Both he and Tytonn wore tunics embroidered with silk; Crispin had chosen a deep, bright purple, and Tytonn a handsome blue. Crispin's heightened excitement made him perspire even more in the thick fabric and high collar than he already did.

Music echoed from two sets of musicians playing across from one another—yet in perfect synchrony—from the twin galleries overhead, while dozens upon dozens of finely dressed couples danced across the black-and-white checkered floor. Many people gathered in groups, gossiping, laughing, and frivolously sharing flirtatious glances, while others snatched fruits and sweets from the many long tables set around the room's perimeter. Orbs of firelight, suspended by magic, floated about the room, washing everything with prisms of shifting colors.

Crispin watched, stunned and almost afraid to step further in, as if the great hall were a forbidden fairy ring and entering might seal his own doom. But the music called, the merriment lured, and the mysterious lights and shadows bouncing across everything beckoned.

"What are we waiting for then?" Tytonn laughed.

He grabbed Crispin's hand and dragged him into the fray. They trailed along the tables, eating a bit of fruit and cake, sampling bits of cheese and wine.

Soon enough, Tytonn engaged in an animated conversation with a group of several young men Crispin recognized but didn't know well enough to join in. Only one person's presence interested him tonight, but as he searched the room, he saw no sign of the girl from the woods. Perhaps, all this time, she had been only a dream after all—

Someone grabbed Crispin's arm, and he jumped. Whirling about, he grinned to see his sister. "Elda! I'm so relieved to find a friendly face."

Elda gave him a sly grin and dragged him over to one of the window seats. They sat together, and she used her lightning to write on her slate: *The way you were looking around so desperately, I don't feel like mine was the "friendly face" you hoped to find.*

"Not you too," Crispin said with a roll of his eyes. "Tytonn's been teasing me relentlessly. But I hardly know the girl…"

I could help with that.

Crispin felt butterflies leap to life inside his stomach and start fluttering against his will, but he remained silent, trying to hide his unexpected elation at the thought.

She's sweet, kind, intelligent. You could do worse.

Elda grinned and nudged him playfully.

"Well, if you consider her a friend, then perhaps..."

I haven't seen much of you these past days. Where have you been?

Crispin shrugged and leaned back against the window. "Been busy with the new responsibilities. How is *your* work coming along?"

Very busy week, Elda wrote. *What with finishing the queen's gown for the celebration. But Gailea proved a great help.*

As Crispin scanned the crowds again, his gaze alighted on the queen. Marlis stood arm in arm with Moragon. He paid her little heed, his attention distracted and wandering, but she seemed not to care as she laughed sweetly at the couple talking to them.

"She looks radiant tonight," Crispin said. "In better spirits. Livelier than I've seen in a while."

Elda touched Crispin's arm, and he read on her slate: *Perhaps that's how you could start a conversation with Gailea. Thank her for her service to our aunt.*

"Mm, perhaps," Crispin said, fidgeting as he again tried to feign nonchalance. "But what about you? Any hopeful suitors to dance with tonight?"

Elda wrinkled her nose.

I've seen relatively few come to call. Which pleases me. She waved her hand over the slate, and the words cleared away. Then, she wrote: *There's talk of Moragon wanting to marry me off to some other kingdom. But of course, I am "damaged," and thus less "valuable" when trades are bargained for between men.*

Crispin rested his hand atop hers. "No, you're *not* damaged."

Shaking her head, she drew her hand away and continued: *I'm only saying what they think. But I'm fine being alone. I'd marry if it would help our family, but I'd rather not have to settle like the queen with someone who hates me.*

"I know, and I wouldn't wish that for you either. It's just...there's been some talk, recently, in regard to your refusal to marry. Some people think you're...that you've..."

That I offer myself to men at leisure? Play the doxy around court? Elda looked at him bluntly and shrugged before adding, *I'm the king's ward, and I have the queen's favor. I'm an easy target for gossip. As I told you before: Let them talk. Soon, it'll be someone else, and everyone will forget all about it.*

"Still, I wish you'd settle down, for your own security."

Even as he spoke, Crispin spotted Tytonn, who stood talking to a group of young men, though his attention had locked solely on Elda. As soon as Tytonn caught Crispin's gaze, he smiled, nodded, and glanced away. Crispin smirked at the rare embarrassment flushing his friend's cheeks.

Turning back at his sister, Crispin said, "What about Tytonn Grayfell? He's a kind and honest man, and a true friend. He'd make a good match."

Elda wrote: *Ideally, yes. But he has no true wealth or political standing. It would never be allowed.*

"If things continue to go more favorably for me with the king, I may be in such a position to raise Tytonn's soon enough."

I do not make choices based upon the whims of "what-ifs" and "maybes." Tytonn is a kind young man, and I would not give him false reason to hope.

"But you might at least grant him a dance?" Crispin's gaze implored. Elda glared at him, scolding, but he took her hand and said, "I sort of promised that you'd grant him just one—out of charity, of course."

Elda sighed but smiled. Playfully wrenching her

hand away, she wrote: *Very well. If he wishes, I'll grant him a dance. My feet are a little eager, to be honest.*

"Of course. I'll be right back."

Crispin hopped up and walked over to the group of young men. Tytonn gave a polite nod and words of parting before drawing to the side with Crispin who said, "Elda fancies a dance, and I told her you'd likely be kind enough to oblige her."

Tytonn glanced over Crispin's shoulder at Elda, who sat watching the dancers eagerly; his eyes widened, and his glance darted to the floor. He swallowed hard, but then he drew himself up and said, "I would be honored to accept a dance with Lady Elda."

"Or several," Crispin called playfully as Tytonn made his way over.

Tytonn glanced back with a scowl, but his face brightened as he faced Elda, asked for a dance, and had soon swept her into the matched lines of dancing courtiers.

Crispin drifted toward a quiet space against one of the walls and watched them wistfully. At first, Elda's movements were flawless thanks to her ability to feel the vibrations of the drumbeats and dancers' footsteps. Yet whenever the opposing lines of dancers crossed to the center to turn with their respective partners, she seemed to rest stiffly in Tytonn's arms. However, as he prattled on, grinning and no doubt charming her with his humor, her face softened into a real smile, her body relaxed in his, and they flowed together like a fluid wave, blending perfectly with their fellow dancers.

As Crispin savored a goblet-full of sweet, red wine, he nearly choked. Several yards away stood the servant girl—Gailea, at last he had her name!—chatting with a slender blonde girl and a brunette. Her simple blue and green gown nicely accentuated her slender curves, and her purple gem perfectly matched the hues of his tunic, if he was honest. The brunette had linked her arm with Gailea's, and Gailea smiled at some story the blonde told, though she shifted now and then, looking uncomfortable. Crispin wondered whether she was unaccustomed to the fine clothes or perhaps the stifling number of people—

Suddenly, she met his gaze, and this time he did sputter, nearly spraying wine all over the floor. He gulped it down, too quickly and thus painfully, but he didn't care. The last way to make a good impression on a lady would have been to approach her with wine all over his clothes like some clumsy drunkard.

As his and Gailea's eyes met yet again, his thoughts whirled into a panic.

She's seen me looking at her. More than once. I should either walk away now or else go over and say...something. Anything. He scanned the crowds for Elda, only to find her engaged in a second dance with Tytonn. *Well...I suppose if Tytonn can manage on his own, so can I.*

Crispin approached, cleared his throat, and announced, "Good ladies, I beg your pardon. May I depart with the Lady Gailea for a few moments?"

The brunette and blonde exchanged looks of curiosity, and an impish light entered the blonde's eyes as she said, "Of course, my lord." She grabbed the brunette's arm, and the two of them drew away, giggling shamelessly.

As Crispin turned back to Gailea, he felt his nerves hitting him anew, as if his sister had struck him with one of her little lightning bolts. Gailea's eyes, so soulful and containing a hint of her wildness and passion, watched him intently; he almost imagined that she could pierce straight into his thoughts.

"Good evening, Lord Crispin."

A bit of relief washed over him now that she was the first to speak. Gathering his thoughts enough to recall

Elda's suggestion, he gave a short bow. "Good evening. I'd just wanted to thank you for being so attentive in caring for my aunt, the queen, especially in such a delicate time. She's looking in better spirits than I've seen in a while."

Gailea smiled politely. "Thank you. The queen is so generous and kind, and I enjoy her company."

"You're Gailea, are you not? I keep hearing your name, but we've yet to be properly introduced."

"Yes, my name is Gailea. Gailea Fleming."

Crispin extended his hand, and as she rested hers gently in his, a thrill rippled through him. He kissed her hand, all the while looking at her and trying to gauge some reaction. If she was anywhere near as nervous as he was, he couldn't detect it.

"A pleasure to meet you at last, Lady Gailea. My name is Crispin Ragnar."

"Of course." Gailea's tilting smile was playful. "I think everyone knows who you are, even if they've spent their entire lives hiding out in the kitchens."

"Indeed," Crispin muttered, inwardly scolding himself. Grappling for something cleverer to say, he added, "You look lovely tonight. Those blues and greens—they look much prettier on you in velvet than when you're covered in moss and leaves. And they accentuate your eyes."

"Thank you," Gailea said. She inched closer to him— the butterflies swirled in his stomach again, and he mentally tried to squash them—and lowered her voice. "And thank you also for not telling anyone about the flute."

Crispin stood caught off guard. His uncles' entire fight about raising her position had stemmed from their discovery of that very flute.

Not wishing to alarm her, he said, "So, they never found it then?"

"Do you think I'd be in such a favorable position now if they had? Instead of being here, at this fine party, I'd likely be rotting in some prison cell."

If only you knew, Crispin thought to himself. *They really are using her as a pawn, an experiment*. A twinge of anger raced through him. This sensation, almost painful, confused him until he realized it for what it truly was—a sudden urge to protect her. Tytonn was right after all: he was utterly captivated and fast becoming smitten.

"Are you alright?"

Crispin noted her frown and followed her gaze to his hands. Tiny flames had erupted from his fingertips. He tried to snuff them out, but in his panic, they only crackled and sparked all the more. He folded his arms, burying his hands in his armpits.

"It's alright," Gailea said. "I won't tell."

The innocent sincerity filling her face soothed him a little.

"Thanks," he said with a grin. "I suppose we both have secrets to hide."

She smiled. "We can hide them together—"

"Good evening, nephew, Lady Gailea."

Crispin jumped at Alistor's unexpected greeting. Although both he and Gailea returned the greeting, Alistor smiled only briefly at Crispin before turning his full attention to Gailea. As he kissed her hand, watching her intently, Crispin had to force the flames in his hands from expanding up his arms. He could feel the embers beginning to singe his clothes and quickly shoved his hands in his pockets instead; it wouldn't do for him to walk about the ball with smoldering holes in his sleeves. "I just came over to congratulate you. It's good to see you rise to a position that comes just a little closer to your deserved station. You've clearly impressed our queen. And our king, of course."

Crispin could sense the curiosity in Gailea's otherwise calm gaze and knew it was reflected in his own. What was his uncle getting at? The other night he had accused her of being little more than a common thief, but now he acted again like she held some secret significance.

"That's a lovely jewel," Alistor continued, lightly touching the red and purple gem hovering just above her breast. As he leaned a little closer to her, her cheeks flushed, but the caution in her gaze intensified. Crispin couldn't resist a smirk, satisfied that she didn't seem to warm toward her uncle as much as she had him.

"Thank you, Lord Ragnar," Gailea said stiffly, "for your kind words."

"Of course. But I can see I've interrupted something," Alistor glanced at Crispin with a coy smile. "I'll let the two of you get back to it then. Good evening."

As Alistor disappeared into the crowd, Crispin edged closer to Gailea and asked, "So, are you? Trying to impress his majesty?"

"Would it trouble you if I was?"

Crispin's cheeks burned. He was being more obvious in his interest than the most lovelorn bard, while she acted so calm that he could hardly detect her emotions. "I would understand. Many ladies aim to win the king's affections in hopes to raise their stations."

"Well, I didn't aim to catch his eye to get to where I am. And now that I'm here, I intend to stay as far from earning his affections as possible. I've no interest in becoming anyone's mistress. So, no, I'm not trying to catch his interest. All I wish is for him to disdain me less."

Crispin's brows rose in amusement, and she hurried on, "Forgive me if I spoke too boldly."

"No, not at all. But I don't think he disdains you, or he wouldn't have appointed you to tend the queen."

"All the same, I hope he doesn't use it as an excuse to

try and see more of me."

"Let's hope not. Though, I wouldn't be opposed if you used it as an excuse to see more of *me*."

As soon as the words spilled out, Crispin wondered at his own boldness and wished he could stuff them back inside, but she granted a small smile. "That might please me. But how would it be possible? I'm a queen's lady now. I can't just go running off to your chambers. The resulting rumors would draw the king's eyes for certain."

He was glad for the over-warm room now—it hid his blush. "Not my chambers, of course not, miss. But perhaps my sister, Elda, could help. She says you've become good friends."

Gailea's face brightened. "Elda? She's been such a help to me."

"I'm sure she could arrange a meeting between us—"

Fireworks exploded right outside the tall, arched windows, shimmering on the glass and illuminating the entire hall with a shower of brilliant color. Trumpets rang from the gallery, and everyone whirled, gasping and whispering words of awe as the king stood on a dais directly beneath the windows overlooking the courtyard, hands raised. As if he were some mystical conductor, all eyes locked on him, and all talking ceased. The trumpets played a final note and then drew quiet.

A moment of silent expectation passed, and then, with a grin, Moragon threw his arms wide and announced, "Welcome, friends of Adelar, to this celebration honoring both my birthday and the rebirth of our realm when I was first crowned as your most gracious king!"

Cheers erupted, and goblets clanked together.

"I would like to offer a contest now, to Adelar's finest magicians. Whoever most impresses me with their magic will win a bag of gold from Master Chevalier!"

Cheers overwhelmed the Hall once more. The king

took his seat on a throne set atop the dais. The queen sat on a throne beside him, sharing a nod and smile with Chevalier who sat on a small throne on the king's other side.

One by one, men and women alike flowed toward the dais. Two or three performers at a time were pulled onto the stage. A woman with a purple gown created a giant bubble and made herself float inside. A band of men juggled lightning bolts and blue flames. A young boy recited a poem, making a light snowfall across the great hall.

A man whose tanned skin glowed copper in the fire-light lifted one hand and seemed to snatch something invisible from the air. He rubbed his hands, cupped them, and then blew into his palms. Tiny sprouts grew from his fingertips, entwining through the air to form a crown of vines and flowers around the queen's head; she touched them delicately as her eyes beamed plea-sure at the man who bowed in her direction. The king's lips drew into a thin line, but he seemed to think better than to insult her in front of the hundreds gathered.

Suddenly, Crispin noticed the king's gaze narrow-ing—and, following the direction of his uncle's stare, he discovered with dismay that it fell upon Gailea beside him. Gailea remained oblivious, laughing and clapping, lost in the wonder of the displays on stage. Crispin moved closer to her, acting as a shield. The king's smile flickered at Crispin; it was not an expression of friendliness.

Moragon rose to his feet then and lifted his hands once more in a call for silence. The crowds hushed, and the magicians ceased their tricks, bowing and standing aside.

"I now make a special request," the king said. "Master Chevalier, astound us with some of your finest magic!"

Chevalier rose from his chair and walked toward the

front of the dais. His long green hair had been plaited into a more intricate braid than usual, and red and purple silks draped over his slender body. His sleeves ended in jagged points, flowing behind him like streamers of fire in the orange glow of the flames hovering overhead.

"I am honored to perform for his grace." Chevalier bowed low toward the king before facing the sea of eager faces. "But this display is best performed with an assistant. Would it please his grace for me to call on one of his guests?"

"It would please me very much," the king said, "and I've already chosen the perfect target—Lady Gailea Fleming. Please, step forward and perform for your king."

Crispin looked at Gailea. Her eyes widened, and she looked as if she would much rather bolt like the fawn in the woods, but then she started forward, graceful and poised, her chin lifted confidently.

Excited whispers turned to anxious mutterings. Crispin caught snatches of accusations about both the queen and Gailea, but he quickly blocked them out, focusing instead on Gailea as she ascended the steps to the dais and curtsied before Moragon.

"Will it please you to serve as Master Chevalier's assistant this evening?" the king asked, extending his hand.

Gailea lightly took his hand and kissed the huge gem glistening on his finger like drops of blood in the firelight. "It is your pleasure that matters, your grace. Though I'm afraid I may not be of much use. I know only simple song-spells, and a few charms for healing and tending plants. I don't know any magic to rival a s—" She hesitated just long enough for Crispin to wonder if she too knew what Chevalier truly was. But she concluded: "To rival such a master of magic arts."

"Fear not, my dear young lady. You're merely assisting. Chevalier will handle the complex work. At any rate, you would not deny the king his birthday wish, would you?"

"No, your grace."

"That settles it then. Chevalier, let the spectacle begin!"

The king returned to his seat and motioned toward the musicians who began to play a raucous tune.

Crispin felt his body tense with anticipation, and he slowly made his way closer to the dais. He nearly growled when the sorcerer touched the small of Gailea's back, but all Chevalier did was gently turn her toward the crowds.

"You say you've knowledge of plants," Chevalier said. His voice never raised above its silvery murmur, yet somehow was clear enough to fill the entire Great Hall. "Can you perform a simple awakening charm?"

Gailea nodded. "I have before."

Chevalier smiled warmly. "Perfect." He began weaving his hands in the air, each turn of his wrist or flick of his hand calculated and precise. His willowy body swayed back and forth as if he performed a seductive dance to charm the air itself. Suddenly, a green and gold light burst mid-air; gasps of delight echoed through the crowd, and the light faded to reveal a bush hovering before the sorcerer. Its large yellow blooms—sweet rosals, Crispin recognized—emitted a faint glow, their petals tightly closed.

Chevalier waved his hands in slow arcs. Vines coiled up from the bush, spiraling high and erupting with more blooms, yet unopened.

"Now, if the Lady Gailea would please be so kind as to awaken the flowers—as a gift for our queen."

Gailea didn't budge a muscle—except for her lips, which parted, then began to move. Moragon leaned forward in his throne, straight and alert, his eyes wild and unblinking as if he probed her mind for the source of her magic. A hush gripped the entire hall, but Gailea seemed not to emit the slightest sound.

Suddenly, the petals of one of the rosals unfurled, emitting a sweet scent. Gasps waved through the crowd. As Gailea's spell coursed up the vines, flower after flower unfolded, stretching their petals like ladies dancing for their king and queen. Chevalier continued to hold out his hands, suspending the plant whose highest fronds now brushed the ceiling. Gailea continued to utter her noiseless spell, and the flowers opened one by one. As they morphed from yellow to pink to purple, it was impossible to tell whether Chevalier or Gailea performed this colorful feat—

A sharp pain shot through Crispin's side.

"*Ouch!*" He glared at the person beside him, prepared to scold them, but his words morphed into a cry as another pain shot from his chest through his arm and down to his fingertips. He winced, bending over. A thick sweat cloaked his body, and the flowers' powerful aroma stirred his stomach, making him want to vomit. His vision faded in and out; the purple rosals blurred into a deep crimson. He caught a glimpse of the king's face, still watching Gailea, fascinated but furious.

Chills gripped Crispin, and he trembled all over. Then, the pain shot through him a third time, like someone had stabbed him in the chest with fire. He yelled and pushed the pain instinctively away from his heart, down his arms once more and through his fingertips—

A brilliant red-orange blaze erupted before him, blinding him; he staggered back and fell to the floor. Cries and gasps surrounded him, but all he could see was black. An overwhelming relief flooded him as the fire faded from his body, and strong hands dragged him up. He stumbled, his feet heavy and numb. Gradually, feeling returned to them, his eyelids fluttered, and then he opened his eyes to stare into Tytonn's face, flooded with worry.

"What...what happened?" Crispin muttered. "Did I pass out?"

"You might say that," Tytonn said. "But not before causing quite the stir. It was the most frightening thing—if only because it was so unexpected—but definitely the most astounding."

Crispin shook his head which ached dully; his vision blurred at this movement, so he held still and said, "What do you mean?"

A flash of bright red caught his attention, and he peered around Tytonn's shoulder with a gasp. Shoving Tytonn aside, he staggered forward and stared at the spectacle before him.

The rosal bush had branched into an enormous tree, still upheld only by Chevalier's extended palms. Dozens upon dozens of rosals bloomed from its twisting branches and coiled vines—and each of the flowers blazed with a brilliant fire. Flames danced along every petal, and yet each flower remained impossibly unscathed.

Beyond the blazing rosal tree, Moragon's attention had shifted from Gailea to Crispin, with the same, all-consuming stare with which he'd watched her moments ago. Gailea gaped at Crispin, whether with fear or concern, he couldn't tell. As he swept a glance across the room, a whole sea of eyes watched him, wide and wondering. Several people uttered water charms to extinguish patches of flame on their neighbors' clothes.

Crispin's heart beat frantically, and his breath came in such short, stifled gasps that he feared passing out again. Staggering, he reached out and placed a hand on Tytonn's shoulder for support.

"It's all right, Cris. It's all right..." Tytonn began leading him from the room, half-supporting him.

"Let me through—my nephew needs aid!"

Crispin was suddenly collapsing against Alistor who helped Tytonn carry him. As Crispin was dragged through the whispering crowds, he glanced back at the dais once more. Moragon's eyes blazed at Chevalier, who dropped his hands. The tree turned to ash, and the ashes collapsed and fell to the dais, but the blossoms floated to the ground and continued to burn in a blazing heap.

Another blur jerked Crispin's attention to Elda who was now before them, blocking their path. Her gaze implored, and she rested a hand on Alistor's arm.

"He's all right, my dear," Alistor said with a nod. "He just needs rest."

With an encouraging smile at Crispin, she let them pass.

As they exited the great hall, exhaustion crashed over Crispin, and he sank down, becoming dead weight as Tytonn and his uncle carried him. He closed his eyes.

He was aware of being dragged up steps, of sinking into a soft, warm spread as he was laid down. Fire pulsed through his body again, steadily intensifying, making him sweat and pant and moan. A bitter tonic was forced between his lips. Cool cloths were draped across his forehead. Muffled voices gave orders and spoke in concerned tones.

Gradually, the heat subsided again, and he opened his eyes. He lay in his bed. Tytonn was gone, but Alistor sat on the edge of the bed, his face drawn into a tight frown. As soon as Crispin met his gaze, Alistor's brows rose, and he released a heavy sigh.

"You gave us quite the scare—while performing quite the finale for Chevalier's pathetic little magic show." Alistor paused to smile. "Between you and me, that is a triumph of which I am exceedingly proud."

Crispin sat up slowly; his dizziness seemed to have passed. "I didn't do it on purpose."

"You could not have done better if planned." His uncle's pleased expression sobered. "I know, my boy. Coming into one's powers can be a tricky matter. But we may as well start cultivating them now. There's certainly no denying their existence any longer, not to anyone—including the king."

"He looked angry."

"Likely envious. Or afraid. Or both. You recall our talk from a fortnight ago?"

Crispin nodded.

Alistor's eyes narrowed intently. "Now that Moragon knows of your powers, it will be vital for you to know how to house and control them, how to best use them to your benefit...and to his. I know it's been a difficult night for you, but if you feel recovered enough, I want to ask you some questions, while the sensations are still fresh in your memory."

Crispin nodded. "I am awake enough."

"Good. Then...what exactly *did* you feel? Have you any idea what might have triggered your fire to show itself?"

"It all happened in such a blur...One moment, Lady Gailea was making the rosals open. Then, this fire just overtook me. It didn't hurt, but it spread through me like a fever and then it just...took control and erupted from me. Do you think it was the presence of so much magic in the room?"

"Possibly," Alistor said. "Though you *are* technically surrounded by magic every day. One would think the heavy saturation of magic found in the protective barriers surrounding the castle would have brought your powers to light long ago."

"What then?" Crispin asked. "Why now?"

"Perhaps it is not the presence of magic itself that has awakened yours, but a specific *kind* of magic that burst open the dam, if you will. You said you only started to feel something when Gailea used *her* magic?"

Crispin nodded. "What would she have to do with me? Unless...unless this has to do with what you alluded to before? About her having some secret value?" He studied his uncle curiously.

Alistor raised an eyebrow. "I *was* rather vague on that point, wasn't I? The timing wasn't yet ripe. But now that it is, allow me to elucidate further. You see, Lady Gailea's magic both fascinates and intimidates Moragon. She is as much an object of desire as she is a threat—in fact, she is both these things, more so than his majesty yet realizes. If he did, he would've made her his mental slave long ago."

"What do you mean?" Alarm gripped Crispin's body, tightening his lungs. "What doesn't the king know about her?"

"If I tell you, you must tell no one. If you reveal this secret, especially before its time, her life may be forfeit."

The urge of protectiveness leapt inside Crispin once again. "I won't tell a soul."

Alistor nodded. "Not only is she a music mage, but through clever research and the aid of trusted servants, I have finally proven my own suspicions and know that she is also descended from the royal line that ruled before the Vorlaires usurped the Adelaran throne."

Crispin stared, dumbfounded. "I thought that lineage ended long ago."

"So did many, for a time."

Crispin tried to grasp the importance of what his uncle was telling him. "Even if that's true, can she really be much of a threat? She has no family or armies to back any claim."

"But her family used to be powerful in musical magic—the one thing his majesty desires most to harness and control. And while the king has no knowledge of her lineage, he clearly suspects she has some special musical skill. It's why I argued against raising her station, to try and keep her away from his watchful eye. Thus far, she's never shown herself willing or able to do much more than parlor tricks. Still, I've been observing her progress—and I intend to do so far more keenly after tonight's performance. Whether or not she used music, I can't yet be certain—though it was well worth seeing the fury on my brother's face. He called her up there to trick her, to make her reveal herself. But if she used musical power, she had good sense and skill to keep it cleverly hidden, even from his mental probing—"

The door burst open, and a servant tumbled in. Gripping the doorframe, he doubled over, breathless. As he looked up, sweat drenched his brow, and his eyes shone wide and wild in the firelight.

"Forgive me, my lords. But the queen has gone into labor. There are complications. The king commands all men and women with a knowledge of healing magic—"

"Take me at once," Alistor said, springing from the bed. He hurried to the door, but before leaving, turned back to Crispin. "Make yourself presentable and come downstairs. If the baby lives and is male, you will be expected to greet your future sovereign."

CHAPTER 10
PLOTS AND POISONS

G ailea sat on the edge of her bed, clutching the sheets; the whole room spun and if she didn't hold on to something, she'd spin out of control right along with it. Tonight had not gone at all as she'd anticipated—especially since Moragon had already made a move to try and sense her musical magic.

A rapid knock on the door sent her jumping to her feet. There was no time for her to move before the door opened and Darice rushed in. She grasped Gailea's hands. "Are you alright?"

Trembling, Gailea sank back on the bed. Darice sat with her, still gripping her hands bloodless. Gailea did not mind the pain: right now her sister's touch was the only thing that rooted her in place and stopped the room from its mad whirling.

"I'm all right. It was a close call. But I'm all right."

"Then he doesn't know about your music?" Darice pressed, bending nearer. "I didn't hear you sing—*did* you sing?"

"I did, but..." She took a deep breath and clutched the gem at her heart. "Lady Aline's gift allowed me to shield my mind. I *had* to sing; I couldn't resist his majesty's orders. So, I used the song I composed when you taught me about gardening charms—"

"You used one of your own songs!"

"He doesn't know, Darice, I promise you. I'm not even sure he knows I sang at all. I could sense him trying to get inside my head, toward the end, but then Crispin's fire..." Gailea shook her head, marveling again at the explosive flames that turned the entire Great Hall and all its attendees gold. "Well, it shifted the focus away from me."

Darice's brows rose, and her anxious face softened with a playful smile. "Oh, it's 'Crispin' now, is it? You'd best be careful; talking so casually could get you into trouble."

"We merely shared pleasant conversation. Although...he does seem interested in meeting with me again—"

The door burst open, and Tory spilled inside, her eyes wide and lit with terror.

"It's the queen. She's delivering. Something's wrong. I was told to fetch you—"

"Take me at once."

Gailea shot up from the bed, shared a glance of new worry with Darice, and then fled from the room behind the young maidservant, who prattled on, "Everything was fine at first. But then she started having these pains. The healers seem at a loss. Lord Alistor went to fetch some potion from his chambers and still hasn't returned..."

Gailea pushed past Tory and broke into a run. The king had surely summoned her to test her. As she touched the gem, she felt its magic diminished; it couldn't shield her now. But it didn't really matter. She had come to care deeply for the queen, and if there was anything she could do to help Marlis, even at the expense of her own safety, she must. She tumbled into the bedchamber—

"Push, your grace—*push!*"

Marlis' eyes blazed feverishly at the midwife. "Gailea—where is Gailea?"

"Here I am, madam." Gailea hurried across the room, shoving between the half dozen healers gathered in an arc around the queen's bed. Sitting on the edge of the bed, she clutched Marlis' hand, damp with sweat. Someone sat on the edge of the bed opposite Gailea, and she gasped to recognize Chevalier. The shock of seeing a man in the queen's bedchamber was subsumed by dread at his behavior. He took the queen's arm, tapped the crook of her elbow by a blue vein, and then sank a needle into her flesh. Gailea followed the thin tube that connected the needle to a bowl filled with a green substance. A pain tonic, she suspected. It would soothe the queen somewhat. The queen's breath came in labored gasps, and her red curls matted damply against her forehead, opposite of the brilliance she'd displayed at the ball. Panting hard, she slowly turned her head toward Gailea.

"Please, help him," Marlis whispered, each word an effort. "Sing one of your songs to ease his way. I can see the stags, standing just there in the window. Don't let them take him…"

Gailea jerked her head toward the window. She almost imagined the shape of a great stag within the moon's silvery glow, but then she blinked and saw nothing. A chill went through her. Of course: The silver stags often appeared visible only to the souls they had come to claim for eternal rest.

No, please, dearest Amiel… Gailea closed her eyes and

prayed that this vision was conjured only by Marlis's feverish mind. Prayed that the stags did not stand there at all.

Gailea's entire body grew numb. The lullabies she'd sung for the queen would not help here. She knew a healing song, but it might do little, if any, good—and it must be sung aloud. Was it worth the risk?

Healers gathered around the bed, their eyes closed, chanting and sprinkling bits of herbs and incense across the queen. Handmaids rushed about the room to bring more water or stoke the fire. Most of all, the queen's gaze implored, fully trusting Gailea. Swallowing hard and fighting back a rush of tears, Gailea opened her lips and sang a quiet melody meant to induce calm inside someone with a fever. She squeezed the queen's hand, hoping the song's power would reach down to the infant. She closed her eyes, focusing—

Then opened them with a gasp. For the smallest moment of wonder, she ceased singing. Then, she quickly started her song again. She'd sensed it: a faint but certain palpitation fluttering to her ears. The baby's heartbeat.

"He's choking!" she cried. "The baby is choking!"

Gailea opened her eyes and frantically searched the room, hoping she was heard amidst the commotion. Briefly, her glance caught that of Chevalier, who continued to feed the herbal mixture into the queen's veins.

"Can't you do something?" Gailea pleaded. "There must be something—a charm—*anything*. *Please*."

Methodically pushing the tonic inside Marlis' veins, Chevalier's sad-eyed stare strayed from Gailea to the wall.

One of the midwives commanded another at the foot of the bed. Marlis groaned and pushed again. She strained so hard that Gailea thought she might crush her hand and then collapsed back on the pillows, panting and sobbing before sitting up to push again.

"The baby's out!" the younger midwife cried, grinning up at the queen and lifting the baby high. The queen smiled and started to laugh.

"He's not breathing," Gailea whispered, her tears releasing as she studied the tiny figure, as still and silent as the stones comprising the castle walls. She sang again, reaching for some sign of life, but his heart no longer matched its erratic beat to her song.

"Give the child here, you fool!" The older midwife snatched the baby into her arms, her face alarmed with Gailea's same realization. She turned the baby over, pounding on its chest. She tried to breathe into its mouth, but its heartbeat did not return.

The queen's laugh choked and faded into a sob. "What is wrong with him?"

"I'm sorry, your grace," the midwife said flatly. "He is stillborn."

"No.... No, let me see him! Please, I beg you."

The midwife walked over and slipped the infantile corpse into his mother's hands. His tiny body was bathed in blood, and his lips were parted, as though he cried out for vengeance for a life cut woefully short. Gailea shivered at the grotesque sight, but the queen held him close to her breast, stroking his wisps of raven curls, his tiny arms and legs curled close to his chest. His hands almost touched, as if praying for the chance to live the life he would never know and to embrace the mother he would never meet.

Gailea started to rise, but the queen clutched her wrist. Gailea resisted as fingernails bit into her skin, but the queen dug deeper, and her eyes begged. "Please, Gailea, help him. You woke up the flowers...I know you can save my child..."

"I cannot, my lady." Gailea's voice broke between

tears. "He's already gone."

"*No*," Marlis sobbed. "The stags—they've left—so he can't be dead…. Wake him up…"

Chevalier's graceful hand rested on the queen's limp arm as he murmured, "No one can wake the dead, your grace. If the stags were here and gone, it is because they have taken the child's soul into eternity and their work here is complete."

Gailea could not help but look at him in surprise. Somehow, his belief in the stags seemed unlike what she expected from such a man, as was his depth of feeling. Regret clung to the edge of his words. He still stared at the wall and seemed to view a world far away from the castle.

"Lady Gailea, perhaps it would be best if you took your leave now," the older midwife said. "His grace will be here soon."

Understanding gripped Gailea, accompanied by fear. Rising to her feet, she hurried from the room, ignoring the queen's pleas for her to return and save her little prince. Tears blinded Gailea as she stumbled down the stairs and into the chamber beyond where a slew of people bombarded her with questions of the queen's welfare.

Gailea pushed past them all without a word; her tears likely spoke enough. Blood stained her hands, and she quickly wiped them on her gown, disgusted. The infant had been just moments away from life. To see him lying motionless in the queen's arms...

Never had Gailea felt so powerless. She bunched the hem of her skirts up and flew through corridors and down steps—

Then she slammed hard into someone and ricocheted back. Catching herself against the wall, she paused to catch her breath, staggering as her sobs choked her.

"Lady Gailea—what's happened—?"

Gailea's sob caught in her throat as she recognized Crispin. His gaze reflected a wild concern and sympathy.

"Please. Tell me what's wrong. My aunt—"

He reached toward her, but she jerked away. Pushing herself up from the wall, she hurried past him, crying over her shoulder, "The queen lives—"

Gailea fled, unable to finish the statement. The queen lived for now, yes...until she died of a broken heart for her dead son and the final severing of any blind hope she might have held to reconcile with her husband.

***

Crispin burst into the garden. Gulping the fresh air, he let its sharp chill fill his lungs, wishing it could numb both his memory and heart to everything that had just transpired. Within a matter of moments, a son had been granted to the king and queen, sealing their lineage. In the next breath, Amiel had seen fit to steal that son away.

Hands gripping his hair, Crispin paced back and forth, hoping that Elda had received his message, when swift footsteps alerted him. Elda ran to him across the lawn, pulling a woolly shawl close about her shoulders. Her ragged breath curled like clouds, and the moon shimmered in her wary eyes. She threw her arms around Crispin, catching him in a tight embrace. Then, taking his hand, she led him to sit on the bench beneath the lofty blue rosal tree.

Drawing her slate into her lap, she wrote: *Are you alright?*

Crispin touched her chin, made her troubled gaze meet his, and nodded firmly.

Elda gave a weary smile. *I was worried, after the performance.*

"Yes. I suppose you saw it—you and the entire court. The fire—it burst from me so powerfully, I didn't know how to react. What awful timing—my magic showing just as the queen gives birth to a stillborn heir..." Guilt struck him in an instant. "I'm sorry. I shouldn't be so consumed with myself in such a mournful time."

Elda touched his hand, drawing his attention back to her. *We're all afraid, in one way or another. It's natural. Only we must not let it shroud our thoughts.*

Crispin sighed deeply. "How is our aunt?"

Elda shook her head. *They are letting few in to see her. I am told she should recover, but I fear her heart will never mend. A child was the one thing granting her hope. But how are you, after everything tonight?*

"I don't know. Alistor thinks Gailea's magic might have triggered my own tonight. That her music might have somehow awakened my fire."

Elda frowned thoughtfully and wrote anew: *I have heard of such recessed powers. Only time may tell. Focus on receiving further instruction from Alistor. Your powers coming to light in conjunction with the babe's death is a sad coincidence, that is all. Worry instead about gaining control of them. A mage out of control is a threat to everyone—not just to kings.*

***

Gailea drifted through the corridor alongside Elda. Morning's light streamed through the tall arched windows, but it carried no warmth, and Gailea shivered.

"The days are growing colder, shorter," she muttered. Then, looking at Elda, she touched her arm to grab her attention and said, "Winter arrives quickly this year."

It had been a week since the king's birthday celebration and the queen's stillborn. Darice had been extra busy with new kitchen duties, but Gailea found comfort in Elda's company.

Elda smiled faintly and nodded. The two girls walked on, Gailea now staring at the patterned tile below, unseeing, as if hypnotized.

Without warning, Elda grabbed Gailea's arm and jerked her toward one of the massive windows. She then nodded ever so subtly before peeking around the heavy velvet curtain out the window. Gailea followed her gaze.

Some yards away, in a large room parallel to this corridor, two figures stood in another room with a large window—Moragon and Chevalier. After what appeared to be a contentious discussion, the king waved his hand in a determined gesture and Chevalier slammed back against the window; Gailea gasped as cracks branched all along the glass. Chevalier stumbled to his feet, and the glass instantly sealed itself, gleaming pure and whole as new in the white sunlight.

Gailea squeezed Elda's arm to catch her attention before mouthing, "Can you tell what they're saying?"

Elda narrowed her gaze on the scene before them, focusing hard. Moragon advanced and Chevalier stepped backward. Gailea wondered why Chevalier looked so utterly terrified. Servant of the king or not, as a powerful mage—perhaps even a sorcerer, if rumors were true—he was strong and skilled enough to match the king. Why did he not fight back?

Elda suddenly jerked away from the window, trembling.

"What did you learn?" Gailea breathed.

The slate trembled in Elda's hands. Gailea grabbed the slate to steady it, and Elda used her lightning to scrawl: *I couldn't catch all of it. But Moragon wanted the queen dead. Chevalier used some kind of poison. I think it killed the baby instead, by accident. Now, as retribution, he's promis-*

ing the king magic that can raise an army of thousands. Elda shook and faced Gailea with wide eyes.

"Some kind of magical poison," Gailea whispered. "That would explain what I felt when the baby died..." Her hands covered her face at the horrific memory. When the moment passed, she dropped her arms.

And now Chevalier was afraid for his life and willing to gamble—and what a large, terrifying wager he'd made! If Moragon was furious over the death of an infant, Gailea didn't want to imagine his fury if Chevalier promised him entire armies but failed.

A tug on her arm drew Gailea's attention back to Elda who'd etched a new message across the slate: *I'm afraid, Gailea. I think Chevalier might have seen us watching him.*

Dread clutched at Gailea's throat, but she shook her head. "I'd be more worried for you than for me."

Don't worry about me, Elda wrote. *But if you want to help us both, talk to my brother.*

"Lord Crispin?" Gailea gasped, halting. "I know he is your brother, but...are you certain we can trust him?"

Elda's gaze urged as she wrote: *Crispin is a good man. He is naïve enough yet to be kind and noble. He will help you, if he can. And he certainly won't bring you any harm.*

"Naivety can be just as dangerous as direct cruelty."

Then teach him. He's intelligent. Convince him. Sway his mind in the right direction before others have the chance to do the opposite. Besides, he is very fond of you, and I can tell despite your fear that you are fond of him too. That already gives you a foot on the path toward his trusting you.

Gailea hesitated. Putting her faith in Crispin was a risk, but at this point, doing nothing was likely riskier. "All right. I will talk to him. Can you help arrange a meeting between us?"

Elda nodded and waved her hand across the slate, the words vanishing once more. With a weary but grateful smile, she turned and fled down the corridor.

Gailea fell back against the wall with a long exhale, hardly fathoming what she'd just agreed to: approaching the kin of her nearest enemies to turn him into an ally. Never mind that he had helped her before. A stolen flute was a trifle compared with murder plots.

"Good morning, Lady Gailea."

Gailea started at the all-too-familiar voice. King Moragon stood before her, tall and straight, hands clasped behind him. He smiled, but no warmth shone from his face. His dark eyes watched her closely but revealed no detectable feeling. Gailea would have preferred Lord Ragnar's presence, even with his all-consuming gaze. At least she could guess what Lord Ragnar desired and how to counter it.

"Good morning, your grace," Gailea said.

"I never did get the chance to commend you," the king said, "for a most brilliant performance the night of my birthday celebration."

"That is more than understandable, sire. You and the queen were likely overridden with grief."

The king nodded. "Yes. We were—and still are. The birth of an heir is something we've long fought for and anticipated together."

Gailea's thoughts lingered on the word "fought." There was likely no love in their bedchamber, not even the lust she'd heard he displayed for many other girls at court.

"Has the queen's condition improved, your grace?" she asked. "It's been a week, and the healers do not permit many to enter her chambers."

Moragon frowned in what might have been some attempt at grief, but even this gesture seemed mechanical, rehearsed. "The queen is still very weak. The healers say it may take her several weeks to fully recover. I too have been troubled over the death of our son. Other of my wife's ladies tell me that you sing to her, to calm her. Perhaps you might do the same for me."

His words suggested, but his tone demanded.

"Those songs were simply old lullabies, nothing more," Gailea said, wishing she wore her necklace with the song-shield inside. While she didn't feel him probing her mind as on the night of the ball, she couldn't be certain if he read her thoughts right now or not. "Shall I go to her now, your grace? I would be glad to assist in any way—"

She had merely begun a curtsey in hopes of being dismissed, but Moragon clutched her arm and muttered, "If you can sing for the queen, you can sing for your king."

Gailea froze still as stone. What harm would singing her lullaby really do? Would the king know it was a song of her mother's, passed down for generations—?

No. Not if she kept this thought and its accompanying fears from her mind.

Gailea began to sing.

The lullaby flowed from her with more passion than usual, and Moragon's grasp loosened. His eyes closed; he swayed and then slouched against the wall, breathing deeply as he slept. Gailea took a few steps back, mortified by what she'd just done. She hadn't meant the song to be that potent; she'd meant to calm the king, perhaps make him drowsy, but certainly not drop on the floor in a slumbering heap—

Brushing up against something soft, she jumped, gasped, and—recognizing the cream-white robes—backed away. Chevalier stared down at her, his refined features pulled into an anxious frown. She stared at him for a moment, hesitating, considering. They were both targets now. Neither was safe from the king's whims and accompanying punishments.

But they were not friends. Gailea turned and fled the corridor, her mind bent on the wild realization that her greatest hope lay with the nephew of her greatest enemy.

CHAPTER 11

A KING'S
INTENTIONS

Crispin stretched his fingers toward the sun, trying to absorb its glow. Wind whistled shrilly through the glassless windows of the old, abandoned watchtower, and as Crispin shuddered, he could almost swear that the sun emitted cold instead of heat. Winter always struck sharpest at the castle, suspended so far above any trees or other shelter that might have blocked its icy sting.

He also shuddered at the still-fresh memory of his aunt's dead infant and Gailea's heart-torn face at yesterday's funeral. He hadn't yet been able to address his fears to his uncle; he didn't know how to breach the uneasy subject.

He concentrated on the sun, staring right into its brilliance and allowing Alistor's voice to drift back inside his consciousness:

"...As a Fyre, you naturally absorb power from the sun on a daily basis. However, to absorb your full potential, you must do so *consciously*. An hour a day is sufficient for most. You can also convert the sun's power into either fire or light magic; some Fyres can do both, others can't. The spell word for controlling fire is '*Rustiék*,' but we'll get to that. We already know you can wield fire. The spell word for light is '*Kaisrah*.' Light is easier to absorb but trickier to use. Go ahead—let's see if you can use light as well."

"*Kaisrah*..." Crispin breathed. He chanted the word over and over again, trying to imagine the light bending to his will.

Suddenly, his fingertips blazed with tiny white flames. They wisped about in the breeze like bright vapors. He stared up at his uncle, who walked closer. "Good. But you're stuck somewhere between fire and light. Try to convert the element fully one way or the other."

Crispin chanted the spell for light once more and pictured the sun's rays obeying him. Gradually, the flames faded and elongated into tiny beams of light. Turning toward the wall, Crispin held up his hand and traced his sister's name. The letters shimmered faintly for a few seconds before vanishing.

"Brilliant! Hold your concentration. Now, try to write something else."

Crispin meant to write his sister's name again but realized that the letters glistening on the wall spelled another's—Gailea. A vibrant heat emanated from his fingers, and suddenly, light transformed to flame, bursting forward and searing the message on the wall. Crispin stared at the charred markings on the old stones, stunned at his own outburst.

"Not bad for a first attempt," Alistor said, and then added with a wry grin, "but you must learn to control your distractions and focus only on the task at hand. I'm beginning to think it wasn't the presence of magic that triggered your fire after all—"

"Give the boy a rest, will you?"

Crispin's head jerked up. Moragon stood at the crest of the steps, arms folded, curt smile directed at his brother. "He's surely not the only one guilty of being enchanted by the Lady Gailea that night."

"Indeed, your grace." Alistor's expression cooled. "And how may we serve you?"

"Actually, I need a private word with my tithe collector. I've some new business that needs attending."

"Today? At this hour in the morning?"

"I am king. I'm a busy man. Surely you can reschedule your little lesson on defiling my castle walls with love letters for another time."

Alistor's eyes blazed with unhidden insult, and Crispin had to hold back the fire yearning to wave through him alongside his embarrassment.

"I am trying to teach our nephew to harness his new-found powers," Alistor said. "Unless you'd rather him burn the whole castle down, allowing him to dictate his thoughts on the walls of an old, unused tower is likely a wise alternative."

Moragon nodded. "Point taken. Well, Crispin, let us be on our way."

Crispin bowed toward Alistor and said, "Thank you for the lesson, Uncle. I look forward to the next."

"As do I."

Crispin turned and wound after the king down the long flight of tower steps.

Upon reentering the main part of the castle, Moragon led Crispin to a large study he had never seen before. The room was decorated in rich crimsons, golds, blacks, and whites, from the ornately carved desk to the flanking bookshelves, to the chairs upholstered in velvet and the thick velvet curtains framing the singular, large window in the back of the room.

A huge fire blazed in the hearth, and its flames glowed bright blue, the hottest kind of fire. As Crispin's chill melted into instant warmth, he wondered how long it would be before he would master such a deeply strong spell.

Moragon sank into a chair by the hearth, casually slouched to one side, and motioned for Crispin to do the same.

Crispin sat across from his uncle, straight and poised, trying to hide his anxiousness. Moragon smiled at him in a friendly sort of way. A strange calm descended, and Crispin wondered if it was a true calm or if the king played some mental trick on him.

"Ah, this is much better," the king said. "I am sorry that Alistor insists on torturing you. That tower is ridiculously cold and secluded."

"He said a high point was vital for my learning, your grace. He said it would be easiest for me to connect with the sun."

"Yes, I'm sure. Still, it seems one would learn best in a more comfortable setting. Alistor is used to hiding in small, cold places—he's virtually reptilian. Indeed, the courtiers call him 'the snake.' Fitting title, in my opinion. He doesn't understand the rest of the world, who thrive on color and warmth and know how to seize what they want—like yourself. I saw how Alistor wanted you to create light, but your fire shone through. You have the potential for great power. It is wise, as my brother says, to know when to control your passion, but it can be just as wise to know when to unleash it with full force."

The king paused, studied Crispin for a moment, and then glanced away, fiddling with the bright yellow rosals set in a vase on the small table beside him.

"You've been doing a commendable job with my tithe collecting. However, a few vassals are still giving me trouble. The Master Weston you and your friend visited, for instance. You showed undue leniency. I must ask you to return and persuade those who did not pay."

Excitement flitted through Crispin. He was still no fan of dealing with the public, but gaining his fire powers had given him an extra boost of confidence to push past that fear and prove himself worthy of the king's trust.

"How do you mean, 'persuade,' your grace?"

The king played with the flowers a little while longer, letting his fingers dance delicately along their soft petals. "Both the Vorlaires and Ragnars have been blessed with strong magical traits. My power of persuasion rests more in powers of the mind..."

He let his hand drop, and one of the flowers curled in on itself; its petals darkened from golden to brown and then broke off, fluttering down to rest beside the other flowers that remained vibrant.

"...Whereas *your* power of persuasion rests more in your physical magic. But both—physical and mental—can be equally powerful and, if combined, unstoppable. Alistor can cultivate your magic, but I can cultivate your mind. You may not possess mental magic, but I can still train you to possess a leader's mind. Your station could rise far beyond that of a tithe collector. An earldom, even a duchy...these are favors and titles I might grant to you, as you have the blood royal. Unlike Alistor, the bastard," he added with a brief malicious smile that vanished almost as soon as Crispin recognized it. "But for such privileges, you must be willing to obey me in all things. Can you do that?"

Crispin stared at the flowers. The rosals had been brimming with life, vibrant and unassuming one moment, and then, in the next, one of their own had died at the king's silent command. He imagined being able to control or even extinguish human life just as easily, and a horrified shiver raced through his entire body. He wasn't certain he wanted that level of power. And yet, if the king considered him for a title as high as Duke, that would grant him his own lands, castles, servants...

"My dear late brother struggled with the same, you know. I tried to help him too."

Crispin's widened gaze darted to the king's face, placid, proud, but otherwise unreadable. He wanted to remain just as composed, but he couldn't help but implore, "My father?"

Moragon nodded. "Merritt was like Alistor in that he had ambition but wasn't always strong enough to take charge and pursue it. He relied too heavily on others. He relied on *me*. And I let him, hoping I could teach him. Unfortunately, his indecisiveness drove him to the accident which culminated in his death. I would not see *you* come to such a fate as well. I would hope you would accept my guidance where your dear father failed."

The king fell silent. Crispin's mind spun with the excitement of the possibilities being offered him. And yet, there remained the lingering fear of what game the king might be playing. Whether for good or ill, Moragon had some agenda; he'd never been known to help someone simply for his own sake.

"What would I be expected to do, your grace?" Crispin asked.

"Only to continue honing your natural talent and to use it to carry out my wishes, to sway the disobedient into submission..." Moragon motioned lazily to the dead flower. "Also, I'm assigning a small band of soldiers to aid and protect you. Your companion, Tytonn Grayfell, might mean well, but I fear he may no longer be best suited for this position."

"But—your grace—his family; I know they've been counting on his new income—"

"I will find other work for him, I assure you. His performance itself is not lacking, and neither is his character. He has proven himself a loyal servant and will be rewarded as such. But in terms of this position, his knowing the vassal Weston might make him too soft and dampen the fire I know burns inside *you*, Crispin. To prove yourself, you must learn if and when to cut yourself off from all distractions—even your closest friends."

Crispin could not respond to such a ruthless suggestion. Instead, he shifted in his chair. "Tytonn *does* have an affinity for taming animals. His powers can calm them, control them. I'd heard that you were in need of a new Master of Horses. Perhaps he might be considered?"

Moragon's brows rose in an expression of amusement. "Very well. I will certainly look into this request." He rose to his feet, which of course meant that Crispin must rise as well. "That should be all for now. I will summon you again once I have decided the course I wish you to take in regard to Master Weston. Meanwhile, enjoy the day, Crispin. I fear it's one of the last before the true dawn of winter's cold."

Crispin thanked his uncle, bowed, and made a hasty retreat into the corridor. At once, a chill shocked his body, absent from the fireplace's cozy comfort. Muttering the word for fire to warm his body, he broke into a run.

Satisfaction made the day seem even brighter. At last, the king turned an interested eye upon him. At last, his powers had opened up new paths, transforming him from a meek, useless boy into a potential leader. A voice inside him echoed a warning of the king's unknown agenda, but perhaps Alistor could help him decipher that mystery.

Later, anyway. For now, he had a far more important meeting to attend with a creature whose company would no doubt prove far lovelier than that of either of his uncles.

***

Gailea followed Elda through the castle toward Lord Crispin's chambers, her stomach twisting inside her like someone wringing out clothes on laundry day. Elda smirked playfully, likely guessing that Gailea's nerves stemmed from an affection toward her brother. Such a guess would not be entirely amiss, and yet Gailea wished that was her worry's only source.

What would she say when she met with the man who had saved her once from the king's wrath and had seemed so eager to make a good impression on her? Was he as sincere as he seemed and as Elda claimed? Or was she blinded by his boyish charms?

Elda was suddenly knocking on a door, which opened to reveal a handsome, smiling face with bright violet eyes and red curly hair.

"Good afternoon, sister." He kissed her cheek before turning a shy grin to Gailea. "And good afternoon to you, my lady."

Crispin took gentle hold of Gailea's hand—his own palm's slightly clammy touch made her smile as she realized he was nervous too—before inviting her and Elda inside the spacious outer chamber of his rooms. The two ladies sat on the chairs beside the luxurious fireplace, while Crispin pulled a chair up close and said, "So, Lady Gailea, my sister tells me you have some serious concerns, though she wouldn't name them specifically."

"She said I could trust you," Gailea said, "and that you might be able to help *both* of us."

Crispin gave her a meaningful look. "I would hope I've already proven my trust."

"Yes, and I am grateful, but with great respect, that was just a silly flute. This is something far weightier. But here you *must* help, Lord Crispin, as what I'm about to tell you places Elda in danger too. And I have no doubt you would protect her with your life."

"Well, what is it then?" Crispin demanded, glancing between the two ladies. "What danger do you wish to share with me?"

His poise and the confident set of his jaw made Gailea think of Alistor, but his eyes lacked the older man's ambitious gleam. Instead, they were full of curiosity and concern, especially as he watched his sister, and some of Gailea's caution melted away.

She explained about the poison, Chevalier's mistake in killing the infant instead of the queen, and his promise of grand armies to make it up to his majesty.

"Shortly after we overheard all of this, his majesty confronted me. He demanded that I show him my magic—"

Gailea stopped short. There was no need to further endanger herself by revealing her secrets before their time.

"Is all this true?" Crispin asked, turning to his sister with a shocked gaze. At her nod, his brows lowered into a frown and his shyness seemed to melt away into a fierce protectiveness toward Elda.

"My sister, Darice, and I, are close," Gailea said, "as I can tell you and Elda are also close. I promise to keep this secret. I wouldn't want any harm to come to Elda."

"I appreciate that," Crispin said, "truly. I wish I could deny that the king would plan something like this, but I won't. I've seen enough myself to know that there is no love in his heart for his queen."

"You and I both."

Gailea glanced away, blinking back a few tears as the infant's lifeless form flashed before her. Elda took her hand and squeezed it gently, and Gailea smiled at her in thanks.

Crispin leaned forward then and asked in a softer tone, "Why did Moragon want to know about your magic?"

Gailea studied him. Again, she could detect no hidden purpose in his gaze, only the lingering gentle concern clearly directed toward her now. "Because the king does not even comfort his wife in the loss of their son. Instead, he now turns his interest to what everyone has been whispering—choosing a new mistress."

"You?" Crispin said bluntly.

"I'm not certain exactly what his grace intends for me. But I fear it."

Crispin watched her a long time. For a while, his expression was unreadable, and she wished he would show some sign of anger, anxiousness, disgust—any slight hint that he was truly on her side.

Gradually, his eyes warmed with a tenderness that made him look more youthful, boyish even. "I want to help. There have been nasty rumors about Elda as well, and if the king is looking for any reason to trade her in some marriage pact, he need not look far if he suspects Elda knows any of this. Only...I'm not sure *what* I can do...."

Elda held up her slate: *You navigate court more than either of us. You might be able to search out any information—the king's intent for us, or for the queen. Anything that may help.*

Crispin nodded. "Of course," he said, squeezing Elda's hand while aiming a reassuring smile toward Gailea that made her face tingle with a blush. "I shall do my best for both of you."

He rose to his feet, and Gailea and Elda did the same. His smile remained on Gailea. "I wish we were able to spend time discussing less heavy matters."

He watched her intently. As the firelight gleamed in his eyes and ringed his curls with a gentle halo, Gailea felt her heart thump faster. But she maintained her composure. No sense in showing the affection that seemed to be growing ever stronger so quickly. He had yet to prove himself.

"I'll send word when I'm able to meet again," he added, "but I do not think meeting here again would be wisest. There are courtiers everywhere, and many are exceedingly loyal to the king."

"Fortunate for King Moragon," Gailea said wryly. "But not good for us, I fear. Do you know how to reach the kitchens?"

Crispin tilted his head. "A strange question from a servant—well, a former servant—to a lord."

"Yes. But even lords, when they were little, had curiosities and, more often than not, no solid opinions of what is right or proper."

His eyes lit up with mischief. "I explored there as a child, yes."

"Then I have a place we could use," Gailea said, "whenever the need arises."

"Very well, then. Till next time, Lady Gailea?"

"Till next time, my lord."

***

Crispin sped through the castle. At first, his path had drifted toward his younger uncle's chambers—not to speak directly about the situation, but instead to pose as the one who'd overheard the conversation between Moragon and Chevalier.

Instead, his footsteps turned quickly in another direction, as did his mind, and he soon found himself headed toward Tytonn's chambers. Even though Alistor had Crispin's best interests at heart, he also had his own interests to consider, his own neck to save if necessary. Tytonn was likely the most neutral party Crispin could share his troubles with at present.

Crispin came to the series of halls stretching less ornately before him. The plain, brown stone walls soothed his mind a little, a pleasing, earthy contrast to the lofty reds and purples always surrounding him.

At Tytonn's familiar door, Crispin was greeted warmly by his friend.

"Crispin," Tytonn said with a raise of his brows. He stood aside and waved his arm in a long, sweeping sign of welcome. As Crispin entered, his foot slipped on something, but Tytonn grabbed his arm to help steady his balance. Glancing down, he frowned at the pieces of white parchment blanketing the floor like drifts of snow.

Tytonn waded with him through the sea of white. They sat on two wooden chairs at a small table beside the hearth. Its embers had died low, emitting little warmth. Crispin lifted his hand and muttered the spell for fire. Thin streams of flame burst from his fingertips, catching the wood ablaze, and he eased back in his chair with a sigh.

"Feel better?" Tytonn asked, cocking a brow with a playful smirk.

"Yes, actually," Crispin said. "That *did* relieve a little tension."

Tytonn leaned forward, elbows resting on his knees. "What troubles you? Your uncles pulling you between their tug-of-war game again?"

"What do you mean?"

"They're both competing to cultivate you—it's the newest rumor afloat, only I'd say it's not much of a rumor."

"You may be right," Crispin muttered. "My sister and Lady Gailea just came to my chambers to speak with me."

Tytonn sat up again, eyes widening. "Whatever for?"

After eliciting a vow from Tytonn to reveal nothing, Crispin relayed his conversation with Gailea before adding, "I don't know what to do. I was thinking of going to Alistor, but…"

"*But*," his friend echoed. "Yes, with respect, I'm not certain Alistor is the best option in this case."

"Why would you say that? I would trust Alistor with my life. I only hesitate to get him involved for his own safety."

"I know you trust him dearly. That may well be the problem."

"What exactly has gotten into you this evening?"

"Nothing. I only meant—"

Crispin rose to his feet and started toward the door. "Never mind. I can see I was a fool to trust you first…"

"Wait!" Tytonn stood and followed him. "I didn't mean it personally against you."

Crispin turned and glared. "Yes, you did. Everyone thinks I'm incapable of making my own choices. The recent rumors—everyone thinks I'm nothing more than some kind of pawn. No one says it to my face, but I feel it."

"I would never think that. I only meant that you have to trust your heart, your gut. Your uncles will tell you one thing, not just for your benefit, but for theirs as well. It's the same with the girl—though, for the record, I'd trust her first."

Crispin shook his head. "Trust a near-stranger above my own family?"

"For that very reason. Gailea is the one who has the most to lose—her life—and she's also the one who has the least cause to lie to you. She can't use you like the others can. She doesn't have that kind of influence—"

"Be that as it may, I'll thank you to stop shaming my family's name—*either* of them. They may soon be responsible for your rise in station."

Tytonn's eyes widened. "How do you mean?"

"I defended your honor to his grace today. I suggested you for the new Master of Horses."

Tytonn's lips parted in a small gasp. "Cris...I don't know how to possibly thank you. The opportunity—it's a true honor, and a job I would enjoy much more than collecting taxes, if I'm honest. I won't disappoint you."

"I'm sure even scrubbing kitchen floors would be more enjoyable than tax collecting at this point." His anger deflating, Crispin sighed and shook his head. "I am glad the king is entrusting me with more responsibility, but it'll be even duller than usual without you..." Crispin shifted his feet, and papers crunched beneath them. With a scowl, he gestured to the floor, "What exactly *is* all this mess, by the way?"

"Music," Tytonn said, a small smile lighting his face. "Mine."

"Yours? In all our years you've never told me you wrote music."

"I've been dabbling around with different things, creating a mediocre melody here and there.... Maybe I could compose something for your new musical friend?"

"Gailea..." Wandering back to the chair, Crispin sank down and stared into the flames. "I've doubted myself for so long. Now I finally have my chance—and then *she* comes to me, places that chance at risk with her accusations against the king. But I must believe her, for my sister's sake. I couldn't bear for any harm to come to Elda, especially due to my own negligence. And Gailea— I can't help but want to help her too. Not just for her affection toward Elda, but for her courage, her wit..."

"You neglect to add her beauty," Tytonn added with a sly smile. But he quickly sobered. "Is there anything I can do? I should tell you...your sister and I have not exactly formed any solid understanding, not as of yet. But I do care deeply about her and would defend her with my life."

"Yes..." Crispin said slowly. "Do you recall Garrison? We took combat training with him when we were lads."

"I do," Tytonn said, face brightening with recognition. "I remember Garrison quite well."

"Have you stayed in contact with him? Do you know if he still works in the dungeons?"

Tytonn nodded. "We talk now and then. Yes, he still works in the dungeons. But why? I see some plot churning in that great mind of yours."

"I was only thinking ahead. Elda—if the time came to smuggle her away from here..."

"In that case, my father might help too. I believe he had some kind of relative who lives in the woods, in seclusion. It may be a place Elda could hide safely..."

"Find out as soon as you can. I'm eager to see my sister far from this place, with so many wretched eyes watching her, accusing her of various vulgarities, and now this new danger. I think she would be happiest living somewhere calm and secluded, as you suggest."

Tytonn's dark eyes shone with determination. "I will look into it."

"Thank you, my friend."

"Of course. And thank you again for offering me up for the new position. May recent events be a good start for the both of us."

"Yes," Crispin agreed. "A start—hopefully to a happy end."

CHAPTER 12

TENSIONS AND TREASONS

As the guards swung the grand double doors open wide, Crispin tripped a little, betraying his desire to turn and flee. While half of him wanted to race toward whatever new challenge the king prepared for him, his other half still feared making a fool of himself—or, worse, that his majesty had somehow discovered his talk with Gailea.

Taking a deep breath and drawing himself up, he reached for the confidence that Tytonn kept reassuring him he possessed and strode inside the council chamber.

Moragon, Chevalier, and several other men, some in expensive robes, others in armor, glanced up from the large table covered with maps and figurines.

"Crispin, welcome," Moragon said, beckoning him closer with a sweep of his hand.

"Your grace." Crispin stopped before the table, bowed, and then glanced briefly about the room. Its splendor mirrored that of the great hall. Rich reds dripped from the curtains flanking the long windows. Sunlight dazzled on the black and white marble squares comprising the floors, and the ceiling shone like gold.

"If you would please excuse me," Moragon said, nodding to each of his council in turn, "I must have a word privately with my nephew."

Moragon motioned toward a golden door carved with ornate pictures of various musical instruments. Crispin followed him inside a small room furnished with a crackling fireplace, a smaller table, and several chairs. Moragon sat, and Crispin followed suit.

"Forgive me, your grace," Crispin said, "if I interrupted something. But I'd thought your message said to come this morning—"

Moragon held up his hand. "It did. Unexpected business arose—hence my absence from breakfast. But I have a moment to spare my dear nephew if he is willing to spare me an extra task during his usual duties tomorrow evening."

Crispin nodded and leaned forward in his chair. The king continued, "Master Weston still has not paid his dues. Ordinarily, I might extend my patience, or else throw him in the stocks for a few days. However, he is not merely guilty of withholding taxes. Word has reached me of several meetings he's held in the woods, where he speaks against my being the true king. He says that because we Vorlaires took this country, he and others like him have the right to disobey what is, in their eyes, a false king."

"That's treason," Crispin murmured in disbelief. "And to do so publicly..."

"It disgusts me as well." Moragon lips curled in a contemptuous snarl. Crispin shifted uneasily; if his uncle's dark eyes were arrows, a single glance could have pierced him on the spot. "We take this realm, protect those too weak to protect themselves, strengthen its forces, improve its trade routes and overall reputation. Ungrateful wretches! But that isn't the worst of it. I've heard it said too that he is one among several who intend to gather an uprising. A riot, perhaps even a war. There is talk of his spies working inside these very walls.

"This kind of tension and divisiveness cannot be allowed to persist. Tomorrow, these traitors will hold one of their meetings, where they'll make speeches and no doubt plot against me. You will go, accompanied secretly by some of my guards, and pretend to be one of them. Then, when the time is right, you will reveal yourself and accuse him. You will promise not to tell me of his treachery if he pays you in full. If he refuses, you will use *whatever means necessary* until he complies. Do you understand?"

Moragon glanced pointedly at the blazing fire in the hearth, then back at Crispin.

Crispin sat frozen in his chair. "Your grace, my magic..." He sought words to replace the ones raging through his mind: *No, I cannot use fire in such despicable manner. Does he truly wish me to burn these men? Or just display the power?*

He licked his lips and ventured something that, too, was the truth. "I'm not certain my magic is advanced enough yet. We've practiced but a few days, really. What if I can't control myself?"

"I think you'll find the strength and will, when the moment comes. But if anything should go awry and you end up mutilating the traitorous bastard, no one will hold it against you. Do this thing for me, and I will know I can trust you a little more. And with trust comes power. You *do* want that—or do you want to become like Alistor, ever dependent on doing others' bidding?"

Crispin recoiled from the vicious wish for such violence in response to mere talk. Treasonous such talk might be, but to *burn* a man for it? That grim fate was reserved for the most dangerous of criminals, the most heretical sorcerers.

But he could not admit his revulsion. Instead, his thoughts sprang to Alistor's defense. But Moragon did speak truth; Alistor, for all his magic and intelligence, wasn't extremely popular—except with the young men he taught and the young women who lusted after his charm and fortune.

There was only one choice. He would ensure Master Weston paid his taxes and convince the men to disavow whatever foolish notion of rebellion might be simmering within their group. It was a risk, defying Moragon, but Crispin felt increasingly inclined to courage. A pair of aquamarine eyes, a sweet smile and lilting voice flashed in his mind before he finally answered—in a lie.

"Yes, your grace. I will do what you ask."

***

Dismissed, Crispin stole to the watchtower and ascended quickly, his lungs constricting from the thin, frigid air.

As he reached the tower's peak, Alistor turned away from one of the tall, glassless windows to face him.

"Good morning, nephew. I began to worry you'd decided to skip today's lesson."

Alistor lifted a hand, and immediately long bursts of flame illuminated from his fingertips, stretching high toward the ceiling. Crispin let flames dance along his own fingertips as he declared, "Forgive my delay. But the king wanted a word with me."

"For what purpose?" Alistor formed the streamers of

fire into a ball and started casually tossing the sphere of flame back and forth between his hands.

Still mimicking his uncle's movements, Crispin said, "To assign me a new task, to be completed on the morrow."

Alistor remained silent, his gaze questioning and commanding in one—today's lesson would not progress until Crispin confided. He conveyed the conversation he had just shared with Moragon.

Alistor snorted and said, "Weston is right, even if he's a fool to declare it—Moragon *is* a false king, in the right sense of the word. But what does the king intend you to do about him?"

"To persuade him to make payment. To threaten him with...with my magic..." Crispin's voice trailed. Uttered aloud, the task made him cringe. He almost lost his grip on the fireball but quickly twisted his hand to regain control before tossing it once more between his hands.

Alistor stared, astonished. Then, quietly, he said, "What is most despicable is that Moragon doesn't even care so much about this vassal's punishment—except where his pride is concerned. The man is likely not even a threat. But *you* are. Don't you see what he's playing at, Crispin? He's testing your loyalty. He doesn't believe you'll carry the task through."

"He might be testing me, but he also believes I'm capable. He's said that I'm every bit as powerful as my father—"

Alistor laughed, loud and sneering. "So now he's been singing Merritt's praises, uplifting him as some kind of saint? Moragon hated your father even more than he hates me—and as much as he likely hates you, or will, if he cannot use you. The best you can hope for from him is tolerance. I don't think the man has ever genuinely *liked* anyone, not even his whores."

Crispin stood frozen to the spot, speechless. Alistor had accused the king of hating his father so freely that it was hard not to believe him. Had the king lied to him? Did Alistor lie to him now? What truth lay in either of them?

Two magnets seemed to pull at his mind, to possibly rip it in half at any moment. Alistor had always been the one to protect and lead him, and he'd done a fair job up until this point. The king's sudden interest was more likely to prove a façade.

"I...I do not intend to follow Moragon's orders," he admitted at last. "Not the full extent of them. It's barbaric. But what should I do, then, if he accuses me?"

"I'm glad to hear of your resolve," Alistor said, letting the ball of flame gracefully roll and circle his hand. As for what to do...you risk being accused of treason yourself or, at the least, being made a fool of, your position given to another without a second thought or chance for glory."

"I know that. How can I prevent either fate?"

"You cannot. If you take this course you must accept where it leads." Alistor nodded toward the nearest window and the icy world visible beyond the narrow tower. "Even out of Adelar, should it come to that."

Crispin was so taken aback at his uncle's blunt counsel that the ball of flame slipped once more from his grasp—and this time, he lost control of it entirely as it slammed straight toward Alistor's face. Alistor swerved artfully, and Crispin ignored the annoying burn of embarrassment in his cheeks as he pleaded, "How can I make such a choice? Leave my home, my friends?" He lifted a hand weakly toward his uncle. "You?"

"There is a cost paid whenever choosing between virtue and power. A friendless life is a lonely life." Alistor clutched his hand into a tight fist, crushing his flame into a spiral of smoke. "It is a difficult and vain life, a pointless cycle that I have grown weary of for many years now. There is no more hope for me—unless there is still hope for you. The stark truth is that if you want to save your life, to improve it and mine, you will obey the king. However, if keeping your virtue is more imperative, then you must be willing to face the consequences. Remember the doe in the woods."

Crispin winced, as if Alistor's words darted out like a venomous snake, stinging sharply. He still admired Gailea for her compassion toward the doe, for her courage where his had failed. But shame bit him more pointedly—both the shame of failing the ceremony's task and the shame of not being able to make the decision of whether to save the deer or slay it.

"Well, you've a day yet to decide what you'll do, don't you?" Alistor said. "Just keep in mind that, at the end of the day, this is all a game to him. He's setting you up, and you can either take control of what he's offering you or, like a captain at sea, drown with your ship when everything falls apart. I wouldn't ask you to do anything against your moral compass, but sometimes, such sacrifices must be made for the greater good—and to survive. Whether you obey him or not, he *will* use you. The question is how and when you wish to be used."

***

Crispin fled back to his chambers. After his talk with Alistor, his lessons had continued to go awry. His fire had blasted out of control, nearly scorching his uncle who was thankfully quick to raise a hand and block the attack. Crispin had tried to wield his light magic instead, but his frustrations made it turn into just as dangerous a flame. The session had ended with a disappointing scowl and

snide remarks from his uncle, and with Crispin doubt-
ing himself more than ever.

The solution to ease his troubled mind seemed so
simple: obey the king, or don't. Two choices. But neither
was easily made. Disobeying the king meant endanger-
ing his life—and thus the lives of his sister and Gailea,
even Alistor. Obeying the king meant torturing another
human being. An atrocity.

Perhaps. Or perhaps he could yet sway Master Weston
and it wouldn't come to that. Perhaps he shouldn't worry about it at all until tomorrow came....

Crispin entered his room and shut the door behind
him with a weary sigh of relief. Perhaps he could search
his father's diaries for some advice. It had been a long
time since he had read them, but surely his father hadn't
been such an epic failure with his Fyre magic and might
offer some insight. As he took a few steps toward his
bookshelf and his eyes adjusted to the dim light, he saw
a figure sitting in a chair by the hearth and tensed—then
sighed further relief as he recognized Tytonn.

"You startled me nearly to death," Crispin said.

Tytonn arched a curious brow. "Rough day?"

"You've no idea," Crispin muttered, breezing over to
the bookshelf and scanning for the old leather tomes he
sought. "But never mind that. Why are you here?"

"I came on Elda's behalf. I've found a way to help
her, as promised."

Crispin perked up. "Finally, a bit of good news in this
gloomy day." Finding what he sought, he snatched the
three diaries, hurried to draw a chair up and sit near his
friend, and began sifting through them for any mention
of fire magic or his father's use of it. "Go on then!"

"You know my father's cousin, the one I mentioned?
She's a seamstress...and more to the point, she is also a
great magician. Elda can learn so much from her, be-

come an even more talented artist. My cousin's willing to protect her, maybe even take her on as an apprentice."

Crispin's heart leapt. "Elda would love nothing more! All she's ever wanted is a peaceful life, a chance to show her talent, to be independent and make an honorable name for herself! What is this seamstress' name?"

"She is known by some as 'the Weaver,' but beyond that, she wishes to remain anonymous. To protect yourself and Elda."

A hint of unease crept into Crispin's mind, but he pushed it aside and returning to leafing through the diaries; if only he could recall where, he knew there was an entry that spoke of keeping one's fire steadier, even under more stressful circumstances that would make it want to go awry like his hand earlier. "Have you told Elda yet?"

Tytonn shook his head. "I thought you might want to be the one to share the news. Meanwhile, we'll need a plan. Garrison is willing to help, but he's wary. He has his own family to protect, and he fears what may happen if we're recognized."

Crispin's mind spun, grappling for some answer, and then stopped abruptly on just the right one. He glanced up pointedly at Tytonn. "Gailea. She has magic that allows her to change the color of her skin, blend in with her surroundings. Maybe she could help with a disguise."

"You think she'd be willing?"

"I think she could be persuaded. She cares deeply for my sister, and she and I have become friendly enough. When I speak to Elda, I will have her ask Gailea..." Crispin sighed and fell back in his chair. "I'm forever indebted to you, my friend. I'll tell Elda as soon as I can. At least *someone's* spirits can be lifted..."

"Something else is troubling you?" Tytonn asked gently.

Crispin hesitated, considering whether to share the brutal request from King Moragon. He knew what Tytonn would say. He'd openly refuse such an order from the king, even if it meant his life. And besides, hadn't Moragon said Tytonn was friendly with Weston's family?

"No, you just focus on your plan to get my sister out of here and let me know the moment we're able to carry it out. Protecting her is all that matters right now."

***

In a clearing within the Delosaian woods, Crispin and all the strangers nearby stood dwarfed by the tall, oppressive evergreens surrounding this open patch of ground. Weston and his companions had chosen well, Crispin had to admit. These same trees provided shadow and privacy to the dozens of men meeting here, appropriate for fomenting such secretive plots.

Crispin inched forward, shifting as the murmuring crowd pressed close about him. He shivered at the sight of dozens upon dozens gathered in opposition to the king. With a glance at the outskirts of the clearing, he located the men clad in golden-brown cloaks and hoods—the king's secret guard—and his nerves eased ever so slightly.

A hush settled over the crowd as a man leapt atop a fallen log and climbed to the crest of its twisted arch—Master Weston. Crispin pulled up his hood, making sure it covered as much of his face as possible, and watched as the man declared:

"Welcome, friends! I thank all of you for coming. The numbers are heartening, more so than I would have expected. For those of you who met with us last, I thank you again for your continued courage. For those just joining us, I thank you as well and will inform you of our purpose here. Any who disagree with what we stand for are free to leave.

"Many of you are aware of the tyranny of King Moragon. He raises our taxes to the point that many families might be better off dead than struggling to survive on such meager means. He steals away our children and women to be used as servants. Some are never seen again, others merely discarded upon a whim when he tires of their use. He has burned many alive under the accusation of sorcery when many were innocents!

"Noble blood may flow through his veins, but it is not Adelaran. We stand here tonight to unite and fight as one. Already, outside aid begins to answer us from neighboring islands..."

As Weston continued, Crispin found himself impressed. This man had seemed so meek and humble when they'd first met, cowering behind the door of his house. But now he spoke with such command and seemed to be amassing whole armies to his side.

Everyone watched him intently, their faces filled with fight and determination. They believed him. They trusted him. Each of them wanted the king destroyed. A flare of defensive anger rose inside Crispin; Moragon would never be his favorite person in the world, but he was family, and he was the king.

"What about the peace he's helped forge with some of those neighboring islands who would now stand against him?" Crispin asked. His voice shook, and as all eyes turned to him, he froze in place and cast a swift glance at the outer edge of the clearing. Moragon's soldiers had now concealed themselves in the foliage, and while he knew they were ready to come to his aid, he wished he could see them. Clearing his throat, he said more loudly, "What about the trade routes he's helped establish? The prosperity he's helped bring to Adelar?"

"The love of money," one man called. "That's always the start of it. People rally behind a leader, thinking he'll make 'em rich. But the king cares nothing of our prosperity, boy. His blessings fall only to those who do his bidding, and only for as long as he needs them. My son was summoned for a possible apprenticeship. We thought he might have an affinity for mental magic. But its traces were weak, and his grace humiliated him, stripped him of what coinage he'd earned. Now, he can find neither work nor a bride. He is shamed, eternally damned by the king."

"Not just a king," a woman accused coldly. "Moragon thinks himself a god."

Struck speechless, Crispin gaped at her. He'd known the king hated poor Marlis, but though the reasons were unfair, at least Crispin understood them. But it became increasingly apparent that he was also unjust toward his people—and every bit as loathed.

"Do not be too harsh on the boy," Weston said. "From the look of him he is young still, and easily swayed. As are all youth—which is why the king's cruelties *must* be made known. He blinds young men and women with lofty promises, and then, when they no longer serve a purpose for him, he dashes them upon the rocks. Think of his own surviving brother. He keeps Lord Ragnar close, hating him, fearing him, even though as a bastard, Ragnar is far from succession, scarcely a threat. But Moragon might execute him merely on a whim at any moment."

He wouldn't do that, Crispin thought, but doubt flickered inside him. Alistor had often said he believed he lived at the sufferance of the king.

"And what about that young boy lurking about the castle?" another man called out. "The king's nephew? Might not the king warp the lad's mind? Do we wish for him to become just as conniving a snake as the Fyre mage, or just as vicious a tyrant as the king? Or even as deadly a tool as Chevalier, that heretic? Shall we not heed the news of the unstoppable blaze he conjured at the celebration, setting light to a score of innocent people for mere entertainment?"

Crispin gasped, his hands clenching into fists. What mad rumor was this? A cruel lie so far from the truth it had to have been maliciously invented. As his mind whirled to find a way to correct them without giving away his identity, he could only listen in silence.

"You're right," a woman called, "perhaps we should be setting our sights on more than one menace. Who knows how the king may be training his nephew for his purposes? Or perhaps Lord Ragnar wishes to use him."

"Perhaps they *both* do," Weston said. "I have met the lad once and heard many reports on him. He is a kind young man, compassionate. But compassion will not win many wars or persuade many kings—certainly not without a strong enough will. He is pliable. He will bend to their wills before long, and the more power we give their family, the more unstoppable they will become together..."

Anger brewed inside Crispin. How dare these people accuse him before he'd done any evil thing? How dare they assume he was too weak to control his own mind, make his own decisions? He was no manipulator like his uncles. He did not harm the innocent. And his will was more than strong enough to choose his own fate.

"If we don't rise and stand against the king now," Weston continued, "before long, it will be too late. He'll have amassed armies of relentless power. He'll spread his poison, ensnaring as many lands as he can. And he'll use his own family to do it—only to kill them too when the time is ripe—"

"Enough!" Heat boiled beneath Crispin's skin as if his very blood caught ablaze. This pain fueled his anger, making him want to release his fire upon everyone gathered, but he focused on Weston, storming forward, pushing through the murmuring crowds.

"I am not the pathetic pawn you claim me to be. I am Crispin, nephew of the king—and I accuse you of treason and command you to step down at once!"

He threw back his hood. The gasps and cries intensified, and several people rushed forward, but Master Weston held up a hand to stop them.

"Lord Crispin, forgive me," Weston said. Apology filled his face, but fear glinted in his eyes as well. "I mean no disrespect against you. But I will not stand down. Your uncle is no king. He is a tyrant and a bully. And I think you know it. You don't have to be afraid of him. Join our side, join our fight—"

"Never!" Crispin spat. "I will defend my king to the death, as should you all. Now, stand down."

Master Weston shook his head. "No, my lord. Imprison me if you must, but my soul would not permit me to—"

"If you will not stand down, then you *will* kneel!"

Crispin lifted his hand and, as a warning, murmured a spell to send several jets of flame into the sky—

Almost the instant the intense heat flowed down his arm and left his fingertips, he knew this was not right—this wasn't akin to the sensations he had read in his father's diary last night. He hadn't taken the time to control the stream. Hadn't gathered his wits to command the fire as to how high to soar, how wide to reach. Panic skittered through his chest and he tried to end the release—but even as he did, the flames resisted like an unbroken stallion. Instead, as if resentful at his attempt to rein it in, the fire rushed back toward him, blazing through his entire body.

Then Crispin *had* to let go. He had to unleash the power he'd conjured or it would consume him. With one tremendous, painful mental push, everything roared into a blast of red, gold and even white flame, which at last plunged from his body with a deafening explosion. The effort sent him slamming to the ground, where he lay stunned, seeing nothing but red as the sky spun overhead.

When his senses returned, strong arms yanked him to his feet and began dragging him from the clearing. He recognized them as two members of the king's guard. Crispin jerked from their grasp and whirled around... only to stare in horror at the sight before him.

Golden-red flames consumed several trees and patches of grass. People scattered, screaming as fire streamed from their clothes. Some threw themselves to the ground, while others hurried to aid them, shouting water charms to create rain and drown the flames.

A tortured cry jerked his attention toward the fallen log, where Weston had been standing; he was there yet, but fire waved high from one of his shoulders, consuming one side of his face. Several men and women dragged him away toward a creek visible not far from the clearing.

People rushed at Crispin, casting ice, water, and various other types of elemental magic. At first staring in mute uselessness, Crispin raised a hand in an instinctive act of defense to block their attacks with fire. This, at least, was one of the first skills he had learned, and maintaining control was well within his capabilities. The mob pressed forward, reaching for him, but Moragon's guards surrounded him in a flash, swords drawn, and the crowds halted.

Crispin pushed past the soldiers and fled into the woods. As the stench of burning flesh followed him, he stumbled, bent over to vomit, then forced himself to keep running. The clank of armor announced Moragon's pursuing guard, but he didn't stop. He didn't want them. He wanted no connection to his uncle at that moment. He had opposed Master Weston, only to make the man's very accusations come true. Something had snapped inside him, and his anger and magic had both gotten the best of him.

Those people had been just as innocent and undeserving as the doe he had attacked in the woods. What would Elda think of him? What would Gailea say when she found out? Would she consider him a monster? Would she refuse to help his sister?

Would anyone help him after what he had done tonight?

CHAPTER 13

PROTECTIONS

Gailea and Elda stood facing each other. They had gathered inside Gailea's chambers for the past hour, sharing both prayers and frivolous conversation to pass the time and try to distract themselves from the anxiety of their fast-approaching mission. Now, at last, the clock struck the hour agreed upon to carry out that mission.

Gailea slipped the precious pendant, Lady Aline's gift, over Elda's neck, looked her straight in the eye, and mouthed, "Are you ready?"

Elda gave a single nod in reply.

Gailea held the red and purple gem and sang her song that would allow Elda to blend more easily with her surroundings. She focused on the girl's gray cloak until her blonde hair had dulled to match its ashen color. Her skin also turned ashen, and her blue eyes darkened to a smoky gray.

Gailea ceased singing. When she saw that Elda's appearance remained altered, she nodded, satisfied that the song's magic had been trapped inside the sealing stone. Elda slipped the jewel beneath the folds of her thick gray dress and followed Gailea toward the mirror. Gailea had already used the same song to alter her own appearance, and Elda's eyes widened as she beheld them both with gray dresses, cloaks and hair, and sickly pallor.

"I'm going to sing another song," Gailea said. "It will make our footsteps quieter. But its magic will only work as long as I keep singing and you hold onto me. Are you ready?"

Elda nodded again.

Gailea grabbed Elda's hand and pulled her toward the door, singing the song quietly in her mind, grateful that she'd practiced enough to master the charm without singing it aloud. After all, what good was a song that could muffle footsteps if people heard her coming anyway as she sang the song itself?

As Gailea grabbed a basket of wood and stopped Elda before the door, she looked at her and whispered, "Remember, if anyone stops us to question us, we're just returning late from stoking the fireplaces."

Such an excuse would make sense for the first leg of their journey, as long as no one recognized them. Short of the king, Gailea doubted that anyone would; no one would expect ladies of the court to degrade themselves so. As for his majesty, Crispin had insisted that leaving at this hour was best because the king was always in his chambers, studying his music before retiring to bed. Beyond that, Amiel willing, the cloak of night would shield Elda beyond the castle walls.

Gailea opened her door and peered out. Then, motioning for Elda to follow, she swept down the corridor. They must move swiftly—not so much as to arouse suspicion, but fast enough that the pendant's magic did not wear off till Elda was well out of the castle.

As they stole through corridors and down stairwells,

they passed a few servants or guards here and there. With each encounter, Gailea's heart seemed to stop, but she forced herself to make eye contact with servants passing by. Sometimes, she would pause the song that muffled footfalls to instead hum her song-shield. While there were no known mental magicians in the castle aside from Moragon, she couldn't be certain who his spies were or what powers they might hold.

Gailea allowed herself to breathe easier as she wound them down the halls and stairs used only for the servants. Anyone they encountered here would be either too weary or consumed in their work to take much notice.

At last, they reached the small closet Gailea had once called home. As they stepped inside and shut the door behind them, she allowed herself to feel relief. This room had always been like an old friend that provided comfort and safety, and tonight it would be that again, if but for a moment.

They did not wait long till a knock on the door made Gailea jump. Then, Crispin's head peeked through, and he motioned them to follow. The two ladies slipped back out into the hall to continue their flight.

"Wait," Crispin said, holding out two strong but thin ropes.

Gailea and Elda held out their arms, and Crispin began binding their wrists. They had all agreed that if they were stopped and questioned, Crispin would say he had caught them trying to steal and that he aimed to please King Moragon by bringing such ungrateful servants to justice and delivering them to the dungeon himself.

As Crispin came to Gailea, his hands fumbled with the ropes, and he muttered a curse beneath his breath. Gailea glanced at his burning cheeks and a flush touched her own face. Despite the incredible amount of possible danger, they prepared to fling themselves into and the weighty nature of their plan, she couldn't deny the spark igniting inside her. That spark flared and grew as she stood so close to him, with his skin brushing against hers.

Crispin was careful to tie the knots so they could break free and run at a moment's notice. Gailea prayed it wouldn't come to that. If it did, the only chance of escape would likely lie in a battle of magics, and she wished no one to come to harm.

"Do you know the way?" Gailea whispered. "The most secret ways?"

Crispin nodded and offered a brief smile. It did not seem to reach his eyes, but she sensed this was due to how intensely he focused on their plan; he likely felt as eager to get on with it as she did. "Yes. I explored much as a boy. I can get us there without any significant eyes watching."

Elda smiled back at him, looking perfectly at ease.

Gailea nodded. She would have to trust him; it was her only option.

Crispin led them through several passages, behind tapestries or through tiny rooms that even Gailea was unfamiliar with. As their journey turned more steadily downward, a cold draft blasted at them. They scrambled down a narrow stairway, and Gailea noted the high windows covered with bars. With no glass to shield the approaching winter's wind, the entire stairway choked in the icy winds, piercing through Gailea's thin dress and cloak with a more bitter cold than she'd felt since before becoming one of the queen's ladies.

They soon emerged into a dank hall with no windows, lit only by torches; they now delved entirely beneath the ground. After winding down another stair, a figure stood at the bottom of the steps, and Gailea instantly prepared any song-spells in her mind that might prove useful to defend them.

"Garrison?" Crispin said.

The bearded man dressed in a simple tunic, breeches, and boots nodded.

"I'll take it from here. Many thanks, Lord Crispin. I assure you they're in good hands."

"Many thanks to *you*."

Crispin then turned to the girls and took one of their hands in each of his. "I'll meet both of you outside, with Tytonn and his cousin. I know this is the scariest part, but you can trust Garrison. Remember that he is Tytonn's friend, and that I would trust my life—or that of anyone I loved—to Tytonn. Stay calm, follow Garrison, and I'll see you soon."

Elda nodded, and he leaned in to gently kiss her forehead.

Then, with a brief glance and nod at Gailea, he sped back up the stairs and out of sight. Gailea stood feeling admittedly abashed. She had expected some token of affection as well—a kiss on the hand, even just a few words of encouragement—especially considering how he was usually tripping over his own two feet for a chance to talk with her show his interest. What in the Five Worlds had gotten into him tonight? Perhaps he was more worried about spiriting his sister safely from the castle than she had realized. Gailea couldn't blame him; she would be just as anxious if she thought Darice was in any real danger.

"All right, ladies," Garrison said, his voice gruff but gentle. "Raise your hoods, keep your heads down, and follow me."

Gailea and Elda obeyed and followed Garrison through the small door.

The sharp stench of mold, rot, and human waste assaulted Gailea's nose, overwhelming her nearly to the point of retching. She covered her face, hoping that Elda would be able to hold back as well. Gailea had encountered her share of revolting smells working the kitchens, but Elda had likely never had to.

They entered a room flanked by barred cells. Torches hanging between the cells cast a sickly orange glow. Some cells held just one prisoner, while others contained many, cramped in the tiny space. While some slept, most lay awake, coughing or moaning.

One man, a scrawny creature with a patchwork of bruises and cuts across his bare chest and arms, threw himself at the bars. His head knocked against the iron, tearing open what seemed a recent gash. As blood trickled down his face, he clawed at the ladies, crying out,

"Mercy, mercy! Please, I beg of you! Show mercy! I am innocent!"

He clutched at Elda's cloak, but a simple threat and raised fist from Garrison sent the man slinking back into his cell.

As they left the man behind, indignation flared inside Gailea. She had spent her whole life hiding who she was to protect herself, but who was there to protect these people? If she ever grew strong enough to stand up to Moragon, she would find a way to make life better for these prisoners. Surely no one deserved such a wretched existence, no matter what their crime.

They wound through another hall, this one flanked by doors with small, barred windows. Most of the guards they passed paid them no heed. A few sent lusting glances at the girls in passing, while others simply nodded at Garrison.

They turned next into a wide-open room where most of the prisoners lay shackled to the walls. A few knelt, bound in wooden stocks. Gailea suppressed a cry as a rat scurried over her feet.

As they approached a door flanked by two guards

talking and laughing raucously with one another, Garrison brought them to a halt.

"Garrison!" one greeted with a warm clap on his shoulder. "And what've you got here tonight?"

"Just a couple little mice that tried to steal some cheese from his majesty's kitchens. They've spent their time. His majesty wants them back to work. But I figured not before I had a bit o' fun with 'em."

The other guard chuckled. "Ah, Garrison. You're always up for a good romp." He lifted Gailea's chin; she felt an urge to bite his finger but only glared at him defiantly. "Pretty little things, and feisty too, this one. Surprised I didn't notice them myself."

"You wouldn't care to tell the difference between a young girl and an old man, as long as they pleased you," the first guard jested. The other guard slapped him, and the first laughed out loud.

"They weren't down here long," Garrison said with a shrug. "Just enough to give 'em a good scare. You know how Moragon is with his ladies. Doesn't want to ruin them before he's had his fill—which works for me, as I'm about to have mine!"

Gailea glanced at Elda, grateful that her friend was keeping her face down and couldn't catch any of their disgusting words.

A familiar sound pricked her attention—or rather, a familiar song, hummed by a voice that cracked but otherwise remained perfectly in tune.

She whipped around and froze, as if she had met the gaze of some creature that could turn her to stone. Amongst the many other prisoners, Lady Aline lay against one wall. Despite her thinning body and once lovely gown now covered in filth, Gailea recognized her as clearly by her looks as by her song. Heavy shackles chained her ankles to the wall, her skin scraped raw from the heavy fetters—an unnecessary cruelty; even had the woman the strength to try, she would never get past the guards.

Bile rose in Gailea's throat at the hideous nightmare. She wanted to call out. She wanted to rush to her teacher's side and rip the shackles from the wall, or at least sing to her to provide some temporary comfort.

Gailea glanced up at Garrison and the other two guards, still engaged in their bawdy jokes. Resisting the urge to run and draw more attention, she wandered over slowly and whispered, "Lady Aline. Lady Aline, can you hear me?"

Lady Aline continued to sing quietly, eyes closed. Gailea wondered if she was half-lost in sleep and was loath to wake her, and yet she didn't know when—or if—they might get another chance to speak. She touched her mentor's shoulder and shook her, ever so gently, hoping she didn't bother some hidden scars or bruises.

Lady Aline's eyes cracked open and shifted sideways toward Gailea. Then, they widened.

"Gailea!" she gasped, whispering. "Is that you, my child? I almost didn't recognize…"

"Yes, Lady Aline, it's me." Gailea grasped the lady's hand, but as Aline winced, Gailea pulled away, wanting to cry as she saw the long, fresh cut.

"You've been practicing your magic, I see." Lady Aline's lips wore the hint of a smile. "But how are you here?"

"I can't explain. There's no time. How are *you* here? Maybe I can help."

Lady Aline shook her head, brushing it against the stone wall. "I can't tell you that. It would only place you in greater danger. But tell me," she whispered quieter still, "do you still have the gift I gave you? Are you making good use of it?"

Gailea closed her eyes against tears. "Yes. Yes, thank you. It's served me well—"

"Trying to extend our stay, are we?"

Strong hands grabbed Gailea from behind, and she struggled against them, crying out.

"I think she'd rather play with us than you, Garrison," said the guard who held her close.

"Stop wasting my time," Garrison said, even as the guard released her and shoved her forward. "Come on, you stupid wench…" He grabbed Gailea by the arm and dragged her through the door after Elda. She turned to catch a final glance of Lady Aline, but the door slammed shut behind them.

They scaled a long winding stair, leaving behind the guards' sneering jabs, but Gailea could not leave behind the agonizing image of Lady Aline huddled against the wall, battered and helpless. The nightmare burned in her mind as vividly as if it hovered right before her.

At last, they emerged outdoors. Gailea gulped the cold winter air and finally let her tears quietly fall.

Another brief exchange was made with the guards outside, and then Garrison led them away from the castle and into the surrounding trees.

Gailea followed numbly. She wanted to scream. She wanted to harness Crispin's fire powers and set the entire structure ablaze. But she must remain silent until Elda was safe. She couldn't bear to see anyone else she loved tortured at the king's hands.

They wound through the trees till they came to a small sky-boat hovering near the edge of the floating island. The king's woods stretched far below. In the dim light of the moon, half covered by clouds, the forest looked like nothing more than a solid, dark green shadow, a great abyss reflecting the overwhelming sadness and outrage flooding Gailea's heart.

They entered the boat and, as Garrison pushed off with the oars, slowly floated down. He pushed them directly under Astyrian, so as to avoid any wandering eyes from the castle lookouts above. An age seemed to pass before the craft landed with a gentle bump on the ground near the woods. When they climbed from the boat, Garrison hid it beneath a canvas and led them on a long walk. At last, Gailea saw the mouth of a cave, where Crispin, Tytonn, and a dark-haired, muscular man waited for them.

Elda flew into Crispin's arms, hugging him close. She then looked to Tytonn, who took her hands and said, "I'm so glad you're safe."

Gailea wanted to be moved by the sweet scene, but all she could picture was the horror of Lady Aline surrounded by cruelty and filth. As she stood, numb, she could almost sense Crispin's gaze on her. She turned and saw his concern, a questioning frown causing a slight line on his forehead. It was clear he knew something was wrong and wished to be a comfort. But Gailea could not bear to voice what she had seen back in the dungeon. So, she gave an infinitesimal shake of her head and cast her attention down to the cave floor. Even then she knew he watched her, and despite her grief, her heart seemed warmed from within by such care.

"Elda," Tytonn said, leading her to the muscular man. "This is Corin, a family friend. He will take you to my cousin the Weaver, to the place where you will be safe. No one will find you there. It's well guarded."

Thank you, Elda mouthed at him, and then at Corin.

Corin nodded. "It's an honor, my lady. I'll protect you with my life."

Elda turned back to Crispin, her gaze full of love and aching.

"I'll miss you too," Crispin said, his smile wavering.

"But you must go. Now. Get away from here as far and as fast as you can—" She hugged him again, and he held her close, whispering, "I love you too..."

Then, as she released him, Crispin looked up at Corin and said, "You recall the way to the portal?"

Corin nodded. "Tytonn showed me earlier."

"Then be on your way. And send word the moment you've safely arrived."

Elda hugged Crispin once more before taking Gailea into her arms and holding her close. Gailea hugged her back; she didn't know when, or if, she might see her dear friend again.

As soon as Elda released Gailea and followed Corin into the cave and out of sight, Gailea could hold back no longer. Trembling, she collapsed to the ground and sobbed hard.

"Gailea!" Crispin cried, dropping beside her. He reached for her but then hesitated, looking at a loss. Gailea wanted to tell him she was all right, that she didn't mean to alarm him, but her words couldn't find a space between her violent tears.

"My apologies," Garrison said. "Some of the guards teased her, tried to get rough with her. They must've frightened her—"

"Is she all right?" Crispin demanded. "Did they harm her—?"

"No," Gailea gasped, drawing a shuddering breath. "They didn't—they didn't hurt me. It's not that—"

"Then what is it?"

Gailea opened her mouth to answer, but tears choked her words once more.

Crispin took her hands and squeezed them, gently but firmly. Shaking her a little, he urged, "Please, my lady, please answer me. What is wrong? Tell me what's wrong, and I can help you."

Gailea breathed as deeply as she could, quelling her sobs enough to look at him and say, "Down in the prison, right before we left...I recognized someone. Lady Aline—I've told you about her, my mentor for years now. She had told me she was going to visit family, but then I saw her in that dungeon, and I—" She gasped again, fighting back a fresh round of tears.

"I'm sorry," Crispin breathed. "I'm so sorry. Surely, if she is down there.... A good woman like that could not have done something so terrible. She will likely be out soon enough, regardless of the cause."

"We both know better, Crispin," Tytonn said. "Don't try to comfort her with lies."

"I don't even care about the reason," Gailea said, drawing her hands away. "We need to get her out of there." She jumped to her feet and flung a wild glance at the jailer. "You can help, yes?"

Garrison looked uneasy and took a few steps back. "I would wish to, but I've a family of my own to protect, and I've already taken great risk tonight."

"Someone either helps me, or I will do it myself!"

"Gailea, think about what you're saying." Crispin stood and walked up to her. He reached for her, but she drew back. "If you return of your own accord, they'd recognize you as the same prisoner; that places Garrison in danger—and Elda. And..." He moved a little closer, and this time she let him tenderly touch her cheek. "It places *you* in danger as well."

Gailea studied the deep concern in his eyes. Her heart ached beyond belief for Lady Aline, but Crispin's gentle caring and obvious sincerity wrapped around her heart, soothing that ache and making it just a little more bearable.

"Forgive me," Garrison said then, "but I must be going." He glanced at Tytonn. "Everything is as we agreed upon?"

"Yes," Tytonn said. "Take your family far from here. Crispin has made all the necessary arrangements."

"You'll be safe in Loz in no time," Crispin said. "Take this for your thanks, and for new beginnings."

He held out a bag of coins, and Garrison took them with a humble bow of his head. "Thank you, my lord. And you, Tytonn, my dear friend. May we meet again someday, under happier times."

"Amiel willing," Tytonn said.

Garrison disappeared into the trees.

"Elda..." Gailea said quietly, gazing into the caves' depths. "They're taking the portal that transports outside the silver barriers, outside the kings' woods? It's in this cave?"

"Yes," Crispin said. "You could go with them, you know. If you hurried, you could catch up and escape as well."

Gailea was taken aback. "I can't—not now. Not until I see that Lady Aline is safe. And my sister—Darice—you must know I could never leave without her!"

"Forgive me," Crispin said, looking surprised and then abashed in turn. "I only thought to protect you. But I can understand your need to stay, and I respect it. It's honorable and brave. If our roles were reversed, I would stay too to protect my sister."

"Have you discovered anything new?" Gailea asked. "About what we discussed the other day?"

"I have some ideas. But now is not the time to share them. We must all return before we're found missing— especially you, should the queen need you. Can you meet me tomorrow?"

"Yes. Do you remember the small room where you met Elda and me tonight?"

Crispin nodded.

"Meet me there, tomorrow around two o'clock."

"Very well. Shall I escort you back to your room?"

"No need. This isn't my first time sneaking out into the king's woods."

She granted him a small, weary smile.

He bid her good night, as did Tytonn, and she sped through the trees.

Soon enough, she came to another cave, little more than a half-collapsed hole in the side of a hill. With the invention of sky ships, portals were used less and less for transport, and many had gone abandoned. Gailea could just squeeze inside the dilapidated cave of earth. Her hair caught in the tree roots twisting from above, but she quickly untangled herself and made her way to the floating disc of light hovering in the small cave's midst. Portals could be unreliable if not properly cared for, but Gailea had never minded the risk. Popping up in some other corner of the world by accident would have often seemed a blessing.

Now, as she stepped inside and was enveloped by the light, only to reappear in the castle courtyard moments later, she felt grateful to be back. Her days for childish fancies of escape were long past. There was too much to do here, too many to protect.

She made her way through the trees and entered the castle through a familiar servant's door near the kitchens. She crept through the castle until at last, she was inside her room, collapsing back on her bed.

She didn't let herself rest long before she sat up and drew her much-treasured wooden box—as always, tucked beneath her pillow—into her lap. Opening it, she ran her hands along the three scrolls, each lesson so lovingly crafted for her benefit and safety. Were these the cause of Lady Aline's imprisonment? Was Gailea herself the cause? No, that could not be; she would have been questioned already, at the least.

Gailea replaced the box and prayed that Crispin would be able to help. In the meantime, she would honor her teacher by using everything she had taught her to help unravel the mysteries around Marlis' illness. She reached up to touch the gem at her neck—

"Oh—oh *no!*"

Her stomach shriveled as if it had been punched. The pendant was, of course, gone: gone with Elda. Elda still wore the protective sealing stone Lady Aline had granted her. In her grief, Gailea had entirely forgotten to reclaim it.

Gailea reopened the box and took out the scroll containing the song-shield spell. With or without Lady Aline, it was time to get to work again. Without the pendant's aid, she must master singing the song-shield inside her mind before Moragon's interests turned to her too fully.

After tonight, she had far too many thoughts that needed protecting.

CHAPTER 14

DISCOVERIES

Crispin hurried toward the kitchens.

At long last, Alistor had released him from his lengthy lesson, during which he had dryly asked if Crispin's haphazard obedience two days' prior had put him at an advantage with the king. Crispin, unable to rejoice—or to admit the whole experience had been an accident—just acknowledged that Moragon seemed pleased. Indeed, when his elder uncle had requested an audience with Crispin, the king had remarked smugly that Crispin's second "hunt" had been far more successful than his first.

Alistor just nodded, apparently believing that Crispin was willing to create submission through fear. Crispin could not decide which was worse: being thought a craven, traitorous coward or someone capable of nearly burning a man to death.

Their disagreement had made it difficult for him to concentrate, but he had managed to perform a steady streamer of fire on a single stone target for a good minute or two. He might have been able to do more if he hadn't grown increasingly distracted as time pressed on. Of all days, this would be the one his uncle chose to push him far into the afternoon on a single lesson.

At last, Crispin paused before the little wooden door and knocked in a rhythmic pattern he and Gailea had worked out together. Soon enough, the door opened, and she hurried him inside.

"I was beginning to worry something happened," she said.

"I apologize. Lessons ran late."

Gailea cleared some candles from the wooden chair before sitting on the dingy straw pallet. She gestured for him to take the chair, but Crispin only shook his head, easing onto the edge of the pallet beside her. They shared a smile.

"How do you know about this place anyway?" he asked. "It's a good little hideout. Hardly anyone seems to come down this hall."

"This used to be my room," Gailea said.

Crispin was taken aback. How could anyone bear to dwell in such a cramped space? He felt trapped often enough between four walls, despite his being much loftier.

"Before I forget," he said, "I did ask Alistor about Lady Aline."

"Thank you. But I hope I didn't get you into any trouble."

"I was more worried at *you* getting in trouble. So, I told him that I'd heard a rumor of her imprisonment and that you had once mentioned her being your mentor. But he didn't seem to know much. Just that she was wanted for treason."

Gailea scoffed. "Treason? The king seems to add more and more whims to his list of so-called 'treasons' lately—" She stopped short. "Forgive me. I can speak my mind too quickly. I know he is also your uncle—"

Crispin took her hands to silence her. "I understand well that the king is not the favorite of many—and why. I'm only sorry that I couldn't find out more."

"I understand. But thank you for trying. If you *do* learn more, please tell me, whether you think I would desire to hear it or not."

"I wish I could help more," Crispin said, feeling a physical pain at the sadness in her eyes, "especially after all you've done for me. I owe you my life. Thank you for helping my sister, despite everything."

"What do you mean? I gave my word to help, and Elda is like my own sister."

"I only meant…surely you must have heard about what happened the night before, with Master Weston. I wasn't so sure you would even want to *look* at me after that."

"I wouldn't like to judge you so harshly before asking you what happened yourself. Besides, you have proven to me by your own actions that you are a kind and compassionate man who values doing the right thing whenever he can, and so I will continue to trust in the you that you've shown me." She squeezed his hands. This simple yet pointedly sweet gesture flooded his heart with a tender comfort, creating a balm that soothed some of his nagging guilt and shame of the past couple days.

"Then you're fairer than most," Crispin said, feeling both awed and relieved. "I swear to you, it was an accident. I never *meant* to hurt anyone…"

Gailea studied him closely. As her lips parted, he prepared himself for some scolding or judgment after all, but none came. Instead, she sang a quiet melody, and a warmth erased the chill gripping his body, a warmth that flowed straight down to his heart, lifting away the remainder of its choking troubles. He watched her in growing fascination.

Even after her song had ceased, he watched her. She looked so tranquil and intent on filling him with the same serenity, and this made her prettiness blossom into a superior beauty that he'd never noticed before, or perhaps hadn't existed before that moment.

"Feel better now?" she asked.

Crispin grinned. "I could likely accuse you of bewitching me, but I wouldn't even be capable. I can understand why Moragon envies your music. But why did you do that for me just now? I don't feel it was deserved."

"If everything was an accident, as you say, then while what you did was wrong, your intent was not. All you can do is keep learning to control your powers so it doesn't happen again. I suppose I just felt a desire to comfort you, that's all. To ease your mind. I don't suppose you have many friends around court to confide in now that Elda is gone. Except for Tytonn—he seems a steadfast friend."

"He is. But it's rather presumptuous of you to assume I don't have many friends."

Gailea smiled sweetly. "I meant no offense. But people do talk. It seems one thing we have in common is a preference for keeping more to ourselves."

He nodded. "You're not wrong about that."

"If it makes you feel better," Gailea added, "I have heard that Master Weston will be all right. He suffered a bad burn on one side of his face, and his hearing may be impaired. But he *is* mending."

If possible, her words warmed him even more than her song's serene loveliness. He sighed in relief. "Blessed Amiel, I am glad. Thank you."

He hesitated with his next words, but her steady gaze prompted him to continue.

"There is one thing more. You've done so much already, and yet I wondered if I might ask you to help with something else."

"Of course."

"It would be even more dangerous than what we accomplished last night."

A corner of her lip quirked into a playful smile. "I can't consider giving you an answer if you never ask the question."

"Well," he said, "I was only thinking that if we wanted to learn more about the king's and Chevalier's plans, that we might try searching Chevalier's chambers. Who better to search, being so close to the king?"

Gailea's face lit up with interest. "You may be right. The queen—ever since the baby, she does little more than sleep and eat a little, only to vomit what she ate. The healers have tested her for any signs of internal bleeding or cancers. If it was something catching, like a plague, the whole castle would be ill by now."

"You think her illness is being directed at her," Crispin said bluntly. "That Moragon still wants her dead, and that he and Chevalier may be involved."

Gailea nodded. "Her strength wanes daily. She has no fevers or sores or other symptoms. It's as if she's just... fading away, being consumed from within. She could just be heartbroken over the babe's loss. But I suspect it's something more."

"Then all the more reason to do some spying of our own."

"But how would we get inside Chevalier's chambers?" Gailea asked. "Surely his chambers are locked and well-guarded."

She hesitated, staring down at her hands, still wrapped around his, before returning the full radiant intelligence of her blue-green gaze to his. "It is said that he's a sorcerer. Is that true?"

Crispin could not speak falsely to her. Her open nature and the intoxicating beauty of her eyes made him feel it would be a sin to hide such a secret. "Yes," he murmured. "But not dangerous. At least—my uncle keeps him at a disadvantage. His powers are not at their fullest; Moragon makes certain of it with some kind of magic device. Please," he blurted, suddenly concerned that he might have given her knowledge that could be harmful. "Do not tell anyone. I know there are rumors, but if the king finds out you know the truth—"

"Of course, I would not tell! And I...I appreciate your trusting me, Lord Crispin."

"Crispin," he corrected gently. Then, daring to speak before he lost the nerve: "If I may have the honor of returning the intimacy...Gailea?"

She smiled, her petal-soft cheeks pinking with a flush. "Gailea," she said with a nod.

He knew he could be lost in her smile for hours but gathered himself back to their plans. "Well," he said after clearing his throat. "As to Chevalier's door... again, I don't think it's impossible to get past any physical or magical barriers. My uncle took me to his chambers once before, to fetch some supplies. There's this trick Alistor uses to unlock doors."

"Do you think you could replicate it?"

"I think...maybe...yes. If I had a day or two to practice and the means. I need something I can melt and reshape that won't go missing."

"What about your friend, Tytonn Grayfell? Isn't he Master of Horses now? I'm sure he could get you some metal scraps to work with."

"Tytonn—of course! An excellent idea. Only...I'm afraid getting in won't be as easy as all that. Chevalier is guarded constantly—as are his entire chambers, especially where he conducts his research. There are more guards, and possibly protective spells..."

"If that's the case, then I also suggest we stop by Lady Aline's chambers. She has many books, potions, powders. We could look for simple charms that might be useful for sneaking past guards and other traps. Is there a time you know Chevalier to be away from his chambers?"

"Sunday afternoons. After the midday meal, he always spends time with the king in his study."

"Let's meet then. We can meet here again." She rose to her feet. "I should get back to the queen now before I'm found missing."

She opened the door but then paused in the doorway to look back, her gaze steady and reassuring.

An overwhelming desire to take her hand, draw her close, and ask her to sing again took hold of Crispin, but she had already disappeared down the hall.

***

"Keep a lookout for me while I figure out the key," Crispin said. "I've only done this a few times, and it can be a bit tricky..."

Gailea nodded and turned her attention to the corridor while Crispin knelt before Lady Aline's chamber door. He cursed beneath his breath, and Gailea glanced down, curious as he fiddled with a piece of metal.

"It's too big for the keyhole," he sighed. "If I melt it now, most of it will just drip all over the floor."

"Here." Gailea reached into her pocket and presented a curved piece of bark. "Use this as a sort of funnel. Direct the metal into the keyhole as it's melting."

Crispin's brows raised in amusement as he took the piece of bark. "You are ever a wonder..."

"I'm sent to the woods often enough, to look for herbs and anything that might ease Marlis's suffering."

"Well, I'm grateful that you're easing *my* suffering right now. Ahh, this is so much easier…"

Gailea glanced up and down the hall again. No one was in sight. She glanced back, intrigued by Crispin's process. He'd laid the small piece of metal on the sliver of bark. Chanting some spell beneath his breath, he tilted the bark toward the keyhole. The metal slowly melted, dripping down toward the keyhole. Crispin breathed another spell, and the metal hardened once more. He tried turning the misshapen key, and after wiggling it around a bit, it turned, the lock clicked, and the door creaked open.

"Well done," Gailea said.

"Thank you." Crispin pulled the makeshift key from the door. Its teeth were slightly jagged, and the rest of it was a haphazard blob.

"It looks ridiculous," Gailea laughed. "But it did the job. I admit I'm impressed."

"It's not exactly how Alistor does it. But it'll do. Come on. Let's shut ourselves in before someone sees us."

As soon as they entered and shut the door behind them, Gailea gasped. The sanctity of her mentor's study was shattered. Furniture lay overturned and splintered. Papers, scrolls, and torn book pages blanketed the floor and clung to the walls at odd angles. A rich smell of scattered herbs stung her nose.

"I'm so sorry," Crispin said. "I doubt this is how you wanted to remember it. But it looks like she at least didn't give in without a fight."

"Or that someone was looking for something," Gailea said, finding her voice. "I'm surprised all her things are still here. Wouldn't the king have had everything confiscated if he feared she was a traitor?"

Crispin shrugged. "Maybe not. Especially if he found what he was looking for. I doubt a bunch of herbs and books would pose much threat or interest. Maybe it wasn't even on the king's orders. Did anyone else have any quarrel with Lady Aline?"

"No..." Gailea shook her head. "But then again, if they did, she likely wouldn't tell me, for my safety. Well, come on then. Let's find whatever we can that looks useful. I'll search her desk, see if there are any powders or potions. Start searching the books for spells."

"All right then."

Gailea waded through papers and climbed over the flipped settee to reach the desk. The massive desk was the one thing that hadn't been turned over, though its mahogany wood was stained many bright colors from spilled potions and powders. Gailea sifted through them, careful not to cut her fingers on the shards of glass from broken vials and bottles.

Many of the potions, powders, and jars of herbs were labeled, while many others were not. A few vials were still entirely intact, and Gailea collected them, stashing them inside the velvet bag hanging from her gilded belt.

"I found a book I think may be useful," Crispin said. He'd perched atop the armrest of a toppled chair, surrounded by stacks of books and papers. "It's missing half its pages. But it's a book for very basic charms—things we could figure out easily enough, with the right materials. There's one here for a simple sleeping charm."

"That could help with any guards," Gailea said. "What are the ingredients?"

"Let's see...lazy lily petals, crushed lazuli stone, and lacy butterfly wings? Elemental magic is such a strange breed."

Gailea riffled through her new pocket collection and found everything but the butterfly wings. It would be impossible to catch butterflies outside in this weather—a fact she was admittedly grateful for, as it would give her no great joy to sacrifice such a delicate living creature. Perhaps the charm could make do without. In a pinch, they would have no choice but to try.

Of course, she could easily lull any guards to sleep with her lullaby—she'd had much practice lately with Marlis—but she didn't feel comfortable exerting so much musical magic. It was one thing to ease the queen's troubled mind. It was another altogether to make possibly dozens of guards fall asleep at once. She didn't know how close Moragon needed to be to detect her use of song, nor did she know what kind of musical magic would most pique his interest. With no mentor now to ask such questions and guide her, she must be extra careful to use her music only as a last resort.

As they continued their search, Gailea collected a few empty vials in case they needed to mix ingredients, and Crispin found another small book on simple elemental alchemy.

Gailea waded through the whirlwind of books and papers till she found a tiny book on slightly more advanced song spells. She glanced at Crispin, who remained enthralled in whatever new spell he read about before stuffing the book in her nearly overflowing purse. Hopefully, she might find something helpful in the way of further guarding her mind from Moragon, especially in her pendant's absence.

Gailea parted the half-hanging curtains and glanced outside. "It's hard to see the sun today with all these clouds...but I believe it's close to noon. We should get back. If either of us is missing for our meal, they might suspect something."

"You're right," Crispin said. "Let's meet here afterward, and we'll head to Chevalier's chambers from there."

***

Crispin walked with Gailea close at his side. It was no secret by now that they had become acquaintances since the king's celebration, and so there was no need to keep a simple stroll through the castle concealed. They talked and laughed quietly, about the coming winter and the weather changes, to appear engaged in regular conversation.

As they curved up a long, winding stair, Crispin paused nearly at the top, pressing himself up against the wall, and Gailea followed suit. Crispin turned to her and whispered, "All right, the next two corridors lead directly to Chevalier's chambers. Any guards in those halls—any people at all—are likely working for him or the king. It's imperative for us to avoid being seen. Do you have the sleeping spell ready?"

"I do," Gailea said.

Crispin moved to Gailea's other side, and Gailea crept forward. Removing a vial from her bag, she uncapped it, tilted it toward the hallway, and muttered an incantation. A pale blue mist floated from the glass and around the corner.

Within moments, moans and thuds sounded one by one, like a giant game of dominoes knocking over. When the last distant thud met their ears, Crispin and Gailea nodded at each other and rounded the corner.

Gailea gasped, and Crispin stared. The guards fell against the walls but remained awake, staggering around drunkenly. Some reeled dizzily and collapsed with a groan. Others reached out their hands, swaying as they tried to catch their balance. One of them lifted his gaze toward Gailea, and Crispin grabbed her arm, prepared to wrench her out of the hallway and run, when Gailea suddenly started to sing, and the guard fell at their feet, snoring loudly.

Crispin's own eyes grew heavy, but Gailea command-ed, "Cover your ears!"

Crispin obeyed and watched as Gailea progressed slowly through the hall, singing. He trailed after her, stepping carefully over the fallen guards and servants. He glanced with remorse toward a girl who'd dropped against a bucket of wash water; she was soaked and would likely wake freezing. He took a moment to roll her out of the water and warm her with his flames as much as he could, hoping to dry her clothes a bit, until Gailea called, "Crispin—come on!"

Crispin darted up and hurried after Gailea. Round-ing a corner, he saw that the song-spell had lulled an-other corridor of guards and servants to sleep—includ-ing several massive guard dogs with impressively large fangs. Crispin shuddered, not wanting to imagine what it might've been like to fight against them.

They navigated through another maze of halls, paus-ing carefully to check around corners. Gailea lulled a few more guards and servants, till at last, they came to an-other stair that wound down and down for what seemed an eternity.

"That was brilliant," Crispin said, "thinking to use that song. Why didn't you just do that in the first place?"

"I—I've only ever used it to soothe Marlis. I didn't think it would work so well on so many. And…and I was worried about his majesty sensing my magic. I didn't want to draw attention to us. But when the guards were about to spot us, I had to react, and it was the only thing I knew to do."

"I don't think the king comes here often; Chevalier usually goes to him. And I can assure you that where they're meeting now is nearer the great hall, so it's not close. I wouldn't worry."

"All the same, we can't be sure. And we might want to make this quick anyway. Chevalier may not have any regular visitors, but if someone finds everyone else asleep, we don't want them to find *us*."

"How long will they sleep for?"

"I don't really know."

Finally, they stood at the bottom of the stair. A tapestry bearing the king's crest—a phoenix spreading its wings wide over a golden harp—covered the stone wall before them.

"Now what?" Gailea asked.

Crispin frowned, moving the tapestry aside and pinning one corner to the wall with a spare bit of metal. "I swear there was a door here before."

"Perhaps it's an illusion," Gailea said. She reached out and touched the wall. "I can feel it—the door. It's here."

Crispin began feeling the wall too. "If we can just find the keyhole...here! I think this is it." He kept his hand on the hole while diving into his pocket for the dilapidated makeshift key from earlier, along with the piece of bark. He tilted the bark toward the invisible hole, placed the key on top, and chanted the spell-word for fire till the metal melted and slid inside. He cooled it, turned the key...

"Nothing."

"Are you sure? I've got what feels like the handle here. But it won't push or pull. Are you certain the key fits?"

"Seems to."

They both began feeling around again.

"It feels like there's another keyhole here in the middle," Gailea said.

"And another on my side as well."

The longer they felt the wall, the more Crispin began to panic. "There's quite a few."

"We need a way to mark the wall, to show which ones we've tried—a way that we can remove later."

"What about your color-changing trick?"

"I can try...I need something a different color than the wall..." She reached into her purse and pulled out a red weed. "This could do. Guide my hand to the keyhole."

Crispin took her hand. Briefly, they glanced at each other, and Crispin wondered if her heart leapt with the same dance that his performed at the subtle touch. She watched him steadily, but her face remained devoid of any emotion except a slight worry and focus on their task at hand.

When Gailea found the keyhole, she touched the red weed to the stone and sang a few quiet notes. A small patch of wall reddened to match the weed.

"Good," Crispin said, reluctantly releasing her hand. "Now we know where we've been."

They repeated their process until they had tried a good dozen keyholes.

"Where can it possibly be?" Gailea demanded. Panic started to fill her face.

"It's all right; keep feeling. We must have missed something."

"The top of the door—it's tall, and Chevalier is tall. Lift me up. I'll search for it there."

Crispin stared at her briefly before shaking his nerves aside. This was a matter of life or death. No time for his knees to buckle like a newborn colt.

He lifted her to sit partially on his right shoulder, flushing when his cheek rested against the curved hip, covered by many layers of her dress. Trying not to think of what truly lay beneath those skirts, he waited while she felt along the top of the door till she cried, "I've got it! If you hand me the bark and metal. Can you do it? Or will you be too far away?"

"I think the charm will still work if I concentrate…"

Crispin handed the tools to Gailea. She fit the edge of the bark inside the keyhole and set the twisted key on top.

"All right then. Ready."

Crispin focused. He couldn't physically see the key from this angle, but he did his best to picture it in his mind while chanting the word for fire. He felt his hands warm, then his entire body.

"Ouch!" Gailea cried. "What are you doing? We're not trying to stuff *me* inside the keyhole."

"Sorry. It's a bit harder to do it this way—without seeing the key, I mean…"

It also didn't help that he held onto her lovely, sweet-smelling body, but he dared not admit this; he was trying to win her good graces, not a slap.

He tried again and asked, "Is it working now?"

"Yes," Gailea said. "It's melting more slowly than before. But it's filling the keyhole. Just a little more, keep going—wait. What was that?"

"What do you mean—?"

A low growling noise made Crispin freeze in place.

"Don't stop!" Gailea snapped. "We need to get inside!"

Crispin focused his spell on the key once more, trying to ignore the padding of approaching footsteps. A series of growls echoed down the stair, coming closer and closer, followed by a bark.

A huge dog burst down the stairs, lunging at them with fangs bared.

Gailea screamed, Crispin lost his balance, and they toppled to the floor. He reached out his arms, ready to wrestle the beast with fire.

But abruptly, all lay quiet. Crispin scrambled into a

sitting position. The dog lay as still as the dead between him and Gailea, who had propped herself against the opposite wall and now stared wide-eyed at the beast, panting.

"How—"

"I sang. I sang, just in time."

Crispin grinned. "Well done. I wasn't looking forward to having to burn that thing to death. But...but why aren't *I* asleep?"

"I don't know," Gailea gasped. "I don't know. I was definitely concentrating on the dog. I've been practicing. Maybe I'm just getting better at controlling my songs, directing them at a specific point."

"Regardless, either way, it was perfect." He rose to his feet and offered his hand. With a shaky laugh, he added, "Honestly—where is Tytonn when you need him?"

Gailea took his hand and jumped up. "What do you mean?"

"He has this gift for calming animals. He's not a musical mage like you, though he does like to compose— oh, no!" His glance fell upon the piece of bark—or what remained of it. It had burst into flames and now smoldered in one corner, turned nearly to ash.

"It's all right," Gailea said. "Look."

She pointed above them. Sticking out from the wall was the bit of metal.

"It must have cooled when my concentration broke," Crispin said. "I'll lift you up again, and you give it a good turn. Hopefully, this is the one."

Gailea nodded, and Crispin hoisted her on his shoulder once more. Gailea turned the key, and a latch clicked. Crispin found the handle and pushed the door.

It swung inward, so quickly that he stumbled forward, nearly dropping Gailea. He set her down, they crept inside, and he the door shut behind them.

They had entered a massive room that served as both bedchamber and study. Along the walls, tapestries with shimmering threads wove to create the image of a stallion rearing amidst a bramble of thorns.

"Chevalier's family crest," Crispin whispered. "We did it. We're here."

Spheres of glowing light hovered all around the perimeter of the ceiling and floor, illuminating the room with a bright white glow akin to sunlight. Windows made of colorful glass lined one wall. Bookshelves lined two other walls, with hundreds of books stacked within. A large desk was situated in the middle of the room, covered with papers, instruments made of various metals, and vials filled with liquids and powders of every color imaginable.

"This is a little daunting," Gailea said. "We're not even sure what we're looking for. But we might as well make the most of it." She wandered further into the room, her gaze dancing sharply across the scattered papers and other items. "All we need is to find something about the queen. Any sign of proof or hope for a cure."

She began rifling through papers, scanning their contents before carefully replacing them. Her gaze scanned along the bookshelves, seeming to read each title. Crispin admired her and then began looking as well. He glanced back often at the wall they had passed through, listening for signs of anyone approaching.

After a while, Gailea picked up a small wooden box with a curious frown. "Crispin, come take a look. I've seen a similar type of box before—meant for hiding items inside, to make them appear invisible. Only this one has a small lock on it. Can you find something else to make a key with?"

"The lock itself looks metal. I'll just try to melt it off."

He touched his thumb to the small lock, and within moments, the heat coursing through him melted the lock away.

Gailea looked at him in a sudden panic. "Can you put it back that way later?"

"I'm...not sure I know how to do that," Crispin admitted, feeling a fool for his impulsiveness.

Gailea shoved the hardened metal blob into her pocket. "Then we'll make it least immediately noticeable as possible. Let's see what's in the box anyway."

She tried to open it, but it remained shut tight. She gripped its sides, struggling to pry it open.

"It won't budge."

"Maybe it's stuck. Let me have a try."

Crispin took the box and tried to open it, prepared to use all his strength.

His fingers had barely touched it when the lid flew open, and as a voice echoed from within, Crispin staggered back, nearly dropping the box. He set it on the desk, and he and Gailea leaned forward, listening intently:

"...how exhilarated I am that we have, at last, unlocked the next mystery behind using the Obscura Shadow magic..."

"Moragon," Crispin mouthed at Gailea who nodded.

"...It has served us well, to keep my nephew's powers in check. A more than fruitful experiment. Once we master it, we might use it to cripple any of my enemies. Meanwhile, I've a new commission, regarding the queen..."

The message continued with Moragon plotting to use this magic—something utterly unfamiliar to Crispin—to murder Marlis upon the birth of their heir. Then, the message began to repeat itself, more faintly this time. Crispin shut the box, silencing its accusing declarations.

"What did he say?" Gailea whispered. "He was speaking ancient Lozolian, wasn't he? I caught a word here and there, but I'm not versed in the old language."

"It would seem the queen was not the only one Moragon has been poisoning," Crispin muttered, his outrage stoking his heated blood until it might have been molten lava through his veins. "All this time—I could have had my powers all this time! I could be as strong as Alistor if only the king hadn't been preventing me!"

"He was *poisoning you*? To curb your power? But why? Did he say?"

"It seems he might have just been experimenting, to see how this so-called Obscura magic works, in hopes to use it against his enemies. Had I died while they experimented on me, I doubt he would've missed me. Just another competing successor, dead. Not that I'd consider myself a true threat. I've no desire for the throne."

"That may be," Gailea said, "but if the time should come, Adelar could do much worse than having *you* as their king. I'd rather see someone like you, who doesn't lust after power, someone who could bring actual justice and fairness to the people."

Crispin snorted. "The people hate me, if Weston's followers are any indication."

"Only because they don't *know* you. In time, if you have opportunity to show them something different than what rumors have fed them, that could change."

"I'm still not sure I deserve your praise, but I appreciate it…" He took a few deep breaths, releasing his anger until his head cleared. With a sigh, he turned to Gailea and took her hand. "Truly, without you, we wouldn't be here now, discovering these important things. I want you to know that I am no longer your lord. I am your friend—we are equals."

As he continued to watch her, passion blazed through his entire body. Gailea flinched, and he wondered if she could feel the heat coursing through him. Her wild eyes lit up. Her breath seemed to quicken, and he wanted nothing more than to pull her to him and kiss her.

Gailea gasped and said, "I hear something!"

"What is it?" Crispin whispered.

"I'm not certain." Her head tilted toward the door, then she shook her head. "I think we should go."

He agreed and they exited through the secret door in the wall. Before scaling the stairs, they locked the door and removed the makeshift key. Gailea returned the stone wall to its normal color, vanishing any signs that they had ever stepped inside, and Crispin replaced the tapestry.

Upstairs, the guards, servants, and dogs slept on. Crispin led Gailea past, careful to make certain no one approached before leading her back into the main part of the castle.

CHAPTER 15

FIT FOR A QUEEN

Gailea sped toward the kitchen. If she knew a charm that could make her fly, she would have shot into the air on the spot. She hardly knew whether to feel more terrified by all she had just learned with Crispin or more elated by how closely they had stood to one another. The tension had felt almost as tangible as his warm hands cradling hers.

But this was not the time to let desire cloud her mind. Upon returning to the queen's chambers, she had been sent to create a tonic to help with a fresh bout of nausea and headaches. Her first task was to procure the proper herbs.

Gailea halted at the crest of the stairs winding down into the kitchen. She and Crispin had been fortunate not to draw any wandering eyes, and she must not do so now. Her slightest display of nerves could give the more gossipy ladies reason enough to fabricate any manner of wild rumor. She took several deep breaths, calming herself.

Then, with a lift of her chin, she rushed down the stairs and breezed into the kitchen.

"Good afternoon, ladies. Is my sister about?"

Muttered greetings rose from the girls who bustled around the kitchen, kneading dough, cutting meats and vegetables, and preparing for the evening's supper. A new face, a tall willowy brunette, had assumed Gailea's old post of scrubbing the floors. Nessa stirred something in the huge cauldron—a savory stew, by the smell of it—and glanced over her shoulder, offering a forced smile and polite nod.

"Gailea," Darice said, grinning warmly as she popped up from the other side of the long, massive table. "I thought that was your voice. But what brings you here? I'm sure his majesty would frown upon one of his queen's new ladies skulking about the kitchens. You don't belong here anymore, love."

"I haven't seen you in so long," Gailea said, "and besides, I've been tasked with creating a tonic for the queen, to soothe her head and stomach. I told Lady Bronia that much of my herbal knowledge comes from you, so she said I could come to speak with you, to find something suitable."

Darice nodded toward the large pantry across the room. "Come on then. I'll help you find what you need."

The two ladies breezed over to the pantry where Gailea began grabbing at the assorted vials and glasses filled with powders, oils, and spices. She opened them, smiling at the fragrance of some, recoiling at the stench of others.

"We've already tried mint and chamomile with little results," Gailea said. "If you have other suggestions…"

"Basil can also work wonders for an ill stomach," Darice said. "You might try it."

"Thank you," Gailea said. "Where might I find it?"

"Second shelf, behind the garlic and cloves."

As Gailea moved the herbs aside, her gaze locked on a vial toward the back. She reached in and drew it out, and the sunlight caught on the name scrawled in a silvery ink: *Dusk*. Inside, a powdery substance shimmered, thin and almost fluid, like a dark red mist.

"What's this?" she asked, holding it out.

"Oh, that?" Darice shrugged. "It's some rare spice we use for the queen—His Grace cannot abide it, but she *loves* it."

"Not shocking, is it?" said a girl snapping peas. "He wouldn't so much as abide his favorite mistress if the queen suddenly took interest in her..."

"Watch your tongue!" Another older woman cast a furious look at the other assistant. "The queen is a gentle lady; she has the most saintly heart for dealing with the king's temperament."

"Don't bark at me! Didn't say otherwise, did I? Facts is facts."

As the banter continued, Gailea glanced at Darice, who was lost in her own search. She eyed the mysterious spice again, contemplating this foreign substance. At last, she made her decision: very slowly, she brought her hand down to her velvet purse. One smooth motion and she'd drawn out one of the empty vials she'd procured from Lady Aline's chamber. She pulled the wax plug of the Dusk and transferred some inside. Despite its powder form, the red material seemed to ooze into the glass container as slow as treacle. *Careful*, she warned herself; *don't take too much!*

Once satisfied, she popped on the corks of both vials and put her own into her purse, returning the originally labeled vial to the shelf. She rearranged the other vials back into place before continuing her search for the basil.

"Ah, found it!"

"Good," Darice said, holding out three other small glass bottles. "Try these as well—ginseng, wormwood, and sage."

"Thank you, sister."

"Of course." Darice grinned but added seriously, "Be safe then. I love you."

"I love you too!"

Gailea flounced from the pantry, smiling and bidding the ladies a good afternoon.

***

That night at dinner, Crispin noticed Gailea looking searchingly over toward the high table, then catching his gaze. He could see she had something significant to pass along to him and nodded, hoping that she caught his own meaningful glance.

The moment dinner ended, Gailea exited the Great Hall through one of the side arches. Crispin waited nearly a quarter of an hour before taking his own leave, using the south door and making haste around toward where he knew Gailea would be waiting.

Crispin followed Gailea at a distance till they had reached a quiet corridor. At last, she sat on the window seat of a secluded alcove, and Crispin hurried over to join her.

"What is it?" he demanded in a whisper, glancing up and down the hall.

"I found something," Gailea whispered back, drawing a vial from her pocket. "Look..."

Taking the slim bottle from her, Crispin held it in his hands and turned it in the candlelight. Its fine, mist-like powder shimmered a deep red hue. With a frown, he asked, "Is it blood?"

"I don't know what its nature is. But it was labeled 'Dusk,' and Darice said they use it only in the queen's dishes. They called it a favorite of hers and said the king abhors it."

"That isn't proof, but it could well be true. Although I've never heard of it before, or seen its like." Crispin held the vial up and shook it back and forth; the red powder moved slowly, like a shifting cloud. "Dusk," he murmured. "A reference to nighttime. Perhaps a sleeping draught?"

"For sleep, possibly." Gailea bit her lip, then quickly exhaled: "Or a permanent sleep."

His widened eyes focused on Gailea, and she nodded. "I think this might confirm all our suspicions. King Moragon is using Chevalier's magic to destroy the queen—to murder her."

"Is it any wonder?" Crispin asked. With a snarl, he shoved the vial back at Gailea, who took it but stared at him, obviously thrown off guard. "He *is* a sorcerer. It's to be expected; who knows what power or titles Moragon has promised him in exchange for the queen's life?"

"What does his being a sorcerer have to do with anything?"

"They are corrupt! Creatures of living, breathing poison!" Crispin stared at the windows above, the waning sunlight turning everything a warm gold. "One of them led to my father's death," he whispered, his heart clearly aching for the man he had known so briefly. "For all I know, it could have been Chevalier himself."

Gailea was silent, respectful of his grief. "I didn't know about your father," she murmured. "I've lost parents as well. It's...I'm sorry, Crispin." She reached for his hand, and he took her fingers, clasping them in mutual comfort.

After a moment, she spoke again. "But...regardless

of whether Chevalier harmed your father...that doesn't mean *all* sorcerers are corrupt. Every single one? It cannot be so."

Crispin shifted uncomfortably but ignored the question. "We are dealing with just Chevalier right now. As for whatever he might be doing to the queen, no doubt at my uncle's command...why poison her at all? She is no threat. And even if Moragon simply wants to be free, why poison her so *slowly*? Even if Chevalier doesn't have his full powers, he could surely strike the queen dead with something as simple as a heart ailment. Moragon could do it himself!"

"I think," Gailea said, lowering her voice as two servants passed by, "that the king is using the queen as an experiment—just like he did with *you*, in dampening your magic. I think this Dusk is the Obscura magic they spoke of and that they're testing it out, to see how it works or how else they can use it."

"Yes..." Crispin said, the wheels in his head spinning. "And that takes us back to Chevalier. Moragon likely wouldn't know about this Dusk at all if not for his pet sorcerer. Dark magic—it disgusts me." He shook his head. "And Chevalier is so seemingly harmless and pious. Pretends to be kind to the queen, when really he's been plotting to kill her for likely months now..."

"Perhaps he is kind to her because he feels some guilt," Gailea said. "We don't know exactly how much control Moragon has over him. Perhaps he only kills her to save his own life. That doesn't lessen his crime—if anything, it makes him a coward. But you didn't really answer my question: why assume that all sorcerers are evil—?"

"Gailea," Crispin blurted. "Your compassion...I admire you for it. But sometimes it might cloud your judgment. They're heretics. Schemers. Killers. It's the law of the realm, and most other civilized realms, that they are to be contained and confined, and ultimately eliminated. They would rule the world and enslave all of us if they were allowed the freedom to do so."

"Then if he believes sorcerers so dangerous, a better question is why the king keeps Chevalier alive? And the answer is likely because he's using him for his powers, for this Dusk experiment. For all we know, Chevalier's days are numbered in correlation with the queen's— hush! Someone approaches."

A group of young lords rounded the corner, talking in hushed, excited tones. One of them smirked at Gailea and Crispin in passing.

The next moment, a flood of servants and courtiers young and old entered the hall, intermingled with a few guards headed in the same direction. Many wore solemn expressions, a few excited, some fearful.

"What's going on?" Gailea asked.

"I have no idea. Let's try to blend in. Maybe we can figure it out."

Crispin and Gailea slipped into the crowds' steady flow. As they rounded a corner, a familiar voice perked Crispin's attention. He strained to catch a glimpse between the sea of people and soon found Alistor demanding of the nearest guard, "What the devil is happening? Has the entire court gone mad?"

"His majesty has ordered everyone to the execution gallows at once."

Alistor scoffed. "His majesty punishes traitors, thieves, and other common scum every day. What's so special about this evening?"

"My apologies, Lord Ragnar," the guard said. "I only know those are his orders."

"Leave it to my brother's narcissism to reach new heights by forcing everyone to watch him deal out death and judgment..."

Crispin took Gailea's hand and hurried past, ducking beside a group of court ladies to shield them. He didn't want his uncle stopping or questioning them.

As they stepped out into the chilled air and reached the execution gallows, waves of people continued to flood the courtyard. It seemed Moragon had managed to clear the entire castle for this occasion. Crispin and Gailea squeezed in, constantly shifting to allow more people to join. Atop the gallows themselves, the executioner waited with a large ax, while several guards surrounded the wooden platform.

At last, the murmuring crowds hushed as Moragon scaled the gallows. The sun began to set, and the skies' vibrant hues ringed the king's head with a blood-red crown. Gailea seemed to pale, and Crispin squeezed her hand, hating to see her so terrified and wanting her to know he was here to protect her, no matter what. He would burst the entire courtyard into flames to keep her safe if it came to it.

"My good people," Moragon announced, throwing his arms wide in a welcoming gesture, his practiced grin gleaming like the bared teeth of a tiger. "Thank you for joining me for this gruesome yet exciting and very necessary occasion. As some of you are already aware, there has been an increasing number of traitors in Adelar as of late—and within our very castle walls. Rebels who would seek to dethrone your beloved king, to bring me and the royal family harm. I have brought you here today so you may witness the deaths of these traitors and to discourage you from any fraternization with such. If anyone knows of someone who speaks out against me, I declare that they make it known. Otherwise, if such connections are discovered, they will be punished in the same manner as the traitors themselves. Now, bring out the prisoners, and let us begin."

As Moragon took a seat in a wooden throne near the edge of the platform, shouts, jeers, and cheers roared from the crowds as several guards began dragging prisoners through the courtyard and up the steps to the gallows. Most of the prisoners were bedraggled, thin and bruised; many looked as though they would welcome death, but a few struggled against their captors, screaming their innocence even as the crowds yelled, "Traitors!" and "Cowards!" and whatever other accusations and lies they hoped the king wished to hear.

Crispin felt disgusted by the spectacle and prepared to pull Gailea from the crowds—there were so many people that they could likely slip away unnoticed—when her hand locked around his, tighter than an iron gauntlet. He grunted at the pain, then staggered as something fell against him—Gailea. Quickly Crispin spun and caught her in his arms, steadying her. She hadn't fainted, but she looked even paler than before, and she watched the gallows with eyes so wide and haunted that he feared she had been struck by some spell of the king's. As his gaze followed hers, he realized that, in the most terrible way, he was right.

An older lady with black, graying hair, clearly Adelaran, stood amongst the rest of the prisoners, hands bound with thick ropes. Her skin stretched thinly over her bones as if she had already met death. Crispin knew without asking that she was Gailea's beloved mentor, Lady Aline.

Beside her, a large man was hauled up the steps by two guards. He fought against them, shouting, "Please! I've a family, and I swear to you, I am innocent! Please, my wife and child! We have no other family to care for them. I beg of you, mercy!"

As Crispin saw the man's face, he felt as haunted as

Gailea. It was Garrison, the man who'd helped Elda escape, the man who was meant to be hundreds, if not thousands, of miles away by now, safe with his family. What did this mean?

One by one, the prisoners were dragged up onto the platform and made to kneel before the executioner as their crimes were declared. They weren't even granted a chance to repent; at some point, Moragon made a speech about how they were not worthy, that working against the king whom Amiel had seen fit to place on the throne was both a treason and blasphemy not worthy of repentance.

One by one, the prisoners fell at the executioner's ax. As the noise of the crowds swelled, Crispin tried to drag Gailea away, but she wouldn't move.

As Lady Aline knelt at the executioner's block, the crowds had worked themselves up into such a frenzy that Crispin could hardly hear the guard's declaration of treason.

"Don't look," Crispin said in Gailea's ear. "We can still leave!"

He tried to turn her away, but she cried out, "No! She never left my side, and I won't leave her now!"

"Please, don't look—!"

The ax fell, along with Lady Aline's severed head and body. Blood sprayed the crowds who cried out for more.

"Come on, Gailea!" Crispin cried as Garrison was dragged next across the platform. He had ceased fighting but still pleaded with the guards, weeping as he implored them for his family. He pleaded with the king, but the king did not so much as look at him. Instead, as Garrison knelt before the executioner's block, Moragon stared straight at Crispin with a victorious smirk. Crispin stared back, stunned, mortified.

The crowds shifted, shielding his view of the king

and forcing it back on Garrison as the ax's blade fell—

Gailea wrenched from Crispin's hold, darting through the crowds. Crispin called after her and struggled to follow, but within moments, he had lost all sight of her.

***

Gailea ran.

She ran till her lungs burned so much she thought they might burst. She sped through the castle until she reached her chambers and there she collapsed, fighting back a wave of nausea as she struggled to catch her breath. Her glance fell upon the box hiding the lessons Lady Aline had given her, and at last her tears spilled over the walls of pure shock and horror that had been holding them back.

She wept violently. As the nightmare of her beloved teacher murdered in the name of false justice replayed over and over, she wondered if her own mind conjured it or if it was some cold trick of his majesty. She wouldn't doubt if it was him, considering the vicious glee that had filled his face at the occasion.

At last, she calmed herself enough to begin planning what she must do next. She must leave. With or without anyone's aid, she must find a way to get far and away from the castle, from Adelar. The king had looked directly at her as he'd killed that poor, innocent man who had helped them smuggle Elda free. Maybe Moragon would never declare it, but he must know the truth, and he had blamed poor Garrison in their stead. It was only a matter of time before he sought a more personal vengeance on them—

A knock at the door startled Gailea so much that she screamed. The door opened, and she flung a wild glare at Tory who stood looking bewildered.

"F—forgive me, my lady, for bothering you. Only it's his majesty—he requests an audience with you at once."

Terror and anger flared inside Gailea. This was it. His majesty would reveal what he knew of her helping with Elda's escape and seek to punish her in his own way. At the least, she wouldn't let him control her without a fight.

She took a deep breath, wiped her face, and followed Tory into the hall. There, two guards waited to escort her.

The guards led Gailea through a set of ornate doors thrust open wide. Gailea stood before the king inside a spacious study. The doors shut behind them, and as the king snapped his fingers, Gailea heard them lock. She swallowed hard but lifted her chin, hoping her attempted confidence erased some of the fear she knew must resonate vividly in her mind and on her face.

"Lady Gailea," the king said. "Thank you for coming, despite your most recent grief. I know that must have been difficult for you to watch. A necessary evil. We must all make sacrifices now and then for the greater good. And you are, unless I am mistaken, very much part of my greater good. Come."

He held out his hand. Gailea walked forward, trying to keep her gaze steady, and took his hand, which closed firmly around hers. He led her to a wooden stand set beside his mammoth desk. On the stand, a book lay open—a book of song-spells. She swayed uneasily, just catching her footing.

"Before she passed," Moragon said, "one thing I learned of value from Lady Aline was the propensity of your musical talent. She praised you more than I've ever seen her praise another student…"

By choice or by force? Gailea wondered.

"Come—play something for me now. Perform a musical charm—in her honor, of course. I've even acquired the perfect instrument for you to borrow for the occasion."

As Gailea took the instrument into her hands, she wanted to both cry and run as far and fast as she could. It was a silver flute. The king could've chosen any instrument, but he chose a flute. His majesty knew. He knew everything. Or at least, he knew enough to damn her. Under any other circumstance, she would have thrilled to hold such a perfect instrument in her hands, but now she wanted to smash it on the stone walls.

"Go ahead," Moragon said, in as gentle a voice as Gailea supposed he could muster. "The spell is right there, in the book."

"Forgive me, your grace," Gailea said quietly, just managing to find her voice, "but I'm afraid I haven't much heart for playing right now."

"Just a little song, for your king. And for Lady Aline, of course."

Gailea glanced at the song-spell book. The song before her was more advanced, the notes fast and complex. With all her recent practice, she could perform the charm, likely get it right on the first try. But she didn't wish to reveal that much of herself to the king.

"I'm sorry, your grace, but this is beyond my skill."

She forced herself to meet his gaze, hoping he didn't detect her lie.

Moragon walked forward till he stood directly over her. He took the flute from her hands and set it aside. Then, quietly, he said,

"I know what you are. My brother thought he was a step ahead of me. And he was, for a glimmer of an instant. But though he has learned to guard his mind against me well, he could not stop me from sensing the desire, the sense of some secret surrounding you whenever he watched you, spoke of you. So, I had my spies follow his, and it was only a matter of time before they discovered, as he did, the truth about your lineage."

Gailea trembled, feeling so weak she worried that she might collapse. She couldn't show her true fear—nor could she allow the king to know more than he did, which was already far too much. She sang her song-shield quietly in her mind—

"Foolish girl!" Moragon boomed, making Gailea jump and instantly breaking her connection with the song. "You think you can shield your mind from me! I admit that the audacity that you should think yourself capable is somewhat commendable; it shows a certain level of confidence that my insipid nephew seems devoid of possessing. But…"

Moragon danced toward her, and as he spoke his next words, a sharp pain shot through her head, as if clawed hands began to pry her mind apart.

"…I see your every thought; I feel your every emotion. Your fear becomes my power and opens your mind like a floodgate. You want to run. You want to make certain no harm comes to your sister. Or to Crispin. You wonder if Elda is safe. You feel guilt over Lady Aline's death, and for Garrison's. You wonder if I intend to kill you—"

"Stop—please!" Gailea screamed. With each new thought or feeling he probed from her mind, her head throbbed more and more till she thought it must explode. Against her will, pain forced fresh tears from her.

"Forgive me," Moragon said, his tone as sincere as his cold gaze was not. "You're not yet accustomed to my magic—but you will be, as we spend more time getting to know one another. Allow me to ease your mind by assuring you of several things: Elda is safe. My spies have yet found no knowledge of her hiding place; for a crippled wench, she is somehow cleverer than her brother. Your sister and everyone you love will remain safe, as long as you obey me. And I certainly do not intend to kill you—rather, I intend to make you my strongest ally. Between my mind and your music, we can rule the world, Gailea, you and I."

Gailea remained silent, all the while thinking how she desired nothing less.

"I know you don't," Moragon crooned. "But you'll change your mind, in time."

Gailea stared at him, bewildered. Would he truly read her every thought now?

"You're right," he said. "I've invaded your privacy enough for one day—only for your own good, of course. I will dismiss you, give you time to grieve, and we can convene another day to discuss my plans for you. However, before then, I would grant you a gift. Come…"

Gailea hesitated but then stepped forward. She already felt exhausted from his mental probing and didn't wish to give him cause to force her to obey.

"Wise girl. You learn fast." As she reached him, he took her hand and slipped something onto her wrist—a bracelet, woven from intertwining bands of white and yellow gold and inlaid with tiny red, purple, and black gems. Admittedly, it was a stunning piece of jewelry, though Gailea would never give him satisfaction by admitting it.

Instead of releasing her hand, Moragon drew her close then and whispered in her ear, "There now. Fit for a queen. And just as a queen is meant to stay ever near her king's side, so shall you stay near mine. For, should you attempt to set foot outside the boundaries of the king's woods, the bracelet's magic will alert me immediately. And should you be captured—which you would—I will have invented another device that will assure you can make no such attempts ever again."

He released her and, with a curt nod, said, "Good night, Lady Gailea."

Gailea turned to leave, thinking that at least the bracelet could not read her thoughts.

"Do not tempt me," Moragon said. "If you disobey me, that may come next."

Without a word, Gailea turned and fled the king's chambers.

***

Crispin hurried after his uncle up the tower steps. After the execution, he had cornered Alistor, demanding to talk with him. Alistor had harshly declared how foolish he was to make a scene in public before agreeing to meet him atop the abandoned tower where they practiced his Fyre magic.

The moment they breached the top, Crispin wheeled on his uncle, ready to burst.

"What in the Five Great Worlds *was* that? I told you how important Lady Aline was to Gailea! You could've at least told me, warned me—!"

"No, I could not!" Alistor thundered. "You're so blinded with infatuation that you would've never listened to me! You would've run to Gailea and schemed some half-formed plot to land both of you in further trouble! Lady Aline knew too much. She had to disappear."

"Why is it that everyone else knows enough to get slaughtered for treason, while I know nothing?"

"Because I cannot afford your romantic fancies of protecting that girl to get you slaughtered!"

"So, you'll still tell me nothing?"

"I tell you as much as you need to know."

Crispin scoffed. "At least Gailea trusts me—respects me, treats me like a man—!"

Alistor rushed up and grabbed Crispin by the collar, shaking him hard. "He knows, Crispin—*he knows*! He knows about her lineage! This is no longer some petty game of cat and mouse. She is in true danger now."

Alistor released Crispin, who fell back against the glassless window's frame, stunned. The frosty air bit him sharply from behind as the horror of his uncle's declaration descended.

"What must I do?" Crispin asked. "How can I help her?"

"You must leave," Alistor said.

"Leave?" Crispin gasped. "Leave *her*? I can't just leave her. The king—Moragon—"

"Will not harm her. He has his own plans for her. I will do what I can to delay them. But her life need not concern you; you should fear more for your own. Moragon has very specific plans for her, and you are not the one he intends her to consort with." Alistor began to pace the perimeter of the tower. "Considering recent events, I don't think I should have to remind you what treason it is to take that which belongs to the king and how such treason may be punished."

Alistor stared at him pointedly. The executions that had happened only moments ago flashed through Crispin's mind, along with fresh fear as he envisioned Gailea pleading for mercy as Moragon tormented her mind with his mental magic till she went mad.

"She *doesn't* belong to him," Crispin said.

"Not yet, no. But don't be such a blind fool as to think that Gailea would never be *tempted* to belong to the king—she may hate him, but she also has royal blood, and if she knows it herself, as I suspect she does, she likely wants to rule this kingdom again."

Crispin shook his head. "No, that's impossible. She cares nothing for the crown—if she did, she wouldn't be working so hard to protect the current queen—"

Crispin bit his lip, so hard he tasted the bitter tang of blood. He'd promised Gailea not to breathe a word of what they'd been up to.

"What do you mean?" Alistor demanded. "And why should the queen need protecting?"

"I meant...I meant only that there are those who would seek the queen's harm, but Gailea is not the one to accuse in that regard."

Alistor's frown deepened. He had circled the tower and now stopped before Crispin, looming over him, his face etched with deep concern and command. "Then who? Who is placing the queen in such danger?"

Crispin hesitated again. He inched toward the door, but Alistor stepped slightly to the side, silently promising that he wouldn't release Crispin until he shared what he knew.

"Chevalier has been using some poison on the queen. It's slowly killing her; that's why she looks so feeble and sickly."

Alistor studied Crispin a long time, revealing no emotion. Finally, he said, in a quiet, even tone, "You have done well to be honest with me, though...there *are* some details you're yet hiding, aren't there?"

Alistor moved to one of the iron sconces holding a flameless torch. Raising one hand, he touched his fingertips it. His fingers caught aflame, blazing bright red and gold, and the iron melted, dripping to the stone floor. Alistor snatched it up, molded it in his hands, and then held up a key.

"I don't understand," Crispin said.

"Ah, of course...." Alistor melted the metal and reshaped it till a much more dilapidated key rested in his palm. "Another sign of your sloppy work and cocky lack of practice."

Crispin's heart seemed to stop inside him, but the next moment, he snapped, "You've been spying on me."

"Only with your best interests at heart. I too have heard things and have begun to fear—for both our sakes. But if you are no longer willing to trust me, then I have no need to disclose my own thoughts."

He started toward the door, but Crispin blurted, "Wait! Uncle—you're right. It wasn't just Chevalier. The king is plotting with him. I think killing Marlis is his idea."

Alistor turned back to Crispin with a cool smile. "Thank you for your full honesty. I shall now continue to grant mine. I am yet uncertain exactly what magic they're dabbling in. But I cannot see Moragon wasting his time on a petty poison. If something stronger is at work, and they bring it to fruition, he will have no further use for us, nor any need to fear us. He *will* find a way to dispose of us; don't you see that?"

"What can I do?" Crispin asked. "How can I protect myself—and protect Gailea—?"

"I have already told you—you must leave."

"But Gailea's far more valuable than I," Crispin said. "She's the true heir. So why not stay to protect her? Die for her even, if necessary?"

Alistor hesitated, looking almost impressed. "She is indeed most valuable. But if you are so bent on protecting her, you cannot do so from the grave. Even if all you say is true and Gailea is loyal, both to you and in preserving the queen's life, that changes nothing of Moragon's plans. Moragon will still endeavor till the queen is dead. And then, he will think to marry no one *but* Gailea, to control her and her music, and to have sons by her.

Once he has his heir, our lives will be forfeit and no longer tolerated. We cannot work here, from within the castle. No one will aid us here."

"So we run away?" Crispin asked. "I'm tired of being called a coward."

"No. We don't run *away*. We run *toward*. We find our freedom and begin rallying those who hate the king as much as we do. We create our own armies and take back the castle as Moragon once took it from Gailea's line. Then, we restore her to the throne."

Excitement flitted through Crispin, but doubt held him back. "That day I was sent to punish Master Weston, I saw how those people hated the king. They hated *me* too—and moreso now that they've seen what I'm capable of. How will we get them to trust us?"

"There are those who'd rather see anyone on the throne but Moragon," Alistor said. "To them, we play the part of being the lesser evil. To those who believe in our cause, we embrace them whole-heartedly. To those who fear us, we show them what we truly are and sway them to our side. And to those who despise us, we eliminate their threat. But I must ask: are you ready to risk all? Have you the strength to leave her, in order to save her?"

Crispin's mind spun in many directions, but he said, "All right. I will go if you think it will help her. But I would speak with her first."

Alistor nodded. "Very well. Speak with her as soon as you can. We'll meet later in my chambers to plan your departure—and what must happen afterward."

CHAPTER 16

SILVER HOPE

Crispin entered the large stone structure housing the stables. His breath curled in thick, white puffs as he drew his cloak tighter around him. A dreary sky permitted only a dim gray light to filter between the straw-thatched roof. The horses' breath issued like storm clouds and their pawing at the floor sounded like little claps of thunder.

Crispin glanced in the various stalls until he found Tytonn, who stood clad handsomely in a thick tunic and cloak of ebony and dark red, with a little white horse embroidered across his breast. He stood beside a brown mare and conversed with a man dressed in red robes—one of the vassals Tytonn had helped Crispin collect taxes from before. Crispin leaned back against the opposite stall, arms crossed, and watched.

"Here you are, sir," Tytonn said, handing off the reins.

"Thank you, lad." The vassal climbed aboard. He patted the horse's flank, and his tired face pulled into a small smile. "It's astounding, what you've done with her in only a week's time. I'd thought her spirits were broken for good."

"What a shame that would have been," Tytonn said. "She's a beautiful creature. Thank you for bringing her to me."

The vassal tipped his hat. Then, with a gentle command, he tugged on the reins and galloped from the stables.

"You're making quite the name for yourself."

Tytonn jumped and glanced up. "Crispin! Forgive me; I'd hardly noticed you."

"Understandable—that mare was a lovely specimen. Though I may have to scold you for devoting your attention so thoroughly to another female in my sister's absence."

Tytonn chuckled. "Much as I enjoy my work, I'd give it up for any other position if it meant your sister's hand. A blacksmith, even."

Crispin smiled warmly. "I wouldn't think too shabbily of being a blacksmith. You have the strong build for it."

"No..." Tytonn held out his hands and shook his head. "These aren't made for molding iron. They're made for taming wild beasts, and for healing. Perhaps I never *was* such a capable bodyguard by your side after all—too soft at heart; I'm sure that's what the king thinks."

"That may be what he thinks of both of us..." Crispin leaned close and glanced up and down the stables; the workers in his line of vision were some yards off, involved in sweeping hay or brushing the horses. "...but we shall both prove him wrong. As Master of Horses, you may yet win my sister's hand. Just as I may soon enough be able to declare my passion for Gailea."

Tytonn's brows rose, and his voice dipped into a whisper. "Gailea? What of her? I've been eager to talk to you, especially after the execution yesterday. She must be devastated..."

"Yes, and I am sorry too for the loss of your friend." Crispin placed a hand on Tytonn's shoulder.

"Thank you," Tytonn said. "If I can afford it, with my new wages, I would like to send what aid I can to his family."

"That is good of you. Elda couldn't find a man with a bigger heart. But I did not come here to simply offer my condolences..." Crispin lowered his voice to a quieter whisper as he explained about his and Gailea's discoveries of the plot against Marlis' life. He finished with a brief account of his conversation with Alistor, including his plan to go into hiding and build allies against the king.

"That's why I came to see you," Crispin finished. "I need to know how to find the Weaver and my sister— and I need a trusty steed to get me to them. The sooner I can depart the better."

Tytonn led a gray horse speckled with dark gray spots to Crispin. After checking to make sure the saddle was secure, he passed off the reins and said, "Go due west from here, deep into the woods, till you find a great silver lake. The Weaver's House resides by its shores. You won't miss it. The House is powerful, imbued with the Weaver's protective magic. It will know you're looking for it, that you have need of it. You'll find it without a doubt."

"How will I know for sure?" Crispin asked, mounting the horse. "How will I know that I've found the Weaver and not some imposter?"

"She'll be able to tell you things. She has a sixth sense, if you will; she can share things about you that no one else could know."

Crispin shivered. "Such magic makes me think of Moragon's."

"It's similar. But definitely not the same. She won't force her mental strengths upon you, nor seek to control you. Don't be afraid. She's powerful, but her powers lie in those of great protection, not harm."

"Thank you. I will do as you say."

Crispin moved the horse toward the door, but there it paused. He urged the horse forward, but when it remained still, he glanced over his shoulder at Tytonn who scribbled on a spare bit of parchment while prattling on, "Keep Elda safe and bring her word of my steadfast affection for her..."

"Of course, but only if you let go of my horse."

"I'm not touching him!" Tytonn insisted, continuing to write.

"Maybe not, but he seems to know your wishes, and he's fighting mine. Tell him to move so I can go to my sister and deliver all your good wishes and lover's promises."

"All right, all right!" Tytonn rolled up the note and handed it to Crispin with a grin. "You can be smart as you please, but you can no longer act like you've never been in love yourself."

"That's why I must go, now—I must find Gailea. If I can, I would take her with me, to keep her safe at my side. At the least, I would bid her farewell."

"Then go, my friend. And may you both be safe and happy together."

***

Gailea drew the shawl closer about her head and shoulders as she stooped and plucked the small patch of witch hazel flowers from beneath the thick bramble and dead leaves blanketing the woods. As something white lightly kissed her thick wool gloves, she glanced up. Winter's first snowfall. She and Darice had once raced through the snow, throwing the powdery fluff at one another. Then, the snow had been an inspiration.

Now, the snow, summoned by the cold, brought only death. Death to the witch hazel flowers that would slow the spread of the Dusk's poison. She and other servants gathered the flowers in the king's woods on the king's orders, but Gailea guessed that he only sought to keep Marlis alive long enough to complete his experiment with the Dusk.

Gailea gingerly fingered the soft, golden flowers then laid them in her basket alongside the half dozen others she'd managed to scrounge. Glancing up at the other servants searching under thick roots and grasses, she read the weary disappointment on their solemn faces. She had volunteered to help in hopes that her knowledge of the wood might prove useful. But no amount of knowledge could hold off winter and make the flowers grow again.

"Gailea?"

She gasped and glanced up. Crispin stared down at her from a gray speckled mare, his intense gaze filled with concern. He wore a thick tunic with at least two shirts beneath. A long fur cloak hugged his shoulders, and the sheen of his sturdy boots reflected that they were new. A sword hung in its sheath by his side, and a leather pack was slung on his back.

Gailea stood to her feet. Petting the horse's velvety nose, she smiled a bit at the creature's serenity. "She used to be so ill-tempered. She wouldn't let anyone ride her, not even when the king tried to force her with a calming charm…"

"All thanks to Tytonn," Crispin said.

"I don't think you could have done any better in appointing him as Master of Horses."

"Indeed..." Crispin ran his hands through the horse's mane, letting his hand trail down until his fingertips brushed Gailea's.

Gailea paused as a warmth that stemmed from something far beyond Crispin's Fyre magic sparked inside her. Catching his glance, she said, "You seem to be going somewhere."

"Yes," Crispin said quietly, "but we cannot speak of it here. Come."

He nudged the horse into a slow gait, and Gailea followed alongside.

"How are you this morning?" Crispin asked gently. "After everything yesterday?"

Recalling yesterday's horrors stabbed Gailea with fresh pain, and she blinked back tears. "Best not to mention yesterday out in the open either..." She glanced around at the trees, standing empty and naked. Wind bit sharply between their branches. She drew her cloak closer around her shoulders, but to no avail. "The trees are dying. The king could likely have Chevalier grow the plants anew, but of course, he won't. Soon, we will have to send for herbs from outside of Adelar to make the queen's tonic."

"Is she faring any better?"

Gailea took a deep breath and released it slowly. "Yes and no. She recovers some of her strength, only to lose it again the next day..."

"Come. Follow me; I know a place where the flowers are still hearty, and you can get all you need there."

"How? I have these woods memorized. I've scoured every inch..."

"I've lived here even longer than you and have been allotted more freedom to explore. Come with me,

please. I was already going into town. I would appreciate the company, and I promise it will be well worth it."

Crispin's eyes shone, pleading with her. Gailea hesitated, but his gaze drew her forward, making her heart
skip as if magnetized toward him. She let him lead her
along.

The trees thinned into bramble, and they spent a
good while weaving carefully between thorns and fallen
branches. Crispin jumped down from the horse to help
Gailea push aside sharp branches. Drawing his long
sword, he sliced through the thin reeds and spider's
webs, clearing a path.

At last, the woods opened into a wide, airy space with
towering trees, their branches tangled to form a close
canopy high above. The light snow barely penetrated,
and the cold wind stilled. A gray light filtered between
the trees, creating a mysterious atmosphere akin to that
found in the fairy rings Gailea had read about.

Crispin released her hand, skipping ahead and
swinging his blade. Grabbing a sturdy branch, he tossed
it to her with a playful grin and faced her, sword poised.
As she swung the branch, memories of play-fighting with
Darice flooded back to her.

She and Crispin parried blows for a while. Then, as
his sword went flying and he watched it arch through the
air, lips parted in speechless admiration, Gailea laughed
and said, "Thank you. I haven't done that in ages, and it
did lift my spirits a bit. But I really shouldn't tarry long.
I'm expected back soon..."

Crispin's smile lit his eyes. "It's just a little further."

He retrieved his sword, and they wove through
the giant trees until their path began to bend upward.
The slope gradually grew steeper, and Crispin offered
his hand. Gailea took it, if only to enjoy the thrill that
skipped through her at his touch. He helped her climb

amongst the unfamiliar stones, thorns, and holes. The trees disappeared, giving way to a large cliff that rose steadily before them.

Crispin began feeling the side of the cliff, letting his hand slide along its rough texture. Gailea hugged the wall, trailing after him. Suddenly, his arms seemed to disappear, and she gasped. When he pulled back, he grinned and motioned her forward. She crept over, peering into the gap between the cliffs, barely visible and just large enough to squeeze through if she turned sideways. Entranced, Gailea slipped inside, and Crispin followed close behind her.

They emerged inside a cave. Light shone faintly through fissures in the ceiling, and snow drifted down as well, more heavily now, forming puddles on the ground.

"This is amazing," Gailea breathed, staring up at the vastness of the cave. "In all my years of searching the grounds, I never knew anything like this existed. But what has this to do with helping the queen? Nothing would grow in here..."

"But beyond, yes," Crispin said, his voice hushed as if he shared the most intimate secret. He smiled brightly at her and took her hand, leading her forward. Gailea's heart sped, matching his excitement, though she didn't yet understand its source.

Soon, their path narrowed and darkened as the cracks above sealed. Crispin raised his free hand, and flames danced along his fingertips. The fire illuminated their path and bounced their shadows along the stone walls, making them dance high and merge as one.

Suddenly, Crispin stopped, squeezed her hand, and whispered, "Look—there it is. Look up there..."

Gailea followed his gaze to the cave's ceiling. A long crack raced along the ceiling, but instead of sunlight, a silvery shimmer shone through.

"What is it?"

"It's the barrier. With just a few more steps, we'll be free, Gailea—free!"

Gailea staggered back against the wall. Scrambling far away from the fissure, she stared at it in horror. Had Crispin not pointed out the barrier, her taking just a step further would have alerted his majesty without her even realizing it. Moragon's wrath would have descended so swiftly that neither of them would have seen it coming.

"I can't, Crispin. I can't."

"Of course you can," Crispin said. "It's all right if you're afraid, but I'll be with you…"

He reached for her hand, but she jerked it back. Tears rushed to her. As much as she longed for his touch, whereas moments before it meant comfort, now it could only mean death—at least for him if he tried to help her flee.

Feigning anger, she frowned at him and said, "You tricked me. You said we were helping the queen."

"We are. But we can no longer keep fighting alone and from the inside. I'm leaving to gather aid. The queen's health is important, yes. But so is her safety, and yours—"

She took another step back. "If you cared anything for my safety, you would not have brought me here. The guards will know—they'll find us—"

"They won't." He rushed forward and grabbed her arms, his gaze pleading. Gailea glanced behind her, and then back to him. Only a thin space stood between them and the wall behind her. She shivered, wanting to wrench away again and place some distance between them, but then a warmth flowed from his hands into her arms. It coursed through her skin and deep beneath it, coiling around her heart and calming it. Her breathing soothed, and her body eased. It was a false calm, created by his magic, and she tried to warn herself of this, but the warmth forbade her fears from returning…

"Everything will be all right, Gailea. But we have to go—*now*."

"*Go*," Gailea gasped, the word jarring her back to her senses. She again drew away from Crispin's touch; the act seemed to cause him pain, and she narrowed her gaze in apology. "I would go with you, but I can't. I must stay to protect the queen. And my sister. The king would surely visit some punishment on her."

"Gailea, please." Crispin stepped forward again, his expression growing more desperate. "Think about what happened yesterday. The executions—I am so sorry that they happened, and if you want to blame me, you can. You can even hate me. But if you don't come—the king—he looked right at us when they executed Garrison. He knows. He knows we helped my sister escape. Who's to say what else he knows? You cannot stay here." He grabbed her arm and pulled her toward the silver barrier.

"Wait!" Gailea cried. "You can't! I must show you something."

Crispin paused but did not release her. "Yes?"

"If I show you," Gailea whispered, "you must promise that it won't make you stay."

Crispin studied her curiously but nodded his agreement and released her.

Gailea pushed up her sleeve and revealed the bracelet, its tiny gems shimmering in the silver glow streaming down from above.

"What is it?" Crispin demanded. "A gift from the king?"

"Not a gift. A punishment. A curse. The moment I set foot outside the barrier, the king will be alerted. If we had taken a few more steps just moments ago, I would likely be captured now, and you might even be dead. I cannot go with you. I won't place you in that kind of danger. And we both know he would find us. We're not that far from the castle..." Her voice broke.

Crispin wrapped his arms around her. At first, she resisted, but as he pulled her closer, she let herself collapse against him, crying and releasing all of yesterday's pain, along with today's fresh fears.

"I'm frightened," Gailea said. "It's not just that he wants to use my music. There's something else, a secret—about my past, about who I am—that he knows now."

"Is it your lineage?"

Gailea gasped and pulled back just enough to stare up at him. "You know as well?"

"I've known for a while now. Alistor told me. But I didn't wish to alarm you."

"How did he find out?"

"I don't know. But Gailea, if the king knows, then you must flee..." He touched the bracelet and snarled. "It's disgusting—he tries to place a collar on you like that dog, Chevalier—a fancier collar, but a collar all the same. Don't you see? This is all the more reason you *must* leave."

"But not now, not like this. The other reasons I gave were also true—I would not leave my sister."

Crispin took her hands. "And I admire that. You love your sister as dearly as I love Elda—that's where I'm going, to find her. Tytonn says the lady she is staying with may be able to help. Then, together, Alistor and I intend to raise an army, march against the king, and throw him from his tyrannical throne for good."

"And then?"

"Then?"

"Well," Gailea said, "you cannot leave Adelar leaderless. It would be in just as dangerous a position as before, when its leaders were divided and Moragon took it in the first place. Does Alistor himself intend to take the throne?"

"I believe Alistor has intentions of trying to restore *you* as the rightful queen."

Gailea stared. "Me? I've never given much thought to wanting the crown. Honestly, I would have thought that *you* would make a fair ruler."

"In that case, we would rule together, for I would take no one else as my queen. At any rate, better me than Moragon, right?"

"What do you mean? You believe Moragon intends to make *me* his queen, once Marlis..." She let the disgusting thought trail, unable to finish it.

"Alistor is convinced that is part of the king's plan for you, yes," Crispin said. "Why would he kill Marlis without plans to marry another, to produce an heir? My uncle thinks Moragon would marry you for your magic. Which is why I wish so desperately that you could come with me..." Crispin grasped her shoulders. "I can't stand the idea of *anyone*, but especially him, calling you theirs. I want to know that you are safe, by my side, in my sight. If I am to be king someday, if that is what you desire, then I would make you my queen, to fight Moragon *with* me."

Gailea drew a deep, shuddering breath. Crispin's warmth began flowing once more from his body into hers. Passion danced in his eyes. He pushed her back, trapping her against the cave wall, and pressed his lips to hers. She stiffened, frozen in shock, but as his warmth flooded her body, so swiftly and completely that she thought she might explode, she kissed him back. She reached up, coiling her hands in his thick curls, panting against him as he suffocated her in ardent kisses.

When at last their kiss broke, Gailea staggered breathlessly against the wall. Crispin's eyes gleamed with unconcealed desire and wonder, and he said, "I must go. Alistor will join me soon; we've arranged to meet in a fortnight. Then, we'll gather our armies and attack Moragon. When that happens, I promise to return to you."

"Be safe," Gailea breathed.

Crispin nodded. "I will. You do the same..."

Gailea glanced at his lips, longing. Crispin stepped forward, holding her close and kissing her again. When they parted, he held her head in his hands. Their foreheads touched, and he stroked her hair, whispering, "Goodbye, my love..."

He stole into the depths of the cave and disappeared into the shadows.

Gailea stared at the darkness that had swallowed him for some moments, bewildered by her new, wild desire.

Then, she fled the cave without looking back.

CHAPTER 17

BEAUTY, DUSK, AND DANGER

As Gailea stumbled back into the place where she had left the other servants, only a sharp chill met her. The snow had begun to fall thicker, turning the cloud-strewn sky to a blur of white canvas. She searched the woods, calling for the others, but no reply met her.

Falling to her knees beside a stream, flushed and panting from her run, she took a vial from her pocket. She'd be in trouble if found missing too long, but her solitude provided the perfect chance to test the Dusk's magic at last. Cradling the vial, she tilted her hands this way and that, watching as the misty crimson substance shifted back and forth, slow and thick like honey, though its tiny granules could be made out like grains of sand.

How should she test it? She wasn't fool enough to ingest it; she already knew what that would do to a person. Her mind reached for the various spells she had begun to learn from the book she'd gleaned from Lady

Aline's study and recalled a melody meant for separating substances into their components. Perhaps, if she focused hard enough, she could separate the Dusk into its various elements. She brushed away a few tears with a smile. If this worked, if Lady Aline managed to help her even in death, then her suffering would not be entirely in vain.

Gailea opened the vial and tipped it over, allowing the tiniest drop to slide onto her finger before capping the vial and slipping it back into her pocket.

As she parted her lips to sing, the words froze in her throat before releasing as a shriek. The drop of Dusk spread, coating her skin like paint. Gailea scrambled backward, trying to fling the red substance from her hand, but it crawled up and up, coiling around her fingers and creeping up her arm. She backed against a tree, breathing heavily. The crimson began spreading across the rest of her, visibly through her gown, as though blood drenched her whole body. Visions began to stab her mind:

*Her as a young girl, being torn away from her mother to come work at the castle, only this time, her mother was slaughtered mercilessly before her eyes; Darice cast from the castle to cower in the snow, starving and friendless; a faceless man breathing in her ear, "You're **my** wife—none other's," and forcing her against a cold stone wall; its rough texture dug into her back like icy needles, and a brilliant light shining from behind illuminated the mysterious man with a golden-bronze, otherworldly glow. He kissed her deeply—*

Gailea screamed as someone's strong arms hefted her up.

It's him. It's him. Moragon. He's found you. His magic has seen your fears and is making them come true—

Gailea kicked and punched. The man spoke to her, but the words were muffled in her terrified haze. Warning echoed inside her mind, begging her to reach for her magic, but she couldn't recollect a single spell.

All of a sudden, she was surrounded by a blue blur and submerged in a shockingly cold wetness. She was beneath water. He couldn't use her magic, couldn't claim it as his own, so instead he would drown her—

As her head bobbed above water, she sang a melody, shakily but with as much force as she could muster. He cried out, and a hard thump told her she'd successfully flung him aside. She scrambled from the water, grabbed her basket of witch hazel, and rushed up the bank toward the portals that would zip her back up to the castle—

Her captor grabbed her around the middle. She screamed and flailed, preparing to sing again, when he whirled her around, caught her firmly by the shoulders, and shook her, shouting, "It's me, Gailea! It's me! Tytonn Grayfell, Crispin's friend!"

Tytonn's face hovered right before hers, his brown eyes wide and pleading. Blood trickled from his forehead where she'd slammed him against the ground. She froze in his arms, bewildered. Then, she collapsed, sobbing, and he caught her, sinking to the ground with her and holding her.

She cried hard, releasing the poison of her terror at the Dusk's touch. Then, wiping away her tears and opening her eyes, she held out her arms and turned them over. No trace of the Dusk remained. She shivered, trying to draw her cloak about her shoulders, but its heavy wetness just weighed her down and added to her cold.

"I'm sorry," Tytonn said, rubbing her back as if attempting to warm her, though he also shivered, drenched from head to toe. "I didn't know what else to do. I tried using one of my calming charms, but it wasn't working. And that stuff...that stuff was spreading like blood all over you. I thought you were hurt..."

"I was testing it, to see what it was made of," she whispered. "But it overpowered me, gave me the most hideous visions. I thought they were real. I thought..." She gasped, forcing back another sob as the fresh memories assailed her mind. "It's more powerful than anything I've ever felt before. I can't dare to imagine what the queen must go through every time she consumes it..."

"Oh, my," Tytonn breathed, his body growing tense against hers.

"What?" Gailea whispered.

"Look..."

Gailea followed his gaze to the stream and flung a hand to her mouth. Fish floated along the surface of the water, lifeless. Their blood stained the water, or else the Dusk did—it was hard to tell the difference. Their silvery scales shrunk, eaten away as if by acid, and the stench of decay stained the air. Gailea covered her face, turning away.

"Come on," Tytonn said. "Let's get back to the castle, get us both warm and dry. We'll just have to hope the kitchens aren't planning on fresh fish for our meal tonight."

He laughed shakily, and Gailea returned a small smile, appreciating his attempt to lighten the mood.

Tytonn wrapped an arm around her and helped her to her feet. He motioned to the gray speckled horse standing nearby, and they started up the bank. "May I ask what you're still doing here? Crispin had said he went to look for you, but then I found the horse here—the one I gave him when he left..."

"So...you know as well?" Gailea ventured. "That he's gone?"

Tytonn nodded. "I hope that he can soon put an end to all this death and madness..."

Gailea grabbed his hand and made him stop beside

her. Looking up into his warm brown eyes, she smiled and said, "You're a good friend—to Crispin, to Elda, and to me. Thank you for saving me." She hugged him. He stiffened at first, but then he wrapped his arms around her, returning the embrace. She sighed against his chest, wanting to cry again, aching for the feel of Crispin's touch and the blaze it had ignited inside her heart. Now she was just cold, wet, and weary...

Someone cleared their throat. Gailea pulled from the embrace, whirling and gasping as Alistor stood leaning against a tree, arms folded, head tilted in his usual nonchalant stance. She pulled the wet cloak closer around herself. The vision of the mysterious man's hands running all over her lingered; perhaps it had been Lord Ragnar, not the king as she'd first thought. With a shiver, she cast a fleeting glance at the snowy ground.

"Forgive me for interrupting," Alistor said. "His grace and I were preparing to go for a hunt, and I require a horse. I must demand you return to the stables and ready the beasts at once—otherwise, I may have to inform his grace that our new Master of Horses neglects his duties to gallivant about the woods rather inappropriately with the noble ladies of his court."

Tytonn bowed his head, looking far calmer than Gailea felt. "My apologies, my lord. I will go at once. May I first see the Lady Gailea safely inside? I'd come looking for her because the other servants were concerned when she did not return with them—"

Lord Ragnar stepped forward and snapped, "Do not think to touch her again. The king would not so easily forgive you, nor would I." With a glare at Gailea, he added, "The portal to the castle is right through those trees. I trust you can find your way?"

Gailea nodded stiffly. "Yes, my lord."

Alistor nodded sharply at Tytonn who began leading

him toward the portal that would land them nearest the stables.

As Gailea watched Tytonn and Alistor disappear beyond the trees, she wanted to rush after, to follow along and make sure Tytonn was safe, even as she knew she couldn't. It was terrifying enough to know that Tytonn walked with a man who held the power necessary to destroy him. Gailea wouldn't risk putting him in even further danger by displaying what could easily be perceived as too deep a concern.

Gailea hurried toward the portal Alistor had indicated, her mind spinning. How much had Lord Ragnar seen and heard, and what new schemes might he plot against her as he rode out with the king? Crispin had promised that Alistor meant to protect her, and yet, in Crispin's absence, Gailea felt naked of all protection.

As soon as Gailea stole back inside the castle, she hurried to her chambers to dry by the fire and slip into a fresh change of clothes—

At the sight of someone in her room, she collapsed back against the door with a gasp. The next moment, as she realized it was Darice, she breathed a sigh of relief.

"Gailea!" Darice cried, hurrying over and taking her by the shoulders. "What in all Adelar is the matter with you? And why are you dripping wet?"

Gailea let her sister lead her over to the roaring hearth. While she held out her hands, drinking in the fire's warmth, Darice knelt beside her and demanded gently, "Tell me what's going on. I haven't seen you since...since yesterday. Lady Aline. I'm so sorry. I know how much you loved her. But I can sense there is something more. Talk to me."

Gailea took a deep breath. Lowering her voice, she said, "Crispin and I made a recent discovery. The Dusk—the spice you said was used only for the queen's dishes—is being used to poison her."

Darice stood struck silent. Her face paled, and Gailea feared she might be sick.

"Oh, Gailea," she breathed at last. "The poor queen...I can't believe it—I can't imagine. I'm so sorry—"

"It's not your fault," Gailea said, taking her sister's hand. "You didn't know. But now that you do, you must find a way to not use it any longer, no matter who commands you. I'll hide it myself if I must."

Darice nodded fervently, all the while blinking back tears. "All right. I'll do what I can. Oh, the poor dear. I knew he hated her, but for it to come to this..." She then touched Gailea's bracelet before looking at her with curiosity. "And what's this? A gift from the young Lord Ragnar, perhaps?"

Gailea took another deep breath. She had neither wanted to worry her sister nor to place her in danger up till now. She still didn't desire to do either, but now that Moragon knew about her lineage, Gailea's mere existence placed Darice in danger by association. She may as well give her sister the truth.

"It's from the king. His intentions toward me are no nobler than they are toward the queen. He means to dispose of her so he can marry *me*. He knows now about my lineage. He's figured it out and wants to use it—and my music—for himself."

"What about Crispin?" Darice gasped. "Isn't he helping you?"

Gailea nodded. "He is..." She considered sharing his escape, but though she trusted Darice with all her heart, any slip of her tongue could be fatal for him, at least till he drew farther from the castle.

"Actually..." Gailea turned her attention wistfully to that earlier adventure, needing a reprieve from such dismal talk. "Earlier today, in the woods, Crispin came to me. He was beside himself with passion, and...and we kissed."

Gailea wanted to smile but refrained, uncertain of her sister's reaction.

As Darice's eyes widened, Gailea felt uncomfortable; did her sister stare from mere shock, or with disapproval?

"How did it feel?" Darice asked at last.

"Beautiful..." Gailea breathed in a sigh of relief. "Whole, complete, but mostly, it felt beautiful. I didn't expect it. I didn't realize how strongly I felt for him, but his kiss awakened something inside me. I care for him very deeply, sister. He's been such a help to me. And if you'd seen how he was today, how much he wanted to protect me..."

"Grand words and passionate kisses make for a good lover—not for a good match," Darice said with a gently warning tone. "Do not confuse romance with love."

"No," Gailea said, "you know I'm too practical for that. But if I loved him simply because he was beautiful—well, that would be impossible. At times, he looks so like his uncle as to terrify me. But he is *not* like Lord Ragnar, thank Amiel. He is far kinder and more compassionate—sometimes, even boyish still. He is so tender with me..."

"I think if he is kinder, it is because he *is* boyish like you say—or a more accurate word for it might be 'naïve'. Worldly wisdom may not fit him well."

"I see no harm in being ignorant toward the world's cruelties."

"Perhaps. But for a king or any other leader, such is impossible. One can be *too* naïve, and such innocence can be easily corrupted. A flower exposed too quickly to winter's frost has no chance for survival..."

"I might have stayed in the woods," Gailea muttered, "freezing to death, and at least dreamed happier thoughts."

"I want to be happy for you," Darice urged. "I do. But I also cannot help but worry. He *is* one of them."

Gailea studied her sister a long moment, knowing deep down that she was right. Hadn't Gailea always resisted getting close to any member of the king's family, for fear that would lead her to betrayal, harm, even death?

"He is one of them," she said, "but he is more than that. He is his own person, not simply a Vorlaire or Ragnar. Even a broken horse who comes from a master renowned for cruelty has some hope of redemption. Crispin is obedient and loyal, so perhaps, with the right influences, his heart may continue to change and grow."

"Then, if you care for him as deeply as you claim, you must make certain he is ever in the presence of the right influences—those who can make him change and grow in the right direction, those whom it is wise to be obedient and loyal toward."

Gailea nodded and smiled. "Thank you. I'll try."

Darice smiled back. "I should get back to the kitchen. I will do what I can for the queen. But tell me—is there anything else I can do to help *you*?"

Gailea hesitated. As the fire melted away the last of her chill, she felt suddenly heavy and wished for nothing other than to collapse into a deep slumber right there on the rug. She glanced about the room as if hoping it might provide her with some clever answer. Her gaze found her special box and an idea sparked inside her.

"Yes...yes, I think there is. Do you still see Sorcha or Macha or any of the other music mages?"

Darice nodded. "Some of them, yes."

"There are a couple of songs that may be useful both for their own protection and to me, should the time come to stand against Moragon. If you could teach them the songs, ask them to practice and teach the others..."

"Of course. Teach me at once."

Gailea explained to Darice about the song-shield, a summoning song she'd recently taught herself, and the song used to magnify or diminish sound. She sang the notes for each. Darice mimicked and, as usual, memorized them with impressive preciseness.

Once satisfied, Gailea said, "Thank you. I like knowing that, if nothing else, they might at least be able to shield the others' minds from the king."

Gailea walked her to the door, and Darice said, "I will start teaching them as soon as I'm able. Amiel bless you and keep you, dear sister."

"And you as well."

***

Gailea paused in the doorway to Marlis' chambers to ascertain that the queen slept soundly. Lately, it took an increasingly long time and effort not just to get the queen to sleep, but to also smooth all the nightmares from her mind. After her own experience with the Dusk earlier, Gailea had been extra thorough with the latter tonight.

Once satisfied with the queen's serene expression, Gailea departed and hurried toward her own chambers; her body felt heavy with exhaustion, and her eyes could hardly stay open. Bronia had been kind enough to exchange watches with her, so she would at least get a full night's rest.

As Gailea hurried down the hall, a shadow rose from the wall before her, blocking her path, and she stumbled to a halt. Lord Ragnar loomed before her. She stepped toward the middle of the corridor to face him head-on, refusing to let herself be cornered.

They watched each other. Her breathing accelerated. Illuminated in the glow of the torchlight lining the walls, he stood before her like a brazen god, not entirely unlike her vision from earlier, and his hair shimmered as though he wore a crown of fire.

As he walked forward, she stepped back, singing her lullaby to calm her nerves but with woefully little success. Her back brushed against the wall, and she found herself trapped between the cold stone and his warmth. He leaned forward and rested one hand against the wall, blocking her path of escape. She glanced at the sliver of empty space on her other side, then back to his face. As his eyes watched her intensely, Gailea hated how alive she felt in his presence.

"Lord Ragnar?" she said quietly. "What did you need—?"

He leaned in and kissed her, briefly, but enough to make her gasp, clutch the wall behind her for support, and stare up at him, dumbfounded.

"That's better—now I've commanded your full attention. Insolent girl, speaking to your master before he's spoken to you. Then again, *I'm* not your master, am I? You pledge allegiance to another these days. Though I'm afraid you're backing the wrong horse, my dear." He caressed her cheeks, and his touch, surprisingly tender, seemed to command her to gaze straight at him. His breath whispered sweet and warm across her face, "He is a weak child, a mere boy. He knows nothing of the world and will destroy himself *and* you before the end."

Gailea hesitated. She almost wanted to relax against Alistor, to fall into his arms as she had Crispin's—though "relax" did not seem a fitting term. Rather than comfort, Alistor ignited a strange passion in her, whether truly or by some spell, she couldn't decipher. Jerking her head away, she said, "You've been using him all this time, feeding him false hopes of becoming king."

"I think we both know I want my brother overthrown. But I don't want the throne for myself. I truly think Crispin would make a far better king; in fact..." He smirked and twirled a strand of her hair; she swallowed hard. "...a better king, I cannot imagine."

"You want to control him." Gailea pulled away from him. "You won't risk taking the throne yourself. You'll use him—and if it destroys him, what harm has it done you? I *won't* let you use him like that."

Alistor laughed softly. He played with another wisp of her hair. She turned her head, but he stroked her cheek instead. His hands trailed down to her neck which he held gently but firmly enough for her to sense the power pulsing beneath his warming skin.

Leaning close so that their faces nearly touched, he whispered, "You see now, *that's* the sad thing. You and I both know how easily persuaded Crispin can be. I love my nephew, but he is not worthy of you. You are above him. Why do you want a child for a husband? Someone whose hand you must hold every step of the way?" His hands danced down to grip her shoulders. "Marry *me*, and we can use our magic to destroy Moragon. If you insist, we will take the throne; I will restore it to you and give you a rightful heir. If that doesn't suit your fancy, we can find some pretty thing to satisfy my nephew and make him king instead."

"He would not be so easily satisfied," Gailea said. "He may be easily swayed in some things, but his heart is not. He loves me. And—and I love him." She added the last words as a whisper, almost in a gasp of surprise as she realized their truth for the first time.

Disgust flared in Alistor's eyes, and his hands scorched her arms. She cried out, but he gripped her harder, forcing the intense heat to fill her entire body. She trembled and opened her mouth to scream, but the scream was stifled by his lips pressed harshly against hers. Forcing herself to concentrate, she changed the scream to a high-pitched note—

Lord Ragnar slammed back against the opposite wall with a hard thud. Gailea stood trembling but poised, ready to sing and attack again. Alistor staggered to his feet, clutching at the wall. As he marched toward her, she shouted, "Don't! Don't you *dare*."

He froze in place, looking alarmed.

"Damn you, girl," he snarled. "Do you not realize by now that it is by *my* hands you even possess such power to begin with? *I* saw your gift long before anyone else did. *I* set you up with Lady Aline, so she could give you a fighting chance against my brother. Once my spies confirmed my suspicions with your birth records, I encouraged her to push you in your studies, send you the private lessons—and this—*this* is how you repay your benefactor?"

Hurt etched his angry, proud tone. For a moment, Gailea felt taken aback and almost sorry. Then, fear grabbed her, along with reason, and she said quietly, "You were manipulating me just as you would manipulate Crispin. Using me for your own purposes. But I won't let you do that to me any more than I will let you do that to him."

"You truly believe you have that much power?" Alistor challenged. "To resist me *and* the king?"

"*You* tell *me*, Lord Ragnar," Gailea said, not bothering to conceal the mocking in her voice. "If your words are true, you created me. How much power *do* I possess?"

Alistor watched her, seemingly stunned. Then, lifting his chin, he said, "I will grant you this one victory, girl. But do not underestimate my magic—nor my ambition. I *will* claim you, one way or another. I will make you submit until I've played your every string. You *will* obey and be mine."

He watched her for a while longer.

Gailea kept her song-spells at the forefront of her mind, ready to defend herself.

At last, he turned and disappeared into the shadows.

Gailea turned and fled the castle, using the portals to zip down into the king's woods. Her feet flew even as her mind raced. If Lord Ragnar was responsible for her magic's cultivation, what exactly did he want from her? What would he gain by obtaining control of her? He was handsome and charming, and perhaps he'd even developed some affection for her after all these years, but she could never trust him to see her as any more than a prize, an instrument to use against his brother.

Gailea bolted through the woods like a wild nymph, feeling almost free as the frigid air filled her lungs.

But the castle's shadow looming over her reminded her that, just like a nymph who is tethered to the trees of her birth, so she was ever bound to the castle. And soon, she may be forced to be more tightly bound. Moragon would not be fooled for long. She could continue stealing the poison for now, but Chevalier could doubtless make more.

She must seek to get closer to the king, to find some way to sway him from killing the queen—at least until Crispin was ready with whatever army he hoped to summon to his side. Perhaps she could befriend Chevalier; they were both powerful magicians, and she did not hate him on principle of his being a sorcerer like most others seemed to.

Her final card to play would be her musical magic. She'd cling to it until absolutely necessary, but if it meant the queen's life, she would pledge to give it up for her—though never entirely. She would never let anyone—neither Lord Ragnar nor the king nor even Crispin him-self—have such utter dominion over that most intimate part of her.

CHAPTER 18

A HINT OF SILVER

Crispin knelt by the trap, inspected it, and breathed a sigh of relief. At last, he'd caught a rabbit. With growling stomach, he reached inside the sticks, grabbed the small, wriggling beast, and sliced across its throat with a dagger-like jet of flame. The rabbit fell limp in his hand. As blood oozed from its fresh wound, Crispin almost dropped it, but then he inwardly scolded himself. He had been hunting like a man and living off the land for a week now. Considering that he'd set his sights on gathering an army to storm Moragon's castle, it was high time he grew used to the shedding of blood.

He curled his other hand, and a ball of flame formed within his palm. After catching it on the pile of sticks he'd assembled, he stood back and watched the flames spread and blaze high. Savoring the rich smell of smoke, he set about skinning the rabbit before spearing and hoisting it between two sticks set on either side of the fire.

A rustle piqued his attention, and he glanced around the small clearing. Nothing in sight, save for bare trees and the snow thickly coating everything. With a shiver, he rubbed his gloved hands together and hunched down toward the fire. It was a cloudy day, not conducive to absorbing as much magic from the sun as he would have liked, and now he gratefully drank in the flames' warmth.

A branch snapped, and Crispin's head jerked up. He had traveled all this time with almost no signs of human life, and those he had seen, he'd ignored. Alistor had warned him to make straight for the Weaver's house and talk to as few strangers as possible.

A branch snapped again, louder this time. Crispin rose to his feet, hands poised, fire dancing along his fingertips. His imagination had run wild the past few days; he'd even convinced himself that a wolf was following him, but it had only been the howling wind. He'd since grown accustomed to the subtly distinctive noises of deer and wolves and other animals. However, no deer or wolf or other beast was likely to stalk this close to a fire—

Several shapes leapt out at Crispin, circling him on all sides. He backed up near the fire, hands aglow with bright flames. The green-cloaked men surrounding him drew back arrows on their bowstrings, and Crispin shifted, ready to hurl his attack, but then something else snapped—something like a small explosion—and bright red and yellow flames burst to life on the tips of their arrows. Crispin froze in place.

"Justice is sweet, isn't it, my lord?"

Crispin whirled, hands still poised. His eyes widened as he beheld Lord Weston, cloaked in lavish purple robes, his grin made all the more menacing by the distorted scars covering one half of his face—the remnant of Crispin's sloppy mishap.

"I will consider giving you your life, if only because I respect Tytonn and know that, however madly, he cares deeply for your friendship. However, I will grant your life *only* if you return to me that which you stole."

Crispin lifted his chin and cocked a brow, trying his best to match the vassal's confident nonchalance, despite the fear churning in the pit of his stomach.

"What do you mean, 'that which I stole'? If you mean the punishment I inflicted, I do humbly apologize, as it was never my intent. My powers were newer and not refined as you see them now."

"I humbly accept your apologies," Weston said with a smirk. "But I do not speak of personal injustice. I speak of you helping to fatten your uncle's treasury so that he can continue enriching his allies and ensure we are never rid of his self-serving reign."

Crispin glanced the lord's robes up and down. "You don't seem to be faring too poorly."

"No. But a great majority of Adelarans are. Our new trade routes may thrive, but most of our people fail. I speak against the king what you would dub as treason, only I would dub it as mere truth, for Moragon *is* no king. I have withheld my taxes to aid the less fortunate, to help carve a path to better lives for them—and for all Adelar."

"You're using funds which belong to the king to plot against him."

Weston nodded. "In a word, yes. But the sum required of others by the king has greatly delayed our plans. Thus, perhaps a donation from your own pocketbook would do. My men will escort you, if necessary. Though, one does wonder what his grace's nephew is doing wandering so far from the castle in the middle of the night. Perhaps you've tired already of the new mistress they whisper about? The Lady Gailea?"

Crispin flinched at this insult but kept his stare steady and calm, trying to stall and conjure some excuse. He couldn't say that he'd fled the castle; if word hadn't yet spread, he wasn't about to share it first with his enemies.

His gaze strayed to the crest embroidered upon the archers' dark tunics—a golden bear crowned with silver stars.

"That sigil—whose is it? I don't recognize it."

"That is the crest of Lord Gareth—the rightful king of this land before your family usurped the throne—and of his son, Lord Donyon."

Crispin scoffed. "The way I've heard things, Gareth aims to become little more than the usurper you claim my uncle to be. He has no power, no real armies or magic. His son, Donyon, once relied on a marriage to King Cenric's daughter, but that failed."

"Bold words for one so ignorant of the times," Weston said. "If you paid any attention to more significant whisperings instead of lavishing yourself in silly gossip, you wouldn't be so quick to judge Lord Gareth's lack of power."

Crispin hesitated. Did Weston say such things just to frighten him, or because they were true? The vassal had no real reason to lie; he couldn't know Crispin intended to build his own army.

Crispin's glance fell upon the archers' blazing arrows, their shafts glinting like black diamonds. If it came to a fight, Crispin couldn't afford for them to make the first move. He could stop the arrows' flames, but the metal would pierce his heart in an instant.

He glanced back at Lord Weston, hoping to detect some sign of a bluff beyond his solemn, steady stare.

He found none.

"My patience thins," Weston said at last. "Do we have a deal? Your life, in exchange for funding our cause?"

"You really think I would betray my uncle for a few coins? Pay you to strengthen his enemies?"

"Come, boy. You may be naïve, but you're not sim-ple-minded. Your uncle cares nothing for you—neither of them does. I care not for your life either, but I at least give you a chance. Besides, what good could come of our success except to save you from your uncles' chains?"

Having Lord Gareth's ranks eliminate the king *for* him was, indeed, a tempting thought. Gareth would likely prove a more complacent master. Then again, might he not try to marry Gailea himself or wed Donyon to her?

Then again, what did it matter? Crispin didn't even possess the funds Weston asked of him. Helping or not wasn't even a choice.

"Very well, Lord Weston," Crispin said, flexing his hands and letting his fire fill him. "I will return to you that which I stole—I will return it to you and your men tenfold!"

He whipped his hands in front of him, and flames blasted forth. Their girth spread wide, scorching several archers. Arrows whizzed past in skewed angles as their masters fell, and Crispin dodged them. Others flew past from behind him, and he dove to the ground, rolling out of the way before leaping back to his feet and dash-ing into the woods.

"After him!" Lord Weston shouted. "And bring him to me alive—I will show him the same mercy he showed me until he relents…"

Weston's voice faded, but footsteps advanced, crunch-ing through snow glazed over fallen twigs and leaves. Arrows sang past Crispin's ears. He dodged some and flung fire at others to knock them off-course.

Crispin ran until his entire body ached with exhaus-tion. Collapsing in the snow, his fire vanished, and he shivered violently at the abrupt drop in temperature. The wind whipped faster, welcoming a fresh barrage of snow mixed with frigid rain. Crispin hugged himself as the intense iciness pierced and spread through him with the same intense burn of a wildfire.

Even so, the truth pierced him far more harshly:

He was no leader. The people hated him. A glance around the woods told him he was lost, alone, with no hope of finding his sister, the one person who might help him.

But his heart didn't ache so much for Elda as for Gailea, to be lost in the warmth of her kisses, to drown in the comfort of her song. Why was he suddenly so useless without her? When he'd pledged his love and begged her to flee with him, he'd never felt more powerful. Maybe his strength had only been a façade created by her presence; maybe she could truly make a queen, but that did not make him a suitable king.

He stood, and some of the snow tumbled from head and shoulders. He squinted against the snow swirling on all sides and inhaled a deep breath. He trudged forward, forcing each step through the thickly mounting layer of snow and ice.

A flash of silver darted through the trees, and he froze still. Another arrow? Did Weston send more of his men?

The silver flashed between the trees again, but this time, its glow lingered a few moments before waning. It emitted again, blinking on and off, slowly like a light-house beacon. Crispin pursued it.

The silver gleams seemed to occur farther and farther away, and Crispin broke into a run, trying to match their pace as they sped ahead of him. It was certainly no arrow; perhaps some forest spirit played tricks on him and sought to lead him to despair.

Just when the silver raced so far ahead he knew he could never catch up, it paused, hovering in place.

Crispin quickened his pace, pushing his sore body and lungs.

At last, he emerged into a wide-open clearing, and there he stumbled to a halt.

A large house stretched high toward the starry sky. Moss and vines encased its ancient stones. The entire structure shimmered in the reflection of the lake nestled right beside it.

Crispin wondered at the glow that the lake emitted; while the raging snows had calmed, the clouds didn't allow much starlight or moonlight to shine through. Tiptoeing toward the lake, he peered inside and gasped. A strange silver liquid filled it, still and smooth as glass. The silver emitted its own glow that rose mist-like from the lake, making everything around it gleam, dreamlike.

Crouching down, Crispin stretched forth a hand to touch the silver substance but then recoiled. It could easily be poison or some deadly magic.

"Go ahead," a voice said. "Touch it..."

Crispin looked up. Some yards away, right at the lake's edge, a woman stood. The lake's silver glow blended with her dark silver robes and highlighted her silvering raven curls. Many wrinkles etched in her deep brown skin showed her age, but her deep brown eyes shone with a vivid alertness.

"It's all right," she said. "It won't hurt you."

Crispin stretched forth his hand and let it hover over the lake, fingers spread wide. He hesitated, frowning as the fringes of the vaguest memory pricked at his mind. What memory or why, he wasn't certain. Perhaps he was just tired. Reaching down, he lightly touched his fingertips to the liquid, and then he lay his palm flat on the lake's surface.

Six sets of ripples expanded from each small point

he'd touched. The ripples glinted with a brilliant silver, and he blinked at their brief yet blinding glow. Cupping his palm, he scooped some of the silver, and it flowed between his fingers, thick as cream but smooth as ice and equally as cold.

"Astounding, isn't it?" said the woman across the lake. "At a glance, its beauty and fluidity make it seem innocent enough, but once fully unleashed, its power can contend with almost any other type of known magic—much like your magic, Crispin, brother of Elda."

Crispin's head jerked up, and he let the liquid slide through his fingers. "You know my sister? Are you the Weaver Tytonn spoke of?"

The lady nodded. "I am Taj."

Crispin narrowed his gaze. "How can I be certain? I have met both friend and foe on my journey, and it becomes more difficult to know the difference. Tytonn said that you were a great prophetess. That you would be able to know things about me that no one should."

"Indeed. I am not a traditional mental magician; I cannot control people as his grace the king can. But I can see things. Gaze into my eyes..."

The silver reflected in the Weaver's eyes seemed to suddenly sharpen, locking his gaze with hers like the strongest magnet. His heart accelerated, and his head hurt as though someone literally peeled back the layers of his mind to peek inside. He felt an urge to tear away but found he could not as she began to speak:

"I see your love for the Lady Gailea. And a quest through the castle, involving many keys and a lullaby. A small closet near the kitchen, a cave, a passionate kiss. I can see further back as well. Your childhood, your sister, Alistor teaching the two of you horseback riding; Elda is casting lightning bolts at targets as she rides past, laughing as you cheer her on..."

Crispin laughed too as the memory flashed before him.

Then, his laughter became nervous as another memory loomed right after it...

Moragon disciplining Elda for riding one of his favorite steeds. Elda's magic too underdeveloped for her to defend herself. Crispin powerless to help her. Alistor interfering, at the cost of his own punishment—

The Weaver released her hold on Crispin, and with a cry, he staggered back, gasping for breath.

"Those were hard times for you," the Weaver said quietly, "but they are long past. Do you trust me now?"

The Weaver tilted her head and studied him closely. What a strange question to ask him after she'd just probed his mind, leaving it very much raw. However, the calm filling her gaze soothed his weary mind, and he knew that the secrets she'd just shown him, however frightening to face at the time, had proven who she was, just as Tytonn had promised.

"I do," Crispin said, able to stand straight at last. "I trust you, Lady Taj."

"Then, come. To the House of Lance. Your sister will be elated to see you."

CHAPTER 19

FIT FOR A KING

Crispin followed the Weaver to the house, matching her slow strides. Even as they drifted away from the glow of the lake, her robes continued to shimmer, and it seemed that more of her wild black curls had already silvered as well.

Upon reaching the house, the Weaver drew a silver chain from beneath her robes and began sifting through a set of keys. Her hands shook, and Crispin almost asked if she needed help, but she soon selected a key and opened the door.

As they stepped inside, Crispin's breath was stolen away. Though a simple stone structure on the outside, the house was magnificent within. A glistening chandelier hung above the wide, winding stairs; candles glowed within the chandelier, as well as in sconces hung at intervals along the walls, washing everything with a friendly orange glow.

Down a hallway on their left, Crispin could make out another room with a blazing fireplace. There, a girl sat in a large armchair, deftly sewing a piece of white cloth with silver threads. Her golden hair swept over one shoulder, she bent down a little more, concentrating on the tiny needle, thread, and fabric.

Crispin glanced with question at Taj who nodded and smiled. He hurried down the hall, his boots echoing dully across the wooden floor and fine carpets.

As he entered the room, his sister looked up. She gasped, dropped her project to the floor, and sprang up with a grin. Crispin caught her in a tight embrace.

"Dearest sister!" he cried, smiling at her and twirling her about. "How have you been?"

As he pulled back, Elda started to smile, but then she frowned and darted back to the chair. Kneeling down, she flung scraps of cloth aside until she found her slate. She scrawled something across and then held up the slate for him to read: *I'm doing wonderfully. I've learned so much here, and Taj is such a dear. It's so good to see you. I've missed you.* They shared a warm grin. Then, she erased the words and wrote, *I knew we had a guest. The House changes appearance when newcomers arrive. I've never seen it so grand.*

Crispin shook his head. "What do you mean?"

Before, we were living in a humble cottage. But as soon as you approached, the House began to tremble and shift. The rooms grew larger. The furniture, food, everything changed to please the tastes of our approaching guest. You aim high. She gave him a playful smile before adding, *What brings you here? And in the middle of the night? I hope no trouble follows you—though if it does, the House will protect you.*

"It will, indeed," Taj said, sitting in the rocking chair beside Elda. "Please, join us." She waved her hand in the air, and a large armchair akin to Elda's floated over from across the room, lighting on the rug to face the two women.

"Thank you," Crispin said, taking his seat.

"And here. You're certainly hungry and thirsty after such a long journey."

Taj seemed to do nothing but blink, and all of a sudden, a small wooden table and tray appeared before Crispin. Roasted pheasant, a soup that smelled strongly of various herbs, and a wedge of cheese rested on the tray with a cup of water.

Crispin's stomach growled, and he took a sizeable bite of the pheasant and cheese. Closing his eyes, he inhaled deeply, savoring the rich flavors before swallowing. Then, he opened his eyes and looked up at the Weaver. "Thank you. I am forever in your debt."

"Well," Taj said, "perhaps you can repay your debt with a bit of story-telling. Elda asked if any trouble follows you. If so, perhaps we may be able to help?"

Crispin cast a hesitating glance in Elda's direction. Elda smiled and wrote: *Don't worry. The owner of the House is bound to secrecy.*

Crispin began, "I've fled the castle. Escaped. No trouble has followed me as of yet—except just now, I ran into some men who despise me and all our family. I got lost after that, but I followed a silver glow. At first, I thought it might be a will-o-the-wisp leading me to my doom, but then it led here."

Elda glanced warily at Taj, but the older woman kept her gaze and serene smile fixed on Crispin.

"The House knows who needs it most," Taj said. "It must have wanted you to find it. Now, tell us why you fled the castle?"

Crispin hesitated again, but only for a moment. A strange warmth began to fill him, and whether it stemmed from his reunion with his sister, the fireplace, or even a spell of the House itself, he felt his fears and doubts melting away. The truth longed to be released and poured easily from his lips. "The Lady Gailea and I discovered a plot against Queen Marlis. The king wishes Marlis dead so he can marry Gailea instead. I would have brought Gailea with me, but he's imprisoned her at the castle with a magic bracelet. Alistor and I intend to rally an army and march against the castle. If we are successful and Moragon is dethroned, Gailea would be free, as the true queen, to reclaim the throne, if she so desired. If not, at least she would be free to live however she wanted."

Elda wrote across her slate: *Wouldn't she need a husband to take the throne, by Adelaran law?*

Crispin nodded. "Yes, but...we *have* recently declared our affection for one another."

Elda's brows rose.

With a tilt of her head, Taj mused, "So, you would aspire to be king."

Crispin had lifted a spoonful of soup to his lips but now paused. "I suppose I've not thought seriously about being king. I don't know if it would suit me..." He ate the soup, letting its fragrant herbs continue the calming spell already at work inside him.

The Weaver studied him, hands folded, gaze curious. Her eyes narrowed a little as if she literally searched inside his mind. "I think that you could make an excellent leader, yes—as long as you listen to your heart and those with its best interests in mind. You are surrounded by many people of varying opinions. Part of being a leader is knowing which counsel is wise counsel, and which should be discarded.

"But there is something else that, whether king or otherwise, any good leader or protector should have ever at their side. Come. Let us visit the lake."

Taj stood and made her way toward the door. Crispin and Elda followed behind her.

As they stepped outside, the winter air bit sharply, and Crispin drew upon the warmth he'd just stored inside him from the fireplace. Crunching through snow, they sloped down to the lake. Taj waded inside till her knees were submerged. Crispin shivered just thinking about placing his feet inside the thick, cold liquid.

The Weaver's tranquil smile and thoughtful gaze persisted, and she began waving her arms over the lake. She swayed back and forth, combing her fingers through the air, circling her arms and rocking side to side. The liquid silver sprang up in small waves before her. They danced together, the Weaver and the silver. Then, the silver began to take shape mid-air. Something echoed dimly in Crispin's memory, something important he could not quite grasp: where had he seen such magic before?

The Weaver's dance with the silver continued until a long shape floated before her. Crispin glanced at Elda, who stood watching with the same wide-eyed wonder. Then he looked back at the Weaver, whose hand darted out, grabbed the long staff of liquid silver, and drew it to her. The silver seemed to flow in constant currents while never dripping. She ran her fingers along the silver, making little waves skip across its surface. Gradually, the waves slowed, and the silver solidified, taking on a more defined shape.

At last, the Weaver held up a long silver sword in her hand. Her fingers danced along its sharp edges a few moments more, and then she released it and let it hover before her. She swayed her hand, and it turned on its side. She placed both hands underneath so that the flat of the blade rested in her palms.

Then, she turned toward Crispin, her smile widening as she declared, "A true leader should enter no battle without a strong and faithful sword at his side. I give you the sword Anwar, born of the moon magic bound within liquid silver. She will guard against both dark magic and minds who would desire to control and consume. Long and well may she serve you."

Crispin hesitated. Then, with a nudge from Elda, he stepped forward, let Taj rest the sword in his hands, and stared in wonder. It felt amazingly light as a feather, but as he clutched its hilt and swung several strokes, it sang through the air, declaring its deadly sharp touch.

"She's wonderful," Crispin breathed. "I understand now why your gifts are so highly regarded. I can never thank you enough. This will be a great help to me. Already, I feel stronger."

Taj nodded. "The sword will strengthen you, yes. Though do not rely entirely upon its strength. Any sword—even a magic sword—is only as strong as its master."

Crispin nodded slowly. Something continued to tug at his mind, some hidden memory or meaning. He ran his hands along the silver blade, smooth as glass. He glanced at the lake. Then, he knelt beside it and rested the sword at his side.

Running the liquid silver through his hands once more, he said, "Liquid silver has its own magic; that's why people envy your creations so. The sword itself... can its power be undone? Does liquid silver have any weaknesses?"

He glanced up at the Weaver. She said nothing for a while. Perhaps his question had offended her. After all, she'd been gracious enough to grant him such a powerful gift; perhaps she took his curiosities as complaints.

But then a calm understanding filled her face, and she said, "Liquid silver *is* one of the strongest magical substances. But it has three known weaknesses, three enemies, if you will, that are capable of undoing its power. First, there is liquid silver itself; if challenged with a purer strain, one can outdo the other. Then, there is liquid sun, another mysterious substance formed of fire, pure light, and, incidentally, liquid silver. And lastly, the strongest types of mental magic have been known to break it, to bend and mold its will—but only the very strongest. Your sword can also fight against mind control; you might say that liquid silver and mental magic are mortal enemies."

Crispin cupped a small bit of the liquid inside his hand. Concentrating hard, he muttered the incantations for both fire and light magic, alternating the spells over and over again. Tiny bits of flame began to dance along his hand, interwoven with thin pillars of light. The flames glistened on the liquid silver, making it shimmer like gold. The silver warmed in his hand, and he continued to utter the spells until his head spun. Once his strength was spent, he quieted and then stared in awe. Strands of a warm gold liquid mixed with the liquid silver in his palm. The two colors swirled, and gradually, the gold canceled out the silver.

Elda gasped behind him, and the Weaver breathed, "Astonishing. Elda told me of your skills. But she did not praise you enough in their extent."

Crispin looked at his sister, whose face shone with awe. "Our uncle has taught me much in the past couple of months. I learned with Gailea that Chevalier had been suppressing my powers all this time, on Moragon's behalf."

"And now they are catching up with tremendous speed," the Weaver declared.

Still looking at Elda, Crispin nodded and said, "Yes. Although I've still got a long way to go in terms of controlling them. I'm surprised I was able to transform a substance as powerful as liquid silver just now."

"It's in your blood," Taj said. "If the king sought to

suppress your powers because he viewed you as a threat, in that much he was wise..."

Crispin's mind reeled as he felt the warm liquid cupped in his palm and tried to fathom his powers' true potential.

"Now," the Weaver continued, "I have a collection of old hilts and belts up in my attic; they may be hard to find, seeing as how your coming has rearranged my entire House, but we can search for all that tomorrow. In the meantime, why don't you spend a moment alone with the sword, get to know its feel? I must speak with Elda privately."

"Yes, my lady."

Taj motioned at Elda, who smiled at Crispin before following the Weaver back toward the House.

Crispin watched them slip inside and then turned his attention back to the sword. As he ran his fingertips along its side, the silver rippled. Remembering the strange bits of gold he'd been able to create, he touched the blade, focusing and pouring his magic inside. His hand quickly warmed, emitting both fire and light. The fire and light danced along the blade, and the sword illuminated with a bright golden glow.

The next moment, the sword weighed heavy as lead in his hands, and he staggered. He fought to maintain the connection between his magic and the blade, but his hand was repelled, pushed away as if by a magnet. His hand burned as if the sword pushed his magic back inside him, and with a cry, he dropped it. Trembling, he clutched at his burned hand, trying to ignore the searing pain, but it seemed to intensify until at last, he plunged his hand inside the silver lake. The liquid closed over his hand, soothing it like healing oil, and when he withdrew, the burn had vanished.

Taking up his sword, he marveled at how light it felt

once more. No traces of his attempted gold transformation lingered on its edges.

Exhaustion pressed on his shoulders, and he heaved a great sigh. It had been such a long day, culminating in a long, dramatic end. He turned and walked back to the House.

The door was unlocked, and he slipped inside. He glanced toward the sitting room. Taj sat in the giant armchair before the fire. Elda knelt before her, head bowed as though praying. The Weaver's hands rested atop her head as if imparting some blessing or spell. Both ladies wore faces of both deep concentration and strange serenity.

Creeping across to the staircase, Crispin set down his sword, sat on the bottom step, and waited. After a few minutes, Elda walked down the hallway and wrote with a smile, *You must be tired. I can show you your room for the night.*

Crispin smiled. "Thank you."

He stood, grabbed his sword, and followed Elda up the great, winding staircase. She led him past many rooms and finally to a spacious one of his own.

Crispin set a great fire ablaze in the hearth and then turned to Elda. "What was the Lady Taj doing just now?"

Elda scrawled across her slate: *Taj has a strong affinity for various types of mental magic. I can share my thoughts with her, and she can share hers with me, without the need for written word.* She waved her hand over the slate; the words vanished, and with a smirk, she added, *It's actually tedious now, having to make special accommodations for you.*

Crispin laughed softly. "You know, I've learned a few new tricks myself, in your absence."

Elda tilted her head in a curious prompt.

Crispin lifted his arms and began waving toward the fire in the hearth, making his fingers dance through the

289

air as if playing an invisible harp. As his fingers began to glow, he glanced at his sister who stared with full captivation.

Slowly, Crispin summoned some of the fire from the hearth, making it coil up into the air like streamers. He wove his hands back and forth, commanding the strands of fire like a puppeteer, making them take shape into two distinct human figures.

Elda drew a long breath. The fire lit up her face, alive with a child-like bewilderment as she watched the portrait of their mother and father hovering in the flames.

Crispin hugged his sister close. Elda laid her head on his shoulder and released a long sigh. Their parents' faces continued to hover before them, smiling from the flames.

After a few moments, Crispin pulled gently back, looked at her, and asked, "Do you think they were really that happy? Or do you think I just remember them that way?"

Elda lazily wrote across her slate, *I do think they were that happy, yes. They loved each other—a rare gift for nobility.*

"Do you think Gailea and I can be that happy?" Crispin asked.

Elda nodded, her face fully hopeful.

"Then I will cling to that hope," he whispered. He continued to watch the flames, imagining that the faces were his and Gailea's, smiling and rejoicing together, all their troubles past.

Suddenly, Crispin remembered the note in his pocket and handed it to Elda. "Tytonn sends his affection."

Elda held it to her heart with a smile. She bid him goodnight. With a nod of Crispin's head, the pictures extinguished, and the hovering flames rejoined those in the fireplace.

Kicking off his boots, Crispin climbed into the large, cozy bed and eased back with a sigh.

Exhausted as he was, sleep would not come. In the surrounding quiet, his mind accelerated. He was inside a magic house. He'd been reunited with his sister at last. He'd been granted a most powerful gift by the Weaver. Within days, his uncle would arrive, and together they would begin amassing an army to remove Moragon and save Gailea...

Gailea. She held his mind most captive, utterly forbidding sleep.

Crispin sat up. His gaze fell on the dresser beside him. A small, reddish box with ornate flower carvings glinted in the firelight. He leaned over and picked it up. Opening it, he jumped as a melody streamed from within, soft and fluttery like a flute. He grinned. Gailea would love such a marvel.

One day soon, the war Alistor promised was coming would be completed. Then, Crispin would bring Gailea to the House himself to meet the Weaver and reunite with the sister she had helped rescue. He would surprise her with this music box, and they would be one, happily ever after together, forever.

CHAPTER 20

PLAYING THE SCALES

❋

Gailea replayed the ascending scale on her flute—C, D, E, F, G, A, B, C, repeat—glancing in turn at the spare parchment pages she'd set on the floor. One by one, each new page she focused on floated up to the ceiling to join the several others already hovering there.

Early morning was the most ideal time for Gailea to practice her magic, while the queen still slept and had no need of her services. There was no sense in directly hiding her music anymore, now that the king knew about both it and her lineage. However, she was yet cautious about practicing and aimed to do so in solitude; no need for his majesty to know everything she had mastered. One of the songs she practiced most often was her song-shield; she could now form a shield that she thought was strong enough to withstand mild mental probing for a couple of minutes on her own.

A loud knock made her jump, and a voice announced from beyond the door, "Lady Gailea, King Moragon requests an audience with you."

Gailea ceased playing, allowing the pages to flutter to the floor like the snow yet falling outside. Gathering them up, she stacked them on her desk then hurried to the mirror to straighten a few stray wisps of hair and smooth out her dress. While she didn't aim to attract the king's attention, she also didn't wish anything to be out of place—especially her thoughts, and she began practicing the song-shield inside her mind.

Outside Gailea's room, a guard waited. Gailea followed him. They walked briskly through the castle, and she gathered her thoughts for the day. Today's focus would be on gaining the king's trust or at least getting him to loathe her a little less. If she had lost Lord Ragnar's favor after their encounter a few nights ago, she would need the king as an ally, however temporary and precarious a balancing act that might be to play.

As the guard led Gailea inside the king's study, its rich golds, purples, and reds seemed to close in on her, choking her with their heavy vibrant hues. Her last and only experience with this room flashed through her mind, and she shivered to remember feeling so trapped by the king's mental strength. The guard departed, and Gailea stood with hands folded, hoping her face did not display her quickly escalating anxiety.

The king stood beside a large table. A map was sprawled open, with several stone figures scattered across. Gailea glanced at the map and saw several markers on the forests that sprawled beyond the king's woods. Did the king summon her because he thought she had some knowledge of Crispin's whereabouts?

Gailea remained frozen in place. She breathed deep, silently reciting lists of herbs to calm her nerves and focus her thoughts. Then, she sang the song-shield in her head, instantly feeling some relief as its soothing barriers wrapped around her thoughts.

At last, Moragon looked up with a smile and said, "Ah, Lady Gailea. Forgive me; I did not hear you enter. Even your thoughts were quiet as a shadow..."

Did that mean they'd grown louder just now? Gailea continued to chant her silent song-shield, forcing the barriers to remain tight in place. She tried looking as serene as possible, wishing to display no fear.

The door opened again, and Chevalier breezed inside, smoothing his golden satin robes. Upon catching Gailea's gaze, he paused, almost stumbling—strange, for his usually fluid, graceful mannerisms. He stared at her with obvious surprise. Then, he lifted his chin, and his emotions faded once more behind his mask of cool composure.

"Master Chevalier," Moragon greeted. "Very good. I now have my two favorite magicians together to consult with—that is, if the Lady Gailea is willing now to divulge the secrets of her magic?"

Gailea swallowed. She must not hesitate too long; that would look disrespectful, suspicious. "Yes, your majesty. I am honored to use my magic to help you in any way."

Moragon nodded and paced around the table, walking toward her and Chevalier. "Good. As I'm certain you're aware, my nephew, Crispin, has abandoned Astyrian, escaping by some sorcery that yet eludes both myself and Chevalier here..." His gaze drifted to the sorcerer, who only nodded curtly, hands folded across his robes. "Crispin's magic, while erratic, has been growing in strength, according to Lord Ragnar. The boy is to be seen as a threat. There are rumors now of his wishing to build an army and usurp me. While the idea is absurd, people *have* been known to follow less likely candidates if those candidates possess the right magic and means of persuasion. I won't take any risks, and besides, Crispin's actions are treasonous. At the least, he must be punished, made an example to others who would dare oppose their king."

He looked pointedly at Gailea. Quietly, she asked, "And how would you wish for me to help you, your majesty?"

"It is my wish, Lady Gailea, that you could teach me musical magic, so I could add it to my arsenal of mental weaponry. However, as I have tried to learn many times in the past and such seems unlikely, I would be satisfied instead with helping you plan and create special musical defenses. Barriers, if you will, to surround the castle, that could only be breached by further musical magic. Since such magic is rare, I believe the security of the castle would increase tenfold."

"Is that really necessary, sire?" Gailea said, keeping her tone light and pleasant. The king knew she wasn't stupid, but she could feign a bit of ignorance in hopes to change his mind or, at least, to better understand his motives. "The silver barriers already surrounding the castle—are they not impenetrable except by the absolute strongest magic?"

"So, I'd thought," Moragon said. "However, unless someone granted Crispin access beyond the barriers without my permission—which is yet being investigated—there must be some flaw in the barriers, some weakness. For he did not use one of the portals; if he had, I would've been able to trace which one and where it led. How the boy could have discovered a different means of escape on his own is beyond me..." Moragon stared hard at Chevalier who kept his gaze steady and unwavering. "...but since he got out, he may be able to get back in—and with any size of an army."

"I understand," Gailea said. "And so you'd have me erect a barrier similar to Master Chevalier's silver one, only with music?"

"Can you?" Moragon asked though the sudden shift in his voice and the sharpness of his gaze declared it was less question and more command.

"It may take a great deal of time and research," Gailea said. "But I think that, yes, it would be possible—"

Trumpets blared outside the castle. The doors to the king's study burst open, and a guard flung himself inside, panting hard, "Lord Ragnar...has just been seen... beyond the borders...We've whole scores of men looking for him—"

"What? He's fled?" Moragon demanded; anger flared in his dark eyes, and his face flushed a bright crimson. "Is that what you're telling me?"

"Yes, your—*ungh*!"

With a flick of Moragon's wrist, the soldier catapulted back through the air and landed against the corridor's far wall with a loud crack; blood sprayed on the gray stone, and his body slouched to the floor, motionless.

The next moment, the doors slammed shut. Moragon banged a fist on the table, and the stone figures scattered across the map. Then he whirled, glaring viciously at Chevalier and snarling, "Damn you! This is *your* doing. You assured me that if anyone else tried to cross the borders, the new alarms would stop them."

"The alarms *did* sound, your grace," Chevalier said, his voice soothing, but Moragon's face twisted with rage.

"Do not mock me," he seethed.

"I'm not, your grace," Chevalier said. "I only meant that Lord Ragnar's escape was not due to my failure to obey your commands. I tried all I could. I created the alarms at your behest—"

"*Are you suddenly an idiot, Chevalier?*" Moragon thundered.

Gailea jumped and thought that Chevalier flinched, however slightly. His graceful figure tensed, drawing as rigid as a mannequin.

"The two greatest threats to my throne have escaped, both within the span of a fortnight! It doesn't matter if the alarms sounded—they failed their purpose of deterrence, as did your accursed barrier!"

Chevalier gasped, sputtering, and Gailea watched as the gold necklace around the sorcerer's neck seemed to tighten, squeezing till his skin reddened. She felt sickened; the collar was a horrible idea when Crispin had mentioned it, but seeing it utilized in person was like watching a helpless animal whipped for some crime it was incapable of committing.

At last, the necklace loosened again, and Chevalier inhaled deeply, coughing and rubbing at his neck. A few moments later, he redrew his elegant composure, but Gailea could sense his embarrassment at having his dignity challenged in the presence of another. He made no further argument for himself, nor did he look at the king.

As Moragon turned to Gailea, firelight shimmered on his red and gold robes, making him look like a wild beast cloaked in the bloodshed of a fresh kill. Gailea fought with every ounce of her will to shield her mind; her thoughts kept wanting to fly to the hidden cave that Crispin—and likely Alistor—had used to escape.

"If I may," Chevalier said quietly, "I do think I know where they are headed. One of my spies intercepted a message from your nephew to Lord Alistor. It seems they are rallying at the House of the Weaver, where the Lady Elda has taken refuge. Should the Weaver grant all of them protection, no magic will be able to breach her safe holds—not even yours, your grace."

Moragon took a deep breath and released it slowly. He glanced at the collection of swords hanging on one wall, and Gailea shuddered. She would hate to see Chevalier's blood staining this room, as did the guard's in the hallway.

Gailea's mind spun. Crispin had been gone nearly two weeks now; surely, he was already secure within the Weaver's House. Lord Ragnar was powerful and clever enough to fend for himself and fight his way there. If she offered the king some aid in this dire moment, it would likely not bring them any harm while elevating his trust in her and granting both her and Chevalier a few more days to breathe a little easier.

"I might be able to help," Gailea said. "They can't stay at the House forever if they desire to challenge you for the throne. They'll come out eventually. I may be able to develop a song that could track their location..."

The king stared at her, his gaze demanding and unforgiving.

Gailea added, "It would likely take a few days' research and practice. But I think it could work."

Moragon studied her a long while more. Gailea studied him back, again chanting mindless lists both to calm her nerves and to maintain a complacent expression. Any hint of fear or doubt could be taken as her lying or omitting truths.

"Chevalier," the king said, "please excuse yourself. Command my guard to send out two extra search parties as you go".

Chevalier gave Gailea what seemed a harsh glare for one who'd just helped him. Perhaps his pride was wounded at being given such menial commands. He let his gaze linger on her a moment more before he turned and swept silently from the room.

A still hush doused the room. Gailea waited. Moragon studied her, for once looking sincerely intrigued.

"So, you would help me find them."

Gailea nodded. "Yes, your grace."

"Why?" he asked bluntly. "We are not friends, you and I. In fact, at our cores, we are rivals for the throne."

"I have no power, beyond my music," Gailea said. "That is not enough to rival you and Chevalier and all your armies. Alistor and Crispin have freedom, and thus the chance to obtain great power. It is *they* I think you perceive as the greater threat right now."

A smirk played on Moragon's lips. "And if they wage war with me and win, what then? You'd still have them to contend with—you cannot be so big a fool as to think they'd grant you freedom any more readily than I would."

"No. But the opposite could very well happen; *you* could triumph over *them*. Best to let the men fight things out and see how they go. After all, I consider *none* of you true friends."

"But you *could*," Moragon said, walking toward her slowly and with a strange grace, as though he almost danced. He towered right above her and placed his hands on her shoulders. Her breath grew shallow as she stared up at him; she could feel strength pulsing through his hands, and a greater power reflected in his dark eyes. With a single thought, he could likely break her bones and rip out her heart.

"We *could* be friends," he whispered; his breath brushed her cheeks, warm and surprisingly pleasant, like mint. "I think you know this. You are intelligent to play the odds of us annihilating one another, but I think we both know how that will likely play out. As long as you are sincere in your ambition to serve me, I think you know how high and how quickly you can rise. I ask you again: can you create this musical tracking device you speak of?"

"Yes," Gailea whispered. She swallowed and said a little louder, "Yes. I believe I can. If you have something that belongs to Lord Ragnar, I could create a song meant to track just him. From there, we may be able to invent some kind of vessel that can house the song. If we can train your men to use it, it will lead them to their target..."

Or away from it, if I so choose...

The thought darted through her mind so openly, but she quickly concealed it, hoping he hadn't seen. He studied her with interest. A cool smile played upon his lips.

Releasing her, he said, "Go then. Use the libraries and whatever other resources you need. If my magic can aid you in any way, do not hesitate to come to me. I will give you two days to learn what you can, and then we will meet again..."

Gailea hesitated. The king wandered back over to the table and set the stone figures back in place, scrutinizing them. When he said nothing more, Gailea curtsied and slipped from the room, hurrying toward the library.

She already knew many of the theories behind the spells she'd proposed. The kind of vessel she mentioned was akin to the pendant Lady Aline had given her. It would likely not take that many days at all for her to prepare such magic. The real challenge would be in buying Crispin extra time by making the king believe that it would.

***

Crispin sat outside the House of Lance, atop a small hill sloping down to the lake. A cold breeze stirred in the early morning, making choppy little waves dance across its surface. The silver glinted like the edges of many swords. Crispin touched Anwar's hilt at his side.

A hand rested on either of his shoulders, and Crispin

sighed, easing into his sister's touch as she began to massage.

After a time, she sat beside him and wrote: *You're very tense. Did you not sleep well?*

Taking her hand, he said, "Inside the House, I forget every fear and doubt. But when I come outside, all my fears and doubts return to crush me with strength tenfold."

Then why do you come out here?

"To remember. To focus on why I am here. I *need* to be afraid. I need to think of her, to try and think of how I will help her..."

Our uncle will be here soon. The Weaver told me she saw him approaching.

Someone stepped through the trees several yards off, and Crispin's mouth parted in a gasp. He jumped to his feet, rushing across the bare ground. The wind tore its chilled claws into his flesh, but as his uncle grinned and caught him in an embrace, a steady blaze beneath Crispin's skin warmed him at once.

Alistor laughed and pushed Crispin playfully away. "Good lord, nephew. You're cold as death. If we didn't share the same features, I'd swear you were an Icean instead of a Fyre."

Crispin laughed and spread his fire through his body more fervently. "Sorry, Uncle. Sometimes I forget what you've taught me, in my passion and excitement."

Alistor grinned. "That is a human enough response—though the time when keeping one's guard up at all times fast approaches. But before we discuss such heavy matters, let me gain some refreshment and share the work I've been about."

Crispin led Alistor toward the House. "What *have* you been about? It took you longer to get here than I'd thought. The Lady Gailea—is she well?"

Alistor nodded calmly. "She is as safe and well as anyone can be under the king's watchful eye—safer likely, considering she is the newest object of his intrigue…"

Jealousy flared inside Crispin, but he only said, "At least she is safe."

"Yes. I told you that worrying about her need not be our first concern. Meanwhile, I've been able to rally a few allies in my short travels. We've set up a camp, not too far from here. From there, we'll start traveling to various cities, gathering more support. Many of those opposing the king keep themselves well-hidden, but if we can show them our determination and the might of our Fyre strength, we may be able to draw them out and to our side."

As they reached Elda, Alistor took her hands and kissed her cheeks. "Dearest niece, it is so good to see you safe as well and, from what I've heard, thriving under the Weaver's tutorage."

Elda smiled warmly and nodded.

Crispin, Elda, and Alistor had nearly reached the House when the door opened and Taj stepped outside. Crispin stopped short, caught off-guard by both her fierce gaze and her appearance; she seemed a little more stooped than the day before, and her wild raven curls had almost entirely silvered.

But her more aged appearance did not temper the sharp glare she turned to Alistor. "He will not enter here. No one makes plans of war within the House, for good or for ill."

"My good lady," Alistor said. "We don't mean to conduct any of our business here. I only wish to step inside for a moment's rest. I've come a long way—"

"There is no rest within your heart," the Weaver said. Her dark brown eyes had silvered as well, and they glinted like daggers. "Crispin, I believe your time at the

303

House has come to an end for now. If you need rest again, do not hesitate to return—but alone." Her sharp gaze darted back to Alistor.

Crispin stared at the Weaver, stunned. He respected her enough not to be angry at her words, but he didn't know how to respond. He glanced at Alistor who seemed to stare at the Weaver with just as hard a level of concentration as she stared at him.

Taj suddenly released a sharp exhale and staggered back against the door. Elda rushed to stand beside her, supporting her with one arm around her shoulder, before turning a solemn gaze to Crispin.

"Good-bye then, sister," Crispin said. "I will be safe. May you be also. When I see Tytonn again, I'll let him know that you are well."

Elda nodded with a small smile. Then, she helped the Weaver inside the House and shut the door behind them.

Crispin let his gaze linger upon the House, which had seemed so friendly mere moments ago but now stood as a cold sentinel between him and his sister and any last hope for comfort. Then, he and Alistor turned and walked away.

Only once under the cover of the woods did Alistor release a long breath. "Less than a cheery welcome, eh? But it's no matter. I'm glad Elda has such a safe haven protected by such strong magic. Besides, as I said, we are not entirely unlucky and friendless."

"Yes, tell me everything," Crispin said. "How did you manage to flee the castle?"

"The same as you—through the passage in the caves. Before that, I overheard talk between Chevalier and my brother. The king seems yet entirely ignorant of the fact that such a simple gap exists in what would be an otherwise perfect defense system."

Crispin shook his head. "That seems so odd to me. If Chevalier is so powerful and the barriers are so secure otherwise, how could they have such a blatant way of escape?"

"How indeed?" Alistor said, arching a brow at Crispin.

"You think Chevalier might have designed things that way purposely," Crispin said.

"Perhaps," Alistor said. "I do not think he would ever choose to run away himself unless he felt there was truly no other choice; doing so could sentence his family to instant death."

"His family?" Crispin gasped.

"His wife and child. Magic isn't the only collar his majesty uses to hold him in check, nor the greatest."

Crispin couldn't decide whether he felt more surprise at the idea of someone like Chevalier having a family, more shame as he realized how Gailea would disapprove of such a thought, or more yearning as he thought of her.

"Perhaps," Alistor added, "Chevalier means to use the cave as a way for Moragon's enemies to get inside someday. Whatever his reasons, I think he knows more than he lets on to the king..."

Crispin glanced back toward the House, but the woods had swallowed it. He felt a sudden pang of longing as he realized that his sister was so far behind already and that, sooner than seeing her again, they'd likely be rushing back toward the castle, toward their enemies—and toward Gailea too, which granted some hope.

"So, our plans, for now, are simply to gather support and then, when we're ready, to march against the castle?"

"Well," Alistor said, "I will not divulge *all* the details until we're back in the confines of our camp. One of the allies I secured is a man named Dulin. He's skilled in various charms, and he's placed silencing charms around our camp so that prying ears may not listen. But I *will* say this for now. There *are* those willing to back a movement against his grace. We just have to know how to sway them to our side."

"And *do* we know how? Do we possess that power?"

Alistor grinned at Crispin. "My dear boy, I am Lord Alistor Ragnar, known by some as 'the snake' for a reason. And you are my nephew. We could turn half the kingdom to our favor if we so desired—and if you will but follow my lead."

A new anxiousness gripped Crispin. They were preparing for a true war. This was no mere coming-of-age hunt. Human lives would be sacrificed. He must be fully prepared, or those lives would be lost in vain. So many would depend upon him and his uncle, not just Gailea—though she mattered most of all.

Crispin's head swam with the immensity of all to be done, but he lifted his chin, trying to feel his uncle's confidence as he said, "Then lead on, uncle. Lead, and I will follow you to whatever end."

"There is only one end, dear nephew," Alistor said, picking up his pace. "To victory."

CHAPTER 21

A SORCERER'S SECRETS

❋

Gailea walked alongside the king, with Chevalier shadowing them close behind.

A few days had passed since her last meeting with Moragon. This morning he had pressed her, and she had calmly assured him that the tracking song would be developed soon. In the meantime, she offered to teach him anything he wished to know about musical magic. Holding his interest and keeping his trust was imperative, and she had determined that as long as she didn't reveal her strongest abilities, she should be safe—as would be the queen.

Marlis had finally started to heal. A soft pink now colored her cheeks. Her body had grown a little fuller since the kitchen had stopped serving her the poison, and she'd even returned to some of her favorite hobbies. In fact, she intended to go riding that afternoon.

Gailea's best hope was to keep the king distracted so that Marlis could continue to improve until Crispin and

Alistor could liberate her—and all of them—from Moragon's schemes. One of the best distractions seemed to be the lessons Moragon had started arranging between Gailea, Chevalier, and himself.

Today, they met inside the great hall. Moragon led them around the room, motioning to each of the musical instruments hovering inside their glass cases and letting his fingers trail along the glass with all the tenderness of a lover's caress—and, Gailea trusted, with more affection than he'd likely ever shown his wife.

"I've learned to play each of these, over the years," Moragon said, "hoping I could unlock their power. But, alas, it seems that for all my mental prowess, an affinity for music has entirely eluded me." He smiled wryly at her.

"Musical magic is rare, your grace," she said, "and not easily copied with potions and powders, as are other types of magic."

"Indeed, we discovered that quickly enough. Chevalier tried all manner of enchantments to allow me to bend music to my will, but to no avail. I can control anything else he creates..." His fingers danced along the glass encasing a flute, and the glass vanished. "...but not music."

"Did Chevalier create them?" Gailea asked. "The instruments?"

Moragon shook his head. "No. My love for music led me to collect them from various lands. This one here..." he tenderly touched the flute, "...was the first in my collection. In fact, it was a flute that led me to my passion for music altogether. I was a young lad, about ten or so. My mental powers are natural-born, so even then, I was keen on honing them. I practiced on mice and other small animals, bending their wills to mine...

"One day, I was out with my father in the market, and

we came across a large crowd gathered around the most spell-binding music. I was a small thing and squeezed easily to the front of the crowds. In their midst, a small band of traveling musicians played. But I knew instantly that it was the flutist who held everyone so captivated; my mental magic was refined enough even then to detect this. I myself felt enraptured by the music, calmed, exhilarated—whatever emotions the flute commanded, I felt them. I was so used to controlling others with my mind, and being influenced thus was a strange sensation for me. But instead of feeling frightened at being manipulated by music, I felt excited. I wanted to harness that power. I wanted to take something so beautiful and create something powerful from it like that flutist did…"

Moragon paused. His gaze and mind looked far away, as though he'd drifted from the great hall to that time long past and could literally see it replaying before his very eyes. Perhaps he could. At any rate, Gailea couldn't help admiring his passion. What a pity that, instead of maintaining his boyish wonder, he'd felt a need to expand his fascination and wonderment into a ruthless lust for power and control.

"I found this flute here," Moragon said, at last, glancing at the flute and seeming to return to the present, "on one of several journeys to Iceania. Like most of the instruments you see here, it's made of Icean crystal, a nearly unbreakable substance—similar in strength to the glass housing them. Now, the glass cases—those Chevalier *did* create, along with my assistance. The glass responds only to my mental command."

"That's brilliant," Gailea said, genuinely impressed. "To be able to create a substance that responds to such a specific imprint."

"Chevalier is indeed a man of many hidden talents." Moragon grinned proudly at Chevalier, though

Gailea felt the king's pride was more for himself than for his servant.

He returned his trained smile to Gailea and continued, "I actually brought you here today to see if *you* might be able to command the instruments *for* me. I have heard that various musical instruments, if mastered by the right magician, can reveal their individual powers."

"Indeed. Any musical instrument has the ability to do all types of spells, but I've also read that they can each have their own strengths. Stringed instruments have been said to hold powers of seduction, ensnaring the mind and bending it to the player's will. Woodwinds..." she nodded toward the flute, "...have the prowess to create physical sensation."

"Like pain?"

"Yes—or pleasure. Desire. Excitement."

Moragon cocked his head, clearly intrigued.

"Show me. Replicate the sensations that first drew me to the flute as a boy."

"I will try, your grace."

Gailea stepped forward, and Moragon moved back to give her space. She took the flute in her hands. Then, closing her eyes, she concentrated and began to play.

The lovely, mournful song filled her, and a soothing warmth coursed through her body.

A hand on her shoulder made her jump, cease her song, and look up.

The strangely subdued look in the king's eyes had made some of his harshness recede.

"Well played," he said quietly.

"It's an old lullaby. Meant to ease troubled minds. It's a favorite of the queen's."

Moragon nodded. "And now of mine. Isn't she a marvel, Chevalier?"

Gailea expected Chevalier to look equally serene, but

his face seemed to have stretched into a tighter frown, and his stare remained distant and brooding, like an approaching storm.

"Chevalier?" Moragon demanded.

"Your grace," Chevalier muttered.

Moragon took a deep breath and exhaled loudly, almost growling; whatever momentary peace Gailea's song had worked within him now vanished. Taking the flute from her hands, he set it back in place where it hovered mid-air, and its glass case instantly reappeared.

"That is all for today, Lady Gailea. We will continue our lessons tomorrow. I must have a word alone with Chevalier, and then I've my usual duties to attend."

"Your grace," Gailea said, curtsying. She curtsied toward Chevalier who ignored her, then exited the room.

As she slipped into the corridor beyond the great hall, her name from Moragon's lips caught her attention. She silently sang her lullaby in her mind till the two guards flanking the door slouched against the wall, breathing deeply. Then, crouching, she peered through the cracked door and sang the charm for altering volume until the voices inside the room magnified just loud enough for her to catch their words:

"...you seem less than enthusiastic today, Chevalier. Is there some distraction that hinders your involvement in our lessons?"

"No, your grace. Forgive me; I am merely tired. I was up late last night, working on our special project."

Moragon started pacing the hall, walking in and out of Gailea's line of sight. "Any word about my dear brother and his nephew?"

Chevalier shook his head. "No, your grace. Rumors say they were last seen leaving the home of the Weaver, though to where, I'm uncertain."

"And last *I* heard, they were still bent on rallying an

army to march against me."

A harsh silence descended.

Chevalier stood still as a statue. "They have gathered a few allies to their side, yes. But most of our people are against him..."

"Even still, I know my brother's powers of charm and persuasion. He can make any morsel look tempting to the right fools—even the hope of standing behind a young fool like Crispin, who has no understanding of warcraft or any kind of leadership."

"Do not trouble yourself, your grace. Even if they *do* manage to amass an army and dare march against Astyrian, they would first have to break through the barrier."

Moragon had wandered over to a large, silver harp. He touched its glass case, which vanished, and traced his fingers over the harp's smooth curves. "They have seen the Weaver. They have the means, if only they find the wisdom to seize them. The Weaver is an old fool, but a powerful one."

"The Weaver is dead, your grace."

Moragon glanced up, letting the slightest intrigue shine in his dark eyes. "When?"

"Just days past. Shortly after Alistor and Crispin were seen departing the House."

Moragon smirked and returned his focus to the harp. "My nephew truly is a bad omen for all he meets..."

"Developments on the Dusk are going well," Chevalier continued. "Even if they are able to breach the barrier, no army will be able to withstand the magic I can provide, especially if my experiments keep proving so valuable."

"You'd best hope so," Moragon muttered, letting his fingertips skip across the strings which trembled with a faint, descending melody. "A second failure on your part will not be tolerated. The queen has outlived her usefulness—for what little it was ever worth. It's high time I wear mourning again. But only briefly, as a new bride will cheer me—as it will also cheer the people of Adelar. They're all soft-hearted fools. They'll adore her as much as they do my current bride. Far more, I should say, wouldn't you?"

Gailea's heart seemed to stop inside her; she knew the king spoke of her. Slowing her breath and freezing perfectly still, she watched on as Chevalier's eyes narrowed with noticeable irritation.

"What's the matter, my friend?" Moragon scoffed. "Surely, an all-powerful sorcerer like yourself is not intimidated by a girl who possesses but a single magical strength?" He stroked the harp's strings, letting its sweet, out-of-place harmony echo throughout the vast hall.

"Your grace," Chevalier said, his voice tight. "My concern is not for myself, but for you. I believe the girl's powers to be far greater than she's letting on—maybe even greater than *she* realizes. She's using your fascination merely to increase her status—"

"Are you suggesting that I am not intelligent enough to decipher allies from foes?" Moragon ran his fingers across the strings again, and they twanged sharply. "For most kings, your counsel might be wise. However, considering my own special abilities..."

Moragon's hand darted out, and he curled his fingers tightly. Chevalier collapsed to his knees, and Gailea covered her mouth to suppress a gasp. As Moragon twisted his hand, Chevalier flinched and grabbed at his skull. He knotted his fingers in his long hair and pulled, shaking his head.

"No, your grace—I beg you—"

"You have ever only told me 'no' once, Chevalier. Need I remind you not to do so again?"

Moragon twisted his hand the opposite direction, and Chevalier screamed, "Don't touch them—leave them alone! They have never once done you wrong!" He shook violently and then fell forward on his face, clawing at the floor.

Gailea trembled, sickened as Chevalier wailed and pleaded. Seeing such a powerful and refined man reduced to a beastly figure begging its master to spare him struck a new terror inside her. That could easily be her if she disobeyed his majesty.

Moragon let his hand fall limp and, in a few quick strides, stood over Chevalier who lay motionless, save for his staggered breathing. The sorcerer reached out, clutching at the fringe of Moragon's robes, but the king jerked them aside and hissed, "For all your other gifts, musical magic was not bestowed upon you. But *she* has it. I want it, and you know I will claim it, with or without your help. Do not aim too high, Chevalier; you'd still make good kindling for a lovely fire, just like the rest of your fellow abominations—you *and* your family. Do I need to show you again what my plans for them are, or do we understand one another?"

"No, your grace," Chevalier rasped, forcing himself onto his knees. Head bowed, he muttered, "We understand each other perfectly. Forgive my insubordination."

Moragon nodded curtly. "See it does not happen again."

He breezed past Chevalier and headed for the door that was on the opposite end of the room. Gailea turned to leave, eager to hurry as far from the hall as possible—

Someone grabbed her by the collar and yanked her back. As she muttered a song beneath her breath, the someone banged against the wall with a groan. She started to scramble down the hall when her body froze, abruptly immobile.

She was spun about, like a puppet on strings, to face Chevalier. He lowered his hand, releasing her, and she collapsed to her knees, gasping for breath. Then, staggering to her feet, she bowed her head and muttered, "Master...Master Chevalier..."

"None of your idle courtesies," Chevalier snarled. "How much did you hear? How much did you *see*?" He drew himself up proudly; with his rumpled robes and hair, he looked elegant but insane as he glared at her. "If you dare ever relate a single word of what you just witnessed, I swear I will find your lover and destroy him."

Pain pierced Gailea at the mention of Crispin, but she merely said, "I would tell no soul—for both our sakes. I don't agree with any of the king's cruelties and wouldn't wish to give him more cause."

Chevalier watched her as if scrutinizing her sincerity. "We are not so very different, you and me. If we were not both fighting against one another for our lives, we might even be companions of sorts."

"I don't want to fight you," Gailea said quietly. "I just want to live."

"But your living requires us to be enemies—don't you see that? As soon as one of us becomes more useful than the other, the weaker is in danger. We both possess something the king desperately wants, which makes us both prizes to win and banes to resent. For the king resents everything he cannot be, inasmuch as he desires it. He cannot be a sorcerer, and he cannot be a music mage. We must always play a careful balancing act, assuring we are more prize than bane..." Fear flickered in Chevalier's eyes, and he glanced away, staring at the wall.

"Why do you continue to help such a monster?" Gailea remembered the magical collar, but she wouldn't embarrass him by mentioning it. "Just now, the king mentioned you having a family?"

"Yes," Chevalier said quietly, "a wife and daughter. Moragon has their estate under close guard at all times."

"Then we are more allies than I thought—equals even, in whatever strange way. I too would protect my sister, and my friends at court."

Chevalier scoffed. "No one has true friends at court."

"I have friends who would help me. If we stood together, we could have a chance."

"A truly naïve notion." He looked fiercely at her. "Do you take me for a fool? Do you take yourself for one, believing yourself powerful enough to stand against him?"

"No. No, my lord. I do not. But even the strongest men have weaknesses. If we could find the king's, then united, we might overcome him."

The sorcerer studied her closely again. Then, glancing up and down the hall, he lowered his voice and said, "Come. I would show you something in my chambers."

Gailea stared, trying to decipher whether he played some trick upon her. Arming her mind with defensive songs just in case, she nodded and followed after him. She remembered the way and had to keep her feet in check, not wishing to cast any suspicion that she'd been to his quarters before.

As they entered the corridor leading to his chambers, Gailea marveled at the complete lack of guards and servants. While she felt more than grateful for the absence of the terrifying hounds, she wondered where Chevalier's guard had all vanished to; perhaps he had secretly sent them away so that they would not see the two of them together.

Once inside the lavish chambers, Chevalier wandered over to one of the colorful windows and rested his hand on the smooth glass. The glass rippled, and Gailea gasped as he dove his hand inside. His hand seemed to vanish inside the window, and upon reemerging, clutched a large round crystal. Its many colors shimmered in the sunlight, and Chevalier said, "This prism may be of great importance to you someday. If anything ever happens to me, you must take it from the window as I have just done."

"Why?" Gailea breathed. "What magic can it do?"

"I am not yet certain," Chevalier said. "But its magic is not evil, if that's what you fear. There may come a time when you have need of a great power, such as this prism is rumored to wield—and if my suspicions prove correct, that time may come soon indeed."

"But why are you helping me?"

"Because, naïve and reckless though you may be, you are merciful. If anyone was to make a righteous leader for this kingdom, it would be you."

Gailea watched incredulously as Chevalier replaced the prism inside the window.

"Where did you get it?" she asked. "And why should I trust you?"

"How it came to me is unimportant. And while it is entirely your choice whether or not you place trust in me, remember that we do stand united in one thing—that we would both wish to see Moragon removed from the throne, for sake of our families."

Gailea studied Chevalier. Here, in the seclusion of his private sanctum, he spoke so calmly to her, almost like a gently guiding father or older brother.

"Master Chevalier, you're from Prismatic, yes? Is that where your family lives?"

Chevalier smirked. "'Live' is a loose term; there are many varying degrees of life and existence and in between. The less anyone knows of my background, the safer I shall feel—for my sake and my family's."

"You miss them, don't you? Do you ever see them?"

Chevalier's smile faltered, and he released a heavy

sigh. "You ask too many questions, girl. Sometimes, silence truly is the best key to survival. Now, run along before anyone finds us here and is given cause to create more vicious gossip. Only remember what I've shown you, should the time come for you to flee."

"I can't flee," Gailea said, holding up her wrist to show the bracelet. "The king says you helped create it. Can you take it off?"

Chevalier shook his head. "Not without his majesty's permission—he would know, and it would mean both our heads. Even though it can't be now, that doesn't mean a time will not come for your escape. But I will say no more. Go now and aid the queen, and we shall pretend as though this conversation never existed."

His gaze shifted toward his door and then back to her. With a curtsy, she bid him good afternoon and hurried from his chambers.

Hurrying to the queen's rooms, she found Marlis surrounded by several other servants who helped her finish changing into her riding clothes.

"Your grace." Gailea curtsied.

"Dearest Gailea, *there* you are!" Marlis grinned. Adjusting the long plume extending from her red velvet hat, she added, "I do miss you in the mornings. But I'm proud of you. It's rare that my husband takes an interest in anyone's education. It might do him some good; I think *he* could learn a few things from *you*, my dear."

The queen turned, and something glinted in her left hand. Gailea gasped and nearly cried out—Marlis clutched a vial filled with a blood-red Dusk sample.

"What is that, your grace?" Gailea blurted, glancing between the vial and the queen's face.

"This?" Marlis held up the vial; the Dusk shifted inside, and Gailea winced. "Why, Chevalier gave it to me. He can be so kind at times. I thought it was quite pretty, and he said it was a bit of new magic he was working on, that wearing it close may help me relax..." With a frown, she began fiddling with the lid. "I've been dying to open it and get a better look at the crystals. See how they shimmer and shift, almost like mist—"

"No, your grace—don't!"

Gailea snatched at the vial. The queen gasped and tripped; as she reached out to catch herself on the vanity, the vial fell and shattered with a shrill ring. The queen reached toward it.

"*No*, your grace!" Gailea cried, reaching for her.

The queen hissed, drawing back her finger and holding it up. Blood shimmered on her fingertip where she'd cut it on the jagged glass. Gailea stared at the queen, holding her breath and waiting to see the Dusk spread across the queen's skin and consume her body like it had Gailea's in the woods. The queen continued to nurse her finger but otherwise looked completely safe. No signs of hellish visions, of the Dusk controlling either her body or her mind.

Gailea looked back to the Dusk spilled on the floor; it seeped down between the floorboards and disappeared. There was no way to catch it now. She prayed the substance was gone and wouldn't spread to anyone else.

She then dove to the floor, using a handkerchief from her pocket to scoop up the shards of glass. The other servants clustered around the queen with rags and a bowl of water, nursing the cut.

"I'm so sorry, your grace," Gailea said, rising to her feet while carefully cupping the damaged glass in her handkerchief. "Forgive my clumsiness. I was only concerned for your safety. Such magic can sometimes be dangerous if handled the wrong way. It may not have been intended for touching..."

"It's all right," Marlis said, waving the matter aside

with her hand. "I'm ignorant when it comes to magic outside that of my people. I'm sorry if I alarmed you. It *is* a shame—the crystals were quite lovely, like little red diamonds..." She glanced at the floor then drew on her riding gloves with a shrug. "But never mind it. I suppose I'll be content enough to ride alongside that handsome young horse steward, Tytonn. Perhaps you'd like to join us? A smart, pretty thing like you could do worse than to be courted by such a man."

Marlis gave a playful smile. Gailea forced a smile in return; she was glad to see her mistress in better spirits and health but still shaken by the near accident.

"If it pleases your grace, may I stay inside today? I am rather exhausted and would appreciate the reprieve."

Marlis looked a little disappointed but said, "Very well, my dear. Until later then?"

The queen breezed from the room. Her ladies departed their separate ways, except one who lingered to resume dusting the room. Gailea stooped down to inspect the floor for any remaining traces of the Dusk. Upon finding none, she breathed a sigh of relief. Despite her clumsy blunder, the queen's life was yet safe.

CHAPTER 22

PREPARATIONS

Crispin raised Anwar, parrying the volley of flame Alistor flung at him, but instead of deflecting the fire, his sword absorbed it. Then, as Crispin swung the blade, the flames burst forth, surging right back at Alistor, who crossed his arms in front of him to draw the fire back inside his body.

Crispin panted hard as they continued to wage flames back and forth. He hurled a giant fireball at his uncle, who leapt aside and threw out his hand to create a beam of light that extinguished the fire right before it slammed into one of the camp's tents.

Grinning in amusement, Alistor said, "Well done, nephew. You almost bested me at my own game. Keep that up, and even Moragon won't see your tricks coming."

"I'm mostly counting on him not being able to read my thoughts," Crispin admitted. "I've never really had to contend with his mental magic."

"And you won't. That sword makes you a god of the

mind. You'll be able to resist him without effort and fight him with ease."

"I wish I could rally supporters with just as much ease," Crispin muttered, swinging his sword to release his frustration. "We've only gathered a couple hundred troops—not nearly enough to storm Moragon's castle."

"Not yet, no," Alistor said. "Of course, numbers are not our only key to success. But they do help. Those who fight by our side now will surely find their loyalties deepened once we lead them to victory over their current corrupt master. You're not just building temporary support, but loyal followers for years to come."

Crispin sighed. "And, just as always, with a few simple words, you set my mind a bit more at ease. Perhaps *you* should remain our chief orator when it comes to persuading others to join our side."

Alistor shook his head. "I've told you why it's necessary that we make the people follow *you*."

"Because of my love for Gailea."

"Exactly. The people will pounce on that sentimentality. You are also young; they may consider you more inexperienced, but also innocent. *You* must convince them what a kind and benevolent master you will make. I could sing your praises all day long, but they are much more convincing coming from *your* lips and displayed in *your* magic. Next week, we'll have arrived in Larkin. The people there are worn down by Moragon's oppression, taxes, and other burdens. They will flock to you if you present yourself in the correct light—"

A flash of silver darted past Alistor's face and paused to hover before Crispin. The silver turned, glistening, and as he reached out to grab it, its glow faded to reveal an envelope in his hands. Writing made from black charring emitted a faint, smoky scent. Crispin turned the envelope over, tore the seal, and opened the parchment. His glance darted to the signature at the bottom, and he gasped, "It's from Elda."

"I'll leave you to take a short reprieve. Let your sister's words inspire you, reinvigorate you."

Crispin nodded slowly, sat down beneath a large tree, and began to read the words scorched on the page by Elda's lightning:

Dearest Brother,

I hope this finds you safe and well; as I do not know your whereabouts, I must trust the House's magic to allow it to find you.

I'm writing to share my grief at the Weaver's passing. Her hair had finally silvered altogether, and then the silver stags came to claim her. She was full of peace and joy as they stole her away to the isle of eternal rest, but still, my heart aches for her missed companionship.

Before she passed, the Weaver bequeathed the House of Lance into my care. Having no children of her own, she said it was her honor to place the responsibility of its magic in my hands. I am going to stay here, carrying on in her name, aiding passersby with gifts of silver and a safe place to lodge. Know that, should you ever need refuge, you will be safe here, being of my blood, as will our uncle.

Watch after him. You know I care for him. However, he sometimes reaches too high. You are capable of great things, but don't let him lead you on a path that neither of you will be able to attain, or safely come back from.

Enclosed is a second message, from Tytonn.

Be safe and strong, dear brother. May Amiel grant you victory, and may we be together soon.

Sending all my love and strength,
~ Elda

Crispin leaned back with a sigh. He smiled, tracing his fingers across her words, rereading them, absorbing their soothing. Then, he drew out a smaller piece of parchment, unfolded it, and recognized Tytonn's writing, equally as neat if not as elaborate:

Crispin,

May this find you safe and well if, Amiel willing, it has first found your sister in the same manner. She wrote to me a few days ago, promising that the House's magic would guide any correspondence that comes from a place of sincerity to its doors.

I thought you might use some words of encouragement, and especially to know how Gailea is excelling. She is so brave and strong. She walks a precarious balance, serving the king while gaining his trust. She does it to protect the queen, and to help turn Moragon's attention away from you. You would truly admire her; I know I do. She is inspiring to watch and fight secretly beside.

Take care, my friend. May we be reunited soon, but as free men, no longer captives of our decadent sovereign.

Amiel be with you,
- Tytonn

Crispin reread Tytonn's note, growing more solemn with each word. It was good to know that Gailea had at least one ally on her side. Tytonn's magic might not be nearly as strong as hers, but his ability to command wild beasts might yet come in handy. If nothing else, his obvious charms should be capable of keeping her encouraged.

"I hope you write as lovingly to my sister as you dance attention on my future bride," he muttered, with half a mind to write Tytonn back and tell him as much.

Crispin shoved the letters back in the envelope with

an inward scolding. His spark of jealousy was likely just boyish foolishness, born from missing Gailea these past weeks. Instead, his concern must turn to the scores of strangers who looked for someone to lead them to victory and a brighter, hopeful future.

Crispin would be that person. He would continue to rise in wisdom and power under Alistor's guidance. Then he would take Astyrian, proving to all, including Tytonn and Gailea and Elda, what a capable and deserving leader he was.

***

A light knock sounded on the door. Gailea glanced up, smiling faintly as Darice entered, before staring out once more at the gray clouds that concealed any trace of the sun. The cushion beneath her shifted as Darice sat beside her.

"What's wrong?" Darice asked. "You look exhausted."

"I am," Gailea said quietly. "It grows more difficult to deceive his majesty. Today I was forced to relinquish the tracking device—though it should at least take his men well out of their way before leading them to Crispin and Lord Ragnar."

Darice took her hand. "Does he still press you to construct a barrier around the castle?"

Gailea nodded. "That is what I fear most; such a barrier cannot be easily undone, not even by me if he also infuses it with his mental magic. I fear for Chevalier as well. The moment I become more useful, Moragon may decide to dispose of him."

"Your compassion is noble," Darice said, "but I didn't know you cared so for the sorcerer."

"He is as much a prisoner as I am," Gailea said. "He has a family. I can't imagine being his wife, never knowing if he's safe, only to receive sudden word her husband is dead…"

"You know," Darice said, squeezing her hand, "at times, I do wish you'd worry a little more for your own welfare."

"I do," Gailea said. "But what about you? Did you come here just to visit?"

Darice grinned playfully. "Perhaps. I suppose I've been rather content, with the gifts of a warmer bed and food."

Gailea grasped her sister's hands. "You were accepted as a new lady-in-waiting after all? Why didn't you tell me? This is wonderful news!"

"It is, indeed. I enjoyed cooking, but I'm glad to be free of the drama of the kitchen. Meanwhile, it may also please you to know that I was able to find Sorcha and Macha."

Gailea lowered her voice to an excited whisper. "And?"

"Macha was skeptical at first, of course. But they both allowed me to pass along the songs you taught me, with a promise to teach the other music mages. I've seen Sorcha once since then, and she says there are many who've been practicing."

"Praise Amiel," Gailea said. "We may yet have hope. Thank you. I'm glad to have you as an ally."

"As I am to have you as a sister." Darice rose to her feet. "Good night, my dear. Thank you for everything, and may Amiel continue to guide you."

"And you as well."

With a final smile, Darice slipped from the room.

Gailea's mind spun, encouraged by the idea of no longer being alone in her fight. After all, the king wouldn't stay patient much longer. In the next few days, she would be forced to construct a new barrier around the castle and hope that, by some miracle, Crispin and Lord Ragnar could still break through.

***

"Lady Gailea! Lady Gailea!"

Gailea stirred and moaned.

"*Lady Gailea!*"

Hands roughly shook her shoulder, and with a jolt, she sprang awake, gasping at the sight of Tory's face hovering near hers, her eyes shining wide.

"What is it, Tory?"

"It's the queen—she won't wake!"

Gailea sat up. "What do you mean?"

"The healers have tried all manner of herbs and charms to waken her. Even Chevalier cannot rouse her. Please—come quickly!"

Gailea scrambled up stiffly; she'd fallen asleep on the window seat, and her body ached. Rubbing her neck, she hurried after Tory. As they raced down the halls, morning's first light peeked between the clouds.

Bursting into the queen's chambers, Gailea excused herself past the healers gathered and perched on the edge of the bed, taking the queen's hand and nearly re-coiling at her icy touch. Marlis' skin had paled again to a ghastly hue, and her chest rose and fell unevenly as she struggled to draw shallow breaths.

Gailea clutched Marlis' hand, singing her lullaby and the newest healing charms she had taught herself. No change stirred on the queen's face, nor in her still body, but Gailea sang on, shaking and fighting back tears.

"Stand aside—move aside for your king, damn you— I need to see my wife!"

Moragon stormed through the gathered healers, shoving past them. They knocked into each other, sharing wary glances. Gailea suppressed her quiet sobs and stood aside as Moragon swept over and knelt by his wife's bed. He took her hand, and Gailea almost wondered at the tender gesture, but then he glared at Marlis in disgust.

Springing up, he whirled and snarled, "This is *your* fault, you incompetent fool!"

Chevalier stood in one corner, poised and straight, hands folded. His eyes widened with visible fear as Moragon marched up to him, but he replied calmly, "The queen was clearly poisoned, your grace. We have done all we can; we even tried bloodletting, but her very blood ate through the metal bowl as if it were acid. You can see for yourself, on her left hand, traces of the poison spreading..."

Moragon walked back over to his wife. Lifting her hand, he turned it in the firelight and then let it fall, stepping back with a grimace. Gailea inhaled sharply; splotches of a shadowy crimson shape just beneath her skin crept up her arm like tiny rivulets of blood.

"Come, Chevalier," Moragon snapped, motioning with his hand and storming from the room. "I must call an emergency council. Lady Gailea, use your music to summon my men to the council chambers immediately!"

"Your grace," Gailea said quietly. She glanced once more at Marlis, pale and still as death, and hurried from the room.

Heading down the corridors toward the council chambers, Gailea sang a summoning song too high for human ears to detect. Moragon had combined the song with his mental magic to create a special vibration that would echo inside the very hearts of his knights; he'd then taught them to respond and assemble whenever Gailea sang it.

Within moments, knights poured toward the council

chamber. Gailea hid in the shadows on the balcony, peering down inside. Moragon paced while the knights clustered in a semi-circle around their king, quietly awaiting his command.

"The queen has been poisoned," Moragon began, his voice tight. "She will not awaken."

Gasps and mutters echoed from below.

"There has been foul play in my hall," Moragon said, raising his voice. "Some spy or other evil-doer who wishes me and my household harm. If any of you have an inkling of who might be responsible, step forward at once."

No one spoke. A hush like a graveyard cloaked the room.

"None of us would bring harm to the queen," one said at last.

"Who would?" another said. "The queen was loved by all, your grace. May whoever has committed this crime be eternally damned."

Shouts of agreement echoed from the knights.

Moragon raised his hand and again called for silence. "Let it indeed be as you say. And let me now give *my* opinion, that such an obvious act of rebellion could only be committed by those serving under the devils who aim to foster a rebellion against me and destroy this kingdom—Lords Alistor and Crispin, a bastard and traitor respectively and no longer family of mine."

Gailea's heart pounded so hard that she thought Moragon must hear it. She slouched back further into the shadows, shaking and gripping the wall behind her for support.

"Let a search go out for the traitors, but let them be brought to me alive, so that I may take vengeance for my queen. If any man standing here should be caught helping them, know that they shall bear the traitor's punishment *and* their own."

"Let it be done as his grace declares!"

"Down with the traitors—how *dare* they betray their queen!"

"We *will* have justice—the streets of Adelar will cry with their blood!"

"Go, my faithful servants!" Moragon commanded. "Send your best men to find the wretches. If you cannot bring them to me, or if they are too well-guarded, then bring report of their current activities. There will be no surprise attack upon Astyrian. We will beat them back before they've managed to step one foot inside our silver borders!"

Cries erupted and calls for blood deafened the hall. Then, as one of the knights started ordering commands, they divided into groups and dispersed from the room.

Gailea remained frozen against the wall. What could she do? Was there any way she could warn Crispin? Only a few weeks had passed since he'd left; he couldn't have had enough time yet to raise a proper army.

The queen's relatives in Hyloria—Moragon would be unlikely to contact them. But perhaps Gailea could; whether or not they cared for their daughter's security was a gamble, considering they'd married her off to such a ruthless man, but if they did, Gailea might be able to convince them to send aid—

Someone grabbed her arms and yanked her up. She shrieked, but the next moment, Moragon had forced her back against the wall. She struggled and muttered a song to push him away, but he pinned her down, tightening his grasp. His dark eyes blazed into hers, and he sneered, "Did you enjoy the little show I put on for you down there?"

Gailea gasped but said nothing, her words stolen away as he squeezed even tighter. She sang the defensive song in her mind again, but Moragon didn't even flinch.

"Do you really think your thoughts have been entirely safe from me all this time? I know how you care for the traitor, my pathetic nephew."

"Yes, but my loyalties are toward you first, your grace—"

Moragon slammed her back against the wall. "Out of fear, not love, as you love him. And I have seen what people will do for love, the sacrifices they will make, the oaths they will sever. Even my fool of a brother, ever incapable of true love, *wanted* you enough to defy me in seeking your favor. But perhaps we could still strike a wager that will please both of us."

"Your grace," Gailea breathed, whimpering as Moragon's fingers dug into her arms. Her head spun for any song that might weaken him, but he slammed her against the wall again.

"No, your tricks won't work today, girl. I may not possess your affinity for music, but I *can* guard against it. Now, hear my bargain. Once this poison of Chevalier's finally fulfills its purpose in the queen, you *will* marry me. Someone must pay for the treason I've declared; my brother will make a nice scapegoat. But marry me, and your beloved Crispin will be allowed his life on the condition of exile."

"Crispin will continue fighting you," Gailea said. "He won't stop."

Moragon scoffed. "What army will rally around a young, spoiled brat who can hardly hold a sword, let alone stand against our joined forces? Because you *will* join me—that's part of the bargain. His life for your magic. You must stop holding back what I know you are far more capable of. I'll even include the life of my deformed niece, for what it's worth to you. What say you?"

Gailea stared up at him, hesitant. "Yes, your grace. I

will teach you all I can."

"Do not lie to me. Do not sing words recited like a little bird. If you deceive me this time, everyone you love will suffer for it."

He released her at last, and she stood braced against the wall, her breathing shallow as he strode out onto the balcony and called down, "You there! Sir Baelor. Go at once and arrest Tytonn Grayfell, the young horse steward. I've just received word of his involvement in the plot against the queen's life."

"Yes, your grace."

The knight's footsteps receded hurriedly from the room. Gailea sprang up from the wall, crying, "No, your grace! What would Tytonn have to do with this? I've already promised to give you what you want—I swear it!"

"Really?" Moragon turned back toward Gailea, who cowered under his fierce glare. He drummed his fingers against the railing of the balcony, and the noise seemed to echo to the rhythm of her pounding heartbeat and throbbing head. "I might have license to believe you, and yet, the young horse steward *was* seen alone with the queen yesterday, while she was out riding. Clearly, *he* is the one Alistor must have enlisted to poison her. Why, what kind of king would I be if I did not arrest this obvious traitor at once?"

"Please, stop," Gailea pleaded, marching up to the king and kneeling before him. "I vow you shall have all that you desire. I prove my allegiance now..." Gailea sang the ascending scales for magnifying sound until the song echoed so loudly that the balcony itself began to quake, and then the entire room. Moragon whirled, staring wide-eyed as bits of stone rained from the ceiling, destroying his throne below.

Gailea ceased singing, and the hall quieted. Moragon turned to her and, with a lustful wonder gleaming in his eyes, extended his hand.

Gailea took it and rose to her feet. "You see, your grace? Together, we shall be unstoppable, as you say. None of your enemies will be able to withstand our magic. Only spare the lives of those I love, I beg you."

Moragon lifted her hand to his lips and kissed it. It was a cold gesture, as rehearsed as her agreeing to help him, but desire burned clearly in his voice as he said, "I will release Tytonn and claim all was a mistake. We shall meet tomorrow, Lady Gailea, in the great hall, where our training shall intensify—just the two of us. We are both beyond the fool Chevalier. His services are no longer needed."

Moragon released her hand and started toward the hallway.

"Your grace?" Gailea called.

He paused and glanced over his shoulder.

"Will you...will you spare Chevalier's life as well?"

Moragon turned toward her, head tilted in amusement. "Have you developed some strange affection for *everyone* in my court?"

"Chevalier and I are not friends," Gailea said, "but I would not see him die on my account."

Moragon studied her a moment more, still looking amused. Then, with a nod, he said, "Whatever you wish. Unlock your musical powers, give all of yourself to me, and I will spare the life of every single prisoner in my dungeons if it pleases you."

"Thank you, your grace," Gailea said.

Moragon nodded, then turned and disappeared down the hallway. Once the shadows had swallowed him, Gailea darted from the balcony, her mind spinning. Crispin and Alistor were safe at present, but Tytonn's life meant nothing to the king, and the moment Chevalier was branded as a sorcerer, his life too was forfeit. Moragon had mentioned nothing of Darice, but she knew he would use her as a mere bargaining chip as well.

She must continue teaching the king, and she must hold nothing back, for he would know if she did; she'd been a fool to think she could outmatch his mental gifts. She must find a way to contact the queen's family in Hyloria and hope they would send aid. And she must pray that Crispin and Lord Ragnar would soon have strength enough to march against the king before she was forced to become his ally with no hope of turning back.

CHAPTER 23

ALLEGIANCES

✳

Crispin lifted the flap of the tent and peered out at the makeshift platform erected in the midst of the town square. Scores of people gathered around, their gazes full of anticipation, some hopeful, others doubtful. Guards stood positioned around the outskirts of the square, along with some of his men. Dulin stood inside an inn window high above, his lips moving rapidly as he maintained his silencing charms; anyone not already gathered who strayed near wouldn't be able to detect a word of what happened today.

"Are you ready?" Alistor asked, coming up to stand behind Crispin.

Suddenly aware that he'd been holding his breath, Crispin released it in a long exhale. While his prowess with Anwar had excelled within the past couple of weeks, he yet doubted in his ability to master the one talent Alistor insisted would prove most vital to their war plans—the power of speech.

"I hope so," he said. "But they all look so anxious. What if I disappoint them?"

"Word has spread of the outcast noblemen gathering forces by the power of fire. Most of the people want to remove the king from his throne for one reason or another. If they see your might, they will stand behind it. Your biggest challenge is to convince them that they will not be bowing to yet another merciless tyrant by placing their trust in you."

Crispin nodded. Supposing he wouldn't feel any more prepared than he did, he strolled from the tent and marched atop the platform.

"It's the king's nephew!" someone yelled. "We've been tricked!"

"It's the traitor—down with him, or the king will have all our heads!"

The people rushed forward and began scrambling atop the platform.

Crispin breathed deeply. Flexing his hands, he let his fire radiate from deep inside his chest, burning and pumping through the rest of him. The flames raced along his body, down through his feet, and spiraled across the wood without burning it, surrounding the platform with a wall of fire. The crowds screamed and pressed back, eyes wide with both alarm and awe.

"Friends," Crispin declared, spreading his arms wide; the fire danced all along his body, and its warmth gave him the courage he needed to lift his head high. "I know you are frightened. It is true that the king has branded me and my uncle traitors—just as he once branded many of your young men as sorcerers and heretics, burning those who were guilty and innocent alike. I have lived closely under the king's watch all my life. I have seen his cruelties firsthand. And now that I am free of them, I wish to lead an army that will bring those cruelties to a swift, certain, and complete end!"

Mutterings sounded throughout the crowd—not the deafening cheers he would have hoped for, but not an outright call for blood as his uncle had been met with in other towns.

"Moragon wrongly took our kingdom," a man shouted from the crowds. "How do we know you're not just another usurper? His family's blood runs through you, after all."

Crispin nodded. "An honest concern. But I assure you I have the highest respect and affection for the true queen, Lady Gailea. She continues to fight bravely from within the castle, aiding the queen and others. The throne is rightfully hers if she will claim it."

"And if not, *you* would?" someone called.

Crispin hesitated. "I might, yes. I am next of kin. My uncle has called for outside aid, and the kingdoms of Iceania and Rosa already stand behind us. We've also gathered about five hundred Adelaran men on our travels, those who grow weary of the constant fear of Moragon's tyranny and the burden of his taxes."

"Why?" a woman called from the crowds. "Why should we follow you? What proof can you offer us of your victory—and that, should you succeed, you won't take equal advantage of us?"

"There is no proof," a man answered. "Every monarch is a gamble."

"I don't ask you to place strength in a man you don't know," Crispin said. "Place faith instead behind the ideals for which I fight. I want nothing more than to destroy Moragon and free both his wife and the true queen."

He made the flames vanish from his body and motioned to the fire still ringing the platform. "You see my magic; this is but a glimpse of its true power. Sir Alistor possesses the same. And once we breach the castle,

Gailea's music, added to the strength of our armies, would make us powerful enough to destroy even Moragon's forces."

Mutterings rippled through the crowds again. Their expressions began to take on a more interesting light, and Crispin's confidence slowly expanded inside him.

"What would you do for us?" a woman called. "For my children? I can hardly feed them a scrap of bread, what with the weight of the taxes his grace imposes on us."

"Moragon's load is heavy, yes. He steals from the poor to fatten the treasuries of nobles already overflowing with more than they can contain. I've seen first-hand what harm this can do; a close friend of mine was born to a less favorable position. I would seek to help distribute wealth. To take from those who have and help those who do not."

"It sounds too good to be true," a man called, and several people echoed him.

"What do you have to lose?" Crispin challenged. "Years of tyranny under a cruel master who cares for nothing and no one but himself? He hates even his queen. I love the true queen Gailea, not as a mere servant, but also as a man. I would protect her with my life and seek to uphold the principles of justice, fairness, and compassion that I know she reveres so highly."

Crispin waved his hand, and the fire surrounding the platform moved instead to hover in the air above him, spreading across the sky like paint. He danced his hands through the air, molding the fire like clay until at last, an image of Gailea hovered before them like a fiery statue.

"*This* is your queen. *This* is she whom I love, and whether she made me her king or her servant, I *will* seek to restore her to the throne."

"What of Lord Gareth and his son, Donyon?" a man said. "They too have been rallying support. They too promise wealth to the common people. In essence, they hold the higher claim over the throne—why should we pledge allegiance to you over them?"

"Because Gailea is the true queen," Crispin said. "Gareth and Donyon are also usurpers."

"Again, you speak only a half-truth. Gailea may be queen by blood, but she cannot rule without a man beside her. Adelar was left to the care of Lord Gareth. The late King Cenric, Amiel bless his departed soul, had meant to join their families through his daughter's marriage to Donyon. Gareth is still king by rights—"

"But not by blood, as you say," Crispin said. "And that raises the question of which is the stronger claim—blood or rights? For my part, I say blood, and if Gailea is willing to bestow the honor of her hand in marriage, whether upon me or another, I am willing to help place her back on the throne and defend both her and her kingdom with my life."

"I would follow you," a man said, stepping forward. "I am willing to stand and fight alongside anyone who claims such affection for the true queen."

"He's bluffing, don't you see that?" someone called.

"No, he's not," the man said, stepping up onto the platform. "His love for her is sincere. Any fool who has ever been in love can see that."

"Love is no reason to go to war," a woman said warily. "He's blinded himself. He cannot stand against Moragon, even with several thousand men."

"Love is better reason than most have," the man returned. Then, walking over to Crispin, he knelt and declared, "I am Fara, my lord. I pledge my allegiance to you and your cause, for as long as it may aid her true grace."

Crispin drew Anwar and tapped the man's shoulders. "Honored I am to have you join me."

Fara rose, and Crispin gazed across the crowds again, lifting his sword high. "What say the rest of you?"

"I still say he is a liar," a woman said. "He means to charm us just like his uncle the snake would. If he is so infatuated with Lady Gailea, then might we not believe the rumors claiming *he* was the one who poisoned Queen Marlis?"

"Nay!" another woman said. "He wasn't even there. He'd already fled the castle; how could he have poisoned anyone?"

"I don't care if he *did* mean to murder the queen," a man said. "She's never deserved the throne; Lady Gailea does."

"How dare you disgrace Queen Marlis!" another man cried, marching up to the first, fists clenched. A couple other men rushed forward, grabbing and dragging him back. He struggled against them, but when their strength obviously outmatched his, he fell still, snarling, "Queen Marlis didn't choose the life she's bound to. She didn't choose that demon for her husband. Fate has not dealt kindly with her, and we should not deal so cruelly against her as well."

"This man speaks truth," Crispin said. "None of this is my aunt's choosing—just as none of Moragon's cruelties are any of our choosing. My friends, I urge you: we cannot continue to stand divided like this. The only hope for Adelar being restored is unity. We have looked for outside aid, and it has answered. Others are willing to stand beside us and fight—but if we fight amongst ourselves, what hope is there for us? We must unite, and we must do so under the true queen—the Lady Gailea. Who will help me free her—free all of us—from the king's tyranny for good?"

A round of cheers erupted from the crowds. Some of the talk rose into arguments, but the guards raised their bows or swords, watching carefully for any sign of disturbance.

Everyone began to divide, choosing sides. Gradually, men and a few women crept forward, offering their services as soldiers, magicians, spies. Crispin welcomed each of them, announcing where they could meet his and his uncle's encampment.

Once the crowds had either pledged their allegiance or began to disperse, Crispin cast a yearning glance upon Gailea's fiery image before waving a hand to extinguish it.

Then, he darted back inside his tent where his uncle waited, grinning with unconcealed pleasure.

"Well done, dear nephew! The people loved you."

"Do you really think so? I still think they more hate Moragon than love me."

"Perhaps some fear you as the lesser of two evils, yes. But all the same, we're growing our army, and that's what counts, isn't it?"

Crispin nodded uncertainly.

"What is it?" Alistor placed a hand on his shoulder. "You should be proud; you put on quite a magnetic display."

"Yes, I'm pleased with how things went, but...Uncle, do you think that I *could* be king? I haven't given it much thought, but if Gailea loves me still..."

"To be king is to bear a great weight of responsibility," Alistor said. "It is a small thing to win a kingdom; it takes but a single battle. It is another to fight the lifelong war of *keeping* a kingdom. I think, between your drive and your magic, you could become more than capable. But you must believe it yourself."

"You've taught me so much," Crispin said slowly. "I

think…I think I'd be powerful enough—with you beside me, to counsel me."

Alistor patted his shoulder. "That's what I would hope to hear…"

He then walked toward the table in the midst of the tent where a map lay sprawled open wide, held open with small stones.

"There is another matter we should discuss. When I corresponded with Rosa, they said that Gareth and Donyon have been steadily amassing their own army. They would likely wait until Moragon is overthrown to determine how weak or strong our own forces are before making any move, but I believe they do pose a threat. I know you are eager to free the Lady Gailea, but we cannot spread ourselves too thin. We must have strength enough to resist them as well when it comes time for it."

Crispin snorted. "Gareth holds no real claim over the throne—any more than Moragon, really. He was too weak to hold the throne in the first place."

Alistor nodded. "In this, we do have an edge. The people love Gailea and, as you saw today, they will come to love us. All the same, do not think that Gareth is powerless."

"No…" Crispin let his fingers trail along the map. "But our numbers are growing. And you must also remember that while Gailea aids the king now with her music, that is only to protect herself. The moment we storm the castle, she will show her true loyalties and fight by our side."

"Perhaps…"

Crispin hated the skepticism on Alistor's face but let him continue.

"…However, even assuming the addition of such a powerful ally, there is still the matter of how to breach Moragon's castle to begin with. The barrier—no army of any size can undo it. Have you even considered that?"

"The caves," Crispin said. "The caves we escaped through. We could send a fleet of soldiers through the caves. While Moragon is distracted with them, I will destroy the silver barriers."

"And how do you intend to do that?"

"With this." Crispin drew Anwar. "This sword can break the barrier. I can use it and my Fyre magic to create a temporary sheath of liquid gold, which can cut through liquid silver. We destroy the barriers, and the castle is easily ours. Without the barrier, the castle becomes no more threatening a challenge than any fortress."

Alistor reached a hand toward the sword, letting his fingers dance along its smooth surface. "It truly might work. If I distract his majesty with our armies, and you focus on destroying the barrier, and if Lady Gailea *does* assist us from within—even Moragon cannot turn his attention to all three of us at once. But we must not forget Chevalier..."

"He's a mere puppet compared to the king," Crispin said. "Do you think he'll choose to fight by the king's side or balk the first chance he gets? If he truly is responsible for creating the cave passage, he might slip out during the battle..."

"Except that if Moragon were to receive any inkling of Chevalier's betrayal, instant death would come to his family. Chevalier will not risk that. He will stay, and he will fight for Moragon. Of course, in considering the caves, Chevalier may very well warn his grace that *we* could use such a passage. However, I think this unlikely; if he tells, he would have too much to explain that could again put his family at risk."

"What then?" Crispin asked. "How can we get past Chevalier?"

"We disarm his magic—contain it, if you will. With the light shield we've been practicing. We can use our light magic not only to protect ourselves but, if we can get to him fast enough, also use it to seal Chevalier's magic *inside* him."

"And you think I still have time to master it? I haven't had much success yet."

"If you are willing to continue our rigorous training, then yes, I believe you can."

Crispin took a deep breath. His head spun, both nervously and excitedly. "When will the rest of our forces arrive from Rosa and Iceania?"

"They should be here within a fortnight or so."

"Very well then. It's a gamble, but I don't think we should wait much longer than that—nor *any* longer than necessary."

"Agreed," Alistor said. "We'll wait for the rest of our allies to arrive and continue practicing our magic in the meantime. Then, we'll attack and bring down the intimidation of Astyrian for good."

CHAPTER 24

THE TRUE QUEEN

Gailea knelt beside Marlis' bed. Clinging to the queen's hand, she wept softly. There had been no change in her, for either good or ill, for many days. Talk of poisoning and treason continued to fly about the castle.

Gailea brushed back one of the queen's soft, red curls and smiled with a shuddering breath. Marlis' pale skin, graceful form, and folded hands gave her the appearance of a statue, perfectly carved to reflect the peace she had never known in her waking hours.

"Gailea?"

Gailea glanced up. Darice stood in the doorway.

"Gailea, the seamstresses are waiting. The king demands your presence."

"Why does he do this?" Gailea gasped. "The queen is not yet dead—why does he make these preparations? He might at least keep up an *appearance* of being a decent husband by tending his wife's side as I do."

"You know why," Darice said, leaning her head wearily against the doorframe. "Crispin and Alistor. Don-

345

yon and Gareth. All these threats of war. Moragon fears them—or at least pretends to. Either way, he uses them as an excuse to have plans for a new bride as soon as the queen dies. He's—"

"Anxious, about having an heir," Gailea muttered. "That's what he says. But that's not his main priority. He wants *me*. He wants me beside him as his greatest weapon."

Darice hesitated and then asked quietly, "And will you still aid him?"

Gailea looked back at the queen and squeezed her hand. "Inasmuch as it might save her life. But, no..." She glanced back at her sister, sharply, "...he will never have full dominion over my magic. I will not become what Marlis has become."

"And we will be ready to aid you," Darice reassured, "me and the other music mages. But for now, you must still come. The king..."

"Yes." Gailea rose to her feet. She released the queen's hand and folded it gently across her chest once more. Then, she met Darice and said, "Let us get through this torment as quickly as possible."

Gailea and Darice headed to the chamber that had become too hauntingly familiar to Gailea within the past few days. It was a small room, and the sunlight flooding it might have made it cheery, but Gailea felt the light mocked her, its brightness ignorant of the shadows encroaching upon the castle and destroying it from the inside out.

Gailea stepped up on the stool, allowing the seamstresses to measure and fit the pieces of the gown that was nearly complete. Its soft, fluid fabric shimmered like gold and seemed to flow between their hands.

After a painful hour, the seamstresses declared their work finished. They need only to sew the remaining pieces together and add the fine embroidery and pearls that the king had demanded.

"It will be a wedding gown fit for the true queen," one of the handmaids whispered to Gailea before departing. Gailea only frowned after her. Even the servants weren't ignorant of the whisperings of approaching war, and already, they chose sides.

"Gailea."

Darice had entered the room again, this time holding a small leather bag, lumpy and bound with several pieces of thick twine. Holding it out, she said quietly, "Responses to your wedding announcement."

Forcing a small smile at Darice, Gailea took the bag. She clutched its heavy weight tightly in both hands and said, "Thank you, sister. For everything. It's good to have you on my side."

Darice embraced Gailea, whispering in her ear, "I'm always on your side."

"I know," Gailea whispered back. "You're the only one I trust anymore, besides Tytonn—not that I see him hardly. It's too difficult and would throw too much suspicion on him."

As they drew back from one another, Darice nodded toward the bag and said, "I hope they help."

"They will," Gailea promised.

Clutching the bag close, Gailea fled up to her bedchamber. Once inside, she hummed her color-changing melody, and the windows darkened to a deep gray that matched that of the stone walls. Her door only locked from the outside, but a quick trill of her voice accomplished the task for her. These were spells that Moragon could easily undo with his mental magic, but not without her knowing—and thus, not without giving her some small chance to hide the bag and its contents, should he seek to enter.

Sitting on her chair beside the fire, she opened the bag, revealing the mountain of gold coins within. Gailea dug deep inside until her fingers brushed against something small and stiff. Removing the tiny parchment, she unrolled it with a smile. It was from Brynn, their mother. Brynn "looked forward to her wedding" and promised to bring flowers from her garden. Gailea skipped ahead to Brynn's signature; beside it, drawn with such precision, was the treble clef.

Gailea had sent out several such pieces of parchment to Brynn, along with instructions on how to use them. She'd infused the parchment with a simple memory charm she'd found in her song-spell book. All the receiver needs to do is touch the treble clef, recite the necessary poem, and record their message before sending it back. With this magic, Brynn had acted as the middle man between Gailea and the king and queen of Hyloria.

Gailea now pressed her thumb to the musical symbol and sang the memory spell. Light poured from the letter, and the shapes of music notes glinted in the rays of light, weaving in and out.

An image flickered within the light and then took shape into the shadowy outline of some person—a man, judging by the shorter hair and muscular build. The image solidified, details and colors filled in, and Gailea stared, mesmerized. The man's face was so like Marlis'. Red and purple dressed him from head to toe, matching the rubies and amethysts ringing his fiery curls. He opened his mouth and spoke:

"Greetings, Lady Gailea of Adelar. I know the risk you take, and so I will make my message brief. I thank you for what you are doing for my daughter. We will answer your call. Our ties with Moragon were made to strengthen our kingdom, but now he abuses his power and disgraces our family. We will send aid to the young

Lord Crispin. We will fight by your side, and by his. Amiel bless you, Lady Gailea, the One True Queen."

The light poured back inside the parchment and then vanished. Gailea sat trembling; the bag of coins nearly slipped from her hands, but she grabbed on tightly. Then, she hurried to the windows, returned them to their normal color, and gazed out. No one watched her from any of the other towers, and she breathed relief.

Footsteps hurried toward her chambers. Gailea shoved the bag of coins and letters inside her wardrobe and sang the charm to unlock her door. Moments later, the door burst open, and Bronia stood in the doorway, breathless. "It's the queen. You must come at once."

"Show me," Gailea said, hurrying after her.

They graced the queen's chambers, and Gailea staggered to a halt. Chevalier knelt beside the queen, holding her hand.

Gailea hurried to the queen's other side, sank onto the edge of the bed, and clutched her hand. As she listened, she shuddered with tears, unable to hold them back; she couldn't stop crying any more than she could stop Marlis' heart from failing. It beat so faintly now, quieter than a whisper, and at uneven intervals. Though she could utter no complaint, Gailea sensed the pain pulsing through her body. Placing a hand to Marlis' deceitfully placid face, Gailea sang her lullaby, pouring every ounce of healing she possessed into the queen. Marlis' pain quelled, but her heartbeat continued to falter.

She glared up at Chevalier. "What did you do to her?"

"Nothing," Chevalier muttered.

Gailea shook her head. "Did you kill her so that you could win back his favor?"

Chevalier said nothing but only seemed to stare straight through her.

"I won't give you that satisfaction," Gailea breathed.

"You both have caused her enough pain..." She sang her lullaby again, only this time, she changed some of the notes. This more melancholy version was not meant for a temporary sleep, but to make the queen's eternal rest come with a more merciful speed.

"You would wish to sacrifice your life to ease her passing?" Chevalier sneered. "Because you know that as soon as she is dead, Moragon will not hesitate to claim you."

"I would not see her suffer any longer," Gailea whispered between tears. "She experienced only torment living in this castle; why should she suffer in death as well?"

Gailea sang on. Her song softened even as Marlis' breath and heartbeat faded, like a music box winding down. Then, at last, they ceased.

For a moment, Gailea's breath stopped inside her.

Her breath came again in a staggered sob as she laid her head upon the queen's breast and wept.

Suddenly, footsteps approached.

"It's him," Chevalier muttered.

"Go," Gailea commanded quietly. "I'll handle him. If he is angry, he's less likely to punish me than you."

Chevalier hesitated before giving her a grateful nod and rising to his feet. "Remember what I showed you in my chambers, when the time should come." He turned and fled the room as silently as a shadow.

The footsteps thundered closer, pounding inside Gailea's aching head.

The door opened. The king strode in and stopped short. He stood still a few moments as if surveying the scene; Gailea didn't look up at him.

Then, he marched over and grabbed her arm, dragging her from the room after him.

"Where are we going?" she demanded, her voice hoarse from tears.

"To your dressing chambers, and then, to the Shrine."

Gailea stared at him, dumbfounded. Her body went limp. Then, as she realized the truth behind his words, she pulled against him. "No, your grace—the queen is hardly dead! What will everyone think—?"

"I don't care what they think," Moragon snarled. He pulled her into the dressing room, where her dress gleamed gold on the wooden mannequin. "It doesn't matter what anyone thinks. We *will* be bound this day. Then, our magic shall be one at last."

"Why are you doing this? Why so sudden—?"

Moragon whirled her around and shoved her up against the wall.

"That is not your concern!" he thundered. "Do not deny your lord and master! You gave me your word; we made an agreement—your music and will for their lives. If you wish me to hold to that bargain, then we must accomplish our unity as soon as possible."

"No, I *won't*—!" Gailea shrieked, wrenching away. "You may not have loved the queen, but *I* do! Can you not give me a moment's peace to mourn?"

Moragon raised his hand, curled his fist, and yanked back; Gailea jerked forward as if commanded by invisible strings. He snatched her wrist, pulling her to him and whispering sharply in her ear, "There will be time for you to mourn *after* the wedding—and much more so if you do not obey me now, for the queen's will not be the only blood you cry out for."

Gailea sobbed; her mind reached for a musical spell that could overpower him, but Moragon yanked her toward the mannequin. He ripped the dress she wore, tearing it from her body, and shoved the golden gown at her, commanding, "Prepare yourself now, or my promise to spare him dies."

Trembling, Gailea gripped the golden gown. She

wanted to tear it to shreds, but Moragon's harsh gaze stopped her, and Crispin's face flashed in her mind. As she envisioned him, she watched till the luster in his eyes faded, as devoid of life as Marlis' abruptly still body, empty of everything. Suppressing another sob, Gailea drew a deep breath and slipped into the dress.

Moragon walked around behind her and clasped the buttons. His touch was deft, swift, mechanical, bent on a single purpose—and he would soon bed her in the same manner. Gailea swallowed hard and let her mind go numb of everything except Crispin and saving him. She could no longer save the queen, but she could save him. She must.

Moragon took her hand and dragged her from the dressing chambers. Gailea quickened her pace to match his so that they might have looked like a couple taking a stroll together, if not for the fierceness in his gaze and the tears on her face.

They wound down corridors and stairs until at last, they burst into the Shrine.

A priest knelt before the altar, praying. He glanced up, alarmed. Moragon grabbed his arm, forcing him to his feet and commanding, "You will marry us. Now."

"Your grace?" the priest gasped. "But the queen?"

"The queen is dead," Moragon said flatly, almost growling.

The priest glanced wildly between Gailea and Moragon.

"Fool!" Moragon clutched his robes and threw him to the ground. "I will do it myself!"

"Your grace," Gailea said quietly, "you do not have the power to marry us—"

"I am king! I can grant myself the power to marry us. You will give yourself to me—body, spirit, and magic—"

Horns blasted loudly outside. The doors burst open,

and a guard staggered inside. He glanced at the priest who lay moaning on the ground, and then turned to Moragon who glared at him and demanded, "What do you want? And what *fool* is sounding the alarm?"

"We're under attack, your grace," the man gasped. "There are forces surrounding all sides of the castle. Lords Alistor and Crispin are leading them—"

"*Those bastards are no lords!*"

Moragon sliced his hand through the air. The soldier flew across the Shrine, burst through the window, and catapulted across the sky. Gailea shielded herself from the shattering glass, wanting to run from the man's fading cries as he plummeted to his death.

Moragon whirled on her then, clutched her arm, and yanked her after him. "Come. Those fools will not breach my forces. You *will* aid me, or so help me, I will kill them all with a single thought—*argh!*"

Moragon's legs crumpled beneath him. He collapsed to his knees, and Gailea tumbled down with him, inhaling sharply as her head knocked against the stone floor. She touched the fresh wound, whispering her lullaby to ease the sharp throbbing. Then, she sat up and glanced at Moragon who'd scrambled to his knees but now swayed uneasily, falling against the wall. He struggled to support himself, gripping at the stones with one hand while clutching at his skull with the other.

"He's trying to sever the barriers!" Moragon cried. He glared at Gailea, and pain glinted visibly in his narrowed gaze and labored breathing. He snatched out at her but almost fell again; Gailea scrambled back, staring in alarm. "Help me, damn you! I cannot hold him off on my own—what devilry is he using—?" He clawed at her and snarled, "If you go to him, I *will* kill him! Help me! Use your music! I will combine it with my mental resistance to keep him out—*ahh!*"

He crumpled again in pain, eyes wide with panic as he struggled to focus.

Gailea realized that he sought to use some mental spell against Crispin but, for whatever reason, was failing. With a lift of her chin, she said coolly, "You won't touch him. He will not lose this battle."

She fled down the hall, ignoring Moragon's cries. He muttered a spell, but as Gailea felt its freezing power spiraling toward her, she sang an ascending scale, focusing on her feet to increase her speed and zip to the side just in time to miss the spell.

Gailea raced down corridors and stairs, her feet flying toward her new purpose. She passed Moragon's soldiers fighting against those clad in armor bearing the crest of a rose—from Rosa, she thought—as well as a blue-haired people whose skin shimmered white as snow—the people of Iceania—along with Adelarans, and Fyres from Hyloria. Crispin's forces had already broken through and infiltrated the castle, but how?

The caves—the ones Crispin had once tried to get her to escape through with him. But there was no guarantee they could all come through the cave—not before Moragon found a way to stop them.

As Gailea ran, she knew what she must do. She began singing her summoning spell, hoping Darice and the others would hear and join her before the king gave up on protecting his silver barrier and came after her instead.

Gailea entered the great hall and stood still, overwhelmed by the mere thought of the immensity of the magic she prepared to try.

Darice burst into the room, Sorcha and Macha straight on her heels.

One by one, more and more children and youth entered till Gailea found herself joined by a good half dozen, along with an elderly man and woman.

"Follow me," Gailea said, "and follow along exactly as I sing. You've practiced this song—but now we must sing it together, in harmony, for this to work."

Gailea led them to the middle of the room. For a moment, she hesitated. If this failed, if someone sang the wrong notes or went off-key, she didn't know what could go wrong. The entire castle might explode, annihilating everyone.

She met Darice's gaze, full of encouragement and readiness. Everyone else watched her readily.

Gailea took a deep breath and began to sing.

She sang loud and full, and the others chimed in, singing the ascending scales over and over—C, D, E, F, G, A, B, C—that were meant to magnify—in this case, to magnify sound. The instruments within the glass cases joined them, quietly at first, but the more passion they poured into their singing, the more vehemently the instruments' passion echoed back.

Strings, flutes, drums, trumpets—all swelled into a deafening symphony. The great hall trembled. The entire castle began to quake. The windows shattered, and lastly, as Gailea pushed a powerful note from deep inside her and the other music mages joined her, the glass encasing the instruments shattered as well. Gailea snatched the nearest one—a flute—and began to play, shakily at first, but soon with the same confidence as one who'd played all their life. The others followed suit, grabbing whatever instrument they could find.

Suddenly, the castle jerked, and a loud explosion sounded, followed by a steady chiming, like raining glass. Gailea was knocked off her feet, as were several of the others, and the instruments fell silent. She rushed to the window just in time to see silver shards cascading all about the castle like snow. Not only had the barrier surrounding the castle shattered, but so had the thick ropes of silver tying the castle to the barrier. Gailea smiled; the silver barrier was broken—

The next moment, she screamed as the castle plummeted downward.

"What do we do?" Darice cried as the other music mages cried in a panic.

"Sing or play after me!" Gailea shouted.

Trembling head to toe, she began playing on her flute. The same song that had sped her footsteps, she now played in reverse, hoping to slow the castle's descent. At first, nothing seemed to happen, but as the other music mages joined her, some with the instruments and others with their voices, the castle's violent trembling slowed to a swaying with an occasional jolt. Its falling slowed, as though gentle arms carried it, and then it landed with a thud and a shiver.

Stones and debris rained from the ceiling, and everyone ducked and dodged, but soon all lay still. Dust and snow rose outside, blinding Gailea's view. Then, as the misty curtain cleared, Gailea made out several flags with a bright red rose and others bearing the crest of a rainbow prism crowned with the sun—the crest of Hyloria—waving between the towers and turrets. She heard the gates raised, the cries of armies, and saw those armies pour inside.

"We did it!" Gailea shouted. "They're coming—we did it!"

Cheers erupted from Darice and the others, and Gailea watched out the window as Crispin led the way, his body and sword ablaze, making his horse's coat shimmer silver. Together, they sped forward like a shooting star.

Gailea smiled, breathless for a few moments, and then fled the great hall. She had helped to start the battle, and now she was ready to help finish it.

CHAPTER 25

FIRE AND BLOOD

"Fall back!" Crispin shouted, raising his shield against the shards of silver raining like needles all around. "Fall back!"

He had drawn power from the sun and struck at the silver barrier with Anwar. Moragon had pried painfully into his mind, trying to stop him, but Anwar's magic had shielded his thoughts from being manipulated, and he had found just enough strength to plunge his sword inside the barrier over and over until it began to crack. Then, suddenly, whether by Crispin's sword or some unseen aid inside the castle, the entire ground had begun to quake, and the silver barrier had exploded, entirely annihilated.

Alistor and several others gave commands. The armies spread out, creating a wider girth as Astyrian floated down. It landed, sending tremors through the earth. Crispin's horse stomped and whinnied, but Crispin touched the tiny vial of magic dust dangling at his wrist and whispered a charm Tytonn had once taught him to settle the beast's nerves.

When the ground stilled at last, the castle stood before them, some of the towers and turrets crumbling from the impact, but mostly intact and ready for the taking. Clouds of dust and debris spiraled up to conceal it, but a loud clanking signified the gates raising. Crispin swung his sword, still illuminated dimly with liquid gold, and spheres of light spun through the air, dispersing the gloom even as the gates finished raising with a loud clunk.

"The castle is ours—forward!"

Crispin raised his sword high and charged forth. With a determined cry, his warriors followed. Moragon's men met them inside, attacking with swords, bows, and all types of magic. More of Crispin's soldiers climbed over the walls and inside the courtyard, aided by ladders and flying charms.

Crispin fought astride his horse. He kept his sword poised in one hand, warding off the occasional foes that slipped between the men guarding him and Alistor. The shields of light he and Alistor had both encased themselves inside only deflected magic attacks like ice or wind, not swords, spears, and arrows.

Alistor called to him. They shared a meaningful look and raised their hands. Then, together, they concentrated, chanting the spell for fire.

Crispin felt the fresh flames boiling up inside him till they burst all along his body. Embers shot erratically across the courtyard, knocking down both foes and a few of his own men. He cursed beneath his breath; the intention had been to illuminate his soldiers' swords, not incinerate them. Several Iceans rushed forward to heal their suffering companions with their cool touch.

Tendrils of flame burst all along Alistor's body and then branched out like lightning, incinerating dozens of Moragon's men while lighting many of their own armies' swords. Alistor emitted another round of flames, this time grappling onto Moragon's soldiers and swinging them about. He coiled the fiery whips around clusters of soldiers and sent them flying through the air, screaming as they burned like shooting stars.

Crispin focused his magic on one foe at a time, not wishing to create another blunder—

"Crispin!"

Crispin's gaze shifted. Some yards away, Tytonn fought atop one of the walls. With his tall, muscular girth, he shoved soldiers aside, spearing others and sending them tumbling from the wall. He hooked Crispin's glance briefly, before the thundering of hooves caught both their attention.

Horses galloped across the courtyard, whinnying madly. Smoke filled the air, and a wild blaze showed where the stables had caught fire. Crispin panicked; most of his men didn't have horses of their own and would be easily trampled by the beasts—

A shout rent the air—Tytonn's—and all the horses froze still as stone. Then, as Tytonn threw several other spells to the wind; Crispin's horse reared, knocking one of Moragon's men down. Alistor's steed kicked out his back legs, eliminating several soldiers. While the madness caught everyone off guard, Alistor hurled fireball after fireball into the crowds, twisting his hands to control the flames' paths, not missing a single target nor harming a single ally. The horses of Crispin's army began fighting while Moragon's horses bucked soldiers from their backs, sending them flying through the air.

An arrow zoomed toward Tytonn, but Crispin hurled it away with a fireball before erecting a shield of light around Tytonn. Tytonn stared, amazed; he could still maneuver, but no magic projectiles would breach his new shield. He grinned at Crispin, nodded his thanks, and then swung his sword, re-entering the fray.

Crispin swept a glance around the courtyard. Some of the Iceans immobilized Moragon's men by encasing them in solid blocks of ice or by freezing their feet and hands. The Adelarans and Rosans fought with sword or spear, while those who possessed magic cast lightning, gusted soldiers away with small whirlwinds, or whipped them away with vines or waves of water. Many still held swords blazing with Alistor's fire. The Fyres from Hyloria fought with both flame and sword. Altogether, they seemed to be overcoming Moragon's forces—

A deafening blend of musical instruments ringing a single note shook the earth, making it shift and split apart. Crispin's horse pranced and released a nervous whinny. Men and women began to fall from their horses. Soldiers from both sides stumbled, falling on each other's swords. Crispin flung a glance around the castle until his eyes locked on Moragon's face leering at him through one of the tall windows of the great hall. Its glass had been shattered, and sunlight glinted along the jagged edges that remained.

A scream pierced the air, and Moragon clutched Gailea to him. She struggled, but as soon as her gaze found Crispin, she held still and stared at him, silently pleading. Moragon bent his head toward her, saying something in her ear. Gailea continued to stare straight at Crispin, and her lips seemed to form the words, "I'm sorry..."

Then, she closed her eyes, her lips began to move, and the next moment, a mighty chord emanated from the great hall, making the entire grounds tremble once more. Stones rained from the towers, crushing both friend and foe. Spooked horses threw their riders. Tytonn looked frantic as he tried to calm the horses to no avail. Crispin's protective shield began to diminish.

An angry fire filled Crispin. Locking his gaze firmly on Moragon, he hurled flame at the window. Alistor did the same, a vicious resolve on his face. Moragon zipped to the side, placing Gailea in the fire's wake. As if sensing its approaching heat, Gailea opened her eyes and flung a song at the fire, making it hurtle straight back toward Crispin and Alistor who each caught the fire in their hands, extinguishing the flames to smoke.

Moragon grabbed Gailea then and, with a glare at Crispin, dragged her into the room out of sight.

Crispin charged forward. Alistor shouted something, but his words were a blur that Crispin could not focus on; he could allow no distractions, even the best intentions, to keep him from fighting his way to Gailea. He spurred his horse toward the castle, but the going was slow around so much fallen debris and fighting soldiers. The horse reared and whinnied in protest—

Flames burst from the horse's hooves, and Crispin panicked. Was his rage at the king so out of control that his fire had ruptured from him without his even realizing, maiming his own steed?

But the horse did not rear in pain. Instead, the flames took shape, spreading wide like an eagle's wings. Then, with a shout from Alistor, the horse jumped up, soaring over the armies. The horse began to buck, but Crispin grabbed the reins and guided the flying beast through the window and inside the great hall.

Crispin jumped off the horse. Shattered glass covered the floor, but the instruments still floated obediently about the room. He hurried from the great hall to begin his search.

Where would Moragon take her? He checked the throne room, the council chambers, and Gailea's chambers but found no traces of anyone. Most of the soldiers had fled to the courtyard, while the servants had likely gone into hiding—

"Lord Crispin! Lord Crispin!"

Crispin spun. A woman with a long dark braid careened toward him, wide-eyed and breathless.

"My sister—Gailea!" the woman gasped. She stopped, bent over, and gulped a few breaths before glancing up and saying, "She's with him—in Moragon's private chambers. He would bind himself to her, to gain complete access to her magic."

"He cannot," Crispin blurted. "He cannot do that—"

"He can. He has spells—the same he used on the queen. It's why she never fought back against him. He had complete control over her magic. And now Gailea—"

"Where did you say they were?"

"His chambers—"

Crispin darted down the corridor.

"Please help her!" Darice called. "Save my sister!"

"I will!"

Crispin careened toward the northern wing, praying he would find them in time.

Screams and shouts soon led him. Large doors depicting ornate carvings of birds and silver harps rose before him. They stood ajar, and he rushed inside.

Gailea and Moragon circled each other around a massive canopy bed. Their curtains had been shredded, and smoke rose from where the furniture smoldered. Other furniture had been splintered. A vase lay shattered.

Gailea's golden gown was torn nearly in two. She crouched low, her eyes wild as a cornered wolf's. As Moragon muttered some spell, she darted to the side, and the bed's headboard exploded, splintering into tiny shreds.

Crispin hurled flame at Moragon, but with a single word from the king, he flew back through the air. Just before hitting the stone wall, Crispin muttered a protective charm that pushed him away from it. He landed on his feet and rushed to Gailea's side, gripping her hand and covering them both with a light shield. His head spun dizzily from the effort, and he side-stepped into the light streaming through the window, absorbing the extra sunlight. This, of all moments, was not the time for his magic to run dry.

"You will not touch her again," Crispin snarled, holding Gailea's hand tight.

"Move aside, boy," Moragon hissed. "Your life is already forfeit. The wench has broken our bargain."

Crispin lifted his chin and lowered his voice. "*Make* me stand aside. You can't, can you? That's why you need her—"

Moragon flung his hand toward Crispin. Pain surged through Crispin's skull, making his light shield diminish, but he clung to it, pushing the light out from his body with every ounce of concentration he could muster. The light consumed the pain of Moragon's spell until it vanished. Moragon's eyes widened a little, but then he flung another spell at Crispin. Crispin countered, burning the spell alive before it had the chance to reach him.

"What *are* you?" Moragon breathed. "No Fyre should have that kind of power. Physical magic cannot undo mental magic—"

"On the contrary, dear brother. For the Fyre who masters blue fire, light magic, or both, has one of the greatest advantages of all magic users, even over the proudest mind rapists like yourself—not to mention, he *does* possess the Weaver's sword..."

A ring of fire surrounded Moragon, who collapsed to his knees with a groan. Alistor stood in the doorway with a sneering grin, hands outstretched. Sunlight poured with a sudden brilliance inside the room, flowing toward

Alistor's hands. The sunlight streamed inside Alistor, illuminating his entire body till he shone like his own sun. The beams of light then emanated from him, and he gripped them in his hands, commanding them as they extended and wrapped around Moragon who yelled and groaned and struggled to stand but could only stumble.

"Liquid silver," Alistor continued, "and its cousin, liquid gold, provide natural immunity to mental magic. I'd have thought you'd known that after all these years, considering you had your precious sorcerer construct your precious barrier from the 'unbreakable' substance. Where *is* your faithful dog anyway?"

"F-fled," Moragon forced between gritted teeth. He groaned and fought to move, but Crispin joined Alistor in redirecting the light to bind Moragon in place.

Alistor glanced at Crispin, amused, and then looked back at his brother. With a broad grin, he chuckled and said, "See there? You always knew his true potential, didn't you? That's why you sought to stifle it..."

Moragon only gasped; the stench of burning flesh began to fill the air, and red marks spread on his skin. They were burning him alive, from inside the core of his twisted heart out to his bones and skin. Crispin almost recoiled but then increased the intensity of the sunlight he commanded. Moragon winced, and Crispin felt a solemn satisfaction. Moragon had burned countless others. He deserved this judgment—

Two soldiers burst into the room, shoving past Alistor and flinging someone inside.

Chevalier.

"We caught him trying to escape through the woods," one of the soldiers said.

With a groan, Chevalier collapsed to the floor. He scrambled to stand up, but Alistor waved one of his hands, and streamers of fire burst from his fingertips in long tendrils, snapping out like whips. They caught around Chevalier's wrists and ankles, chaining him to the ground.

Chevalier muttered a spell at Alistor. Crispin hovered a light shield between the sorcerer and his uncle, and the spell rebounded, spiraling into Chevalier who'd started to stand but now crumpled to the ground.

"Impossible," Moragon seethed, growling and snatching toward his brother; he fell forward and caught himself with both hands. His skin began to bubble and distort, and his hair began to recede, singed away by the heat radiating from inside his body.

Alistor twisted the hand keeping Moragon in check. Flames burst from Moragon's arm, and he howled. The fire vanished just as quickly but left the ruined king doubled over, clutching his mangled arm to his breast, muttering what Crispin imagined were insults and curses.

Alistor grinned in satisfaction. "Why impossible, brother? After all this time, you still consider yours to be the superior family. But the truth is that the phenomenon that created Crispin happened by *my* family's blood, not yours. But don't worry, brother. It will all end soon..."

"No...it won't," Moragon rasped, glaring viciously at his brother. "Not for me...and not for you...You'll see your folly—" He flinched and swayed uneasily on his hands and knees. Then, he stared straight at the floor, seeming to concentrate hard on one of the wooden planks—

And vanished. Crispin gasped and let his hands drop. He flung a glance at Alistor who still stood illuminated by fire and sunbeams, keeping Chevalier in check.

"Don't worry," Alistor said. "I knew he would likely flee. A coward at heart. He always accused *me* of relying on others, but you see what he is in the end."

"Where will he go?" Gailea asked. "Should we pursue him?"

Alistor shook his head. "He will find some new ally to deceive. We may see him again, but for now, we have bigger matters to contend with..." He turned toward Chevalier.

Crispin focused on Chevalier, trying to erect a light shield around him to keep his powers in check, but the shield flickered. "Uncle, I don't think I've power enough left in me to help you."

"No matter," Alistor said. "A light shield would not have contained him for long anyway—but this memento from my brother will."

Alistor lifted his hand to show the ring he now wore. It glistened, both with Moragon's blood and the many facets of its huge, dark red gemstone. As Crispin glanced to the floor, his eyes widened at the sight of a severed hand, warped and blackened from fire and lying in a pool of blood.

"No," Chevalier gasped, looking wild and desperate. "No—no, it can't be..."

He struggled to stand again, straining against his fiery chains, but Alistor swung his free hand and embers spiraled through the air, knocking Chevalier to the ground. The sorcerer tried to push himself up but only collapsed, shaking violently. Alistor glided forward and hovered over him. He raised his hand, letting fire fill his palm; small flames darted from his fingertips, teasing along Chevalier's skin and tattered robes.

"Please," Chevalier begged, his eyes wide. "Please, I beg you..."

"I shall gladly appease you," Alistor mocked. "Nothing shall give me greater pleasure than to personally burn you for the heretic and coward that you are. If you feared the pyre, you shall fear my presence tenfold before I am through—"

Alistor drew his sword and lit it with flame. Crispin cringed, and a sickness twisted his stomach. Alistor brought the sword down toward Chevalier—

"No—*stop*!"

The blade rested just above Chevalier's ribs. Alistor narrowed his gaze at Gailea.

Gailea clung to Crispin's arm. "Please, Crispin. Let him live. He *is* a coward. And he may have done evil—but he is not evil himself. He had his reasons. I beg you—let him live."

Chevalier's gaze darted wildly between Gailea, Alistor's blade, and Crispin. Alistor narrowed his gaze a little more and shifted it to Crispin, silently demanding.

"Why would you show him this mercy?" Crispin asked her gently.

"Because he has a wife and child. And because I can understand what it's like, to feel forced to do horrible things to protect those you love. I only obeyed Moragon just moments ago to protect you. How is what he's done any different?"

Crispin studied her, overcome with the tenderness in her eyes as she watched him.

Turning back to Alistor, he said, "Moragon has fled, and Marlis never was the true queen. Lady Gailea is now queen of all Adelar, and you must obey her."

Alistor's gaze blazed with loathing. Turning back to Chevalier who now trembled, his body jerking from the fiery bonds searing his flesh, he said, "Then I ask permission to escort him to the dungeons and have charge over his personal welfare."

"If I grant you this, you will not mistreat your power," Gailea said. "You will see to it that he has all he needs. If I find you have misused this responsibility, my retribution will not be light. He will be given a chance, and you will not torment him further."

Alistor nodded stiffly. He yanked back his hand, and the fiery ropes turned to beams of light that jerked Chevalier to his feet. Chevalier released a weary exhale and closed his eyes. As Alistor walked away, the bonds of light commanded Chevalier's body, making him float along behind him.

As soon as Alistor and Chevalier had disappeared from sight, Crispin turned to Gailea and clutched her hands in his. "It was a noble decision, sparing his life."

"Perhaps not," Gailea muttered. "Perhaps he would have welcomed death. But his family...I know he wouldn't wish to leave them like that..."

She glanced away sadly, but Crispin lifted her chin, drawing her gaze back to his. "I've had my own fears these past weeks. The fear of losing you, of never seeing you again. My aunt—she must be so very proud of you..."

Gailea gasped. Tears filled her eyes, and she let her head fall on his chest. "Marlis is dead..."

She wept softly. Pain tore at Crispin's heart. He hugged her close, stroking her hair.

"I could not save her," Gailea whispered against his heart.

"She was not yours to save. You did your best. She would be proud..." He drew her back, holding her shoulders and gazing into her somber, blue-green eyes. "As am I. You saved me. You saved *us*. You bought us time, sent the armies from Hyloria—you've no idea what a welcoming sight they were."

Gailea smiled a little and wiped her tears. "I knew you would come. I knew you would find your courage and strength. And your magic, Crispin—it's incredible since we last parted. I think you have quite a special gift indeed—and..." she stretched up her hand to caress a wild curl away from his face, "...you will use that power to protect your kingdom. You will make the noblest king that Adelar has seen in many years. You will provide it with the protection and strength it has yearned after for such a long time."

Crispin drew a staggering breath. His hands trailed from her shoulders, down her arms, and wrapped around her waist, drawing her to him. Their bodies pressed close, and his face bent down, hovering just above hers so that their lips nearly brushed and her breath tickled his cheek. "I would be honored to be your king. But first and most importantly, your husband. Marry me, Gailea. Today. Let us not waste another moment."

Gailea stared up at him, her breathing shallow. "My dress is torn..."

"We'll find another."

"My mother—she wouldn't be able to come, what with the war. And your sister—"

"Battles will linger for some time. But I don't want to wait. We can always have another celebration to honor our families. But let our kingdom be united at last—let *us* be united at last."

He let his lips brush hers, ever so lightly. She shivered and then pulled his face to hers, kissing him deeply.

After a while, she let their lips part just enough to breathe the words into him, "Very well, my king. I accept your proposal. Let us be married—but first, we must announce our victory. This is not a victory to celebrate just for us, but for all Adelar."

CHAPTER 26

A SONG OF PASSION

Gailea laughed and clapped as the acrobats twirled their partners in the air and caught each other. Then, she squeezed Crispin's hand to catch his attention. He smiled warmly at her and kissed her hand before delving back into an animated conversation with Alistor.

Gailea sighed with contentment. A month had passed since the night of their whirlwind marriage celebration, and she could hardly believe the change of atmosphere that had descended in the great hall in Moragon's absence. The chatter rising from the courtiers was more jubilant and sprinkled with laughter. The joy and peace ruling the great hall was such a stark contrast to the constant anxiety of being under Moragon's probing gaze that sometimes she felt amazed that it wasn't all some wonderful dream.

"…hello, Gailea? Gailea, love, are you in there?"

Gailea jumped and turned a sheepish grin to Darice. "Sorry. My mind wandered off for a moment."

Darice grinned in turn, her gaze playful. "You've been daydreaming a lot lately." Leaning across the table, she lowered her voice and asked, "Have you shared the good news yet?"

Gailea shook her head. "Not yet; I haven't…"

"My love!" Crispin grabbed her hand and sprang to his feet. "Thank you for being so patient in allowing me and Alistor to bore each other with political matters. But now, come. I've a surprise for you."

"A surprise?" Gailea's brows rose. "For what occasion?"

"For my love for you—isn't that occasion enough?" He smiled and kissed her hand before drawing her to her feet.

As Gailea followed Crispin outside, she marveled once more at the change that had occurred in both the castle and the grounds within the past few weeks. After their wedding and coronation, their first decision as king and queen had been to restore the castle to the best condition possible. The Abalino people had been summoned from their floating kingdom to suspend the castle in the air until any rubble and debris could be cleared away. A space had been cleared in the woods, and then the Abalinos had safely returned the castle to the ground. Repairs of broken towers and turrets were yet underway, but at least the castle no longer sat lopsided like a broken doll's house.

Gailea's breath puffed in white clouds as they crunched across last night's fresh snowfall. As a sharp wind blew, she shivered, but the next moment, Gailea felt Crispin's warmth flowing into her, easing her body and spirit as he drew magic from the bright sun overhead.

They soon reached the stables and passed several stalls where stablemen spread fresh hay, cleaning and brushing the horses and supplying them with fresh blankets. A familiar singing perked Gailea's attention, till at last, they stopped before a stall where Tytonn sang gently to a horse whose gray coat was speckled with light tan spots that shone almost pink in the lamplight.

Crispin folded his arms, feigning a scolding stance. "And what have I told you about wooing other ladies with your songs in my sister's absence?"

Tytonn looked up with a laugh. "Forgive me, sire. I simply cannot help myself."

"Tytonn Grayfell—the greatest ladies' man at court," Crispin teased with a shake of his head. The two men embraced, and he added, "How've you been, my friend? We haven't been able to meet as much as I would like lately. There's still much to fuss over in terms of the war."

"Yes, how goes all of that?" Tytonn glanced between Gailea and Crispin, all the while brushing out the horse's coat.

"Things have started to die down," Crispin said, "but Gareth and Donyon's numbers are still growing. They've gathered enough armies to begin infiltrating some of our smaller fortresses. But thanks to Alistor, we've got it under control for now."

"Yes, I'd heard about his new title—Duke of Turn-worth, eh?"

Crispin nodded.

"What an honor. I must congratulate him next I see him." Tytonn paused in his work with a sigh. "I must also tell him to help end these battles as soon as possible. I'm eager to see Elda return to court."

"As am I," Crispin said, hugging Gailea close to him.

"As are both of us," Gailea said, "but she wrote recently, and she's doing well. She's very focused on her sewing. And she's been able to use the liquid silver to craft weapons and armor for our armies."

"I'm glad she's content," Tytonn said. "Such a job suits her. She always wanted to do something with meaning and purpose. And as long as she's safe..."

"I assure you that the House remains well under guard," Crispin said. "There's no safer place for her to be."

As he hugged Gailea again, she looked up at him and said, "Are you going to tell me now why we're here? Or will you leave me in suspense all day?"

"Why, isn't visiting our good friend here reason enough to enjoy a walk around the grounds?"

"You mentioned a surprise. Don't think I've forgotten."

"But I've already shown you the surprise." His eyes twinkling, Crispin nodded at Tytonn who passed him the reins, and he held them out toward Gailea. "She's all yours."

Gailea took the reins and stared up at the horse in awe. Removing a glove to stroke the beast's velvety nose, she said, "Oh, she's the loveliest creature. Thank you."

"Of course," Crispin said, "I was thinking that perhaps we could go riding together. It's been a while, but no time like the present, eh?"

A flush touched Gailea's cheeks as she glanced up at him uncertainly. "I love her; truly, I do. And I do miss riding with you. But I don't think I can today. I'm not feeling quite myself and fear that riding may make me ill."

Crispin arched a brow. "This mysterious illness wouldn't be the sort that lingers for, say, nine months or so, would it?"

Gailea's eyes widened. "You—you know! You've known all this time, haven't you?"

Crispin chuckled. "Keeping secrets around court is near impossible, as you should know by now." He held out his hands, and she took them. He pulled her close and twirled her about, and they laughed together.

"You're not upset then?" Gailea asked. "I was waiting for a good time to tell you, but you've been so busy."

"How could I be upset? I have my queen, my throne—and now I'll have my heir, with the woman I love most in the entire world."

As he set her back down, Tytonn caught him in a huge embrace.

"Congratulations, my friend!"

"Thank you," Crispin said, clapping him on the back. "And I've already decided to name you our honorary godfather. If you're up for it."

"Indeed! What an honor." He hugged Crispin again and then hugged Gailea, who stood taken aback.

"My apologies," Tytonn said. "I'm just very excited to be part of the family."

"And we're excited to have you," Crispin said.

"Of course we are," Gailea said. "You only caught me off guard."

Crispin laughed again. "You're acting as skittish as your new horse here before Tytonn tamed her. When only weeks ago, you were standing on a parapet singing an entire castle to the ground."

"They do say pregnancy changes everything," Tytonn said.

"But for the better," Gailea assured Crispin.

"Yes," Crispin agreed, smiling down at her and drawing her close, "all for the better."

***

Crispin strolled through the Adelaran marketplace with his arm wrapped around Gailea. Gailea chatted gaily with Darice, who walked at her other side. Alistor trailed behind, along with a couple of guards, but Crispin paid them little heed. This day was about his wife, and thus far it had been perfect.

A few days had passed since his revelation of her special secret, and he had insisted they go to the market to look together for gifts for the coming infant. While the child wasn't expected for another good eight months, Crispin's couldn't hide his enthusiasm, and Gailea couldn't deny it. Besides that, she had been thrilled to leave the castle grounds at long last. That had been one of their proudest moments together—Moragon's enslaving bracelet exchanged for a crown of freedom and peace.

Already, they had found some little velvet and silk frocks for the babe, a music box that Gailea could store her own songs inside to play, and a few toys that might suit for either a boy or a girl. Crispin had thought to bring Gailea by her mother's house, to share the good news, but Darice said that Brynn was out of town on business, delivering one of her seamstress' orders. A letter would have to suffice.

Instead, they turned their sights to the main square which bustled with conversation, laughter, and, as they drew nearer, upbeat music played on strings, flutes, and drums. They reached the square, and Gailea strained to see between the crowds. Crispin looked too and caught a glimpse of several musicians playing, with many of the townsfolk joining hands and dancing in rings around them.

Gailea's foot began to tap, her body swayed, and she looked at Crispin eagerly.

"Shall we?"

Crispin frowned in concern. "Are you sure it's all right?"

Gailea rolled her eyes. "I'm pregnant, not on my death bed. Of course, it's all right. If I start to feel ill, I'll take a rest. Come on then—dance with me!"

She grabbed his hands and pulled him through the crowds. He laughed out loud, yelling over his shoulder for Alistor to join them, but the sight of him was soon swallowed by the throngs of clapping, cheering towns-folk.

Crispin, Gailea, and Darice entwined themselves with the rest of the dancers, holding hands while skipping, hopping, and twirling around the musicians. One of the musicians darted through the crowds, extending a hat that folks tossed coins inside, and Gailea threw in several.

Crispin and Gailea danced till he felt breathless, and even then he danced on, giddy with the joy of sharing such a jubilant experience with his wife, who didn't seem winded in the least. Their first dance had come at their wedding feast, but that had been a formal affair. Here, Gailea seemed in her element. The music flowed wild and free, just as she and Crispin could now be.

At last, the song ended on a high, cheery note, and the dancers dispersed, laughing, cheering, and throwing more coins at the performers who announced it was their last song of the afternoon.

"Glad we were able to catch it," Crispin said with a wide grin.

"So am I—"

"As am I—Gailea, how good it is to see you!"

The man who had collected the coins in the hat pranced up, grabbed Gailea's hands, and pulled her into a warm embrace. Crispin watched in mild alarm at the man's boldness, but the next moment, he bowed his head and said, "Forgive me—I forgot for a moment that you are now queen. I was only so excited to see such a friendly face."

"Think nothing of it," Gailea said, waving the matter

aside with her hand. "It's good to see you as well—Gerry, isn't it? I used to see you about the kitchens at the castle. You were always kind to me, offered me your breakfast on more than one occasion…"

"Oh!" Darice cried. "Yes, I remember too! You were always coming up with the most ridiculous songs to cheer us up…"

As the three chatted gaily, someone placed a hand on Crispin's shoulder, and he jumped before recognizing the touch as Alistor's.

"Uncle," Crispin said merrily, "you should join us next time. You missed out on a splendid romp. I haven't felt so refreshed in a long time."

"Forgive me for spoiling the fun," Alistor said quietly, "but I prefer my 'romps' to be a bit more refined. But are you certain it's wise for you to allow your bride such familiarity with this man? There are many eyes about, and watchful eyes can quickly turn to rumors."

"He's just an old friend of hers," Crispin said. "Do calm yourself, uncle. Have a bit of fun."

"I believe that young man is having more than a bit of fun speaking with her majesty…"

As Crispin continued to watch their animated conversation, his joy began to cloud with doubt, but he quickly shook it aside. "It may be your duty to look out for our welfare, but I would not ruin my wife's happiness, not when she is free after being trapped inside that castle for so many years."

Alistor clicked his tongue. "Hardly king for a month, and you would let her authority surpass yours already?"

Crispin turned to frown at his uncle. "I'll thank you not to patronize me in front of my bride or her friends—"

"Crispin?"

Gailea touched his arm, drawing her attention back

to him. She beamed, and a healthy red flush touched her cheeks. Crispin's irritation at Alistor melted, and he could feel only joy for his wife once again.

"You look so radiant. Have you enjoyed yourself?"

"Very much so. But I think I've finally tired myself as well—and the baby."

"Then come." Crispin linked his arm in hers. "Let's go home and have a fine dinner prepared—for the both of you."

***

After dinner had concluded, Alistor announced that he had some news of war preparations to share.

As Gailea followed Crispin inside the council chamber, Alistor glanced up from the large table covered with sprawling maps and figurines. With a frown, he asked, "What is the queen doing here? Shouldn't she be resting?"

"Why does everyone insist on treating me like some invalid just because I carry a child?" Gailea joined Crispin on the opposite side of the table. "Women have been doing so nearly since the beginning of time."

"You carry no mere child, but a royal heir. You shouldn't be troubling yourself with matters of war."

"This is just as much my kingdom as it is Crispin's," Gailea said. "And besides, my mind will be far more greatly troubled if it wastes away with boredom."

Gailea shared a challenging glare with Alistor before he recollected himself in his cool manner, hands clasped behind his back, and studied the maps.

"There have been skirmishes recently here and here," Alistor said, pointing to various towns across Adelar. "Rumors begin to solidify into truths as Gareth and Donyon build up their allies. I am of the mind that we should continue building our own armies and attack them as soon as possible, strike them down before they have a chance to become an even bigger threat and waste to our resources."

"What of Elda?" Gailea asked. "Is she still crafting weapons and armor from the Weaver's House?"

Alistor nodded. "Faithfully so."

"Then is there a need for immediate war? Honestly, with Elda's craft, we could well defend ourselves if an attack arose. I think we should focus on peace. Has anyone tried to speak with Gareth or his son? Suggest a treaty?"

Alistor snorted. "Of course not. It is futile to destroy some enemies without eliminating the remnants of all."

Gailea touched Crispin's arm and gazed up at him tenderly. "You've always been a compassionate soul. What does your heart tell you?"

"Compassion does not build a kingdom," Alistor said.

"She did not ask you," Crispin snapped.

Alistor bowed his head. "Forgive me, sire."

Crispin watched Gailea, fear and doubt lingering clearly on his face. His gaze then strayed to the maps, and he heaved a great sigh. "You really think I should consider granting them pardon? I admit that I'm not keen for another war..."

"Love reunited this kingdom," Gailea said, "not fear. True power does not come by fear—you've seen this, with Chevalier. He obeyed Moragon because he feared him. But had he loved Moragon, he'd likely still be by his side, aiding him. 'Humble in defeat, merciful in victory.' Let *that* be our motto. Keeping Chevalier alive—it hasn't harmed us, has it?"

Alistor scoffed. "The only wisdom in keeping Chevalier alive is the hope of learning more about the dark magic he was creating with Moragon; the last thing we need is that nuisance running amuck or landing in the wrong hands. We're not even certain what all it's capable of."

"The Dusk?" Crispin said. "Have you been able yet to learn anything of its whereabouts?"

"No. Chevalier remains silent as stone. If he didn't possess such knowledge, I'd just as soon destroy him along with Gareth and Donyon. It's foolery to place stock in the hope of peace with such repulsive contenders—"

"Leave us," Crispin said curtly.

Alistor stood taken aback.

Crispin repeated more sharply, "Leave us."

Alistor bowed, muttered words of respect, and took his leave.

Gailea touched Crispin's troubled face and brought it toward hers. Gazing into his eyes, she sang softly, watching as his fears and doubts drifted away—though not entirely this time.

Crispin exhaled deeply. "It seems the more and more I tap into my Fyre powers, the less sway your music holds over me—and I hate that. Sometimes, I feel as though my mind is consuming me from the inside out—as if, even in his absence, Moragon has found some way to curse my gift as a burden..."

"I don't think your Fyre magic burdens you; it's the confusion of so many councils. And I don't wish to confuse you further. But I cannot agree with your uncle's suggestions and will speak out for what I believe to be best for our kingdom—and us."

He smiled down at her, a weary but sincere expression. "Which is one of the many things I love about you. I *have* considered your idea, of granting them pardon. I've toyed with it, much as I've toyed with Alistor's arguments of war. They each seem so possibly right, in their ways..."

"I think pardoning them would be the noblest decision," Gailea said. "Of course, there could be certain terms and conditions to protect us from any further thought of rebellion on their part. But if you grant them amnesty, you may have gained powerful allies. Fight them, and you've created enemies anew."

"And if they didn't accept? Or if they betrayed such a treaty and attacked anyway?"

"It's taking them much longer to raise support than it did you. That says something for your leadership; the people love you, Crispin..." She placed her arms around him and drew him close. "*I* love you. I wish you didn't worry so. We are safe and strong. Nothing can destroy us. Our combined magic alone could sustain this castle's safety for weeks on end."

Crispin sighed and wrapped his arms around her. "When Moragon fled to Carmenna, I thought I'd seen the last of my enemies. But Alistor is right—holding a throne is a much trickier balance than obtaining one. There are still those who hate me, those who would rip me from this kingdom—rip *us* apart...."

"But they *won't*," Gailea said, resting a hand over his heart. "They do not bear your strength, nor the people's allegiance."

Crispin smiled down at her again. "I wish I could possess your calm and confidence—but in the meantime, I thank you."

"Remember that you need make no hasty decisions," Gailea added. "We are in no immediate danger. Tend to quelling any skirmishes that might endanger our people, and take what time you need to decide the rest."

"I will. But for now, the only decision I wish to make is to smother my wife in affection for being such a strength and comfort to me this evening..."

He swept her up in his arms, and she squealed in surprise before laughing. Crispin quieted her laugh with a kiss. Then, with a meaningful look in his eyes that filled Gailea's heart with a song of passion, he carried her toward his bedchamber.

CHAPTER 27

A KING'S CONFIDANTE

Summer's wind warmed Crispin's face as he made his way toward the stables. The past six months had seemed to literally fly by. Snowy drifts had been replaced by the new, green life surrounding him. Birds sang sweet songs akin to his Gailea's. He gulped a deep breath of honeysuckle, letting its sweetness caress his throat and refresh his spirit.

As he entered the stable, familiar voices drifted toward him. He caught a glimpse of Tytonn and Gailea at the far end, leaning close together. Gailea glanced up and smiled briefly at Crispin before turning back to Tytonn with a solemn expression and finishing their conversation, too quietly for Crispin to decipher the words.

Tytonn looked up as Crispin approached. "Morning, your grace."

"Morning, Master of Horses." Crispin kissed Gailea's forehead. "Morning, my love."

She grinned up at him. "Morning."

"Are you sure you should be here? Engaging in such an arduous trek in your condition?" Crispin frowned, half-pretending to scold her.

Gailea turned to the horse behind her and caressed its muzzle. "The horses calm me. Tytonn's taught me some of his charms, and I've made my own song to gain their trust. I think it's good for the baby too..." She cradled one hand to her stomach. "...He seems to dance inside me whenever we visit here."

Crispin smiled gently and hugged her close. Then, he turned to Tytonn and said, "I came to find you because I was thinking of Elda last night. I'll be sending word to her soon, and I'm sure she wouldn't mind hearing from you either."

"Actually," Tytonn said, leaning against the stable wall, "we still write frequently."

Crispin nodded. "Good. With a sufficient guard, I could escort her here without harm. She'll likely insist she is needed more at the House, to continue creating armory and weapons. Such creations were at my own behest. But my heart aches to see her. Gailea can tell you how weary I've become after months of war talk."

Gailea snuggled against him, and her head brushed against his chest as she nodded. "I think a visit from Elda might do us all some good."

"Indeed." Crispin released his hold on Gailea and kissed her hand. "I'll leave you to your fun, my lady. I've many duties to attend. Till tonight?"

Gailea nodded and smiled. "Tonight, my love..."

"Crispin, wait."

Crispin turned to Tytonn.

"Crispin—your grace—if I could have just a moment with you privately?"

"Tytonn." Gailea placed a hand on his arm, her gaze

imploring. "Not yet. We don't know anything for certain..."

"And by the time we do, it may be too late."

"What's going on?" Crispin hovered over Gailea and took her hands. "Is it the baby? Is something wrong with our child?"

Gailea shook her head. "No, not that. It's another matter entirely..."

She glanced once more at Tytonn, her gaze reflecting urgency; then, she nodded to the side, away from the stables.

Tytonn glanced beyond Crispin at the workers milling about. "The queen is right. Not here. The woods, further in."

Tytonn slipped from the stable. Crispin rested his hand at the small of Gailea's back and led her after his friend.

When only the whispers of the wind in the trees surrounded them, Tytonn brought them to a halt. As Tytonn and Gailea watched each other closely, Crispin's frustration began to brew. What important secrets had they been keeping from him?

At last, Tytonn said, "I overheard talk the other day of some foul play happening in the dungeons. Lord Ragnar's name came up, and at first, I thought how you wouldn't wish any ill word to be spoken against him. I thought of defending him. So, I followed him. He went to see Chevalier. He used his Fyre magic on the sorcerer; I thought he meant to burn the man alive. He was inquiring about a type of magic called 'Dusk...'"

"It's been so long, I'd almost forgotten we were still searching for it," Gailea said, squeezing Crispin's arm. "Or perhaps I'd just hoped it had vanished altogether by now. It's a terrible magic. If it still exists..." She shuddered and looked back at Tytonn.

Compassion filled Tytonn's gaze as he studied Gailea.

Crispin held Gailea a little tighter. "Go on, Tytonn."

"Yes. Well, once they'd finished arguing and Chevalier still refused to relinquish any information, Alistor healed his wounds and left."

Crispin tried to stem the anger simmering inside him; Gailea flinched, and he pushed back the rush of fire. He hardly knew whether his wrath was kindled more against Alistor, or against his wife and friend for keeping this secret from him. Then again, he had been so exhausted lately that perhaps he was just blowing things out of proportion.

"Alistor is ambitious," he said. "But I cannot believe he would defy me so blatantly—and defy my queen. But even if it's true, my uncle is not a man to act without cause. Perhaps...perhaps if it *is* true, Alistor knows something we do not. This Dusk poison—perhaps Chevalier still means to use it. He could have spies in the prison, servants..."

Gailea shook her head. "Remember the charms we placed on the prison, my love. Chevalier cannot use magic. And if he or anyone else in the prison is questioned, any lies will be detected. Secrecy in that cell would be impossible."

"And yet, if Alistor isn't asking the *right* questions, Chevalier's secrecy could yet prove lethal."

"Chevalier once meant to alter the Dusk so it could create a terrible army for Moragon. Perhaps Alistor means to use the Dusk to do the same—not necessarily for evil means, but as a means of helping you, of easing your mind in the possible war against Gareth and Donyon."

Crispin nodded slowly. "Yes...yes, that might be very possible...Alistor might do something of that nature..."

"*But*," Gailea added, "I do not think that would be

the best path. The Dusk magic is dangerous. It's forbidden magic—blood magic—and not easily controlled. Even if Alistor intended to use it for a noble purpose, I think it might easily corrupt."

"We truly don't wish to suggest anything severe against Alistor," Tytonn added. "Nothing along the lines of intentional treason or betrayal. Only that he may have hopes and plans for far-reaching conquest that he fails to discuss with his king."

Crispin shook his head. "He would not hide anything so monumental from me."

"I would at least exercise caution," Gailea said. "He plotted behind Moragon's back. He may have affection for you, but we have also seen what he's capable of…"

Crispin pulled away from her, his frustrations mounting again. "My uncle may have overstepped his bounds, as you suggest; I *will* look into it. But I strongly forbid uttering another word against him—either of you." He glanced at Gailea but rested his stare upon Tytonn.

"Sire," Tytonn said, bowing his head. "Forgive me if I've offended you."

Crispin nodded curtly. "And forgive me if I came across too harshly. I'm exhausted from my duties. I think a small rest would do me well. Join me, my love?"

He offered his arm, extending his affection once more, and Gailea took it.

Crispin started to turn, but then he glanced over his shoulder and said, "We have always been friends, Tytonn; I have always looked out for your welfare. Do not make me lose my patience should *you* be the one to overstep *your* boundaries."

"Of course, sire," Tytonn said.

Without another word, Crispin turned and led his wife back toward the castle.

When they'd disappeared from Tytonn's view, Gailea

stopped before Crispin, making him stop too. She frowned, her gaze brewing with anger and hurt.

"Gailea—what in the world—?"

"How dare you embarrass me like that," she snapped, her voice tremulous.

"Embarrass you? Perhaps the baby is just making you full of emotion..." He reached out to take her hand. "I would do nothing to embarrass you—"

Gailea stepped away. "Wouldn't you? I know what you were suggesting back there, between Tytonn and me. It was *I* who went to *him*. He said he would follow Alistor, and I asked him to meet me afterward. But if you wish us to end our friendship, I would rather you express that before you start telling yourself such hideous lies."

Her narrowed gaze sliced deep into his heart. He hated for her to look at him with such accusation. He wanted nothing more than to bridge the sudden gap between them, sweep her into his arms, and make their troubles fade away with sweet kisses.

"I know there is nothing unclean between you and Tytonn. I was upset because I felt like you'd kept secrets from me."

"I spoke to him about the Dusk because I knew he would understand," Gailea said, a bit more gently. "Months ago, when you first left Astyrian, I was experimenting with a bit of Dusk, trying to help Marlis. It spread over my entire body, gave me the most realistic nightmares. Tytonn was the one who found me thrashing like a madwoman. He helped me to calm down. He saved my life. You should be indebted to him, not jealous."

"I'm sorry," Crispin said. "I didn't know. You're right—I was too quick to judge. Can you forgive me?"

"Of course," Gailea said, "if you will also forgive me

for speaking against Alistor. I know he is your kin, but as he is also Moragon's, it's difficult yet for me to fully trust him. But I truly meant no ill against him. Only that he is ambitious and has been known to keep secrets in the past."

Crispin took a deep breath but held silent. Gailea was right, but Alistor had since proven his faithfulness. He'd helped Crispin take Adelar in the first place; why would he do anything that would possibly risk losing it?

All the same, doubt lingered in the back of his mind, and he said, "All right. I will talk to Alistor at once regarding the Dusk if that will please you."

"It would. Though pleasing me is not as key as is protecting our kingdom and new family. *That* is what concerns me most."

"And me as well," Crispin said, placing his arm around her waist to steady her as they continued up the hill toward the castle. His hand rested on her stomach, and he felt their child kick against him. He grinned in awe, and Gailea smiled warmly.

"The child knows it too," she said. "She already has a great loyalty toward protecting her people—and her family."

"She will take after her mother in that regard."

He kissed the crown of Gailea's head and hugged her a little closer.

***

Crispin rested atop the small balcony overlooking the great hall, smiling as his wife engaged in animated conversation with a group of young women. As she had never been able to grow up with luxuries like parties and meeting new faces, he enjoyed indulging her now.

Often, he enjoyed indulging at her side, but lately,

the crowds overwhelmed him, and he preferred solitude here on his private perch.

"Crispin? What are you doing up here?"

Crispin turned and arched a brow at Tytonn.

"I could ask you the same thing. Shouldn't you be skulking around the stables instead of lurking up here in the shadows, Sir Horse Master?"

Tytonn laughed lightly. "Perhaps. But at the least, it smells far better up here than amongst the horses. I may be able to tame them, but there are no spells to sweeten their smell."

Crispin laughed, but the pungent aroma of beef, vegetables, fire smoke, and sweat made him wrinkle his nose. "I'd beg to differ with your first statement."

Tytonn chuckled before announcing, "I'm up here because I was looking for you, actually. I wanted to let you know that I've just written to Elda, urged her to join us for a reprieve here at the castle."

"Thank you. The messages should reach her quickly, via the House's magic. I've already decided to send out an escort tomorrow morning of my best swordsmen and magicians to bring her safely here. She may be reluctant to leave her work, but I think she will obey her brother and king. Besides, she'll come for you, and for Gailea…"

Crispin leaned against the railing, distracted by the spectacle below him. Swishing gowns, thumping boots, colors constantly swirling, mixing, turning. Laughter and banter mingled with strings and flutes, swelling into a strange symphony. Hovering up high above the madness, removed from the constant entourage of questions and prying gazes, Crispin could somehow see Gailea more clearly. A smile filled him as she watched the dancers with a serene grin, cradling her stomach.

"You must be the absolute proudest," Tytonn said, leaning forward on the railing beside Crispin. "You have truer cause than most to rejoice—as does the kingdom. A thriving country, a lovely wife and queen—and a child on the way."

"Yes..." Crispin released a long sigh. "Yes, I suppose I *should* be proud, shouldn't I?" He glanced over at his friend.

"Are you not?" Tytonn's smile fell into a frown. "Does something trouble you?"

"It's just...at times, and forgive me if this sounds a little insane, but at times I actually wish for the days *before* Gailea and I were crowned king and queen. When we were struggling for our lives. We struggled for each other then too. Now, my days are often filled with routines, councils, magic lessons, and possible war preparations. I feel like the joys of new marriage were cut too short, not for lack of passion—we've always had that in bounds—but because those wretches Gareth and Donyon are a constant distraction."

"Do you want to talk about it?" Tytonn asked. "Unburden your mind?"

Crispin turned and leaned back wearily against the railing. "I would tell you. But I'm advised to speak as little of such matters as possible to those outside my most intimate council."

Tytonn crossed his arms and gave a playful smile. "You're implying that I could be a spy."

Crispin grinned back. "You never know. But Tytonn?"

"Yes?"

"I truly am sorry—about earlier, in the woods—losing my temper, accusing you. I don't know what's gotten into me lately..."

"The pressures of being a good husband, father, and king," Tytonn said. "The simple plight of a man fighting to do right by everyone and forgetting to take time to care for himself. Truly, there is nothing to forgive."

"Thank you. You are too good to me."

"Whatever our positions, we are yet friends first and foremost. Meaning that, should you need to discuss anything with me at all, I would truly breathe a word to no soul, on my life. Even a king needs someone to share his troubles with at times. Becoming king doesn't mean you stop being a man…"

"Contrary to how some would behave," Crispin muttered. A bitter sort of whimsy flitted through him, and he added, "Do you remember when we were young, Tytonn? When we used to play-fight with sticks in the woods and imagine the glories of battle?"

"When did we ever imagine the glories of battle?" Tytonn chuckled. "*I* only wanted to ride a great warhorse. And *you* only entertained the notion of carrying a fancy sword. Now I think on it, I suppose we both got what we wanted, in a way."

Crispin smiled faintly. "I suppose we did. And yet… it's so different. Pretending to fight as a child versus being responsible for an entire kingdom. Whole armies looking to you for guidance. Being afraid to wake in the morning to find your castle under siege, or to receive word that all your allies have joined your enemy, or…" He paused as Tytonn studied him intensely. "I'm sorry. These burdens are not yours."

"They are; as I said, we're friends."

"Yes. It's just…I would normally unburden myself to Gailea. But I hate to trouble her lately, in her condition."

Tytonn smirked. "Do you think she'd allow it to be any other way?"

Crispin considered for the briefest moment. "No, you're right. She—"

A brilliant crimson streak shot by, its warmth grazing Crispin's skin. Stunned and a little irritated, he whirled to see a ball of flame hovering nearby. A moment later, it vanished into a puff of smoke.

Crispin scanned the crowds below and found Alistor standing next to Gailea. Alistor met Crispin's gaze, nodded, and then slipped through the crowds and out of sight.

"I must speak with my uncle," Crispin muttered. "I'll see you later, Tytonn."

"Your grace," Tytonn said, bowing at him.

Crispin hurried back down the stairs. As he breezed past the great hall, he paused and peered inside one of the doors, finding Gailea who yet caressed their unborn child. How he longed for her company and the soothing of her sincere happiness and song.

***

Crispin approached the ornate doors of his uncle's lavish new chambers. Since becoming king and naming Alistor a duke, Crispin had insisted on a more suitable room for his uncle than his previous underground dwelling.

Crispin knocked on the door, and it swung open. He stepped inside the massive room ringed by huge, floor-to-ceiling windows. Since Crispin had insisted on new chambers, Alistor had insisted on chambers with the largest windows, perfect for a Fyre to constantly absorb sunlight.

Alistor stood behind his desk, examining several maps and letters scattered across.

Impatience spiked inside Crispin, and he cleared his throat.

Alistor glanced up. "Ah, your grace. So good to see you."

"I'm not certain I can say the same today," Crispin said.

Alistor frowned. "Are you troubled? Does sleep evade you again? I can give you some of my herbs—"

"No, thank you. They make me sick."

Alistor stared as if trying to examine Crispin's mood. Then, he walked around his desk, letting his fingertips trail along the maps. "Have you thought further on our discussion concerning Gareth and Donyon and what is to be done with them?" His gaze questioned yet commanded at once, as if his mind had already made up the answer and expected Crispin to make the same.

"Yes, I have." Crispin lifted his chin. "I don't want to create enemies where I have none. I don't trust Gareth and Donyon enough to allow them back into Adelar freely, but nor do I wish to call for their blood. Let them be free for now. Let them raise their small armies and trust in their false hopes."

"This is Gailea's doing. Her mercies will raze this kingdom to the ground yet."

"On the contrary, her mercies may preserve it. I have no desire for war. I may have won a battle, but I have no true taste for blood—as *you* do."

Alistor scoffed. "Do not play games; say what you intend."

"And do not patronize me, uncle. You summon me here to talk as if I am still some mere boy—but I am your king—"

"Then *act* like one. Your display of cowardice revolts me; you'd let every kingdom just swoop in and take over out of sheer politeness—"

Crispin flung his hands toward Alistor, and fiery whips darted from his palms, sending Alistor spiraling over his desk and knocking against the far wall. Crispin yanked the whips, and Alistor's body jerked up. Crispin slammed him back, binding him against the wall as if chained. Alistor's body glowed a pale crimson as he tried to fight against Crispin, and pain began to show on his face.

Marching over, Crispin glared his uncle straight in the eye. "Is *this* what you want? Is this what a king does? Is this what you've been doing to him—to Chevalier—behind my back?"

Crispin released Alistor and drew his fire back inside him. His uncle collapsed to his knees, trembling and panting. Alistor muttered a few spells, and the scorch marks on his skin and clothes vanished. Then, he rose to his feet, looking just as whole and every bit as proud as before.

"Chevalier alone knows the whereabouts of the remaining Dusk. You should not punish me, but rather thank me. As long as that poison exists in the world, it could prove fatal if fallen into the hands of our enemies—including Moragon. He may have no friends now, but he will, and when he does, we don't want him to obtain yet another tool to wreak vengeance against us. The sacrifice seems worth it, doesn't it? To torment one soul in order to spare thousands?"

"You still should have come to me first. Disobeying direct orders to leave Chevalier in peace could be considered an act of treason."

"Forgive me," Alistor said, bowing his head. "I only meant what was best for the realm."

"And for yourself?"

Alistor flinched, for once showing a hint of surprise, and Crispin added, "There are those who suggest that you might desire conquest of other lands and that you could you use the Dusk for that cause, if it has the ability to command such armies as Chevalier once promised."

"I would have to raise my own army," Alistor said. "And that would, indeed, be a direct act of treason. But I have entertained the idea of harnessing the Dusk for war. With its help, you could make war not only upon Gareth and Donyon. There are other traitors as well. You could extend your reach to the nearby lands that did not come to your aid in the fight against Moragon. You could show them the punishment earned by disobeying Adelar's true king. You could make them fall to their knees, submit to you as a true lord to be feared."

"Perhaps that is what you wish," Crispin said. "But we are at peace, and I do not desire further warfare. I would not make myself hated as Moragon was."

"Not hated—*worshipped*," Alistor said, his eyes gleaming. "The people love you, and they love Gailea. You could become the most powerful ruler in all the Spectrum Isles. You wanted to be king; this is what kings do—"

"Not *this* king," Crispin snapped. Fire pulsed beneath his skin again as his impatience grew. "And you will stop presuming to know what I desire. I've made up my mind. I will not punish the innocent for power's sake."

"No. You would let Gailea rule through you—*over* you, instead of beside you. You would let her control you and make you weak. She falls on her back and her knees, and you obey her every whim—"

Fire erupted from Crispin, dancing along every inch of his skin. He clenched his fists, forcing himself not to attack Alistor who stood perfectly still, watching cautiously.

"You will not disgrace my wife again. You will not defy me in matters of war again. You will not touch Chevalier again, nor will you seek to bring such an evil magic as the Dusk anywhere near this castle, or I swear, the punishment will be more severe than any you could ever envision."

Crispin lingered a moment more, letting his warning sink in. Then, he fled the room and slammed the door shut.

As the flames receded back into his body, he trembled with the excitement coursing through him. He had detected the fear in Alistor's gaze. At last, he could prove his worth, and no one could stop him—not even his uncle. He was strong. He was more than capable.

He. Was. King.

CHAPTER 28

DISCORDANCE

"My lord—my lord! An urgent message from your sister—"

Crispin sprang wide awake.

Gailea sat up beside him, muttering, "What's going on? What's wrong—?"

"Elda," Crispin gasped, flinging back the covers and jumping from bed to follow after the messenger. The rustling of covers and light footfall announced that Gailea trailed close behind.

Within moments, they'd burst into the council room where Alistor stood with his hands sprawled on the large table, leaning forward and studying the maps.

Tytonn tumbled in behind them, breathlessly demanding, "Elda—where is she? What's happened?"

"I don't know," Crispin snapped. Then, whirling on the messenger who stood wide-eyed and panting for breath, he demanded, "Well? Where is my sister? Is she—?"

He choked on the words. He couldn't imagine her being harmed, much less dead. Gailea placed a hand on his arm and began whispering a soothing melody, but Crispin jerked away. If anyone had laid a hand on Elda, he did not wish to be comforted. He wished for blood, for vengeance—

"She is unharmed, your grace," the messenger said. Relief washed over Crispin; Tytonn closed his eyes and heaved a large sigh. "However, on the way here, she was attacked by a band of Gareth's followers. Your men bravely defended her. A few were wounded, none killed. Gareth's men fell or were chased away. Elda was moved back to the House and her guard increased."

Crispin nodded slowly. "Good, good..."

"Good?" Alistor echoed, his tone superior and mocking. He scrutinized the maps a moment more before glancing up. "I see nothing 'good' in this incident—beyond my niece going unharmed, praise be to Amiel. But this was no accident to merely brush beneath the proverbial rug. This was a threat, not simply against Elda, but against you, your grace, and the entire realm. Gareth's followers grow too confident. They would make a mockery of us—unless we put them in their place at last."

Crispin folded his arms and held his head as it began to throb. "And what would you suggest?"

"What I have suggested from the start—war. They have already initiated one by daring to lay hands on your sister. That is cause enough; would you still sit idly by, blinded by the hopes that Gareth and his son will simply fade away in peace?"

Alistor's demeanor was clearly condescending. Crispin waved a hand at the messenger, dismissing him. The man hurried from the room, and Crispin shut the door behind him. Then, meeting Alistor's gaze head-on, he said, "How dare you make a fool of me in front of my servants and especially my wife."

"Your wife?" Alistor crossed his arms, cocked a brow,

and turned his gaze to Gailea who stared at him, looking wary but determined. "Are you sure the queen isn't the one who's made a mockery of you? After all, things devolved to this state in part by her counsel."

Crispin looked at Gailea. "You know I don't desire war, but perhaps it's time."

Gailea tenderly touched Crispin's arm. He began to draw back, but she shook her head and said, "I would not sway you with my music; I am not Moragon. But I wish you would calm down and think clearly. You're making decisions based upon feeling, not logic and what's best for the realm. It's true that this would not have happened if we'd already gone to war and defeated Gareth. But one could also say that this would not have happened if we'd already offered amnesty and come to some peaceful agreement..."

Crispin's nerves eased a little at the sincerity emanating from his wife's face. "I know how much you desire peace. I admire it. I don't blame you, but much as I've loathed the idea of further war, I can no longer heed your counsel. Gareth and Donyon have made it plain that they do not wish for a simple treaty."

"Have they?" Gailea challenged. "You haven't ever *tried* to extend amnesty toward them. How can you be so certain they wouldn't accept?"

Crispin rubbed his aching temple. As usual, the two people he cared about most made such valid arguments. He wished that they could somehow both be right, that he didn't need to choose.

"I know you care dearly for Elda," Crispin said. "Does it not trouble you that she could have lost her life?"

"Yes, but that does not mean exchanging other lives for—"

"My sister is worth scores of theirs. And scores *will* fall, at our hands, if necessary."

Gailea's lips parted as if to argue further. She glanced briefly at Tytonn who studied her with a sort of apology. Anger flitted through Crispin; friend or no, Tytonn had no business forming opinions on such lofty matters, and certainly not with the intent of persuading his wife to follow them.

"Alistor," Crispin said, "meet me after breakfast tomorrow. *Immediately* after. We must work to strengthen our forces and prepare for war."

Alistor nodded. "Your grace."

"Till then, you are dismissed."

Alistor bowed and departed the room.

"Let's return to bed, Crispin," Gailea said, reaching for him again. "It's been a difficult night. Sleep will heal all our minds for the morrow—"

"You are dismissed as well," Crispin said, drawing away from her.

For a moment, Gailea stood frozen in place, seemingly dumbfounded. Regret sliced through Crispin, and he almost turned to comfort her, but a final glance of concern exchanged between her and Tytonn made him stand firm.

Gailea turned and quietly left the room.

Crispin studied Tytonn closely. Tytonn stood with hands folded and head bowed but watched Crispin in return.

"You are rather bold," Crispin said at last, "staring your king so squarely in the eye as though you were his equal."

"Forgive me." Tytonn glanced down. "But we *were* once equals—"

Crispin grabbed Tytonn by the collar and slammed him back against the wall. Tytonn stared up, alarmed, his attention fully focused on Crispin who snarled, "Do you forget your place as easily as you forget the queen's?

404

Are you jealous of how far I've risen above you?"

"No, my lord," Tytonn said. "I only mean that, when you and I are alone, we might yet be able to think of ourselves as equals in that we are friends—just earlier tonight, we spoke of our continued friendship. I would seek to bring no disrespect against you or the queen. I love both of you; you, as my closest companion, and her because she is your wife. For that reason alone, would I defend her to the death."

"If your intentions are as sincere as you claim, if you still held half the affection for my sister as you do for my wife, you would be ready to rip out the hearts of those who attacked her—"

"You don't think I am?" Tytonn took a step forward, seemingly overwhelmed with a sudden flare of passion. "You don't think I would desire to do just that? I encouraged Elda to come. I can't help but feel partly responsible for the attack. But taking revenge will not truly help Elda, nor will it aid others—"

"*Enough!*" Crispin yelled. "I think you *are* jealous. Is having my sister not enough for you? I don't need to remind you that treason can be whatever the king perceives—especially if I continue to perceive that you associate with my wife more intimately than as a mere friend."

"Crispin—"

"You *will* address me with the proper titles, as would any other subject in this castle."

Tytonn's eyes narrowed in hurt for the briefest moment. Then, he said, "Forgive me, your grace. But I assure you my intentions toward the queen are simply that of purest friendship and comfort. I seek no ill against either of you. I still consider you a close friend, even if you no longer share that sentiment. I'm only trying to help."

Crispin's anger ebbed. Guilt tried to steal in, but he

had no room for it at present; duties called, and he must stand strong.

"You are dismissed," he said quietly. "I will trust you for now. Just see to it that your relations with my wife give no one any reason for suspicion—including myself."

Hurt flickered in Tytonn's eyes again, and Crispin knew that his words were not the absolution he'd likely hoped for. Without a word, he bowed and left the room.

Crispin listened until Tytonn's footsteps had receded. As a chill tip-toed through the room and up his spine, he spread a gentle burn through his body, warming himself.

What now? His mind was set. He had teeter-tottered between the choice of peace versus war for months now, but the hideous attack on Elda now tipped the scales in the favor of war.

But what was his way forward with his wife? Gailea would not approve of the war, nor the way he'd shunned her earlier, nor even his firm warnings against Tytonn. She would understand none of it.

Crispin tore toward his chambers. He hated this new wall between him and Gailea. He loved her with every fiber of his being and wished to regain her approval with every flame that burned inside him.

Inside their chambers, he found her sitting on the window seat, gazing at the stars. White moonlight veiled her face, reminding him of their wedding night. Passion flared inside him, and he walked quietly over, sitting beside her. She looked up with a gasp, and he grasped her face in his hands, pressing his lips close. She slipped easily into the kiss. He leaned her back, trapping her between the wall and himself, deepening the kiss...

After a while, her passion seemed to wane into a mechanical routine. Irritation ripped inside Crispin, and he found himself jerking back. "What is it now? Can I not be with my wife without you making me feel guilty for that too?"

"That's not my intention," Gailea said, her blue-green eyes darkening. "I would gladly succumb to your passion, only my mind cannot help but be distracted with the idea of war; I've always loathed it. I simply don't understand how you can think that is the best way forward, when a treaty—"

"There will be no treaty. How can you even consider it, after what they did to Elda?"

"So, we spill blood for blood, repay fear and violence with more fear and violence? How can that be the best way?"

Gailea reached for him, but he pushed himself up from the window seat and stepped back a few paces, fighting to ignore the hurt illuminating her gaze.

"I must do what is best for you and for our kingdom—and for our child."

"I wouldn't wish to teach our child that war is the solution—"

"I am king, and I have made my decision. I would thank you not to interfere in these matters again."

Gailea flinched as though he'd slapped her. "'Interfere?' How can I do anything *but* interfere with the matters of my own kingdom? You are not the sole ruler—"

"But I *am* the greater of the two. I am king. You are queen. You need concern yourself with protecting my heir and nothing more."

Accusation shone in her eyes, but he couldn't allow that to sway him from his choice.

He turned, crawled into bed, and waited for sleep to carry him like a wave far from the castle, to a dream where he and Gailea could be at peace once again.

***

Gailea watched Crispin for a long time until he'd drifted to sleep at last. Then, she rose to her feet and padded silently over to the bed. His face peeked from beneath the covers, and the moonlight seemed to dissolve the cares so often etched upon his brow as of late. Gailea stroked his wild curls and kissed the crown of his head.

Then, she wandered over to her desk, set a quill to parchment, and hesitated.

Writing to Gareth and Donyon to extend an offer of amnesty could either entirely save their kingdom and her bond with Crispin or make it unravel more fully than it already began to. She did not wish to see her kingdom torn apart again, but Crispin was changing and would continue to, as long as he allowed Alistor to influence his decisions. She must start making her preparations.

She dipped the quill began her letter, imploring Gareth and Donyon to meet with her and her husbands' ambassadors to consider a treaty. She promised that Crispin's wrath was bred from simple fear and misunderstanding, and that his heart could yet be changed.

Gailea slipped from the bedchamber, made the trek to one of the old, unused towers, and sang a song into the night. The letter took flight, and the breeze shifted to carry it to its destined reader.

CHAPTER 29

WHISPERS

Gailea stood stroking her horse's soft gray coat, whispering a gentle song.

"Good morning, your grace," Tytonn greeted warmly as he approached with a saddle crafted from green leathers. "I come bearing gifts from his majesty."

Gailea grinned in turn. "The child is jumping with excitement. And I admit this warm spring weather has me eager for a ride myself."

"Well then," Tytonn said, "best get this fitted. By summertime, the little one will be here, and you can both ride to your heart's content."

Tytonn began fitting the saddle. The horse pawed at the ground, but both Gailea and Tytonn hummed a tune to quell her nerves.

"How handsome she looks," Gailea said, once the saddle was secured.

"Indeed. The colors were a solid choice on Crispin's part."

They shared another smile, but Gailea's soon faded.

Lowering her voice, she said, "May I speak with you for a moment about a more serious matter?"

"Of course," Tytonn said.

"Crispin continues to ignore my suggestion to offer Gareth and Donyon amnesty—especially after the attack on Elda. I don't think the attack would have even come about if Crispin had already extended an offer of peace, but Alistor swayed him completely against the idea..." Gailea glanced about to ascertain no wandering eyes or ears lingered nearby. "I have written to Gareth and Donyon myself, asking if they would consider such an offer."

Surprise flashed across Tytonn's face. "That is risky."

"Perhaps. But I am queen; there is little Crispin could do to me. The real problem is that Alistor has swayed Crispin back into his clutches. And I do not think it is entirely for Crispin's good. I've never told this to anyone, but some time ago, Alistair tried to pursue me..."

Shock flooded Tytonn's face. "Romantically?"

Gailea nodded. "Yes."

"I suppose I can believe that, saw hints of it...but does Crispin know?"

"No, I never told him either. I suppose, with us being together at last and so happy, that I forgot for a while. Now, I think telling him would only upset him—if he even believed it, which I doubt. My point is that Alastair acted in his own interests then, and I believe he does so now. I think something must be done about him—and about Chevalier. And there is also the matter of the Dusk itself. If Alistor was to get a hold of it, he'd be terribly powerful. I don't want to imagine what consequences that might create for Crispin...for *all* of us...That day by the stream..."

She shuddered.

"I know," Tytonn said gently. "I know how that terrified you. I was scared too. I didn't know *what* the Dusk was, or if I could help you."

"Something must be done," she whispered sharply. "The Dusk exists, and what matters now is whose hands it falls to. In releasing Chevalier and offering amnesty against all sorcerers, we could make him a powerful ally. Chevalier may be a coward in some respects, but I believe he does pledge allegiance to those who help him, and I think he would serve us better out of love than fear. I may try to speak to him myself..."

The sounds of raucous laughter jarred her attention as a group of young men entered the stables, toting large bales of hay.

"Crispin has promised he has meetings with Alistor all day," Gailea said quietly. "I think I will pay Chevalier a visit while I can."

"Might that not raise suspicion?" Tytonn asked.

"As queen, I have the right to come and go as I please, in any part of the castle."

"That may be so, but with all due respect, the jail is one of the most common places for rumors to run rampant. Any rumors spoken against you, even those based in truth, could further strain things between you and Crispin."

"Then what would you suggest?" Gailea asked.

"A bribe perhaps? I still know many of the guards. I'm even friends with a few. My wages have greatly improved since Crispin's rule. Allow me to persuade their silence."

"No. I would not have you sacrifice your own wages to aid me. I will provide the funds out of my treasury. If you wouldn't mind being the one to deliver them and speak to the guards on my behalf..."

Tytonn bowed his head. "It would be my greatest honor to help you, my queen."

"Not just your queen—your friend first," she reminded gently. "Now, let me set about getting you what you need so you can help me—and so I can help Chevalier as best I can."

***

Gailea crept down the spiraled stairs, shivering as the prison's damp draft hit her like an icy wave. As she pushed herself through the jail, memories of Lady Aline's tortured face flashed through her mind. Her one comfort was the lack of inhabitants. Since becoming queen, she had been able to release many prisoners who were either altogether innocent or whom Moragon had forced to overextend their stay.

Thanks to her generous gift of gold, Tytonn had succeeded in swearing many of the guards to silence. Gailea had then approached the jail, demanding an audience with the man who continued to defy both her husband and Lord Alistor and thereby insult the mercies she'd extended by allowing him to live in the first place. As queen, she had rights to visit him, but making her wrath against him seem more convincing would hopefully throw less suspicion upon her, should Crispin or Alistor find out after all.

As Gailea rounded a bend and the cell at the far end loomed into view, she ordered the guards stationed throughout the hall to clear out and grant her some privacy. As they slipped through a door into the corridor just beyond, Gailea noticed someone sitting near the bars of the cell, head lolled back against the wall.

At a glimpse, Gailea didn't think the thin wisp of a man slouched limply in the corner could be Chevalier, but then he turned his face toward her, his green eyes met hers with their cool pride, and she inhaled sharply. It was most definitely Chevalier, his tall and once-graceful figure existing inside skin stretched taught over bones and silken, tattered robes. His eyes continued to watch her, staring steadily but revealing no emotion.

"And why does her grace lower herself, in her condition, to bestow a monster like myself with the honor of her presence?" Chevalier's voice rasped with hints of mocking and accusation. "We both know you'll be chastised if found here—though of course, it is I who'll get the whip for it. Congratulations, by the way. About your child."

"Thank you," Gailea said, easing down to the cold floor and making her eyes level with his. "But I did not come here to exchange idle flattery. I've little time, so I will be frank. I come to extend an offer of amnesty—toward you and all sorcerers in Adelar."

Chevalier laughed; the sound croaked like an old bullfrog before morphing into a harsh cough. Once he'd regained himself, he looked sharply at Gailea, his gaze rent with cynicism. "And what can I presume is the price for such an offer? My magic? My soul? The heads of my wife and child?"

"I wish no harm against you," Gailea said. The baby shifted inside her as if it felt just as uncomfortable as she did at the sight of his cheekbones, grown so defined that he might have been a statue chiseled from marble stone. "I'm truly sorry that things have come to this. But I wish for nothing for myself—only for the safety of my kingdom. I want the Dusk or the remnants of it. To know where it is, so I may destroy it. Or, if it cannot be destroyed, to hide it away from those who would misuse it."

"How can I know that?" Chevalier snapped; despite his body's apparent weakness, fight edged his voice. "How do I know you haven't succumbed to your husband's desires and would use the Dusk to tear this kingdom apart? And how can I trust your intentions toward me and my kind? No one has ever made us a promise that they did not go back on the moment they perceived us as a threat."

"Do you not recall our conversation before? When I said we were allies, equals?"

Chevalier scoffed. "Our positions have since been altered. I cannot know what you have become, but I must see you as one of them—like Crispin and Alistor, lofty and in a place of great power."

"But I am not like them," Gailea said firmly, though guilt darted through her. She was not like Alistor, but openly admitting the recent discord between her and her husband made its truth vibrate more painfully in her heart. "I would help you and am quite willing to do so. Your family—perhaps I could free them. Have you any clue where they're being held?"

"No," Chevalier said, "nor would I tell you if I did. Even if your intentions are for good, information can easily get passed to the wrong messengers."

"Then perhaps that should be my next goal, to prove myself to you: to find your family and move them to a safer place."

"You'd be wasting your time," Chevalier muttered. "Only Alistor will know their location, possibly the king by now. And even if you were to aid them, I cannot give you what you seek. I don't know what has become of the Dusk; Moragon himself may have taken it when he fled."

"Even were that the case, you yet retain the knowledge of how to create and use it—and thus how to stop or destroy it, should the need arise."

A loud thud echoed distantly as if a door had been opened and closed. Gailea pushed herself up and said, "I should go."

Chevalier nodded and released a long exhale as if

he'd spent the remains of his much-needed energy on their conversation.

Gailea started to walk away, but he called to her, "Your highness."

She turned to him. "Yes?"

"If things should go awry for you, remember what lies hidden in my chambers. If you obtain that, then whatever else happens, I will know my vengeance approaches. At least then, I can die in peace."

Gailea studied him, surprised by the sudden resolve and almost-gentleness in his voice.

"I promise," she said quietly, before turning and hurrying from the dungeons.

***

Crispin barged inside the castle and stormed through the corridors, trying to make sense of what he'd just witnessed. Gailea and Tytonn in the stables, whispering closely. Why did his wife speak once again with his best friend about important matters before himself?

Stopping before his uncle's door, he knocked hard.

Footsteps announced someone's approach, and then the door opened. Alistor's face loomed in the doorway. He stood aside and waved his hand. "Come in, your grace. How can I help you?"

Crispin strode inside. He paced to one of the large windows and back. He sighed loudly, almost growling. "I don't know, uncle. I begin to wonder if *anyone* can help me. My kingdom, and now my wife—all is in confusion..."

Alistor frowned. "What do you mean? The Lady Gailea—how could she possibly cause you such visible grief?"

"I have just seen her with Tytonn Grayfell. They were

whispering closely. They mentioned something about the Dusk—and, once again, your desire for it. I heard little else, but that was more than enough..." Crispin glanced up sharply at his uncle, uncertain whether to look more questioning or accusing.

Mild alarm showed on Alistor's face. "I can say little of your Master of Horses, either for ill or good; rumors surrounded him when Marlis was queen, though I think she may have just found comfort in his company where she could not find it in Moragon's. As for the Dusk, we've discussed this. No one knows where Chevalier hid its source, and he has yet to speak on the matter. The idea of me or anyone else coming across it is absurd. I would not concern yourself at present with such an un-attainable relic. I think the danger you should focus on rests much closer to home..."

Alistor studied Crispin pointedly before glancing away and fiddling with a feather quill on his desk.

"Gailea—you think she's planning something, don't you? But what? She helped me save this kingdom and build it to what it has become."

Alistor scoffed and glared up at Crispin. "So did I, if you'd recall every once in a while. But I don't think the queen means any ill against you or your kingdom—not intentionally. But perhaps through another, one who would give threatening advice..."

"Tytonn," Crispin said.

Alistor lifted his chin. "Yes...Tytonn. They spent many weeks together during your time away from the castle before I joined you at the House of Lance. She relied much more on him for advice and comfort than I think you realize."

"What are you getting at? Tytonn may be a bit too comfortable when it comes to titles of respect around court. But we are still friends. If my wife is to form a friendship with anyone, Tytonn is not a poor choice."

"That also does not make him a wise choice," Alistor said. He twirled the feather, caressed his fingers along its long plume, and bent it so that it formed an arc. "Besides, doesn't her majesty's belly seem a little larger than it should for one at her stage of pregnancy?"

Crispin frowned at his uncle in confusion. Then, as understanding lit inside him, it spread through him with the velocity of lightning.

"How *dare* you," Crispin snarled. "How dare you suggest that the queen would betray me to such a hideous degree. What you say is treason; I could have you burned along with that filthy sorcerer Chevalier—"

"The sorcerer who alone knows the source of the Dusk that could destroy us all? The sorcerer who lives only by your wife's mercy? Tytonn has connections to the jail's guard; recall how he helped Elda flee. How do we know he won't help Gailea set Chevalier free as well?"

Crispin shook his head, disgusted. "Gailea would not do anything to endanger our kingdom."

"Yes, but even the wisest person may be swayed by the right sort of 'counsel'. And if you wish to speak of treason, it is treason to take what rightfully belongs to the king—even if you were not *yet* king, your grace. Perhaps the one who you would still call 'friend' has already done so. I've seen your distance from him lately. You suspect—"

"I suspect nothing," Crispin snapped, "and neither should you. I should punish you for insulting both my wife and him—*and* my sense of judgment."

"My apologies then, your grace," Alistor said, lifting his hands, palms out in a submissive gesture. "I only meant to protect your best interests." He bowed his head and folded his hands before him, looking almost humble, though a hint of pride lingered in his gaze.

Crispin turned, storming from the room and slamming the door without a backward glance. Sunlight dazzled through the windows, and he soaked it up, letting it soothe him. Perhaps a walk would do him good.

Once outside, he delved into the woods. Breaking a branch from a tree, he swung it in the air, whacking through tall grass and bits of bramble. He and Tytonn had used to play-fight this way not long ago, and yet now it seemed an age past, another world away, another lifetime away full of entirely different people and places.

Crispin could hardly fathom that such a time had been real. Perhaps his old naivety had been a blessing after all. Now he knew both too much of some things and too little of others, and both were equally frustrating.

It all had to end. He must get to the core of what was going on, with his friends, his enemies, sort out who was who. Deciphering his uncle was all but hopeless. He loved his wife, but he didn't wish to trouble her, as she had their child to look after. Tytonn was a dear companion, but his intentions regarding the queen were proving gradually more suspicious. Crispin hardly knew which to sort out first...

Chevalier. The sorcerer. He held both Alistor's intrigue and Gailea's pity. Perhaps he was the next pawn to be removed. Alistor had tortured him in the past, to try and persuade information from him.

Two could play at that game.

CHAPTER 30

MIRACLES AND MURMURS

✳

G ailea stirred from sleep.

Nightmares had assailed her all night, visions of blood and deafening screams that haunted her even now as she woke. She groaned and clutched her stomach; it burned as though on fire, and panic roused her more fully from slumber. She'd felt no similar sensation in all her pregnancy, and the baby shouldn't come for two months more besides...

Sharp pains seared through her whole body and she curled in on herself, wishing she could hide from the intense throbbing. Wetness seeped beneath her, flooding her gown and the bedsheets.

"Crispin?" she called, her voice trembling. "Crispin!"

"Gailea? Gailea! What's going on?"

Crispin sprang up and scrambled away from her, his eyes shining wide and alarmed.

Gailea parted her lips to ask him for help, but pain stabbed through her stomach again, and she could only moan. She reached toward him and then let her hand fall, again touching the wetness. She glanced down; blood stained the bed. Trembling, she flung a wild look at Crispin and gasped, "The baby! I think something's wrong—summon the healers!"

Crispin lingered for a moment, horror frozen on his face. Then, he fled the room, shouting orders.

Gailea laid on her back and breathed deeply, trying to stave both her tears and her terror. Last night had gone so smoothly. She'd enjoyed a nice supper with Crispin. They'd read together by the fire and fallen asleep together. She'd woken later in bed, tucked warmly beneath furs and blankets. But then, as she had drifted back to sleep, the nightmares had attacked her mind, and now this. What could have happened between now and then? What could she have done so wrong?

The stabbing sensation surged through her abdomen. Groaning and suppressing a scream, Gailea reached back, gripping the pillows hard. The baby was coming. She prayed that her child would come alive.

Footsteps echoed down the corridor. A whole string of healers burst inside, as well as Darice and several other handmaids. Darice ordered the other girls to fetch hot water and then sat on the bed, holding Gailea's hand.

"Don't," Gailea gasped. "There's blood everywhere..."

"Hush," Darice said sharply. She dipped a cloth in the bowl of water set by the bed and laid its cool comfort across Gailea's forehead. "I'm your sister, and I *will* help you through this. Do not even think to send me away."

Gailea started to smile, but pain gripped her again, and this time she screamed.

"Push, your grace," the midwife said, standing at the foot of the bed.

"Your grace," said another of the ladies. "Here—hold onto this."

Gailea gripped the rope that had been tied to her bedpost, grateful for something to dig into as the pains repeated more intensely. Darice took her other hand, holding on tight. Gailea tried to concentrate on her lullaby, but the song evaded her, and she supposed it wouldn't do much to ease her pain anyway. Several healers stood nearby, chanting; Gailea didn't know what spells they uttered, but she prayed they might make the baby come faster.

After what seemed an impossible age, the midwife shouted, "Keep pushing, your majesty! Push hard! I can see the crown of the head!"

Gailea pushed and gripped Darice's hand so hard she feared she might wrench it off, but her sister only watched on, breathing words of comfort. The healers stood around, repeating incantations, and one rested an herb to Gailea's lips, saying softly, "Eat this, your grace. It will help dull the pain."

Gailea opened her mouth and chewed. She coughed on the dry leaves but, as her pains began to subside a little, forced herself to swallow. As the pain faded even more, she glanced gratefully at the healer. Then, she focused on pushing again.

"You're nearly there," the midwife said. "He's almost free. Just a few more pushes..."

"Push, dear sister," Darice said. "You can do this..."

Gailea pushed, straining her entire body. When her whole body quivered until she felt it would collapse and fall apart, a baby's crying tore across the room. The midwife cut the cord and then held the baby up; blood covered him, gleaming in the firelight, and his face twisted into a wrinkled frown. The midwife passed him to a servant who wrapped him in soft cloths, all the while commanding Gailea to give the last few pushes to release the sack that had held the baby inside.

Gailea pushed again, and her head reeled dizzily. Her vision blurred, but she tried to stay focused. She couldn't lose consciousness now. She must see her new babe, feel that the child was alright in her arms...

Healers rushed to her side, chanting spells to clear away much of the blood. Her pain turned to a dull ache as they sealed the tear where too much blood had left her. Another healer tilted a bitter drink to her lips. She sputtered but made herself swallow; soon her senses began to return to her, and she sat up a little, demanding, "Where is my baby?"

"Right here, love. A beautiful baby boy."

The servant had passed the babe to Darice, and she now passed him to Gailea who cradled him close and looked down on him. The pain and exhaustion gripping her body seemed to fade away. She smiled at him and sang softly; his cries quieted, and his blue eyes squinted up at her. Gailea shuddered, and a few tears fell down her cheeks.

"He will be called Merritt, after Crispin's father. It's what we agreed to."

"Merritt," Darice said. "It means 'renowned.' It's a strong name for him."

Gailea nodded and caressed his soft head. "May he be strong in body and in spirit..."

"Your grace." The midwife stood beside her. "We should get you and the baby cleaned up now. The king will be eager to see both of you, but it is customary that the men should not enter until mother and child have been cleaned."

Gailea sighed and clung to Merritt, reluctant for him to leave her arms. Passing him to Darice, she said, "Let's get this done quickly then. I want my husband to see his son."

Darice tended to Merritt, soothing his whimpers. The midwife and other ladies brought in several bowls of hot water, sponging away sweat and the remaining blood that the healers had not cleared away. As one of the girls mopped Gailea's brow, she glanced up and recognized Tory.

"Congratulations, my lady," Tory said. "He is so beautiful."

"Thank you," Gailea said, granting the girl a weary but true smile. "He is indeed, as beautiful as his father."

At last, she was considered clean enough. Resting on fresh linens and propped up against a mountain of fresh pillows, she searched eagerly for some sign of her son. Darice breezed into the room, beaming and holding him to her breast. She sank onto the bed beside Gailea and placed him in her arms again. Gailea touched his tiny nose and each of his tiny fingers. He looked clean and smelled just as fresh, as if the messy affair had never occurred and there was only them and this perfect moment.

"He's lovely," Darice said. "He cried a little while I was washing him, but I sang to him, and music certainly seems to settle him. He's definitely your son."

Gailea's grin widened. Then, as she turned to Darice, her smile faded a little. "Sister, is he well? Did the healers say anything?"

"They examined him. He seems to be in perfect health and fully grown."

"I wish that could please me, only I don't understand it. He shouldn't have come for another two or three months..."

Darice shook her head. "Don't worry about things you can't control. Praise be to Amiel, for he is a wonderful child. Besides, you and Crispin are two of the strongest magicians I've ever seen. Who knows what magic may have spawned this miracle?"

Gailea tried to smile but again faltered. If magic had indeed created the early birth, she feared it was neither hers nor her husband's doing.

The door creaked open then, and a woman servant announced, "His grace wishes to see his wife and son."

Gailea nodded and glanced at her sister who smiled warmly and squeezed her hand before rising from the bed. As she left the room, Crispin rushed inside.

Crispin froze still, staring across the room at Gailea and the baby. Morning's gray light began to tinge the sky and dance upon Merritt who squirmed and clutched at Gailea's gown. Gailea smiled down at him, then up at her husband who hurried over, his eyes wide as though she held a ghost instead of a child.

Gailea patted the bed beside her. Crispin eased uncertainly onto the edge of the bed, continuing to stare down at the baby. Gailea's heart fell a little; she'd hoped for a warmer reception, but perhaps he was just overwhelmed.

"Isn't he beautiful?" Gailea prompted. "I've called him Merritt, after your father like you wanted..." She held him toward Crispin.

"He certainly has your looks," Crispin muttered. "Especially his eyes. And his hair is fair as the sun..."

"Are you disappointed?" Gailea asked quietly.

Crispin studied the babe a moment more. Then, as his eyes found Gailea's, his face warmed with a smile. "Forgive me. I suppose I did hope that our first son might bear some of his father's resemblance. But he truly is beautiful. And if he is healthy, then I am glad..."

"Good," Gailea said, "and besides, with time, he may start to take on your likeness more than mine. And even if he does not, he shall be the most handsome prince Adelar has ever seen. Please, won't you hold him?"

As Merritt cooed and curled his hands around Gailea's hair, Crispin's expression softened a little more. A child-like curiosity and tenderness touched his gaze, making him look almost like the sweet, mischievous creature she'd made love to on their wedding night.

Crispin gently traced the babe's soft brow. Then, he bent low to kiss his forehead and breathed, "He truly is a marvel..."

"*Our* marvel," Gailea said, allowing both her smile and her hope to grow a little.

Crispin wrapped his arms around Gailea and Merritt, and a steady warmth pulsed from him into them. Together, they let warmth and peace fill them. As Crispin leaned them back against the soft pillows, Gailea sighed with sleepy contentment.

For the first time in a while, she was able to drift to sleep in her husband's arms as, for the first time ever, their child fell asleep in hers.

***

Crispin delved beneath the castle, winding down the drafty stairs leading into the dungeons. He had left Gailea sleeping soundly with their son. While he wished that he could focus solely on the joys of his new-born heir, even such monumental joys were tainted by fears of betrayal and treachery, fears which would go unabated until Crispin dug down to the very core of their truths.

After trekking through a maze of cell-lined corridors, Chevalier's cell rose into view. Crispin commanded the guards into the next corridor, to grant some privacy.

The sorcerer sat against the leftmost wall with his head drooped forward against the bars, his eyes closed. As Crispin reached the cell, he stood taken aback at how thin Chevalier's form had become. His skin stretched as thin as paper that might tear any moment. His face, once pink with health, was nearly unrecognizable. Shredded robes hung limply on his frail body, faded and stained with dried blood.

Crispin called Chevalier's name. When no response came, he called louder. Finally, he cast a ball of flame that slammed Chevalier straight in the chest before dissipating in a puff of smoke. He woke with a start, doubling over, gasping for breath.

Crispin gripped the bars and leaned forward. "I can make your heart stop entirely if you continue to be so uncooperative."

Chevalier panted, clutching at his chest as if afraid Crispin had already ripped it open. When his breathing began to subdue, he straightened with a sort of ghostly grace. "And to what occasion do I owe this fine visit, your grace?"

"A bargain," Crispin said. "A bargain, and its terms are not negotiable, so if you desire a bit of freedom, listen well. I need the location of the Dusk, as well as some information on how I can protect my family and kingdom from its possible harm. Do this, and I will improve your living quarters. You'll have your own chambers in the castle. Your magic will still be tempered, but you will have proper food and other needs met, without my uncle's constant watchful eye."

Chevalier continued to stare at Crispin, unmoving, unblinking. The hint of a smile pulled at his lips, and he said, "You know, you are not the first of your family to make such an offer. And those other offers promised a far greater level of freedom—"

"*I am king.*" Crispin pressed his face close to the bars, glaring at Chevalier. "Forget whatever offer my uncle may have pledged you. He may have the power to aid your escape, even to help your family. But I have the power to destroy you and him both."

"But you wouldn't dare destroy him," Chevalier said, almost sneering, "if he hasn't driven you to it by now. And besides, I did not speak of your uncle."

Crispin's mind spun to grasp the sorcerer's meaning. Then, it hit him like a thunderbolt, and rage illuminated his heart. As he stretched forth his hand, tendrils of flame burst from his fingertips, pinning Chevalier against the wall. The fiery vines latched onto the sorcerer's chest, right above his heart. Crispin pumped fire inside Chevalier who began to writhe, destroying the last ounce of his beauty and grace.

"I don't know what truths you've twisted to make my wife so keenly defensive of you, but I promise that if you do not leave her alone, I will hunt your wife and child to the grave."

Crispin slammed Chevalier back and then released him. Chevalier slumped over and lay very still, breathing shallow. Crispin waited; he had all the time in the world to get past this traitor's lies and stubbornness.

After a time, Chevalier tried to push himself up from the cold floor. His limbs shook violently, and his breathing came in heavy rasps. After several attempts, he grabbed the bars with one hand and braced his other hand against the wall. Just as he'd nearly pulled himself into a sitting position, Crispin touched the bars; they glowed a bright red-orange, and Chevalier jerked away, howling and collapsing in a heap once more—

"Crispin? What are you doing?"

Crispin jerked his head over his shoulder. Tytonn raced toward him, wide-eyed.

"*You*," Crispin said, rising to his feet and facing him. "I should have known you might be involved in this. Did you come to make some kind of wager with the sorcerer behind my back as well?"

"No!" Tytonn cried, shaking his head, clearly insulted. "Crispin—your grace—No one conspires against you, or if they do, it is certainly not me or the queen—"

"Then why has she been down here?"

"I think she was trying to discover where he'd hidden the Dusk. And she feels sorry, I think, that his state has sunk so low when she promised him the opposite."

Anger rose inside Crispin again; fighting back the accompanying fire, he muttered, "I wish that my wife spoke so intimately to *me* on these matters anymore. You seem to know her every thought and desire."

Tytonn took a few steps forward, compassion warming in his eyes. "Gailea misses you, Crispin. She speaks to me and her sister because she fears the two of you are growing distant. I think she's afraid to tell you, but she worries how much time you spend in your uncle's presence—as do I."

"Why is everyone so against Alistor? How else must he prove himself? You and Gailea extend mercy to this sniveling heretic, but you'd accuse my uncle of being a more dangerous enemy?"

"Chevalier is a survivor; Lord Ragnar is a fighter. He once desired Gailea. Are you so certain he doesn't still? Or that he isn't using you to control the throne, or—?"

Crispin grabbed Tytonn's shirt and slammed him up against the wall.

"What lies are you feeding my wife?" he demanded. "What—have your efforts to seduce my sister failed, and you would have my wife, instead?"

"No, Crispin, I—"

Crispin pushed him against the wall again, snarling, "You *will* call me 'your grace.' And you *will* stop talking to my wife."

Tytonn stared in shock, and a twinge of guilt tugged

inside Crispin. A part of him missed his friend, however much they'd both changed in recent months.

Crispin released Tytonn, who staggered back. Tytonn watched him closely, looking hurt but displaying no fear. This angered Crispin more, and he said, "I will not be so merciful again. First, befriending Weston, and now Chevalier. Clearly, I've been a fool to place absolute trust in you. What are you even doing down here?"

Tytonn's face fell at Crispin's harsh words, but he answered, "I came to get you because your sister—the Lady Elda—is here to see you."

Surprise flitted through Crispin, followed by elation.

"Then go," he said, "and have her sent to my chambers at once."

***

Crispin and Elda stood on one of the walls spanning between two of the castle's many towers. Elda sighed deeply and leaned forward, propping her elbows on the half-wall. As they stared out at the vast forest, in the glow of the setting sun, the trees glistened like many brilliantly colored jewels.

"It's beautiful, isn't it?" Crispin asked quietly.

He smiled at her. Everything about everything felt so jumbled lately—his uncle, his wife, his closest friends. Elda alone remained constant, unchanging.

She smiled back at him and wrote: *Certainly not as beautiful as your new son? I can't wait to meet him.*

"I can't wait for the same. You'll love him at once."

I already do. She waved the slate clean, and her expression turned more somber as she wrote, *I didn't just come here in response to your summons. I need to show you something. I've had a lot of time to learn some new skills.*

Lifting her hands, she began weaving streamers of lightning. They sparked and crackled mid-air, taking shape until the Lady Taj's face formed. Wisps of silver leapt within the yellow and blue lightning tendrils, forming her wildly curly hair and making it shimmer almost like pure gold.

The image panned out to show Elda kneeling before Taj, head bowed. Taj rested her hands on Elda's head, and suddenly, Taj's thoughts echoed aloud, as clearly as though she stood before them:

"The House of Lance is a wishing house. When the renowned Alistair Lance created the house, he placed certain protective charms upon it. The House is able to move at will; if its owner is in danger, it has the power to relocate in an instant. Or, if its owner is lost or in some dire need, a strong enough wish will bring the House back to him or her.

I have no children to pass the House on to, and it would be a terrible shame to let its powers die. I have seen the silver stag, child, as you know—he came to me the eve your brother did. Soon, the stag will return for me, and I will go to my final resting place.

I, Taj, now bequeath the House of Lance to Elda and all her kin. May it come to you in times of greatest need."

The lightning flickered, obscuring the memory. Elda let her hands fall, and the scene vanished altogether.

Crispin stared at his sister, awed and a little daunted.

Elda wrote: *The stag came for her that next day.*

"And now you're the owner of the House. I knew that—but I had no idea how ancient was its magic's history."

Elda nodded. *It will not only protect me but all my kin. I thought you might appreciate a reminder.*

Crispin took his sister's hand and squeezed it. "Thank you for that offer of comfort."

It's an offer I intend you to think seriously upon. Taj said also that you have exceptional magical talent. She said you would rule kingdoms one day, but she warned also that you should guard your heart against those who might lead it to despair.

Crispin's hand felt suddenly cold in his sister's, and he pulled it back. He gazed out at the trees spanning toward the horizon and meeting the ocean there. They seemed to merge and become one, and yet, they were two entirely different entities, the solid earth and the wavering sea.

"It's hard to tell anymore," he said, "who is false and who is true. Everyone pulls me in different directions. I don't always know who to trust. Even my wife; I know I should be doing nothing but rejoicing, with our son's birth, but things have been strained between us, and that weighs on me..."

Elda wrote: *Trust me. Trust our love and friendship. Through everything, it has not changed. Trust Amiel, for his mercies are also unbending. Trust Gailea and Tytonn, and all the others who love you.*

A pain tugged inside Crispin's chest, as if the mention of each name forced a dagger deeper inside his heart. "I wish I could be so assured. But the only one whose love I trust as constant and true right now is yours. I'm so confused and angry at times, I doubt Amiel Himself could love me right now."

You must never doubt Amiel's love. He created you for a purpose; you must embrace that and let it shine through, above your fears, above whatever doubts people may whisper about you. Do not turn from Him, nor yet Tytonn and Gailea.

"Tytonn and Gailea...strange how those names seem so intertwined as of late..."

Elda's frown was scolding. *Tytonn loves me. He would do nothing to harm you. He loves you too.*

"Are you so sure?"

Taj's warning rings true, brother. Someone breathes falsehoods in your ear, and you too readily accept them. Think of

Tytonn, and Tytonn alone; think of everything you know about him. Even if he had any affection toward Gailea beyond that of a friend and sister, he could never be so unfaithful to his friend and king. He regards you so highly; that much is clear in our correspondence.

Crispin's gaze lingered on her words. He waited for the accusations against Alistor; that seemed to be everyone's excuse for his confusion as of late.

But no accusations came. Instead, Elda rested her head on his shoulder. He gently laid his head on hers, and together they drew warmth from the sun as it faded into the west.

CHAPTER 31

HIS FATHER'S SON

As the months passed, Gailea still received no word from Gareth or his son. Still, she was unable to discover any inkling of Chevalier's family's whereabouts. War preparations progressed, and Crispin was continuously more absent, involved more intimately with those plans than with anything else.

Her greatest joy rested in watching Merritt grow. He had started to crawl and even tried to pull himself up. Every now and then he would succeed, but then his chubby little legs would wobble and he'd plop back down, looking stunned but ever determined to try again.

It was warm for a winter evening as Gailea sat in the garden beside Elda. Together, they watched Merritt scurry about, crawling after insects, leaves, and other small wonders.

Elda wrote: *He is such a beautiful child. But you still seem worried about him.*

"Crispin hardly pays him any attention, hardly *looks* at him—he hardly looks at *me* lately. It's just him and

Alistor, locked up all day together. Ever since he spoke with Chevalier..."

She took a deep breath and released it slowly. Crispin had never mentioned that day to Gailea, but Tytonn had.

"...I think he will never trust me again."

Elda squeezed Gailea's hand and wrote with her other: *He may yet. I'm sorry that my counsel does not do more to help him. He's consumed with this war. He's paranoid about his throne.*

Gailea's gaze strayed to Merritt. "Yes, but he is threatened for all the wrong reasons."

Merritt is his son. Crispin will bring him no harm.

"I think Crispin still suspects the child isn't his."

If he is so adamant, then why does he not work to create another heir?

Elda's smile was playful, but Gailea couldn't absorb her lightheartedness. Elda made a valid point, but validity was not Crispin's chief quality as of late.

"Crispin is no longer rational. He would see fear and enemies everywhere."

All the same, I think you should try talking to him. Perhaps the suggestion of another child may ease his mind and make him a little warmer toward you.

Gailea nodded slowly. Such an idea was certainly worth a try. She prayed that, at least for tonight, his mind would not be too consumed and exhausted with talk of battles and glory to listen to a simple plea from his wife.

***

Crispin paced around the table and studied the map closely. The imaginary troops had been set. Aid had answered from many of their neighboring islands. They were well fortified against Gareth and would soon be ready to launch an attack on his forces, scattered as they were.

"It looks solid," Crispin said. "I think we've done all we can. Good work, uncle."

Crispin gave Alistor a weary smile and turned to leave the room.

"Your grace."

Crispin turned back. "Yes?"

Alistor walked toward Crispin, his expression serious. "There *is* one matter more. My spies intercepted a most intriguing letter this afternoon. I thought you may wish to read it for yourself..." He presented the letter from beneath his cloak.

Crispin glanced uncertainly at his uncle. Then, he pulled the parchment from the envelope and began to read. Anger and hurt mounted inside him until he flung the letter to the floor and demanded, "What is this?"

"It would appear to be a letter from Gareth and Donyon, expressing their interest in heeding the queen's counsel to meet and discuss the possibility of a treaty."

Crispin took a deep breath and released it slowly.

Alistor continued, "You've always known she had the propensity to plan against your wishes. First, in talking with the traitor Chevalier. Now she would bring our enemies to our doorstep—the very same enemies who attempted to murder Elda—and offer them peace. She is queen; she has the power to do these things. But you are king. You are above her. She must be stopped, or everything we've fought so hard for will unravel—"

"Everything *I've* fought for," Crispin snarled.

Alistor's brows rose and it seemed that, for once, he stood struck speechless.

Good. He deserves to be put in his place.

Crispin snatched up the letter and stormed from the room without another glance at his uncle. His mind churned, blind to any other purpose except speaking with Gailea and getting to the bottom of things. For months now, she'd spoken not a word regarding either war or the sorcerer. Now, he knew why—she'd been plotting behind his back all this time.

Crispin barged into their chambers where Gailea had just lowered Merritt into his bed. The child slept soundly, and Gailea smiled down at him. Longing flitted through Crispin at the scene, its beauty almost perfect. But the parchment crumpled in his hand reminded him of his far-less-than-perfect truth.

"What is this?" Crispin demanded, raising the letter.

Gailea glanced up, looking surprised and then perplexed.

"What are you talking about, Crispin—?"

"*This*—this response from our enemies to your supposed gesture of amnesty toward them."

Gailea's brows rose. "I sent them word months ago. I'd nearly forgotten."

"That does not answer my question." Crispin marched forward, waving the letter at her. "Why? Why this treachery?"

"There was no harm in writing them," Gailea said, "on seeing how—or if—they might respond. Do they show interest? Because if they do, then your war may not need to happen. No further blood need be spilled—"

"You insist on forgetting that they nearly spilled my *sister's blood*!" Crispin threw the letter at her feet. "I suppose you would bring Chevalier into this as well, let him loose to use his Dusk to annihilate every kingdom in the Spectrum Isles, Adelar included?"

"I don't think Chevalier desires dominion. I think he only desires freedom. And for the right price, we could grant him that as well. He would make a most powerful ally; that you cannot deny."

"Yes, I can. What other secrets do you keep from me—?"

Cries rose from Merritt's crib. Gailea lifted the child into her arms. Cradling him close, she swayed and sang a calming tune. His cries soothed almost instantly.

Yearning tugged on Crispin's heart again, and he muttered, "You used to soothe *me* with such gentleness..."

"And I would still if you would let me." She looked at him, clearly hurt. "Or perhaps you would feel comforted if you held him. You don't hold him anymore..."

Gailea held Merritt toward Crispin, but he started to cry again. Gailea drew him back to her breast, singing softly and rocking him, but his cries culminated into shrieking wails.

"See there?" Crispin growled. "He rejects me."

"No—likely he knows that *you* reject *him*..." She shook her head. "Why are you doing this? Why are you being so cold in what should be the pinnacle of our celebration? I know we've been distant with talk of war and duties, but our child should unite us. Rejoice with me..."

"*Rejoice* with you?" Crispin scoffed. "When the child is a continual proof of just *how* 'distant' we've grown in these past months? The healers said he was fully grown and healthy as any newborn child. How is that possible, when we'd been married hardly six months upon his birth?"

"I don't *know*, Crispin. Don't you remember how terrified I was when he was born?" Gailea cuddled Merritt closer to her heart. "I didn't know what was going on. I thought I'd lost our son. Now that he is here and fully healthy, you act as though he carries some kind of curse. I know you're disappointed at his looks. But better he look like your wife than be hideous—"

The doors burst open. Two guards stumbled inside.

Crispin whirled and shouted, "How dare you come in here and disturb the queen! She is resting with our son—"

"Chevalier has fled," one of the guards gasped. "He's nowhere to be found. And your sister, Lady Elda—someone saw them together—"

Crispin roared, and fire blasted from his hands. The guards flung back into the corridor and knocked against the wall. Merritt wailed, and Gailea rocked him, snuggling him closer still.

Crispin glared at her. "Is this *your* doing? Do you betray me twice in one day?"

"No, Crispin—please—I have no idea—"

"I'm going after them. Elda has no time to waste if that monster has taken her."

"Chevalier won't harm her—"

"He is a sorcerer," Crispin said flatly, "and contrary to whatever he has convinced you of, he is capable of the darkest magic. I'm going to my sister, the one person who has been faithful to me in all things."

***

Crispin had left Gailea with only the morning's dawning gray and her baby's whimpering to comfort her. Gailea sang a new melody, rocking Merritt even once he had fallen asleep and staring numbly out the window. She felt her heart begin to break inside her and could only pray quietly that Crispin's anger had been some dream, that Elda would be all right, and that he would return to her and their son with open arms.

A knock sounded on her door. As Gailea bid the person enter, a guard opened the door and announced that the Master of Horses requested an audience with her. Gailea turned toward the guard with a curious frown but nodded. The guard stepped away, and Tytonn breezed inside.

His eyes were wide and wild, and he clutched his hat

close to his breast. Then, as his gaze rested upon Merritt, tenderness washed away his alarm.

"He is wonderful," Tytonn breathed. "And getting so big..."

"I wish his father thought he was as wonderful. I wish his father watched him with even a fraction of the same adoration. But why are you here, Tytonn? You shouldn't be; Crispin is in a bad temper right now..."

"That's why I came to you," Tytonn said; he let his glance linger upon the baby a moment more and then turned seriously to Gailea. "Crispin left with a small guard to search for Chevalier and Elda. He was so furious, he set the stables on fire; we just managed to save the horses. He wouldn't even *look* at me when I tried to calm him. He was so reckless... I've never seen anything like it."

"I fear that he hates our child..." Gailea flinched; speaking the words aloud made them too real and caused physical pain. "Sometimes I think...I think he really believes that *you*..." She bit her lip and glanced away, unwilling to speak the insult.

"He's mad if he thinks I would do this to you—to him. And he *knows* I love Elda. I would not be unfaithful to her."

Gailea nodded. "I know. But he's been spending all his time with Alistor. Alistor never wanted the crown, but he wanted to control it from the inside out. And he's doing that now, through Crispin. I vowed that I would never let him, but I think that Crispin may be too far turned now to turn back. The thought terrifies me..."

Tytonn reached up and touched her shoulder. The gesture was gentle, pure, and made her ache for Crispin's tender touch.

"I've never placed love or faith in many people," Gailea whispered, "only my sister, my mother, and the queen. Because I knew I could trust them and their love; such trust seems rare to find in this world. But Crispin— loving him was a gamble. I suppose I've always known that, deep down. I just didn't want to admit it. I've given my heart to him so fully; do you think that it's possible to love someone *too* much?"

"Love is never an evil," Tytonn said. "But who we choose to love—that can be a virtue and a vice in one. I have no regrets in loving Elda, even though our being together has never been likely. I can't help how I feel. But what I *can* choose is what to do with that love. I can continue working hard, hoping someday I'll be worthy of her. Or, I can let her go..."

Tytonn watched Gailea closely. She drew a staggering breath. "I can't stop loving him, just as you can't stop loving Elda. But I *can* make a choice, as you say. I can remove myself from his poison if it continues to spread."

"We both love Crispin. But what we love is a different man from what he's become. I pray it will not come to that, but I will help you if the need arises. Do not fear to come to me for aid."

Gailea nodded. Tytonn reached toward her, and she let her head fall on his shoulder. His arm wrapped around her, and she cried gently. His touch, so safe, held more affection than Crispin had shown her in many weeks. She nestled a little closer to him.

"I wish he still held me this way," she whispered. "We are friends, Tytonn, and I value your comfort. But it's not the same."

"I know, dear Gailea," Tytonn said quietly. "I know..."

CHAPTER 32

A HOUSE UNBROKEN

✳

Crispin and his fleet galloped across the beach toward the House of Lance. As some movement stirred in one of the upstairs windows, he pushed his horse harder, bursting ahead of the others. Though the House had since relocated, whether by its own will or by those inhabiting it, Crispin's kinship to Elda had allowed him to sense and seek it out.

Upon reaching the House, Crispin tugged the reins hard, bringing the horse to an abrupt halt. Crispin jumped down and rushed toward the door—

The door flung open, and Chevalier stood pale and thin as death. Clutching Elda's arm, he forced her to stand in front of him. Her lightning began crackling along her skin but vanished as soon as Chevalier muttered some incantation and then held her close, shielding himself.

"You cannot harm us while we are within the House," Chevalier said, his voice hoarse. "But I *can* harm her. The House has taken *both* of us in. Leave now, your grace, or she will suffer."

441

Elda glanced at Crispin, pleading with him fiercely, but without fear; rather, she seemed to command him to leave.

Crispin's heart lurched toward her. Then, he glared at Chevalier and demanded, "Let her go. Your life is already forfeit. I can promise you a swift death, a painless one—but only if you let her go now."

Chevalier chuckled darkly. "And why would I? You've already declared me dead either way, haven't you? And for what? What crime have I committed against his grace except fleeing the hell of his prison to reclaim what little freedom I am bidden in this land?"

"You did not have to take her with you."

"But I'd be dead already had I not, wouldn't I?"

Crispin narrowed his gaze at Chevalier who returned a haughty glare.

"I will allow you that," Crispin said. "But such is not the only crime stacked against you. You are guilty also of bewitching the queen into helping you escape. My uncle was right in that all sorcerers are truly worthy of death for their treachery."

Chevalier laughed again. "Your uncle, eh? I see he's not hovering by your side for once. If you had any wisdom of your own, you might look to *him* with your ridiculous accusations. He has more motive than your queen for setting me free. He's always desired the crown, the Dusk—he desired my magic too. Are you so certain he isn't seeking it even now, in your absence, to build his own army and overthrow you—?"

"Silence!" Crispin hurled a ball of flame at the House. Chevalier ducked and drew Elda out of the way. The fire exploded against the doorframe and disintegrated into a shower of harmless sparks; the faintest trace of charred wood showed but quickly faded.

Chevalier stared at Crispin, all amusement vanished from his face.

"I too am the owner of this House," Crispin declared, "not just my sister. Do not think your life to be as safe as my wife may have promised it. Her intelligence can often be blinded by her concern for her lovers..."

Chevalier blanched. "What do you mean? How dare you even suggest—?"

"How could I not?" Crispin snarled. "She has already birthed a child whose features I am certain cannot be mine. She wanted to spare you for some reason. You were with her in my absence, before she was queen. How do I know you didn't use your charms to lure her into your bed so she would do your bidding? Give me one good reason why I shouldn't burn you alive right now and grant you the death you've always deserved. You never cared for Moragon, only for your own devices. You'd hoard the Dusk to yourself until it has the strength to destroy us all—"

Crispin...

The solitary, electrified word hovered in the air, shimmering. Elda wriggled, trying to release herself from Chevalier to say more, but he jerked her back and pinned her arms to her sides.

Crispin took a few steps forward, letting his fire fill his palms. "Unless you'd prefer I handle you with the same 'gentleness,' I would let her speak."

"I tire of the lies of kings. I desire no more talk, only solitude..."

A green glow spread across Chevalier's skin; it began to magnify, and Crispin squinted against its blinding glow. Chevalier lifted his chin, and a smile spread across his face. Glee danced in his green eyes, and a sort of pride seemed to glint beyond their steady, resolute stare.

"...but I am ready, knowing that my vengeance shall be repaid upon you and your kind. One day, you will be brought down by those who gather around your queen; it will not take many to do so, either—only as many as there are colors in a prism—"

"Insolent fool!" Crispin shouted.

He stretched forth his hands. Fiery tendrils erupted from his wrists, and he grasped them, swinging them about like whips. They crackled against the House's roof, setting it ablaze. He snapped one out toward Chevalier, and it coiled around his ankle. Chevalier roared in pain, releasing his hold on Elda who collapsed back against the doorframe, and the green glow enveloping him vanished.

"Elda, run!" Crispin shouted as fire flooded him and prickled along every inch of his skin.

Elda remained frozen in the doorway, staring as Chevalier writhed. More of the fiery chains wrapped around his arms and legs, pinning him down. The stench of burning flesh filled the air, and the blazing House began to smoke.

"Elda, please!" Crispin shouted, panting hard and bracing his feet, fighting to contain the fire mounting inside him.

Elda bolted down the stairs, but Chevalier snatched out, grabbing her ankle. Elda crashed to the ground, shooting tendrils of lightning at Chevalier; they just missed him, instead exploding into the doorframe which crumbled around them.

"*Elda*—!"

The fire filled Crispin to the point that his skin seemed literally to boil. Nearly passing out from its intensity, he closed his eyes and released a low, guttural growl. His body shook. A scream pierced the air, and his eyes shot open. Volley after volley of flames poured from his body at the House, and its every surface blazed. Red and gold danced high. A body writhed on the ground. Neither Chevalier nor Elda was anywhere in sight.

Crispin tried to tame the fire streaming in involuntary waves from his body, but they would not cease. He darted forward and reached toward the blazing body on the ground, turning it over and searching. It was already burned beyond recognition, but its small frame promised it was more likely his sister's than the sorcerer's. With a roar, he darted inside the House, searching for any sign of Chevalier, but there was none.

Bursting outside again, he watched as the flames receded from the House of their own will—or perhaps by the will of the House which soon stood singed but unbroken.

Crispin collapsed to his knees beside the charred skeleton. He reached out a trembling hand, imagining where her long hair had framed her pretty face. He shook all over, unable to say or do more.

Then, as the harsh truth struck him, he roared and emitted another burst of flames. The House caught fire for but an instant, then extinguished itself once more, as if mocking him. He could not harm its wood and stones, dead and unable to defend themselves as they were. But he had murdered his sister...

No. No, *he* had not killed her. That viper Chevalier. In stealing her away, Chevalier had murdered the only true and loyal family Crispin had ever known—

Family—a chord of remembrance jarred Crispin's mind, resonating violently. He yelled into the cloud-strewn sky, "I'll find them, Chevalier! Your wife and your child—they will be dead long before you can ever reach them!"

Yes, Chevalier would pay. But the sorcerer had not acted alone. Gailea and Tytonn, those scornful lovers who had freed him—they had released the monster who had now caused the deaths of two innocent women. Crispin could not punish his wife; the people would surely rise against him. But Tytonn could pay for both his and Gailea's crimes.

"Your grace?"

Crispin whirled on the guard who approached. With a growl, he drew his sword and swung it in a wide arc. Flames erupted from the sharp blade, slicing through the man's neck as easily as scissors cutting thread. The headless corpse collapsed, and blood sprayed, staining the brown dirt to midnight black.

Crispin's tears came at last. Weeping bitterly, he yelled and flung the sword from his hands; Anwar spiraled and landed far out in the lake. There, it hovered for a few moments before sinking deep inside the silver and being swallowed whole, never to be seen or held ever again—just like his sweet Elda.

"Your grace?" one of the guards called again.

Crispin turned a seething glare upon them. They stood several yards off, their eyes wide and wary, various magic spells poised in their hands, ready to defend themselves.

Rising slowly to his feet, Crispin said, "Elda will not return with us. She loved the House. We will bury her here. Then, we will prepare ourselves for the war which we bring back to the castle; there are traitors who *will* pay for my sister's death."

***

"Close your eyes, my precious little treasure;
When you wake, the dawn will shine anew.
May you nestle safe beneath the covers,
And may Amiel show mercy on you..."

Merritt shifted in Gailea's arms, emitted a soft coo, and then lay still. His subtle, warm breath touched her breast, and she adored the rhythm of his tiny heartbeat. Laying him gently in the cradle, she turned toward her bed—

"Lord Ragnar!" she gasped.

Alistor leaned back against the bedpost, arms crossed, staring with his sultry gaze. A smirk pulled at the corners of his lips. "Good evening, Lady Gailea."

"You have no business being in my chambers. Leave now, or I'll have you removed."

"*Will* you?" Alistor challenged, pushing up from the bedpost and circling Gailea. His shoulder brushed hers, and fire danced dimly along his skin. Its warmth radiated into her, making her shudder, and she drew a long breath to steady her nerves.

"Does *he* touch you like that anymore?" Alistor whispered, stopping right before her; Gailea swallowed but held her ground. "Or is it merely the power he's granted you which ignites such passion inside you? Enjoy it now, dearest Gailea, for your reign is about to come to an end."

"You cannot frighten me," Gailea said, quiet but firm. "Crispin is scared and upset. He carries the weight of many burdens, and they blind him. But in his heart, he knows I remain loyal and true to him, and that Tytonn does as well."

"Mmm...*does* he?" Alistor turned his head and frowned. "And will he trust you so well now that the sorcerer is loose? Especially considering the secret chats you've had with your alleged lover?"

"You know I have not betrayed the king," Gailea said. "Your poison will not consume him. I vowed once not to let it—"

"A vow you've failed to uphold."

Gailea froze still; her lips moved, but no words came to her. There were none. She could not argue with such a hideous truth.

"I might worry more about your own life if I were you," she said at last. "His grace's mind may have become warped by your counsel. And perhaps that's what you want. But don't think it will work entirely in your favor. Don't think that he will stop at eliminating just one or two people he thinks have betrayed him. As things crumble, he'll need someone else to blame."

Alistor nodded. "That may be true. But even once things come to that, my suffering will be brief. It will pass quickly. But yours, my dear..." His voice dipped into a breathy whisper. He crept forward and allowed his finger to trail along her cheek and jawline. "*You* will endure. *You* will suffer, and far worse than me. Crispin once loved you and perhaps still wants to. Bitterness and heartbreak will be his final weakness, and from them will emerge his greatest strength—a thirst for vengeance. He will not deal lightly with you—or your bastard." He flung a seething glance at the child and back again. "At least if you'd chosen me, your child would not have to suffer such a fate and title."

"He is no bastard," Gailea said with a lift of her chin. "He is the king's true son."

"You and I may know this. But it only matters what the *king* says and knows, doesn't it?"

Gailea stared at him solemnly. No matter how much she wanted to protest, she could only agree with him.

"Good evening, Lady Gailea. His grace should return within the fortnight—for your sake and that of your child, I would pray he does not return in the same state in which he left."

Alistor bowed and then slipped into the shadows, seeming to become one of them.

Gailea turned back to the cradle where Merritt still slept soundly. She lifted him into her arms and held him close to her breast, needing to feel his warmth, his presence. Her mind flew to Chevalier's promise and the gift he'd hidden inside his chambers for her. Alistor was wrong; perhaps she would suffer, but if the sorcerer's promise held firm, she would ascertain that her child suffered for nothing.

***

Crispin led his men solemnly through the woods. The journey home had been hellish; he'd pushed them quickly at first, eager to place as much distance between him and his sister's death as possible. But the nearer they drew to the castle, the more he realized he was not keen to embrace it either. His sister was dead. His wife and closest friend had betrayed him. His uncle cared for nothing but his own profit.

There was nothing left for him there. He did not return home, but to prison, the same prison he had once believed the castle to be for Gailea, the same prison he'd freed her from—and *this* was how she repaid him...

"Your grace—I said I think we're being watched."

The guard's voice had floated to him at first like an incoherent mumble, but now the words broke through clearly. With a growling sigh, Crispin slowed his horse to a halt and listened.

"I hear nothing. Only the wind screaming through the naked branches. Same as we've heard the past few nights."

"Dulin insists..."

Crispin glared back at Dulin. "If you're wasting my time, you'll meet with the same fate as your comrade on the beach."

"No, my lord," Dulin whispered. "There are footsteps. And the stretching of arrows along bowstrings. I sense danger—some enemy approaches—"

Arrows sang between the trees. One struck Crispin's shoulder like icy claws digging deep and spread a sharp cold through his entire body. With a growl, he tore the arrow from his flesh. Blood oozed out, and after a glance at the arrow's shimmering blue tip, he flung it aside, disgusted.

"They've got strong elemental magic, whoever they are!" Crispin shouted. "Arm yourselves and make for the field!"

Crispin and his men raised swords, shields, and bows and burst through the trees. Arrows continued to whiz past, and hooves thundered. Crispin winced and groaned, clutching at his arm which seared with an icy pain. He tried to push his healing fire inside the wound, but the pain wouldn't subside. His horse turned side to side as he led clumsily, making him lag behind the others. Whipping his head over his shoulder, he narrowed his gaze at the sigil inscribed on the flanks of the pursuing horses—a golden bear crowned by silver stars—Gareth and Donyon's men.

Crispin made his horse turn. The beast whinnied in protest at the sharp movement and nearly fell over, but Crispin had already flung himself from the horse's back. Landing on his feet and throwing his good arm before him, he catapulted wave after wave of flame at the approaching army. Their horses reared, throwing their riders from their backs. Flying embers knocked others from their steeds. Trees caught ablaze until the forest was a sea of blood-red flame. Most of Crispin's pursuers died instantly, though a sparse few managed to turn and flee.

Crispin continued to release his fire, yelling, "Traitors and murderers! You will not take my kingdom from me! I am Crispin, King of Adelar! You have stolen my sister and my wife—but you will not claim my kingdom for your own!"

He trembled all over, emitting fire until he thought he would explode and almost wishing that he would. Flames poured from his body, morphing from red into a bright purplish-blue. Then, at last, he collapsed to his knees, breathless, head spinning.

"Your grace, are you all right—?"

"Get away from me!" Crispin slammed the man aside with a fiery fist, panting hard. "I am your king, not some infant who needs looking after. Bring my horse—I want to see to Tytonn's arrest at once! And then I must speak with my uncle..."

One of the servants led Crispin's horse over. The beast jerked and resisted as he drew near the flames, and Crispin snarled; likely Tytonn had injected the horse with some charm of disobedience. He placed a hand to the creature's side and soothed it with a gentle warmth before swinging himself up. He then burst into a gallop, commanding his men to follow.

Within a few hours of straight riding, they'd exited the woods and reached the small patch of the field surrounding the castle. The gates raised, and Crispin thundered through, pushing his horse toward the stables. Their rebuilding had begun, and a large number of men were hard at work, hammering, sawing, reconstructing.

Crispin galloped inside, flung a wild glance around the stables, and demanded, "Where is he? Where is the Master of Horses? His king demands an audience at once!"

"I believe he was last seen inside," a man said, "visiting the queen—"

Fire surged from Crispin at the man, knocking him

against the stall where he slouched down, motionless. Then, turning his horse, Crispin rushed from the stables and toward the castle doors. Dismounting, he hurried inside, scaling corridors and stairs until at last, he burst inside his wife's chambers—

She stood by the window, holding the baby and laughing at something the Horse Master had just said. Tory stood nearby, hands folded, smiling at the scene. Tytonn grinned at Gailea and reached out to cradle the baby's head—

Crispin rushed at them. Rings of fire burst from his fingers, slinging around Tytonn's wrists and ankles and binding them like fetters. Tytonn cried out and stared wildly at Crispin.

"Crispin, what are you doing?" Gailea demanded.

"Stop, now, *wife*, or I will throw the bastard right out that window."

Gailea froze in place, her face drained, and Tory crept up beside her.

"This man is under arrest," Crispin said; the sound of clanking armor met his ears, and several guards thundered inside the room.

"Why?" Gailea asked, quiet but firm. "What has he done?"

"He bewitched my wife and conspired with her to release another traitor, Chevalier."

"No, Crispin—"

Crispin struck Tytonn across the cheek. He staggered, knocking back against the wall. Crispin latched a fiery rope to the bonds on his wrists, yanking him and making him stand up straight. Studying the burn marked across the Horse Master's cheek, he said, "I have given you enough allowances, but now we are no longer friends. I have warned you before to address me with the proper titles of respect."

"Your grace," Tytonn panted, keeping his head bowed. "The queen and I have committed no treason against you. We did not release Chevalier."

"Then what of the conversations witnessed between the two of you?"

"We did discuss the possibility, yes. Lord Ragnar is a powerful man—he'd be even more dangerous if Chevalier's Dusk landed in his hands—"

"And the Dusk would not be more dangerous in the hands of the sorcerer himself who created it? What kind of fool do you take me for? I was a fool to listen to you in the first place, to keep him alive instead of burning him as my uncle would have counseled—*and now she's dead, because of you!*"

Fire erupted from Crispin, making him collapse while scorching Tytonn who cried out and stumbled back against the wall. Gailea handed Merritt to Tory— the baby began to whimper—and then fell at Crispin's side, touching his arm. Her touch was hesitant, and he recoiled, snarling, "Do you touch your lover with such disgust?"

"Crispin," Gailea pressed. "Why are you so upset? And who's died? What happened—where is Chevalier? Where is Elda?"

"Elda is dead," Crispin spat, "and Chevalier has fled."

"Dead?" Gailea gasped. She swallowed hard, clearly fighting back tears. She gripped his arm as if needing to support herself; he stiffened and almost wrenched away but didn't. He wanted her touch to soothe him as it once had, even though he knew such a hope had almost entirely slipped away from his grasp.

"Crispin...what happened? Who—?"

"You should know," Crispin said sharply, and then turned to Tytonn. "Have you nothing to say for yourself?"

The Horse Master's face had drained of color, all warmth vanished from his eyes. "Elda...Elda, she..." he trembled and wretched and then broke down, sobbing.

"Yes, she's dead," Crispin said coolly. "Thanks to you."

"I did not kill her," Tytonn said shakily, before crying out, "I did not let the sorcerer go—nor did the queen! I will kill him myself if I ever find him!"

"You'll find no one and do nothing ever again!" Crispin shouted. "Not under *my* watch, in *my* castle. Guards, escort him to the dungeons at once. I will declare his sentence shortly."

The guards hurried forward and dragged Tytonn from the room. His face went blank, devoid of any feeling, as though he became an empty shell, no longer human. Crispin tried to comfort himself with this idea— that Tytonn *was* no human, but a monster, worthy of whatever punishment befell him.

The baby's cries culminated then, seeming to synchronize with Crispin's wildly pounding heart and head.

"Take that creature from my sight, will you?" he snarled, glaring at Tory.

Tory glanced briefly at Gailea who nodded, and Crispin rose to his feet, yelling, "No—you answer to *me*, *without* her permission. *I am king*!"

Tory jumped and fled the room, cradling the child close to her breast.

"Crispin, I'm so sorry," Gailea breathed, standing beside him. "I'm so sorry...Elda...she was like a sister to me as well..."

Her voice broke, and she reached a trembling hand toward him. He sidled closer, almost letting himself melt into her touch and the musical soothing of her voice. But then the baby's cries echoed, dimly but certain, from the adjoining room. Gailea's hand closed around his, but he flung her aside. She caught herself against the wall and stared up at him, wild and poised, like an animal ready to spring.

"I should have always seen you for what you are," Crispin seethed. "You saw me as nothing more than a way out. A way to rise to power and gain your revenge on my family when all I've ever done is love you and try to help you—"

"I love you too, Crispin—you *know* I do—"

"No. You *want* me. You love what you think I should be. You don't know *me*. You don't love *me*. You bewitch me, make me weak, but no more. I am strong. From now on, you are my wife alone, and your place is in the bedroom, not in matters of war, or of the kingdom..."

Crispin turned and stormed toward the door, but Gailea called, "What right do you have to forbid me to grant aid and counsel? This is my kingdom too—more mine than yours by rights, if you really want to be reminded."

Crispin paused in the door but didn't turn back to look at her. He breathed deeply, using every ounce of his remaining strength, however feeble, to refrain from turning his fire on her. Whatever the extent of the wrong she had done him, she was his wife, and he would not harm her. But he could not allow her to control him any longer.

"Your ideas as queen have nearly razed this kingdom to the ground, torn it in two. From now on, I fight alone."

When Gailea said nothing, Crispin glanced back at her. She'd opened her mouth as if to retort, but after taking a breath, she merely said, "Elda? What of her body?"

"Her remains are already buried. I must meet now with my uncle. Our enemies grow stronger—I was nearly killed today on my way home, it may please you to know. Lord Gareth's spies linger near our gates. I must go now—I must be king."

Crispin tore from the room, blocking out his wife's haunted gaze, her bastard's cries, and the visions of his sister's perfect, serene face. Damn them all. There was no one left he could seek counsel from—except his uncle.

He might not fully trust Alistor, but his counsel was all he knew, all he had to turn to. Besides, they were the same now in that they were friendless. Alistor would know best how to help him answer the war knocking at his gates.

Then, if even he proved false, Crispin could destroy him, just as he would destroy all others who'd betrayed him. Tytonn would die a slow and painful death, and if Gailea did not change her loyalties, she would live a long and painful life.

CHAPTER 33

THE ONLY RAGNAR

✳

Crispin melted the lock to his uncle's chambers, flung it aside, and burst into the room.

"What news of Gareth and Donyon's coalition?" he demanded.

Alistor glanced up from his desk and set down his quill. He took a deep breath and released it slowly. With a lift of his chin, he said, "In your absence, we did receive word from our spies. Gareth and his son have been gathering more armies in secret than we originally thought. They will likely arrive within the week, declaring war."

"*Damn it!*" Crispin snarled, blasting fire at the desk. Alistor jumped aside; papers caught ablaze and trinkets scattered on the floor. "Can we do nothing to stop them?"

Alistor waved his hand over his desk to quell the flames. "May I ask where this sudden blaze of passion comes from? You seem even more on edge than usual—"

"Elda is dead." This very declaration made Crispin's anger burn anew. How many times must he say it? How many times must he be forced to confront its hideous truth?

"What?" Alistor gasped, for once looking truly alarmed. "How can this be?"

"Chevalier," Crispin spat, believing the lie even more fervently now that he shared it with another, breathing its falseness to life. "His family—surely you know of their whereabouts?"

"I'm afraid not," Alistor said. His voice was tight with something like remorse, certainly a strange sound to Crispin, but he supposed that even Alistor must feel some emotion over the death of a family member. "Only Moragon knew their whereabouts—and perhaps Chevalier himself. What of the sorcerer?"

"He escaped my grasp," Crispin admitted bitterly.

"I can have search parties sent out at once. She *will* be avenged."

Crispin nodded curtly. "In the meantime, we must deal with the enemies drawing nearer our borders. I was thinking...could we not create some kind of barrier around the castle like Moragon and Chevalier once did?"

"I'm afraid that such magic is very rare; we would need to mold liquid silver to our will to reconstruct such a barrier."

"We have liquid silver in droves, thanks to the Weaver's House."

"But no true knowledge of how to utilize it. It may be possible to construct some kind of fire wall around the castle, but even that will not hold forever. You *will* need to go to war."

"I tire of war," Crispin growled. "I tire of the costs—both in bloodshed and my treasury..."

"She knows you hate war," Alistor said quietly. "She knew it would come to this."

"Do you suggest that I cannot make my own decisions?" Crispin spat. "Do you think I must rest so heavily upon her opinions?"

Alistor said nothing, his expression unreadable.

"It's true," Crispin muttered. "She once held me under her spell. Her music—I shall now claim its power as Moragon once tried to do. She will mock me no longer; she *will* pay in this war to come..."

Crispin's words suddenly pained him. Despite the anger fueling them, something else tugged at his heartstrings, something that he couldn't quite pinpoint, a distant longing he'd nearly forgotten. Why had it come to this? Why had she betrayed him so? It hurt him to consider tethering her spirit and its essence—her music. After all, her wild and free spirit had once made him love her.

"Ready our armies," Crispin said at last. "We will meet tomorrow to discuss warfare. You will help me to construct a wall of flame about the castle. That may discourage them for a time and work to our advantage. Good night, uncle."

"Good night, your grace."

Crispin nodded curtly and stole from the room.

His feet hurried as if guessing his desires even before his mind caught up with them. He missed his wife. The only words they'd exchanged lately were words of discord and mourning. Perhaps she'd been unfaithful, but she wasn't entirely at fault.

The traitor, Tytonn—curse his so-called friendship—had lured and overpowered her. She'd been only a servant at the time. Who knew what lies Tytonn might have spun to convince her? He, her lord and husband, was the one she truly loved, wasn't he?

***

Gailea lifted the fussing infant from the cradle, eased down onto the bed, and set him to her breast. As he fed, she rocked and sang gently.

The door creaked open. She glanced up, and her heart fluttered with joy as Crispin walked in. Then, as she noted his stooped frame and the frown filling his face, her heart spiraled. How old and empty he looked.

"Crispin?" Gailea said quietly. "How are things with your uncle?"

"Fine..."

"Do you wish to talk about Elda?"

"Why would I?" Crispin snapped. He looked away and stared at the floor, brooding.

"Because it may help with the pain. I miss her too. She was like a sister to me—"

"But she wasn't. And you have a sister still."

Gailea inhaled deeply. Brushing aside the harsh comment, she said, "Please, come to bed. I can sing to you, comfort you..."

Crispin met her gaze, seeming to consider. Then, his gaze drifted to Merritt, and he said, "I'm tired of going to bed beside that thing. I want to go to bed with my wife."

"Once I've finished feeding our *son*, that may be possible."

"*May* be?" Crispin stood up straight and took a few steps forward. "Would the possibility be more definite if it was another's arms offering to hold you?"

Gailea flinched but held her ground. "I only meant that perhaps we should talk first. We've both gone through a lot today. I think it would be best if we could talk as we once did—as king and queen, and especially as husband and wife."

"You would aim to grant counsel," Crispin said with a sigh.

"Does my counsel exhaust you?"

"What does it matter? Gareth and Donyon's war will soon be upon us, regardless of any counsel you might grant."

Gailea hesitated. In truth, Crispin had never heeded her true counsel, to extend an offer of amnesty toward Gareth and Donyon. But arguing would not provide the comfort he needed right now.

Gailea shifted Merritt in her arms, walked over, and reached a hand toward Crispin. Their fingertips brushed, ever so lightly. Crispin looked at her with a sudden yearning, and she wrapped her hand around his.

"I miss this," Gailea whispered. "I miss the man I fell in love with. He was happier, with so many fewer burdens to bear. You can still walk away from all of this and find happiness again. You could even give up the throne. I never wanted it; I only wanted to make things better for our people. But it isn't worth seeing my family so torn. We could go and live at the House of Lance and be happy there, just as Elda was..."

"I could not dwell in that reminder of my sister's death," he whispered, but he drew closer to her, wrapped his arms around her. Gailea melted against him, basking in the steady warmth radiating from him. How right this felt—her, her husband, and their child, all as one. "But I do envy that life sometimes. To abandon it all and just be free..."

"You are king. You have the power to do everything— including the power to *stop* being king. It wouldn't have to be immediate. We could take time to choose someone worthy of taking the throne for you."

"And how would we choose? Our enemies exist around every corner..."

"Crispin, at times...your enemies exist only where

you imagine them to," Gailea said gently; Crispin's hold on her tensed, but she added, "Release Tytonn—you know he never committed any crime against you. He loves you—"

Crispin shoved Gailea aside with a snarl. "How *dare* you. I come to you for comfort, but you can't turn your thoughts away from him for an instant."

Merritt had finished feeding and began to cry. Gailea cuddled him and said quietly, "You truly don't intend to murder him. Banish him if you must, but I beg you not to kill him. He has not betrayed you, and in time, once your grief is past and you don't need someone to blame, you will see that—"

"Insolent wench!" Crispin yelled, and Gailea shielded Merritt. "After all the humiliation he has brought to *me, your husband,* and still you defend *him*, ask pardon for *him*—"

Crispin strode forward and wrenched Merritt from her arms.

"What are you doing?" Gailea cried, hurrying after him. She began singing a charm to slow his footsteps, but he flung his arm toward her, and a stream of fire spiraled forth, knocking her back against the wall. Her head spun, but she heard the door open and Crispin declare, "Take this and get it out of my sight at once!"

As Gailea's head cleared, she pushed up from the wall and watched as Crispin shoved Merritt into Tory's arms. He slammed the door on the baby's cries, and they receded as the servant fled down the hall.

"You're mad," Gailea breathed, shaking with tears, not knowing whether anger or fear dominated her more. "It's one thing for you to lose your temper with me. But to push your anger onto your own son—"

"My son?" Crispin sneered, any hints of affection vanished from his face. "No, I will not play that game any longer. That brat is not my son—I am surer of it with each passing day. He was born too early, and all signs point to you having betrayed me with that bastard I once called friend. I've tried to give you credit, but I should have known just how wily you can be. You whored with Tytonn, and once you'd lured him into your web, you conspired with him against me. You set Chevalier loose and spared Gareth and Donyon, so that now, all my enemies are free and war knocks on my doorstep. *You* did that! Your music bewitched me into sparing their lives! You claim to care nothing for the throne, but you would destroy me and take it solely for your own!"

Flames leapt across Crispin's body and shone in his eyes, making them glow like burning coals. He stormed toward her, but she sang a high note that flung him back against the wall.

"Stop it, Crispin! Why will you only choose to accuse those closest to you? This *must* be your uncle's doing—*he* let Chevalier go. Chevalier probably gave him some spell to affect my pregnancy; remember what he did to Marlis—"

"My uncle has ever stood faithfully by my side," Crispin declared, staggering up from the wall. "He has only wanted what was best for me and this kingdom—unlike you, who would steal it for your own, reign with your lover, allow all manner of traitors to roam free and wreak havoc—"

"They could be friends. *Allies*—"

"Like *you*? Alistor warned me it would come to this. I didn't want to believe him. I wanted to believe that our love would endure. But look at you—you *disgust* me."

Gailea inhaled sharply; his words cut straight into her heart, twisting and digging deep. Fighting back tears, she pleaded, "Please, Crispin. This is *me*. You *know* I love you—"

"No, you don't. Not in the way a king needs to be loved—the way a *man* needs to be loved. You've *never* cared enough for me; you've always placed others first. First the queen, then Tytonn, and now, your love for his son would override all else."

"I never asked you to pursue me. You made that choice. If you wanted me to love *only* you, then you should have chosen another bride."

Crispin lifted his chin. "Perhaps I should have."

"But," Gailea persisted, "I do still love you. After everything—and above all others." As she spoke, she realized the lie for what it was—her love for Merritt was greater than anything, but such a declaration might mean the child's life.

The anger in Crispin's gaze wavered as he said, "Then *prove* it. Say you want Tytonn dead for showing disrespect toward your husband and king."

"I cannot," Gailea whispered, "for that would be to deny who I am at my innermost core. I love you, but I will not lie to you—nor to myself."

Anger flared afresh on Crispin's face.

"Tytonn really *has* warped and twisted your mind to his loyalty. Well, I will put a stop to that and rid you of his witchcraft."

Gailea stepped back as Crispin advanced, his strides long and purposeful, thundering as loudly in her ears as did her wild heartbeat. She began singing again, but he waved his hand and a fiery shield leapt between them, just long enough to block her song-spell. He grabbed her wrists, shoving her on the bed and pressing his body close, trapping her.

"No more," he whispered in her ear. "Moragon had the right idea. You will be mine or your bastard's life will be the sacrifice you pay..."

His warm breath made her shiver. His hands were

like a stranger's roaming her body, but she held still and fought back her tears, thinking of Merritt.

"Your lover *will* be tortured and killed as a traitor, for hiding powers of sorcery all this time and using them to seduce my wife and thus betray his king. His bastard Merritt will meet the same fate if you don't start caring more for your king and husband than your lover. You wanted a king—you encouraged me to become this—and now you have it. This time, I'll get what I want. This time, I'll *know* the child is mine."

***

As the first gray light of morning dawned, Gailea slipped silently from the bed, stole inside her dressing room, and donned a simple, warm woolen gown. She had no more need for lace and jewels and other frivolous adornments.

She braided her long blonde hair and glanced into the mirror. Her face looked solemn as death. Tears crept down her cheeks, but she rubbed them quickly away. A bruise had begun to form beneath her left eye since last night's struggle, and she powdered it, hiding the mark.

Then, she stole from the bedchamber. Pausing by her son's room, she made certain he still slept. One of her handmaids sat by his cradle, rocking it and singing. Gailea granted a sadly wistful smile and then continued down the hall.

The rising sun dazzled through the tall arched windows, while fire blazed beyond—the wall of flame surrounding the castle that Crispin and Lord Ragnar had constructed late last night after Crispin had finished with Gailea. He had fallen back into bed early that morning, exhausted.

Gailea descended into the depths of the castle, and the

façade of warmth vanished, replaced by an iciness that seeped beneath her skin, chilled her bones, and froze her heart. She fleetingly wished for Crispin's warmth to comfort her, but it had abandoned her long ago, as completely as the castle's warmth avoided the dungeons.

She hurried past the cells, ignoring hands that reached out to her and voices that pled for mercy. She could not release them, but hopefully soon, a kinder master would. As guards let her through to the various sections of the jail, she didn't care this time if they saw what she was about. This was her last chance to help Tytonn.

She focused on the thick iron door at the end of the long stretch of corridor. Guards flanked either side and as she approached, their watchful gazes seemed to stare straight past and through the wall beyond—except one, whose gaze shifted uneasily to her for a moment before glancing away again.

Gailea walked up to the door and peeked in the small sliver of a window. Straw scattered across a cold stone floor. Faint gray light filtering through a crack in the back wall illuminated the small space's emptiness.

"Where is he?" Gailea demanded, striking her gaze at the guard who'd looked at her. "Where is the prisoner Tytonn?"

The guard hesitated.

"I am your queen! You will answer me."

"They have already taken him, your grace," the guard answered.

"What?" Gailea gasped. "It's too early for a public execution..."

"His grace gave the orders last night. He wanted the job done in secret—"

"Where is he?" Gailea demanded again, biting back tears.

"Come. I will take you to him."

The guard started forward, and Gailea followed. They wound through corridors until cries of pain echoed down the hall. As they neared, the cries weakened, and Gailea hurried her pace, flying past the guard and glancing inside each open door until at last, she stumbled to a halt before one and peered inside, gripping the doorframe for dear life.

Tytonn was strapped upright to a long wooden pole, hands bound behind his back. The masked executioner whipped Tytonn with long black cords; fire spiraled up the cords each time. His cries had quieted into moans, and his head lolled. Gailea burst forward and fell to her knees beside him, taking his hand.

"Your grace," the executioner said. "His grace's orders—"

"Silence," Gailea whispered sharply. "You can see that he is through. I will finish the job for you."

The executioner hesitated and then let his weapon slip to the ground. It fell with a dull clatter, and he watched Gailea with remorse as he stepped back and said, "I am truly sorry, your grace. But his grace ordered a private death. He said he wished to spare the Horse Master public humiliation, as they were once friends..."

Gailea wept. Even in this, Crispin played the coward; he wished Tytonn to die quietly in hopes that everyone would forget he'd existed, including her. He couldn't even bring himself to watch, perhaps out of some last shred of guilt, or perhaps simply because he cared so little now for Tytonn that he'd allowed himself to forget and sleep right through.

But she wouldn't forget—nor would she let anyone else.

Squeezing Tytonn's hand, she listened carefully for his heartbeat, his breath. Both labored and rapidly faded. She could not save him now; he was beyond her aid.

"*Gailea*," he forced her name. His voice was hoarse and foreign in her ears. Still clutching his hand, she let a few tears fall and whispered back, "Yes? Yes, Tytonn?"

"You and Merritt...protect yourself, and the baby..." His voice contorted into a wheezing cough as he struggled for breath.

"I will," Gailea whispered. "We are already on our way."

Tytonn's head moved in what might have been a nod. His lips twitched as if attempting one of his warm, kindly grins.

"Good. If Crispin ever knows he loves you again... help him remember me too, that we were once friends..."

"I will..." Gailea spoke the lie as fervently as she could.

Tytonn's breath labored again. He opened his mouth as if to speak again, but Gailea said, "Sh, no... No more. *I* am going to comfort *you* now..."

He looked at her a moment more. Then, he closed his eyes, ready and accepting.

Gailea forced her sobs to grow still.

Quietly, she began her lullaby.

Just as before, when she had brought the castle crashing from the sky, she varied the melody to create something new, inflecting the song into his very heart and lungs. His mind quieted and lay at rest. His body calmed until his heart beat a final note and fell still.

Gailea remained kneeling for a time, holding his hand, weeping and saying good-bye.

When she rose to her feet, the guards surrounding the room watched her, silently begging her forgiveness for the lover they believed she'd lost. She *had* lost a lover, though not the one they imagined. She'd lost her own husband and now, in Tytonn, a dear friend.

Gailea emerged from the dungeons. She crept back

into her chambers and donned a thick cloak. Then, she bundled Merritt and lifted him from his bed. The servant who'd rocked his cradle had drifted to sleep—as would everyone else, soon enough.

Gailea swept through the castle, weeping quietly and singing her lullaby over and over. Letting her grief empower her, she pushed her music out into the very walls of the castle, inside its windows and tapestries. She fused her magic with that of the castle until it quavered, so slightly that she could just detect its shuddering breaths. Windows cracked. Stones shifted, though not enough to crumble. Fires dimmed and then died. Servants and guards fell to the floor in a deep slumber.

Gailea pushed harder, making her music flow in culminating waves beyond the walls to the woods just beyond. All the while, she strayed toward her final destination before leaving the castle behind—Chevalier's chambers.

The puzzle with the keys yet remained intact, but Gailea sang a charm she had researched in one of her books to unlock the door.

His room struck Gailea with an icy cold blast. Merritt whimpered against her, and she drew the blankets closer about him. Despite the fact that all the castle now lay doused in her command of sleep, Gailea felt certain that Chevalier's domain had lain dormant far longer. Here, the cold bit sharpest, the shadows seemed to stretch the longest, and dust and cobwebs cloaked everything like a mourning veil. A glimmer of sadness touched Gailea; if Chevalier's chambers had once reflected his grandness and elegance, they now most certainly reflected his despair.

Gailea wandered to the window made from colored glass. She touched the glass, and it wavered like water rippling, but her hand did not pass through. Chevalier had given her no specific instructions for retrieving the prism. She'd have to figure it out on her own and fast. Terrified to end her lullaby and risk destroying everything she'd worked so hard to set up at such a vital moment, she focused more fully on the glass, hoping to lull its protective magic to sleep. It quivered as if fighting against her but then finally lay still. Gailea's hand reached through this time, and she extracted the prism. It glistened in the fresh light filtering through the other windows. She tucked it carefully in a pocket inside her cloak, close to her breast. Then, still singing, she fled toward the kitchen.

She took a moment to survey the kitchen, strangely quiet as all the servants and cooks and even the stoves slept, and she thought of her sister. At least Darice would be free from this life as well; she was away visiting their mother and would have no reason to return upon learning of Gailea's departure.

Gailea exited the kitchens. Picking up her pace and clutching Merritt tightly to her, she darted like a shadow toward the stables. Finding Silver, her speckled gray mare, she took one of the blankets slung over the stall and gently laid it over the horse's face. Blinded to anything that might cause her alarm, Silver followed Gailea willingly.

Gailea flew toward the gate, stumbling as the spell's immensity weighed down on her. One last barrier waved just beyond the gates—the wall of flame encircling the castle.

Gailea tried to connect mentally with the fire. Its heat crept along her skin, making her shudder. She slowed her pace; she was fast growing tired, and her grip on the lullaby's magic waned. But then Merritt stirred against her breast. His tiny fingers clutched her dress, silently cheering her forward. She picked up speed and concentrated.

As the flames danced close, so close that their heat made her breath come in staggering gasps, Gailea sang fervently, overriding the fire's fear and hatred with her song. A section of the flames lowered, then extinguished. Gailea mounted Silver and dashed across the charred ground into the woods beyond. She was free at last. As she delved deeper into the woods, footsteps thundered toward her. Glimpses of flags flashed past, Lord Gareth's emblem waving high. Adelar would soon be free again. She prayed that her husband might also find freedom and peace.

***

Crispin groaned, turned over, and felt the bed. He recoiled, cursing beneath his breath. Why was it so damn cold? Had the servants been fools enough not to stoke the fires in the middle of such a chilly night?

Crispin gripped the covers beside him. His hand groped, reaching for comfort, but there was none. His eyes flew open. The bed was empty. His breath seemed to freeze inside him for an instant. Then, he sprang up, dressed, and barged from the room.

He stormed down the corridors, rubbing his hands vainly and watching his breath curl like smoke before him. Where had she gone, and what devilry had she struck upon his castle? The torches' flames had also died. A stillness like death clung to every corridor, and he felt as though she watched him from the shadows, taunting. Had she run off to be with her lover in the middle of the night? No, he should be executed already. Perhaps she'd gone to grant him some final comfort...

Rounding a bend, he gasped and staggered to a halt. Along the length of the hall, guards and servants alike had collapsed and lay motionless. He hurried to the girl nearest him, turned her over, and placed his ear to her breast. Her heartbeat pulsed steadily; she only slept. He shook her, slapped her, hovered a hand over her breast and burned her flesh, enough to scar and certainly to waken. But no traces of pain showed on her face, let alone signs of waking.

Crispin jumped to his feet and scurried down the corridors. He broke into a run, shouting and straining for any answer to meet his ears. None came—until a flash of red streaked past the window and caught his attention. Crispin whirled and peered out. One of his banners caught ablaze, snaking like a red-gold dragon across the gray sky. Crispin peered closer—an arrow had woven itself into the banner's fibers.

Crispin stormed down the corridor and climbed stairs until he emerged atop one of the outer walls spanning between two of the highest towers. He raced to the middle, stopped short, and gripped the wall as he gazed out.

Armies spanned as far as he could see, streaming from the woods like a flood toward a singular point— a gap in his wall of fire. Golden bears ringed by silver stars waved high on hundreds of flags. Armor and weapons shone in the sunlight struggling beyond the clouds. Shouts and commands dimly reached his ears; ladders were hoisted, and men began to clamber up. It would be mere moments before his castle was overrun. He thought to shout to the guards, but they'd be asleep as well—

Some movement made Crispin glance up. Alistor stood on the wall some yards away, also staring at the approaching armies, wide-eyed.

Anger blazed inside Crispin as he marched toward Alistor.

"How are *you* yet awake? What part in this did you play?"

Alistor glanced up. "Nothing, your grace. I only just woke moments ago myself."

Crispin flung a wild gaze back at the armies surrounding his castle's gates. "Can't we do anything? The wall of fire—how could she have extinguished it? You promised it was invincible except by the strongest magic—"

"Both you *and* Moragon always had a habit of underestimating her—and, apparently, even I made that mistake. Now she's fled with her bastard and taken her revenge by allowing our enemies to crawl inside our gates with all the ease of scavengers cleaning up after a wild beast's kill. Don't you see? She *wanted* it to be just the two of us, in the end. Even now, she tries to manipulate you, to turn you against the one person who has ever claimed utter allegiance to you." He folded his arms and lifted his chin. "I always *did* try to warn you about her..."

Something snapped inside Crispin. Absorbing power from the sunlight above, he flung his hands in front of him. Fire darted through the air so quickly that Alistor had no time to react before fiery bands strapped him to the wall. He groaned, grimaced, and pulled against the bonds. Crispin strode forward, fire brandished in both hands and filling his entire body.

A steady, red-gold glow spread through Alistor's body, likely canceling the pain from Crispin's bonds, though he did not break free. He panted, and his face twisted into a feverish grin as he chuckled darkly, "At last, the boy finds his strength and evolves into a man—perhaps even a true king—now that it's too late, now that his kingdom will be taken—"

"Silence!" Crispin yelled. "You will no longer patronize your king. You have destroyed my life—it was you, all along. You may have been right about Gailea, but she was doubly right about *you*. It's your fault she's turned against me, your fault that Elda is dead—"

"And what about *you*?" Alistor challenged. Flames erupted all along his body, shattering Crispin's bonds. As the sun continued to rise behind him, he shone like a brazen god. No fear flickered in his gaze, only a deep contempt. "Do you truly think she loved you as much as she said? Then why did she flee? Why did she leave you—?"

Crispin sent another wave of fire at Alistor, but as a sharply icy pain shot through his shoulder, his fire wavered. He cried out in frustration, lowering the arm that yet suffered from where Gareth's ice arrow had struck a few days ago. Perhaps the fool would take his kingdom, but Crispin would not allow him this final humiliation.

Throwing his good arm in front of him, he flung another wave of flame at Alistor who countered by raising his hands to form a fiery shield. As the two Fyres pushed, each vying for their magic to overcome the other, Alistor continued, "I argued once that being feared is more powerful than being loved. But you will be neither; you will simply be hated. You will continue to breed hatred, blaming others for your own mistakes—your own weaknesses. *I* didn't create this disaster, boy—*you* did. You couldn't control your own powers, nor your queen, nor shall you ever control this kingdom. You're no ruler, but Gailea was. *She* knew how to act. And she made the wisest choice of us all in fleeing you—"

"You're wrong, *snake*," Crispin hissed, pushing his fire through his body until it morphed into a bright blue.

Alistor's eyes widened with bewilderment right before the coils of blue flame snapped against his shield, shattering it, and lassoed around both his wrists and neck. His skin continued to shimmer with a faint red glow, but the smell of burning flesh signified that he could not long defy the might of Crispin's blue fire. His breath came in rasping gasps. His eyes shone with fear. He opened his mouth to speak, but no words came out.

"That's right," Crispin said. "Gailea is not the only one who was underestimated. You have always under-estimated my own abilities, uncle. Or perhaps, like Mor-agon, you feared them and sought to conceal them away. But no more. If I cannot control anything else, I *can* control whether you live or die. Bow before your king at last—"

Crispin lifted his hands, and Alistor rose into the air, pulled along by the fiery noose. He clawed at the noose, glaring at Crispin. His lips moved, and Crispin decreased the intensity of the flames. "Yes, uncle? Have you some final repentance to share, to ease your soul? I will allow that, but speak quickly."

"Repent," Alistor croaked, and even beyond the pain flooding his gaze, a hint of pride gleamed. "You would still blame me for all this. But in the end, young unwor-thy king, the reflection you see when you look in the mirror is the only one to blame for your downfall."

Crispin's anger flooded him like a whirlwind, and his fire poured violently into Alistor's body, consuming him. Alistor clawed at his bonds, jerking violently mid-air un-til at last, he fell limp.

Clanking armor made Crispin look up. A guard barged onto the wall, staggering as if still heavy from Gailea's sleep-spell. Collapsing, he gasped, "Your grace—the castle—it's under attack—"

"I know, you fool. What hope is there of securing it?"

"None, your grace. Most are still sleeping. Gareth's men are not killing those who sleep, only imprisoning them—"

"Weak fools," Crispin sneered. "Gather what men you can and smuggle them out of the castle. I will meet you in the caves."

The guard nodded. Then, as he turned to go back, he staggered again, gripping the wall. "Your—your grace—what has happened to Lord Ragnar?"

Fire flared inside Crispin. With a disgusted scowl, he flicked his hand, and Alistor's corpse flung through the air and fell toward the woods.

"Lord—Lord Ragnar, he—"

Crispin whirled, slammed the guard back against the wall, and declared, *"I am the only Ragnar now! There is none other!"*

A CHANCE SOUTH

Gailea finished gathering dried fruits, meats, and canteens for water into the large satchel. She checked her pouch for the humble supply of silver coins—enough to grant her passage to Hyloria. She wished she could sail farther, entirely from the Spectrum Isles, but any distance placed between her and Crispin was safer than none.

A little over a month had passed since she'd fled the castle, and she knew she could not stay at the House of Lance much longer. By now, Crispin was either still contending with the war on his castle or else had fled. Either way, the House might be the first place he sought refuge—or even sought her. She wasn't yet certain where she would go once she reached Hyloria, but better to risk her life to build a better one for her and her children than to stay on as sitting targets begging for the kill.

Gailea checked the cradle by the fire. Merritt slept on, clutching the quilt under his chin. She smiled and ran a hand through his wild curls; their gold had begun to deepen into a more handsome red. He looked more and more like Crispin each day, a sight which both tore at Gailea's heartstrings and yet made her hold him closer to her heart. She could not be with Crispin anymore. She could not love him anymore, but neither could she hate him. Instead, she would love their son, give him a chance, and hope that he embraced that chance where his father had not.

Gailea placed the satchels by the door and then sank into the armchair before the fireplace. They would depart soon, in the cover of night and while Merritt slept on, but as she touched her stomach—and the new baby inside—she knew she must first grant herself a few moments' rest.

She let her fingers trail along the music box she'd found on a little table beside the armchair. She opened the lid and let a few tears fall as the wistful tune played. Lifting the folded parchment from within, she unfolded it and let her gaze linger upon its words once more: Crispin's promise that the House belonged to her as much as it did him, and a story about the song inside the music box, the song that had spun the House's magic into existence and kept it alive. The letter ended with sweet words about how much he loved her and wished he could share the House with her in person one day.

That hope was long past. She must now rely fully on her own strength.

Rising to her feet, she lifted Merritt from his bed, cradling him in the soft quilt. She slung the satchel over her shoulder and drew her cloak close about her.

Then, she stepped outside and hurried down to the lake. Moonlight dazzled the sand and water, making them shimmer like silver and gold. Silver stood waiting along the shore. Gailea smiled a little as she caressed her muzzle and saw Tytonn's warm gaze reflected in her calm, brown eyes. Tytonn was at peace now, rejoicing in the Forever Havens with Elda. Darice was secure with Brynn; she would worry, but at least she was safe. There was nothing left to do except protect her children. Gailea hefted herself atop the horse's back, rested Merritt securely against her breast, and sang a gentle command.

The horse galloped away, into the woods, and toward Adelar's southern shores.

Dear Reader,
Thanks so much for taking the time to read *Serenade of Kings*!

The Gailean Quartet was inspired by the choir class I took in college and especially my choir teacher, who provided a refuge for me during a very difficult time in my life.

If you'd like to help me out, please leave a review for me wherever my books are sold. I absolutely love hearing from my readers. Discovering a new review and reading what others have to say about my work truly makes my day. It also helps other awesome readers like yourself discover my book so they can enjoy it too.

On that note, God bless, happy reading, and may you be inspired!

I look forward to seeing you in my next book.

~ Christine E. Schulze

The Chronicles of the Mira Free Download

Dear Reader,
I have a special gift for you! Get your free copy of my young adult fantasy, *The Chronicles of the Mira* (usually $2.99), when you sign up for my newsletter that features exclusive content for subscribers only. Just follow this link to sign up and download your new book! https://www.authorchristineschulze.com/free-ebook

Happy reading,
~ Christine E. Schulze

More Books
by Christine E. Schulze

*T*he *Amielian Legacy* is a vast fantasy comprised of both
stand-alone books and series for children and young
adults. *The Amielian Legacy* creates a fantastical mythology for North America in much the same way that Tolkien's Middle Earth created a mythology for Europe.
While it's not necessary to read any particular book or
series to read the others, they do ultimately weave together to create a single overarching fantasy.

Young Adult Books

The Amielian Legends: A Young Adult
Fantasy Collection
(Can be read in any order)

The Chronicles of the Mira

The Crystal Rings

Serenade of Kings

Bloodmaiden
Lily in the Snow
Tales from the Lozolian Realm
One Starry Knight
The Pirates of Meleeon

The Gailean Quartet

Prelude of Fire
Serenade of Kings
Symphony of Crowns
Requiem of Dragons

The Stregoni Sequence

Golden Healer, Dark Enchantress
Memory Charmer
Wish Granter and Other Enchanted Tales

Children's Books

The Adventures of William the Brownie

The Special Needs Heroes Collection

In the Land of Giants
The Puzzle of the Two-Headed Dragon
The Amazing Captain K
Puca: A Children's Story About Death

Lozolian Timeline

B.Z.S. = Before Zephyr Split

A.Z.S. = After Zephyr Split

This method of naming refers to the sacrifice that the great fairy Zephyr made in order to split the original Loz apart into multiple islands, thus saving it from being destroyed in flame during the first Age of Dragons. Queen Grishilde the Silver later declared that the new islands be named in Zephyr's honor, hence the name "Zephyr's Islands."

This became a sacred turning point in Lozolian history. Thus, all important historical events in the Lozolian Realm and surrounding area are referred to as happening either **B.Z.S.** (Before Zephyr Split) or **A.Z.S.** (After Zephyr Split).

I. First Age of Dragons, 1325 B.Z.S.

Wars led by Grishilde the Silver against the Great Dragon, 1325-1327 B.Z.S.

II. *Zephyr Split*, March 9th, 1327 A.Z.S.

The wars led by Grishilde the Silver culminated when the fairies of Loz (at this time there was no official Council) joined together to split Loz into separate islands, thereby stopping the massive fire that the Great Dragon would have used to decimate the entire land. To complete the spell, the fairies had to disperse at the last moment, barely escaping destruction by fire themselves.

One fairy, Zephyr, was unique in that she was born without the ability to fly; because she could not fly, she could not flee the small piece of island that was consumed by flames and thus died, sacrificing herself to help the other fairies complete the spell.

Zephyr's Islands include Hyloria, Aquanitess, Spaniño, and Carmenna, amongst others. The largest island, which yet housed the capitol of Iridescence, took the name of "Loz" in place of the much larger predecessor from which it had been formed.

III. First Age of Peace, 1327 A.Z.S.

IV. Surpriser Curse, 1330-1430 B.Z.S.

Books: *The Legends of Surprisers* (or *The Legends of the Seven Kingdoms*)

On the massive mainland east of Zephyr's Islands lay the Seven Kingdoms. One of the kingdoms, Labrini, sought to make itself lord over the other six kingdoms. The kingdoms were soon divided. War broke out. The seven peoples who had once loved each other as brothers and sisters slaughtered one another.

The three great fairy sisters who guarded the Seven Kingdoms, Keziah, Gemimah, and Kerennah, intervened, placing a curse upon the peoples which gave them animal-like features. Until they stopped quarreling like beasts, they would look like beasts. But more than that, if all seven kingdoms did not reunite peacefully within one hundred years, the curse would complete itself, the people would turn completely into beasts, and their humanness, their kingdoms, their history—everything they held dear—would be lost forever.

V. Age of the Mass, 1410-1443 A.Z.S.

Mass War, 1440-1443 A.Z.S.

During this time, a sect of fairies known as "the Mass" came to power through the use of a dark shadow magic that would later be known as "the Dusk." Their primary focus was on using the Dusk to usurp Loz and purge from it all those born without magical blood.

To protect against this growing threat, the first official Lozolian Council was formed. The Council consisted of various magical leaders from all across Zephyr's Islands and the Seven Kingdoms. The renowned Lynn Lectim herself was one of the core founders of the Council.

A year later, Lynn Lectim's Academy was established at the behest of Lynn Lectim. She believed that, in order to properly defend themselves and their homes from dark magic, magical peoples should have the chance to be educated by those with expertise in various magical fields.

During this time, it was also revealed that Zephyr was still alive. She had been disguising herself as the phoenix Brandi. This was how she escaped the flames during the Zephyr split, by shape-shifting into a phoenix at the last possible moment; while she could not fly in fairy form, she could fly in phoenix form. She remained in phoenix form for some time, letting many believe she was dead, in order to elude certain enemies and carry out certain tasks. She was quite useful to various quests leading up to the breaking of the Surpriser Curse, as well as in the Mass War.

* Formation of First Lozolian Council, 1440 A.Z.S.

* Founding of Lynn Lectim Academy, 1441 A.Z.S.

* Mass Defeat by Queen Grishilde the Red and Sir Willard, 1443 A.Z.S.

The Mass was originally founded and led by Sir Willard of Loz. Toward the end of the Mass War, he was entrusted with the care of his niece, Aribella, a brave youth with a keen desire for both mercy and justice. Through Aribella, Willard came to see the error of his ways, left the Mass, and joined the Lozolian Council to fight against the evil entity he had originally created. In the last battle, which occurred on the grounds of his mansion, he sacrificed his life to complete a magic ritual that would ultimately allow Queen Grishilde the Red's armies to triumph over the Mass.

Willard left everything, including his estate, to Aribella. Aribella in turn gave the house to Lynn to use as the Lynn Lectim Academy's first actual building; before then, the students had lived in tents and tree houses and conducted their studies in the woods. To this day, Willard's Mansion still stands and serves as Lynn Lectim's middle school. An elementary school, high school, university, and chapel have been built on the grounds as well, offering all magical students a full education.

VI. Age of Music, 1450 -1487 A.Z.S.

Books: *The Gailean Quartet*

VII. Second Age of Peace, 1487 A.Z.S.

VIII. Second Age of Dragons, 1491-1493 A.Z.S.

Books: *The Gailean Quartet*

IX. Third Age of Peace, 1493 A.Z.S.

X. Age of Shadow, 2325 A.Z.S.

Books: *A Shadow Beyond Time* (*The Hero Chronicles* reboot)

About the Author

✳

Christine E. Schulze has been living in castles, exploring magical worlds, and creating fantastical romances and adventures since she was too young to even write of such stories. Her collection of YA, MG, and children's fantasy books, *The Amielian Legacy*, is comprised of series and stand-alone books that can all be read separately but also weave together to create a single, amazing fantasy.

One of her main aspirations for *The Amielian Legacy* is to create fantasy adventures with characters that connect with readers from many different backgrounds. Her current focus is to include racially diverse characters and also those with disabilities. The latter is inspired by Schulze working with adults with autism and other developmental disabilities at Trinity Services in Southern

Illinois. She also donates 25% of her royalties to ALFA, a local charity that supports many of Trinity's programs.

Schulze draws much of her inspiration from favorite authors like Tolkien and Diana Wynne Jones, favorite games like *The Legend of Zelda*, and especially from the people in her life. Some of her exciting ventures include the publication of her award-winning *Bloodmaiden*, as well as *The Stregoni Sequence* and *The Amielian Legends series*. Her books for younger readers include *In the Land of Giants* and *The Amazing Captain K*.

Christine currently lives in Belleville, IL, but you can visit her on her website: http://christineschulze.com

CPSIA information can be obtained
at www.ICGtesting.com
Printed in the USA
JSHW021755250623
43721JS00002B/98